PRAISE FOR SARAH MLYNOWSKI
As Seen on TV

"A fun and telling look at the world of reality TV
and the lure of fame."
—*Booklist*

"*As Seen on TV* is funny.... The book is filled with
witty characters and Steve, a lovable boyfriend
whom you can't help rooting for."
—*Columbus Dispatch*

"*As Seen on TV* is simply irresistible—
one of the best reasons you could find for reaching
for the TV remote and hitting the off button."
—International bestselling author Nick Earls

Fishbowl

"An original and very funny celebration
of friendship between women."
—*Waldenbooks, Best of 2002 Women's Fiction*

"...Mlynowski is out for a rollicking good time from the start."
—*Arizona Republic*

"Undemandingly perfect...wonderfully bitchy."
—*Jewish Chronicle*

"A fresh and witty take on real-life exams in love,
lust, trust and friendship."
—Bestselling author Jessica Adams

Milkrun

"Mlynowski is acutely aware of the plight of the
20-something single woman—she offers funny
dialogue and several slices of reality."
—*Publishers Weekly*

"This *Sex and the City*-style story
is chick-lit for the modern age."
—*Heat*

sarah mlynowski

monkey business

**RED
DRESS
INK**

™

First edition October 2004

MONKEY BUSINESS

A Red Dress Ink novel

ISBN 0-373-25071-1

www.RedDressInk.com

Printed in U.S.A.

ACKNOWLEDGMENTS

Many, many thanks to:
my mom, Elissa Ambrose, because she reads each word
I ever write, no matter what time it is, and always makes
my sentences sound prettier; my editor, Sam Bell, for
putting this book on the Slim-Fast diet and showing me
how to punch it up; my agent, Laura Dail, for being
superb in every way; Corinne Gelman, for still being my
favorite interview subject, and for taking the time to read
early, cryptic drafts of this book; Lynda Curnyn, because
she is one of the nicest editors around, as well as being
a fabulous writer and my favorite lunching companion;
the RDI team: Farrin Jacobs, Margaret Marbury,
Laura Morris, Stephanie Campbell, Margie Miller,
Tara Kelly and Tania Charzewski, for their excellent
work; my friends and little sister: Jess Braun,
Bonnie Altro, Robin Glube, Jess Davidman and
Aviva Mlynowski, for always answering my
Is-This-Funny?/Does-This-Sound-Too-Canadian? e-mails
within thirty seconds of receiving them; and Todd Swidler,
because with him beside me, everything makes sense.
Life, love and even arbitrage pricing.
Okay, he had to explain that last one
multiple times and ver-r-ry slowly.

For my dad and stepmom,
Larry Mlynowski and Louisa Weiss,
with love.

orientation
(primarily academic)

kimmy's big blunder

He aims, he shoots, he scores—all over my silk duvet.

"It's okay. Not a big deal," I lie.

"Give me two seconds, Kimmy, and I'll be ready for round two."

"Don't worry about it," I lie again.

And then he rolls over and passes out.

He's sleeping, I'm still in my jeans, and my goose-feather duvet—a gift from my father and the only thing I own of any worth—has a puddle on it.

I can't believe how gross this is. And to make matters worse, this guy I've chosen as my one-night stand—make that five-minute stand—is in my class. I can't imagine spending the next ten minutes with him, never mind the next two years.

Besides being incapable of holding it in long enough to make it to the condom, a lesson the girls were supposed to teach him when he was an undergrad, he's flabby, short and has a unibrow. Also his penis is smaller than my PDA, and that fits in the palm of my hand.

For the first time ever, my mother was right. I hate that. She nagged me to put a cover on my duvet, one nag among millions, but did I listen? No, not me. My reasoning? I liked the feel of the satin against my skin.

Apparently so did Jamie.

He's comatose on top of my comforter, his jeans and checkerboard boxers bagging around his hairy thighs. His eyes are closed, his mouth slightly open, and a trail of drool leaks onto my pillow. Hasn't he already soiled enough of my linen?

The devil-red numbers on the alarm clock beside my single bed say 12:01 a.m. Or is that 1:21? I can't see too well, as I'm a bit on the dizzy side.

Okay, I admit it. Drunk dizzy.

Dread dribbles through my half-dressed body like nausea after one too many beers. From my uncomfortable position (back pressed up against the thin wooden wall, legs straight like a clothespin to avoid making contact with his), I analyze the situation's gravity. There's a balding, tire-around-the-middle, quasi-naked man in my bed. Correction, *on* my bed.

Oh, God, what did I do?

My class of two hundred is divided into three Blocks (aka sections), A through C, and all my classes are within the same Block. The way to impress my new classmates probably wasn't to take one home the first night I'm here. Especially not one in my Block. Block B. It sounds like a prison.

His bloated lips are slightly open, his breath gentle and wet. This embarrassment will probably sit two rows behind me ten times a week. It's going to be a long two years.

Why did I invite Jamie back to my room? Oh, right, I was trying not to think about Wayne. And I thought he could be my replacement boyfriend. I'll give Jamie cute in a worn, teddy-bear sort of way. He said he was twenty-six, but he looks almost middle-aged. Like a forty-year-old who buys a Corvette and gets an earring to stay hip.

Spew all over my comforter is not cool. Okay, it's not all over the comforter; it's relegated to a one-inch Italy-shaped boot on the right side of the bed. But still, what am I going to do, bring it to the dry cleaner? Wash it in the sink? I don't even have my own sink. I share three sinks with the thirty other people on my floor. I'm not Linus. I can't start dragging my comforter around the dorm. I'll have to wait until the middle of the night to sneak through the halls, covert-operation-like.

I have to pee. Too much beer. I swing my legs over the comatose body, onto the raggedy red-and-blue throw carpet, which was the first thing I unpacked when I arrived this morning. (I like a warm ground under my feet.) Then I blow out the potted candle on my desk. That was the second item I unpacked. Unfortunately, the wick didn't get much of a workout tonight. *I* didn't get much of a workout tonight, and you can blame that on *his* wick.

I open the closet door and disappear inside. The massive space reserved for my wardrobe is the anomaly of my minuscule eight-by-eight-foot room. My bed, desk and chair are squished practically on top of one another, yet my sweaters, jeans and shoes have a huge suite. Go figure. I don't even like shopping.

I can't believe I'm here. In the closet. At business school. *At business school.* What am I doing at business school? What am I doing in Maplewood, Connecticut? Wayne, jackass Wayne, is the one who wanted to attach the letters MBA to his name. I was more interested in the letters MRS.

So we studied together for the GMATs, the standardized business school exam. And then I took the test and scored in the eighty-ninth percentile. Wayne only scored a fifty-seven. And then we separately filled out six applications and wrote the obligatory Why I Want to Go to Your School essays ("I want to go to New York University because New York is the financial capital of the world…I want to go to

Stanford because San Francisco is the technology capital of the world…I want to go to the University of Miami so I can have a perma-tan…" Kidding about that last one. Sort of).

I was accepted by four of the six, including LWBS, Winsford University's business school, one of the top business schools in the country. Wayne didn't get accepted anywhere.

Wayne then told me we were getting too serious. He wanted space. I want to take a break, he said. I need to focus on my future, he said. But then I found out that what he really wanted to focus on was my friend Cheryl.

No, we're not friends anymore.

I hope he and Cheryl have a nice, happy, uneducated life together.

I decided to come to LWBS anyway. Why not? I begged my dad to loan me tuition money. I would find myself a new boyfriend. The ratio of men to women here is three to one. *Three to one.* I read somewhere that single women should head up to Alaska, but this is a billion times better. And a billion times warmer. Well, not that much warmer; it's Connecticut, not Florida.

In the mirror on my closet door I see that the eyeliner around my eyes is smeared, making me look as if I'm auditioning for an anti-smack ad.

At least my nose is perfect. My father bought me this nose for my eighteenth birthday. I begged him for that, too. In the tenth grade the boys in my class used to rank the girls. I got eight out of ten in personality, seven and a half for body, and five for face. I spent the rest of the day crying in the girl's rest room.

If pre-nose job my face was a five, post-nose job, I'm at least an eight. In *three to one* B-school, where the average woman cares more about a flawless résumé than a flawless complexion, my eight translates into at least an eleven.

I should clean up in this place.

I slip on a pair of shorts and look for a sleep shirt. My

ripped class-of-2001 college shirt? Nah. That's best left hidden from the public eye. Instead I squeeze my latest acquisition, a new aqua T-shirt patterned in miniature Playboy Bunnies, over my head. It brings out the blue in my eyes and shows off my curves. I bought it specifically to be my wear-to-the-bathroom-in-the-middle-of-the-night-in-case-I-run-into-a-hottie shirt.

I look slutty. But in the good way.

My head starts to pound. I shouldn't have brought Jamie back to my room. What was I thinking? I wasn't thinking. I was wearing beer goggles.

"How many MBAs does it take to screw in a lightbulb?" he asked me.

"I don't know," I said, finishing what was left of my drink.

"Trick question—MBAs won't do manual labor."

For some reason (too much beer?) I thought he was funny and I thought, that's what I need. Wayne isn't funny! I need someone funny! Then I felt his hand on my arm and I thought: This is it. He's the one! I met *the one* on my first day, lucky me! When he asked me if I wanted to get some air, I was elated. And then when he said he was in Block B like me, that sealed the deal.

Thank God I didn't actually sleep with him. I'd be branded as the class slut. And not in the good way. Hopefully he's embarrassed by his performance and he'll keep his mouth shut.

I slip my enormously revolting size-ten-and-half feet into my pharmacy-bought flip-flops. I exit the closet to see that the flabby half-naked man is unfortunately still sprawled on my bed. Then I open the door to my room. It groans. I jiggle it back and forth in an attempt to cause an ear-exploding screeching sound and thus rouse him from his post-orgasm nap.

CREEEEEAK.

Light from the hallway floods the room, but his eyes don't even flutter.

Shaped like the letter *H,* the dorm is made up of a hundred and twenty rooms, thirty on each floor. I live on the northwest side of the top story. I slip into the hallway and quickly close the door behind me to shield any potential hookups who happen to be passing by from seeing my exposed new classmate, then maneuver my way around the sharp corner in the hallway toward the bathroom. The coed bathroom is in the dash in the middle of the *H.* I push open the bathroom door to three sinks, five toilet stalls and three showers. Apparently people spend more time peeing than washing.

One of the showers is occupied. So far I haven't met any of my neighbors. Is it a guy? A hot guy?

What would he do if I took off all my clothes and sneaked in there with him?

He'd run his hands down my body, telling me how gorgeous I am.

Yeah, right. He'd probably be repulsed by my seven-and-a-half-rated fat ass.

I open the door to the stall against the wall. Since I moved in yesterday, I've tested all of them. I think I like this one best, since it means I get one potential stall neighbor instead of two. It's one thing to be in the shower with a hot guy; it's another to be sandwiched between two strangers while you're peeing.

My stomach feels queasy at the thought of a guy in the stall next to mine. There's no way I'd be able to pee. And what if I fart? I can't fart with a guy next to me. What if it's smelly? I can't deal.

Again, what am I doing at business school?

I flush and wonder if the shower just got cold. The water stops, and I take a deep breath, compose myself and prepare to meet my future.

Maybe a six-foot, brown-eyed, big-smiled, dimpled god of manhood with a tiny white towel around his waist (he'll be slightly bronzed) will slide open the shower stall door, water dripping down his naked chest. He will smile, maybe say hi, and the two of us will start talking. Maybe we'll stand in the bathroom for ten or so minutes, and then, so immersed in the conversation, we'll stop in the hall to talk some more, sharing and baring our souls until dawn, and just as the sun pours through the hall window onto the faded stained beige carpet, he'll kiss me gently on the lips, tell me I'm beautiful and wrap his arms around me. I'll pull the keys out from my pocket, pull him into my room…

Oh, yeah, Jamie.

Jamie is going to ruin everything. First my reputation and now this.

The god of manhood is still in the shower, probably drying himself with that itsy-bitsy towel. I hurry over to the sink and turn on the water. His first impression of me can't be in front of a toilet.

The man of my dreams turns out to be a tall and voluptuous woman in a maroon terry-cloth bathrobe, a matching towel perched on her head, holding a pink basket filled with at least two shampoos, three conditioners, numerous unidentifiable bottles, an electric toothbrush and a shower puff. Damn.

She sets her cosmetics down beside one of the sinks and pulls out her toothbrush, toothpaste and floss. "Hi!" she chirps as she rolls the bottom of her Crest tube and applies an overdose of paste to her brush.

"Hi," I say. "Nice privacy in here, huh?"

She nods enthusiastically. "It's pretty good," she says, and turns on her toothbrush.

Yikes. I was being sarcastic. Where did this broad grow up that she thinks this is private? On an airplane? "I was kidding," I say, and splash some water on my face. "We're like animals in here." Maybe that's why they call it the Zoo. If only Wayne were here for me to live with…those with domestic partners are eligible to live off campus. Bastard, Wayne.

"It's not ideal," she continues. "I was trying to be positive. I'm concerned about the excessive bacteria."

"Uh-huh." What is she rambling about? Damn. I forgot my cleanser and toothbrush in my room. I point to her face wash. "Can I use some of that?"

She spits into the sink, rinses. "Of course." She squeezes a drop into my palm. Maybe she doesn't want me touching the tube in case I have bacteria. "One of my nannies always said that the trick to having good skin is that no matter where you are, you have to wash your face before you go to sleep, every single night. I'm Layla. You?"

Her nanny? I've never liked girl-bonding, and getting info about this broad's nanny is just weird. Most of my friends have been guys. Except Cheryl, and look how that turned out. I don't trust women. "Uh, Kimmy," I answer. My voice sounds a bit strangled, I think.

The girl smiles, reapplies her toothpaste and sticks the toothbrush back into her mouth. A blond strand slips from her head towel and into the foam.

I pat the creamy cleanser over my face until it's thick. Just as I lean to wipe it off, the door flings open. There stands Jamie, shirt unbuttoned, hairy, flabby chest protruding, beige pants haphazardly done up.

"Hey, gorgeous," he says, strutting into the bathroom. "I was wondering where you were. You okay? I'm zonked. I'm going back to my room to sleep."

I know I don't like him, but that doesn't mean I want him to see me looking as if I've dunked my face in whipped cream. Why does he want to go back to his own room? What, now he doesn't want to spend the night? Did I do something wrong?

"See you later," I say as he strolls toward one of the stalls. His urine tinkles into the toilet bowl.

Shower girl gives me a nod and then leaves. She must be judging me, thinking I'm a stupid slut for hooking up with someone on the first night.

Bitch.

jamie wants a replay
so he can amend his foreplay

I bang the palm of my hands against the walls as I sprint down the hallway. Who knew I'd be the business school stud?

I hit the jackpot.

Fine, I might have hit the jackpot a little earlier than intended, but Kimmy didn't care. And I'll make it up to her next time and then some.

Kimmy could have taken home any of the guys at the beer bash, but she chose me. The shmuck in the corner. My dream girl. Almost. My dream girl is Deborah Messing, but Kimmy's a close second. And I was in her room. In her bed. In her pants. Okay, *on* her pants. And on her comforter, but that's not the point. Why was it so easy for me? I wouldn't hook up with me if I were a girl. I don't get it. (Actually, I did get it, which is what I don't get.)

Russ and Nick, the guys I met yesterday, decided to go out for wings before the party, but I declined. I wanted to get a head start checking out the ladies. Who there weren't too many of. After a dozen rounds of hand shaking and "Hi, I'm Jamie Grossman, I'm from Florida, I used to work in hospital management, and you?" I switched it up to keep the night lively. I was Jeremy from Iowa, former accountant. And then Bill from Dallas, former gun retailer. I even added a modest twang for effect. My mother had been wrong. The college drama course I'd taken was good for something.

The party was a total sausage fest. In the common room, the three couches shaped like a horseshoe around the big-screen TV were swamped with men. For the occasion, welcome signs and sagging balloons in the school's royal-blue had been taped to the freshly painted white walls, which probably destroyed the paint job, but who cares?

After my fiftieth introduction, a few bowls of pretzels and four plastic glasses of lukewarm Coke, I was bored. Most people were piss drunk, which only heightened their pompousness. Making conversation was like talking to a parrot on Prozac. The people I met couldn't have cared less about what I had to say. They only wanted to talk about themselves. Which was probably a good thing. I don't want them to know too much about me anyway. They may start getting suspicious about what the hell I'm doing here.

I don't drink. Alcohol makes me depressed and stupid. I prefer my screwups to be done on my own merit. Like failing my first semester of college because I was too in love with Mia Brottman to go to class, or getting fired from my first postdropout sales job because I told my boss he was a dickhead. (He *was* a dickhead.)

Anyway, the party was lame. And I was exhausted—I only slept about four hours last night after driving for twenty-four hours from Miami and then partying all night. I was deliberating escaping to my room to relax and watch a DVD. I have three hundred in my room. I am a major movie buff who has wasted many a day enjoying theme specific marathons, such as a Clint-Eastwood-athon, Three-Stoogesathon, etc. (Which might have contributed to my failing my first semester that year.) But as I swallowed the last drop of flat Coke in my cup, in walked a movie star.

A pint of cold beer to a group of men who'd been chomping on salted pretzels all night, she was wearing a purple silk wraparound top that exposed a liberal expanse of glistening cleavage. Brown curls framed her creamy face, swirling onto her shoulders. I wanted to run my hands over her voluptuous behind.

I had to talk to her. I was in lust. I maneuvered my way so that I was standing near her, and then, when she looked sufficiently bored with the computer nerd beside her—"D-d-do you know that integrated wire-l-l-less LAN de-de-devices…"—I jumped in with a joke.

A few drinks (flat Coke for me, beer for her) and several jokes later, my hand was firmly on her arm. And then I asked her to get some air.

Love that. Air. A euphemism for let's get it on.

When I told her I was joining Hillel, the Jewish campus organization, and she said she was thinking of checking it out, I knew I wanted to spend the rest of my life with her.

Gorgeous, in business school and Jewish. My mother would be so *farklempt.*

Then we were sitting next to each other, almost touching, in the courtyard behind the dorm. She was chewing a piece of gum and I couldn't tear my eyes away from the sexy way her lips weaved with each bite. I felt like I was in my own porno movie.

Me: Is that the real color of your eyes, or are they contacts?
Her: Real. Do you like them?

She blew out a bubble and then sucked it back into her mouth. I wanted to be the piece of gum moving in and around her lips. I wanted to be that bubble. And when she turned away from me to stretch her legs onto the bench beside her, polishless toes pointed, feet arched—holy foot fetish, I had to have this woman. I couldn't stop myself from lightly kissing the back of her neck. When she tilted her head toward me, smiling with her juicy, bite-able mouth, I leaned forward and kissed her, savoring the mix of beer and cherry gum in her mouth.

She grabbed my hand and led me up the stairs to her room. She lit a musky scented candle and turned off the lights. I pulled her shirt over her head, then unfastened her black lace pushup bra and let it drop to the floor. A set of gorgeous breasts stared up at me, their nipples like headlights in the dark.

"Good evening," I said to them.

She unbuttoned my shirt, and then nibbled, bit and kissed my neck, shoulders, chest, nipples, stomach…and then she unfastened my belt, unzipped me and pushed me onto the bed.

I ran my fingers through her hair.

She sat up and licked her lips.

I was as hard as a mezuzah. Which she hadn't put up on her door, I noticed. I decided that maybe now was not the time to discuss her religious values. Especially since if she wanted to have sex we'd have to do it soon. The cork on my little man was about to pop. "Do you have a condom?" I asked. Or begged, to be more precise.

"Yeah, one sec." She leaped off me, her fantastic breasts jiggling, opened her desk drawer and pulled out a Trojan. Wow, we'd just moved into the dorm—she must have un-packed them right off the bat. My kind of woman.

She leaned beside me and licked her hand, and used it to play with me while she opened the condom wrapper with her other hand and her teeth.

She had to stop. Don't stop. Stop. Her hand felt so hot. Don't stop.

Oy.

I came.

She surveyed the damage. "It's okay. Not a big deal."

What a sweetheart.

So tired. Needed to rest my eyes for just a moment. Took a nap. When I opened my eyes, she was gone. And I was still exhausted. I found her in the bathroom, said good-night and headed to my room.

And now, here I am, inexplicably wide-awake, pounding my hand against the bathroom wall. I love B-school. Who knew? I want to scream out to the world how much I love this place. But I don't want to tell anyone why. I'm not the type who boasts. I can hold my tongue, just not my cum. Ha-ha.

Maybe I should U-turn to Kimmy's room for another go. Nah. I don't want to overwhelm her, or, God forbid, appear too eager (I already scored too high in the eager department). I can wait until tomorrow. We have all year to shtup. Tonight was just a warm-up.

But I'm too hyper to sleep. Should I watch a movie? Or read? I have a drawer full of movie scripts in my room. I've been buying and reading scripts of famous movies since I was ten and I wanted to be an actor.

Nah. I'm suddenly too hyper to sleep.

Maybe Nick and Russ are back. Instead of making a sharp left to my room, I hang a right toward the southeast side of the dorm, hoping they're still up.

Still up? Under the circumstances, I should probably re-phrase that.

russ floats and forgets

I'm contemplating taking off to call Sharon so she doesn't go ape-shit, when someone knocks on Nick's door. "Who is it?" Nick asks, eyeing the glass tube of hash on his desk.

"Jamie," a deep, low-pitched voice responds.

Nick inhales from his joint and then exhales out the open window. "Come in."

"Good evening, gentlemen." Jamie pushes open the door and nods at Nick on the computer chair, and then at me. I've made myself comfortable, sprawled across the wooden floor. Oh, man, I'm way too relaxed. My arms, legs and ass are numb. I try to raise my hand in a wave, but find that my body won't cooperate. Instead my fingers feel like they're floating on the floor.

"Russ?" he says to me. "Are you conscious?"

Jamie's voice doesn't match his body. He's like an Ewok with Darth Vader's set of pipes. His rumored sexual prowess doesn't fit, either. Do women really go for the geriatric look?

He looks at the TV. We've been watching the security video. Some rich alumni donated the money for a camera in the entranceway, and now anyone with a TV in his room can watch the entrance on channel two. Sure to provide hours of stoned entertainment.

Nick rolls his chair over to Jamie, then slaps him on the back. "Whassup with you, Mr. Stud?"

Jamie smiles coyly. "Great time at the beer bash, I tell you."

"You got action, eh?" I say, attempting and failing to lift myself up by my elbows.

"How'd you know that?"

Nick laughs. "People talk, dude."

I'm not crazy about the word *dude.* Too wanna-be surfer-boy. Nick's from California, so maybe he's allowed. His pale skin and skinny body, however, suggest that the only kind of surfing Nick does is for porn.

But he's a good guy. A cool guy. He has a guitar in the corner of his room, and cigars on his desk. I've always wanted to be friends with the "cool" guy. After making a small fortune at a start-up five years ago and then blowing most of it on two failed ventures, he decided to invest in an MBA.

As for me, I'd planned on coming to B-school since I started watching *Family Ties* and wanted to be Alex P. Keaton. Later, I wanted to be Bill Gates. I also wanted to be a superhero but decided that Bill was the more realistic role model. And I wouldn't have to wear tights. I slaved over my B-school application for months and then agonized for even longer while I waited for the schools to get back to me.

I met Jamie and Nick yesterday. They came up to school one day early to settle in. I came one day early to attend the international student orientation. Canadians should not have to sit through a four-hour international student orientation. I learned how to use American money. Thanks. The international student orientation also taught me that in *Amerika,* people have to tip. No shit.

The only entertaining part of the boredom marathon was the bit about greetings. The lecturer asked two male students, one from Brazil and one from Japan, to come up to the podium and say hello as if they were at a business meeting. The Brazilian guy jumped the lecturer and kissed her cheeks. The Japanese man bowed and wouldn't go near her. She then taught us that in this wonderful country, you shake hands. Thanks again.

After a full day of more useless instruction, I headed back to my room, pushed my duffel bag off my slightly stained mattress and stared at the wall, feeling overwhelmed. As I lay on the bare, squeaky mattress, I congratulated myself on finally getting here. Of course, I'd paid a price. I'd given up a top-paying consulting job in Toronto. And left my girlfriend. And taken out a massive loan.

Hoping that someone would come by and make me feel better, I left the door open. Ten minutes later Jamie stood just outside my room. When he invited me to join him and Nick in wandering around, I gladly accepted. Nick and I quickly led the group to the closest bar, where we got pissed.

We'd sat together at the dean's welcoming address today. Nick had occupied himself by reading the *Wall Street Journal* on his PDA while Jamie checked out the women and promptly fell asleep.

I listened in awe, rubbing the felt of my chair with adoration and amazement. I was sitting in a top B-school auditorium. I was finally here. A B-school student majoring in…well, I don't know yet what I'm majoring in. There are so many amazing choices. Finance, Marketing, International Business, Entrepreneurship…

"You are the future Fortune 500, the future entrepreneurs of America, the future CEOs of the world," the dean had told us, sending chills through my spine. I had expected him to look more like Dumbledore from *Harry Potter,* but he looked more built than wizardly, with his wide shoulders and buff upper torso. Kind of like The Hulk. Sharon would have thought he was hot.

Oh, man. Sharon. "I gotta take off," I say, carefully rolling myself off the floor. I don't want to touch the tissues strewn around. I'm not sure what's in them.

Nick pushes me back down. "Come on, dude, finish this joint with me."

Why not? I'll stay a few more minutes. Arm officially twisted, I inhale, hoping it'll help me sleep. I've been too excited to get any rest. "So," I say to Jamie, "while we were at the sports bar, you were getting laid, eh? We stopped by the beer bash, but someone said you'd left with a chick."

I pass the joint to Jamie, but Jamie motions it away and grins. "Your information is correct, Russ. I did leave with someone, but I don't like to kiss and tell."

Nick boots up his sleek-looking laptop. "What's her name? Was it the tall blonde?"

"Nope." Jamie sits down on the corner of the desk. "Oh, why not. Her name is Kimmy. She just got here today."

"I'm going to need her last name, dude."

"Kimmy Nailer."

"Come on!" I laugh. "Nail-her? That's her name?"

Nick clicks away on his keyboard, and I peer onto the screen. "Are you going to Google her?" I ask.

"Much better than that, dude." He clicks on to the LWBS Web site. Then he clicks on to a section labeled Calling Card. A list of names pops up on the screen. "Every person in our class is on here. With photos."

"Why are some of the names purple and some blue?" I lean toward the screen to take a better look. "Why are all the girls' names in purple?"

"Because I've checked them all out," Nick says.

"Someone's been busy." Maybe that's what the tissues were for.

"Hey, Jamie Grossman," Nick says, then pauses. "Why don't you have a picture up? I thought you might be a babe."

The term babe might be just as annoying as dude. I prefer "chick"—Sharon hates it.

Jamie looks away. "I keep forgetting to bring it in."

Nick clicks on Kimmy's name. A sexy brunette with significant breast exposure flashes across the screen. Nick whistles. "Nice work, dude."

I nod. "Hot." Too bad it's not a full-length picture. Nice top. She'd look great in matching tight white pants. Love it when women wear white pants. Don't know what it is about the white, but it turns me on.

Nick clicks on me. I'm making my best "I'm serious" face. I got a haircut specifically before taking the picture and put on my favorite suit and tie.

"Bet you were wearing jeans underneath that jacket, Russ," Nick says. "Like everyone does."

Now why didn't I think of that? I wasted a clean pair of pants. Stupid. I have a twenty-thousand-dollar tuition loan over my head, and dry cleaning is a splurge. I nod so I don't look like a moron.

Nick clicks back to Kimmy Nailer. "I didn't think babes like her went to B-school."

"They do," Jamie says. "And she's mine, so keep your grubby hands off."

"You two already a couple?" I ask.

He half nods. "Working on it."

"That sucks," Nick whines, kicking the side of his bed, jolting me. "I wish we hadn't gone to Moe's for wings. Then I could have had a crack at her. That rack is A-plus."

I shrug. "I thought the wings were A-plus."

"What do you care?" Nick says. "You have a woman."

Jamie looks down at my hand. "You married, Russ? I don't see a ring."

Married? Oh, man. "No wife," I answer. "Girlfriend."

"Serious?"

"Pretty serious."

He accidentally knocks over an empty binder from the desk, then leans to pick it up. "Do you date other women?"

"No."

"Even if you don't tell her?" Nick asks, eyebrow raised.

"Never have." Nope, never cheated on Sharon. And since Sharon was my first real girlfriend, that means I never cheated on anyone.

She wasn't thrilled with my plan to come to the States. She didn't understand why I couldn't go to B-school at home. There are some great schools, like Western and U of T, but I've always dreamed of going to an American top ten. I promised her I'd come home after I graduated. Go back to my old job or get a better one in Toronto. She's not a big fan of living in the U.S. Hates the health-care system, thinks the corporations run the place. Her family is all in Toronto, and she wants to buy a house next door to her sister, get married and have kids. Lots of kids. There are pictures of other people's babies all over her apartment.

I take a longer look at the hot chick's cleavage. What if I come across a BBD (translation: Bigger Better Deal)?

"What's your girlfriend like?" Jamie asks, making me feel like shit.

"She's…she's great." Then I lower my gaze from the cleavage to the clock on the bottom right side of the screen. What kind of jackass am I? I've been in school for one night and I'm already looking to trade up? Did Clark Kent try to trade up Lois Lane when he became Superman? Don't think so.

I stay slumped on the floor for the next while, imagining myself metamorphosing in a phone booth. It's a bird, it's a plane, it's B-schoolboy!

One-eleven. Shit. Sharon's going to murder me. "I gotta go."

"See you tomorrow," Jamie says.

Nick continues clicking on his female classmates' attributes. He zooms in on the breasts of a woman named Lauren. "I heard this babe is bi. Later."

When I return to my room, I immediately pick up the phone and punch in Sharon's number. One ring. Two. Three. Clank, clank. Smash. Clank, clank. "Hello?" She sounds more drugged out than I am. Not that she would ever smoke pot. She hates when I get high, even though she's the one I tried it with in college. She thinks that now that I'm a professional I should act mature. I haven't smoked in a long time, and probably wouldn't have if I hadn't met Nick. Thing is, it relaxes me. Stops me from worrying. Helps me sleep. I've got to keep my voice steady so she won't be able to tell. Luckily she's not here. My thumb and index finger still smell of it.

"I woke you, eh?" Of course I woke her. Sometimes I'm such an ass.

"What do you think?" she murmurs.

"Sorry, hon. Go back to sleep."

"No, wait. How was your day?"

I lie back on my unmade bed. Crunch my head against a pillowcase stuffed with T-shirts. I forgot to bring a pillow. I don't know how I did since pillow was definitely on the Do Not Forget list that Sharon made for me. Sharon makes a lot of lists. They're taped all over her apartment. Floss is also on her list. Which I didn't forget because my dentist made me promise I'd floss every night. Unfortunately, I did forget to do it last night and tonight.

"Good," I say. Voice remaining steady. "We had orientation. Hung out with the same guys I met last night. Took a campus tour. A library orientation. Set up our Internet. Got our class schedules."

"Yeah? How is it?"

"Monday and Wednesday I have Organizational Behavior at nine, Accounting at ten thirty, Statistics at one... one...one-thirty." My body has sunk into the mattress, and I feel numb again, but I continue talking. "Tuesday and Thursday it's Strategic Analysis at ten-thirty—that's a sleep-

in. Economics at one-thirty, IC at three. But IC is a half-se-
mester course, so it only runs until the end of October."

"What's IC?"

"Integrative Communications. Presentations and stuff."

"Sounds fun."

She's being sarcastic, but the truth is, I'm excited. "Fun,
fun, fun."

Silence. "Did you smoke?" she accuses me.

Oh, man. "No."

She sighs. "You swear?"

"No."

She sighs again. "You have to stop. You know what pot
does to your attention span. School's for real now."

"What?"

"Your attention span, Russ."

"I know, I know. You're right." She *is* right. What am I
doing? When I smoke I have no attention span. I can barely
remember five minutes ago. Where was I five minutes ago?

"So no more?" she says.

"No more," I promise. She's right. I can't screw this up.
She's always right and I'm an idiot. "How was your day?"

"Good. I prepared. Tomorrow is my first day of school.
I'm giving my grade-ten class a surprise pop quiz on the details leading up to Confederation. They're going to thrilled."

At sixteen I wouldn't have cared what test a hot teacher
like Sharon gave me as long as I could keep looking at her.
Thank you, miss, may I have another? With my zit-infected face
and scrawny pipe-cleaner body, watching her teach would
have been the most action I'd get. "But it's only the first day,"
I say, regaining my senses. "A test already?"

"If I don't whip them into shape at the beginning, they'll
walk all over me."

"Wanna come over and whip me into shape?"

She laughs. "Is that an invitation?"

"What do you think?" Don't think she'd be too impressed with the saggy single bed, shit decor and hike to the showers.

"You miss me already, don't you, Russ?"

"Uh-huh."

"I figured. Okay, I'm going back to bed."

"Good night," I say. "Good luck tomorrow."

"You, too."

"Thanks. We meet our Blocks in the morning."

She yawns. "Good. And, hon?"

"Yeah?"

"Can't you call me slightly earlier tomorrow?"

I knew I was going to get flak for that. "But you told me to phone before I went to sleep."

"I did. But it's a school night. You should be going to bed earlier."

"Sorry. I won't call you so late tomorrow."

"Good. Go to bed now, okay? Love you. Be good."

"Love you, too." I press the end button on the cordless.

Now what? Clock says 1:40. Still excited about tomorrow. And worried. I thought pot is supposed to make me sleepy.

Maybe I'll visit Nick. Oh, yeah. Already did that. Maybe I'll call Sharon.

layla applies herself

I'm pacing outside the door to the Carry the Torch Committee office on the third floor of the main MBA building, the Katz building. I've been here for forty-five minutes. Someone better arrive shortly or I'm going to be late for orientation. I'd sit on the floor to wait, but who knows when someone last swept the hallway.

I hear the click-clack of a woman's heels coming down the hall. A short redhead in a black Theory suit turns the corner…finally. Yes!

I stretch out my hand. "Hello, I'm Layla Roth and I'm here to apply for the committee." You can judge people by their handshake. Firm means strong personality, trustworthy. Limp means weak, whiny. The woman's hand is flaccid. No matter. I still intend to apply. My mentor at Rosen Brothers Investments did this job when he was in business school, and I want to do it, too. It sounds fun. The committee chooses ten people to read over next year's applicants, and I want to be one of those ten.

The redhead looks as though she's surprised someone is

waiting for her before nine in the morning. "Layla, like the Eric Clapton song?"

"Yes, like the song." If I earned a dollar for every time someone refers to the Eric Clapton song when I introduce myself, I wouldn't have to work a day in my life. Not that I could stand not working. Not that I have to work for financial reasons. But what would I do all day? Volunteer for the Salvation Army? Please.

"Well, Layla, you're my first applicant. But you didn't have to wait for me." She points to a box marked Applications beside her door. "That's what the mail slot is for."

What if everyone else handed them to her in person? What if I crammed my application inside the box and she didn't check? What if it got stuck to the side of the box, like a chewed piece of gum, and was never seen again? Just in case, I'll take the extra two minutes, thanks. "I prefer to introduce myself."

She tilts her head and smiles. "Aren't you a go-getter! I'm Dorothy. Nice to meet you."

We chitchat for a few minutes about school, and I peek inside her office while she turns on her lights and boots her computer. I give her my application, then shake her hand—firmly—and say goodbye.

In the elevator I glance at my Rolex. I meet my Block in an hour! The back of my neck tingles with excitement. I can't believe this day is finally here. I'm going to be surrounded by kindred spirits. Imagine, networking every day. These are the people who will help me find jobs, help me move up the corporate ladder. These are the people who will one day rule the world, the people who will one day hire my children who will one day rule the world.

These are *my* people.

I stop at the admissions office to pick up my schedule. I already reviewed it online, but I want to have the original hard copy to post in my new room.

The next time I glance at my watch, it's nine-twenty. Forty minutes! I'd better get a move on if I want to get a good seat in orientation. I stop at the women's bathroom, which isn't coed and therefore less germ infested. The bacteria propagation is the one thing I'm not looking forward to about the coed dorm. I've never shared a toilet with a man, and I've heard it's not a pleasant experience. When I lived at home, my mother always complained that my father had lousy aim. Good thing they have his and hers bathrooms. And a housekeeper who takes care of the spills.

I squat over the toilet so I don't have to touch the seat. Who knows how often they're disinfected? Then I flush with the heel of one of my new Prada shoes. I wash my hands, retie my long blond hair into a pony off my face and take a paper towel to protect my hands from the microorganisms on the door handle.

Last week I did a virtual "First Day" walk on the LWBS Web site, so I know precisely where the orientation is being held. Room 107. The door is open, the ten-row auditorium empty. Eager to begin this next stage of my life, I sit in the front row and set my plastic name card at the front of my desk.

"Was that online Economics workshop really, um, necessary? Because I didn't do it."

I do not believe the guy in the back row. Isn't it a little late to be asking a question of that nature? I did the workshop back in June. And it took me thirty-three hours. Poor boy. He's going to be so lost.

The second-year student leading the orientation fingers the mole on his cheek. "It's a good way to brush up on your skills," he says. His voice cracks like a twelve-year-old muddling through puberty. "But I don't think it's something that will be tested."

Oh. But still. I'm glad I did it. I learned a lot, and that's the point.

"If you have no more questions," our mole-leader says, "we'll move on to the get-to-know-you exercise."

Yes! At last, an activity designed to help us bond with our classmates. I wish I could have been here for the beer bash last night, but one of my best friends back home was having a birthday party, and I couldn't miss it. So I drove in late last night, and went directly to my room to start decorating. I hope my fish, Martha, likes her new home. I put her right by the window so she gets lots of sunlight. Yes, I named her after Martha Stewart, and I don't care what anyone says, I'll defend her innocence to my death.

The second-year leader walks through the rows, passing out index cards. "Please write down your name, where you're from, where you worked and an interesting fact about yourself. Then pass up the cards and I'll read out the information. Stand up when I say your name. And then to lighten the mood, please tell your Block something embarrassing that happened to you."

Being a leader next year would be a fantastic experience. So would the Carry the Torch Committee. I'd be able to help shape next year's class. Maybe I should drop by the office again after orientation to reiterate how badly I want to be part of the program.

I must stop obsessing.

The Japanese woman with dyed orange hair sitting to my left looks dazed. I begin writing the information on my index card. She taps me on the shoulder. "What I do?" she asks.

Poor girl. How is she going to manage this year? I show her my sheet. "Name. Layla." I point to myself. "Where I'm from. Manhattan. Job. Rosen Brothers Investments. Interesting fact." I haven't answered that question yet.

"Oh! Thank you." The girl smiles and nods. "My English not so good."

"Don't worry. It will be." I have to think of an interesting fact and something embarrassing. Can it be the same thing? What if I can't think of something? How embarrassing! Could I use that?

Let's see now. Embarrassing…embarrassing… The time I was supposed to introduce a guest speaker in the third grade and was so overcome with stage fright that I refused to go? No, can't say that. I don't want them to think of me as the girl who cracks under pressure. After that little disaster, I forced myself to be in two performances to conquer my fear, and I did just fine. What about the time at summer camp when I was a counselor and had so much to drink that I passed out and wet my pants (so they said) in front of the five other staff members who later had to take me to the infirmary? As if I'd admit to that.

When everyone has passed up their information, the mole-leader begins to randomly read out names. I try to pay attention but instead think about my Carry the Torch application. It was good. Perfect. There's no reason for me not to make the cut.

"Jamie Grossman," the mole-leader says, "is from Miami. He worked in management at the children's ward at Miami General, and of late was a freelance reporter."

That hospital sounds familiar. What have I heard about it? The mole keeps talking but I can't concentrate. Where do I know that hospital from? Oh, right. From a deal I worked on when I was at Rosen Brothers. We merged two hospitals. Recommended a bunch of layoffs. I wonder if he was one of the "superfluous" personnel. Perhaps why he became a freelance journalist? That's what I hated most about my job. Knowing my recommendations often ended with people getting axed. What can I do? That's my job. I'm in mergers and acquisitions. And that's where I want to go back to after I graduate. That's where they'll pay me the big bucks. And I get to wear those cute Chanel suits.

I daydream about putting on my favorite Chanel suit. I love my Chanel suits.

"Kimberly Nailer."

Suddenly there's whispering and rustling from the back row. Kimmy, the woman I met in the bathroom, stands up, and the male students in the back row give each other knowing looks.

Tell me I didn't see that. I'll give the men here the benefit of the doubt and assume they'll be treating women as equals and not as second-class citizens or as sex objects. I wave to Kimmy as she stands up. I'll always stand behind my fellow females. Thirteen years at an all-girls school teaches you to take pride in the sisterhood.

"Kimmy is from Arizona and worked in leasing. An interesting fact about her," the mole-leader continues, "is that she was in a TV commercial when she was a baby."

Lighthearted laughter wafts through the class.

"What's your embarrassing fact?" the leader asks.

Kimmy blushes. "They were diaper commercials."

That is so cute. Do I have anything that adorable? True, calling attention to one's bare behind probably isn't the way to curtail the sex-object problem, but still, everyone will remember her, and isn't that the point?

She sits down, and the leader continues listing names.

"Layla Roth."

I jump from my seat and stand at attention.

"Layla grew up in Manhattan and worked for Rosen Brothers Investments. Her interesting fact is that her mother was one of the first women to graduate from the Leiser Weiss Business School. What's your embarrassing moment, Layla?"

Someone in the back row is humming the tune to the Clapton song.

"I was in London when I was nine, and I was at a party that Princess Diana was also attending. When it was my turn to meet her, I was so overwhelmed I couldn't speak. My parents had to take me home." I shiver at the memory.

"So you never met her?" the leader asks.

"Oh, I did, but not until four years later at a benefit."

I loved Diana. Instead of pictures of Kirk Cameron, I had posters of the princess of hearts up on my wall. Not on my wall proper, obviously—the tape would have ruined the paint. I thumbtacked them to the corkboard inside my closet.

Ah. That's what I forgot to buy. A corkboard for my schedules. Dorothy had a terrific one in her office with a gorgeous chrome frame. I must remember to ask her where she got it when I inquire about the job.

She must have read my application by now.

kimmy contemplates the random acts of the universe

What am I doing here? Jerry, the guy sitting four seats diagonal to me started a multimillion-dollar paper company. Juan, sitting in the corner, is an international student from Colombia and has two degrees in neuroscience. The woman I met in the bathroom at the dorm is an investment banker and hangs out with British royalty in her spare time.

I was in a diaper commercial.

I'm not sure why I couldn't come up with something a smidgen more intellectual than discussing my crap, literally. I am so pathetic. I must have been an admissions mistake. Stapled to a worthier application by accident. That's the only explanation. I don't know how I aced the GMATs. I must have gotten an easy version.

The class is laughing now, while my knuckles are gripping the sides of my desk in panic. They're laughing at a joke where Arbitrage Pricing Theory is the punch line. What am I doing here? I don't even know what Arbitrage Pricing Theory is.

Something pings me in the head. A paper airplane is nestled between my freakishly long foot and the leg of the desk. I look over my shoulder to see my nightmare from last night demonically smiling at me.

I've been successfully avoiding him all morning. When returning from the shower this morning, I spotted him standing by my door, knocking and hollering, "Kimmy? Kimmy, you there?"

I ducked back into the bathroom.

When I heard him searching inside the bathroom, I sneaked into a stall.

How could my potential husband have turned into my personal stalker in just twenty-four hours?

What does he want from me? I thought all men wanted was action, and then they took off. Why was this one still around?

I rushed into orientation, claimed a desk with my sweater and pen and then disappeared back outside. I correctly assumed that he wouldn't be able to sit next to me if he didn't know which desk I'd taken.

Unfortunately, I didn't take the law of random act of chance or whatever it's called into account. Until he threw an airplane at my head, I'd managed to pretend to concentrate on the lecture with intensity usually reserved for a *Details* magazine. (I love men's mags. Women's are so annoying: "What do I do? My mascara is clumping!" Who friggin' cares?) I spin around and there he is. Two rows behind me.

The jig is up.

The entire auditorium is ogling me like I'm butt naked. Nice work. It's only my second day and I'm the class slut.

I give him my best thin smile.

"How are you?" he mouths.

"Fine. And you?" I mouth back.

A goofy, buoyant smile is plastered on his face. "Want to hang out tonight?" This time his mouth has sound, and the entire room is in heat waiting for my response.

Ahhhh! What kind of question is that? Hang out? As if *hang out* could mean anything but *hook up*. If I say yes, I'm a slut. No, and I'm a bitch. It's like I'm at a witch trial.

Blink, blink. What to do, what to do. I skim the back row to see what the peanut gallery is expecting. And then my eyes lock with the bluest eyes I have ever seen. I feel like I just fell headfirst into a bucket of rich blue paint. They're opaque and beautiful and I lose myself in them entirely.

I snap back into focus and check out the rest of the man with the magical gaze. He's wearing a blue-collar shirt that matches his hypnotic eyes, and he's leaning forward, his elbows on his desk. Yikes, his tie has miniature Superman S's plastered all over it. But…his hair is dark, black almost, and those piercing blue eyes—I bet he could easily play Superman in any upcoming remake.

I'm in love.

Okay, I know I've thought that before, but this time I mean it. And this time the object of my love is looking at me while I'm looking at him. I smile, then turn back to the front of the room. The best way to flirt is to make eye contact, smile and then look away. Screw you Wayne, I've found someone else!

"Um…Kimmy?" Jamie asks.

I crane my neck backward again. "Yes?"

"What about tonight?"

Oops. If I want to marry Blue Eyes, I can't say yes. But if I say no, the peanut gallery will condemn me for life. What kind of girl fools around with a guy then refuses to see him? Sure, if I were a guy the act would have earned me kudos, but face it, I'm a woman struggling to survive in a testosterone terrain.

I take a politician's platform. "We'll see."

The goofy smile returns to Jamie's face.

I spend the next hour looking straight ahead, feeling the hairs on the back of my neck prickle as if it were cold in here. Actually, it is cold in here. I'm a bit nippy.

Of course that could be because of Blue Eyes.

Maybe when the bell rings, he'll smile at me, and we'll chat about school and then he'll ask me to get a coffee and I'll say sure and we'll grab a cup to go and park ourselves under a tree on campus. He'll spread out his jacket so my beige pants won't get stained with dirt. Damn, I don't think he has a jacket. What will I sit on? His lap? Wrong. Too early—I don't want to repeat the Jamie experience. I guess I could sit on my notebook. Anyway, we'll smile shyly at each other. The wind will blow through my hair. And then we'll sit together in all our classes and fall madly in love. (Then I can sit on his lap. His chest. Anywhere I damn well please.) We'll spend the next two years studying in the library, giggling together. He'll explain to me all the things I don't understand. Like Pricing Arbitrage.

Pure bliss. One day we'll tell little Blue Eyes Junior how we met on the first day of orientation.

Once again, I might be getting a smidgen ahead of myself. He might have taken a look at my fat ass and decided I was repulsive. Or he might already be married. He might already have a Blue Eyes Junior. I should know by now that you have to look at a man's left hand before you look in his eyes. Unfortunately, since he's sitting diagonally behind me, two seats over from Jamie, from my position there's no way I can get a good look at his ring finger.

He doesn't look married.

"Okay, guys," the class leader says, "it's time for you to divide into groups of five. Remember, you'll be working with these people for every group assignment this semester. LWBS's policy is to allow students to choose their own work groups within their Blocks. Some B-schools assign the groups, but LWBS believes you are capable of making the decision. I would suggest that you talk among yourselves, to get better acquainted. Each group should be made up of people of diverse backgrounds so that you'll be able to attack assignments from various angles. For example, you don't want five engineers in one group."

Panic. This must be how the heavy girls felt in gym class. No one will pick me. What can I add to a group? Uh, nothing? How's this: two accountants, one engineer, one banker…and a diaper model. I slouch in my chair. Through the slits in my eyes I watch my fellow students mill about. I don't look up in case they're pointing at me and shaking their heads. No, not her. No morons in this group.

What happens to the people who don't get picked? Will we be rounded into the corner to become the loser group? Maybe I'll be the only one left. I'll have to do all the assignments by myself. First I'll struggle to understand them, then I'll fail them, and then I'll get booted back to Arizona.

"Psst, Kimmy."

I practically pirouette at the sound of my name. Jamie. Sweet Jamie.

"Want to work with us?"

As far as I can tell, us includes himself, (gulp) Blue Eyes who has now moved to sit next to him and a skinny bleached-blond guy making a beat with his pen on the edge of his desk.

"Sure," I say, way too quickly to appear nonchalant. Wow. They want me. They want *me* to work with *them*. Maybe there's some merit to being the class slut, after all. Three boys and me. One boy who wants me, one who's a stud, and one who looks like fun in the musical I-have-a-garage-band way. This will be awesome—until they realize that I'm totally useless and start to hate me. What if they have secret meetings and vote me out of their group, *Survivor*-style?

But awesome until then.

I catch Blue Eyes' gaze and exude my best come-hither smile. He grins back.

Jamie jumps out of his chair and sits on the table. "Excellent. She's Kimmy, by the way," he says to the other guys.

"We figured," Musical Blond Boy says, smirking.

"The smart ass over there is Nick. The beautiful Lauren is on his right—"

Lauren? No one said anything about a gorgeous Lauren. I take one look at the stunning African-American beauty and want to cry. She towers over Nick and is sitting with perfect posture, her perfectly perky breasts at attention. Her hair cascades in jet-black curls down her back.

I noticed her when I walked in. How could I not? Every eye in the room followed her when she strutted to the back of the room, parading through the rows like she was on a catwalk.

Bitch.

I know it's wrong to hate women just because they're better looking than I am, but I don't care.

"Hey," she says, leaning into her palm, her elbow on the desk.

"Hi," I say, trying to infuse my greeting with enough suspicion so she'll know I'm on to her.

"And," Jamie continues, "the ugly guy sitting next to me is Russ."

Russ. I smile and lock eyes with Blue Eyes once again.

"Nice to meet you," he says, extending his right hand to shake. His fingers are soft and warm. And how is his left hand?

Ringless.

The year is looking up.

russ omits one significant detail

Need better reading material. But I feel like a hoser walking to the washroom with a newspaper. Everyone on the floor doesn't need to know when I'm planning on pinching a loaf.

"Hey, Rena," I hear a chick say. I know Rena from Toronto. She's a friend of Sharon's older sister. She's a second year, but lives on my floor. I've been told I'm supposed to call her and get together, but she's seriously annoying. Speaks in a nasal voice and wears ties. Thinks she's Avril Lavigne. Why would a woman wear a tie if she's not in a music video? I think she thinks it's sexy. It's not.

"Hey. How are you?" she replies in a voice so nasal, if there were any windows in here it would shatter them.

Oh, man. Just what I want to listen to. Nasal female voices while I'm taking a dump.

This whole coed deal is not for me. Yesterday I watched a chick from my Block tweeze her eyebrows. Did Superman ever watch Lois Lane groom? I don't think so. And then she took a *People* magazine to the toilet. That's just gross. I don't want to picture chicks taking a dump.

In junior high I had the unfortunate experience of watching Linda Stalwart, a girl I worshiped from afar, burp the alphabet. It was nasty. Not that she cared—she wouldn't have looked twice at me then. Ha. She should see me now. Well not now, as in on the throne. Now, as in at LWBS. Built. No longer known as Pizza Face.

My little cousin once called me that. Wasn't trying to be obnoxious. He was only five. Came over for Christmas dinner and pointed to my face and told me I looked like a pepperoni pizza. My aunt tried to shut him up, but he was laughing and pointing and jumping up and down.

Oh, man, my aunt felt so bad. Tried to convince me it was a compliment. Pepperoni pizza was my cousin's favorite, she said. I hid in my room for the rest of the night with my comic books, picking my face. Disgusting habit, but I couldn't stop. Once there was a piece of available skin I'd play with it and end up pulling it off. When I finally went on medication and kept my hands in gloves to stop picking, my skin took a year to heal.

Linda Stalwart. I wonder what she's doing now. Probably married and fat and teaching little kids how to belch.

Once when I stopped by Sharon's, she opened her door with that white stuff on her lip. You know, mustache bleach. "That's something I wish I hadn't seen," I said, shielding my eyes.

"Then don't come over uninvited." She slammed the door in my face.

I apologized a million times. Then she went on a rampage about how she could stop bleaching if I preferred, let it get dark and style it.

The talking chicks finally leave. To keep myself occupied I stare at the bathroom wall graffiti. You'd think that by this age, people would stop using the wall to express their inane thoughts, but no. In green marker, it says:

Sweet Kimmy,
  Violets are blue
  Roses are red
  Let me marry you
  And I'll please you in bed
Yours forever,
Jamie

What a hoser. The way to get the girl is not by writing cheesy-ass poetry on the back of the bathroom door. I'm not sure if he's kidding or serious. Kimmy knows he wants her. Everyone knows he wants her. Thursday night a bunch of us went out for dinner, and he dove into the seat beside her and kept telling her how hot she was. She laughed and smiled at him, but I doubt she was interested. She didn't go home with him, that's for sure. He was back in Nick's room after dinner, watching us smoke joints.

Yesterday, one of the get-to-know-your-group activities was a scavenger hunt through Maplewood. We were given questions like, What address is city hall? How many floors are in the library? How much are ten wings at Moe's? Six bucks. That one I knew. But anyway, Jamie wouldn't stop bugging her the entire activity. He asked her to marry him four times and serenaded her with Air Supply songs. I'll admit, it got laughs from the rest of us, but does that act work?

How do I know? Sharon's the only serious girlfriend I've ever had. And Jamie did manage to get two of the best-looking chicks in the class to be in our group. According to him, Lauren is bi, and currently prefers females. How hot is that? Lesbian eye-candy.

I flush, wash my hands and let them air-dry as I head outside. Think I'll take a nice Sunday afternoon nap. Not that I've done anything today to merit a nap. I woke up at eight, stared at the ceiling, had brunch with Nick, bought some pharmaceuticals at the drugstore and spoke to Sharon.

As I push back the door, Kimmy is pulling it open. She's looking pretty damn hot. Wearing tight black spandex shorts, a black bra that exposes her flat stomach, a red sweatshirt slung around her hips, little white socks, bright white runners. My guess: Going to the gym. Her brown hair is pulled back into a high ponytail, exposing soft-looking triangular ears. I love women's ears. I can spend hours running my fingers through Sharon's hair and playing with her ears.

"Hi, Russ," Kimmy says.

"Where you off to?" I ask like an idiot.

She smiles. "The gym."

"Yeah? Have you been already? I've been meaning to check it out." I can't believe I haven't gone yet. Any build I have is going to melt if I'm not careful.

"I've gone a few times this week. It's pretty good. There's a wait for some of the machines, but not too bad." The sweatshirt slips down her body exposing a fine-looking ass, but then she reties it. "Want to come with me?"

Why not? Sounds like a constructive way to spend a Sunday. "Sure. Do you mind waiting two minutes for me to grab my gym stuff?"

She smiles and takes a sip from her water bottle. "No problem. I have to use the bathroom anyway. Why don't I meet you in the courtyard and then we'll head over together?"

"Give me five," I say, trying to mentally block out the bathroom part. I sprint back to my room and grab the gym shorts and T-shirt I wore yesterday to play basketball with some of the guys. I suck, but it's fun. I started playing postcollege to help pump up.

Wonder if Sharon would care that I was going to the gym with a chick. Probably, eh? What should I have said, no? I can't go to the gym with you, I have a girlfriend? She wasn't hitting on me. Probably knows about Sharon, anyway. I must have mentioned it.

I spot Kimmy staring into the sunlight in the courtyard. She's wearing sunglasses. I need to buy new sunglasses. Left mine in Toronto.

"Let's go," she says, now wearing the sweatshirt. Shame.

It's getting cold. Wish *I* had a sweatshirt. "Where is this place?"

"At the back of the Student Services Center. Not far."

She walks fast for a girl. Her ponytail swings from side to side like a tennis ball in play. Sharon is the slowest walker ever. If I don't pay attention, I leave her a half a block behind.

"So how do you like school so far?" she asks.

"It's cool. I went to University of Toronto, so I lived at home."

"Were you in a frat?"

"No, no frat. Not my thing." I decide not to tell her that I didn't have much of a life in college. I preferred my calculator and comic books to beer kegs. Of course, that changed in my last year, when I met Sharon. "I bet you were in a sorority, eh?"

"No way. I'm not a gamma, gamma, gamma, can I help ya help ya help ya type girl."

I can't help mentally casting her as one of the sorority girls in *Revenge of the Nerds.*

"How do you like the dorm?" she asks, and takes another sip of her water. "Want some?"

I shake my head. "The dorm is all right. Not used to sharing a floor with so many people." Not used to sharing a water bottle, either. Sharon doesn't like when I take sips from other people's drinks in case any of them are sick and then I get her sick.

"I know. I feel like I'm eighteen again." She motions to a sprawling stone building. "We're here."

We climb the stairs to the top floor and show our student

cards to the scrawny kid at the front desk. The gym caters to the entire school, not just the business school, so it's packed. Puffing women on treadmills are lined against the window.

"Do you lift weights?" Kimmy asks.

"Yeah." Truth is, I've been slacking on my workouts. I feel a wave of panic that my muscles have all disappeared.

She stretches her leg in front of her. "Do you want to run with me?"

Even though I'm feeling anxious about the state of my muscles and want to get to the weights, the idea of watching her jiggle beside me is too appealing to pass up. I stretch out my hamstring beside her. "Sounds good."

We find two unoccupied treadmills in the corner, facing the window. She sets her speed to seven. I set mine at nine.

Shit. That's fast.

We run in silence. The sun beats through the glass, and I'm starting to sweat faster than usual. Oh, man. I must be out of shape. The wall of window makes me feel as if I'm running off a cliff. I wonder if the miniature students below us can see us. Maybe the windows are tinted. I'll have to check next time I walk by.

It's interesting watching below. Groups stopping, laughing. Someone doing a handstand against the side of a building. What is that guy doing? "Is that Jamie?"

Kimmy peers out the window, then grabs the handlebars and ducks. "Yikes, hide me."

"Hide you? Why?"

"I can't escape him. What's he doing?" A group of three girls are standing around him, laughing. He flips over and sits on the pavement. Two of the girls sit next to him. I think one of them is Rena.

"Gymnastics of some sort. Maybe he's working out."

Kimmy smirks. I'm pretty sure we're both thinking that

he doesn't look like a guy who works out. "So does that mean you're not interested in him?" I ask.

Her mouth flies open. Closes. Then it opens again. "Jamie? Nooo."

"What about what happened last week?"

She's flushed from my question. Or from the workout.

She bites her lip. "You know about that?"

"Ah…no?"

"Very funny. Did he tell everyone?"

"Didn't you see the ad in the LWBS paper?"

"Hilarious."

I'm worried that I've upset her, but then she laughs and adds, "What a blabbermouth."

Now I feel bad for Jamie. "Don't be mad, we forced it out of him. Tortured him, if you want to know. Tied him up then performed Japanese water torture."

She raises an eyebrow. "I'll bet."

"So, you interested in him or not?"

She shakes her head no, and her ponytail swings again. Game, set, match. "That night was a mistake. He's not what I'm looking for."

"What are you looking for?" I ask, now watching her pump her arms. She gets very into her workout.

She turns toward me. "Exactly what I'm looking at, actually. You."

I miss a step and almost trip into the handlebars. As I steady myself, I think, *me,* eh? This hot chick, breasts heaving, is interested in me?

Now might be a good time to mention Sharon.

Okay, now.

Now.

Kimmy reaches over for her water bottle, pulls up the tab with her teeth and sucks the water into her mouth.

Now.

"Do you want some?" she asks.

I nod. I know, I know. Shouldn't share water bottles. She hands me the bottle and our damp fingers touch. I swallow a mouthful, not unmindful of the bulge in my gym shorts. I'm hoping for those tinted windows. I wouldn't want this entire scene being described to Sharon via her sister via Rena.

Bad business this sharing of water bottles.

first semester

jamie comes late (literally)

Love that I'm late for my first class. Partially my fault, partially my mother's. She called me at eight-thirty this morning to complain about the new development in my sister Amanda's love life.

Mother: Apparently Amanda has a secret boyfriend. Did you know that, Jamie? I'm not a happy woman.

Me: I thought you wanted her to meet someone.

Mother: I do, but I'm worried because he's not Jewish.

Me: I thought you were worried because you didn't think she'd ever get married. You certainly have a lot of worries.

Mother: Don't be a smart mouth. How's school? Are you going to screw it up and not go to class?

Me: If you let me off the phone, I'd go to class.

Mother: Sue me for wanting to talk to my son who lives on the other end of the country.

Me: I thought my being accepted to B-school was the proudest moment of your life.

Mother: I am proud, but that doesn't mean I wouldn't have been prouder if you had gotten accepted to school in Florida.

Me: Oy. Great talking to you, Ma. Always love hearing first thing in the morning about all the things I'm doing wrong.

That conversation made me late. The muffin and coffee I stopped to pick up made me later. Not that it matters. Organizational Behavior is a joke anyway, but not in a ha-ha kind of way. Professor Matthews is supposed to be a bastard.

When I open the door, he's already started the class. I climb up the auditorium stairs and slip into the seat beside Kimmy in the fifth row. She's wearing an adorable back-to-school outfit: a short brown corduroy skirt, a tight white turtleneck and knee-high brown suede boots. Schoolgirl sexy.

The classroom has stadium seating, so everyone faces the professor in the middle, the professor who looks like an angry Morgan Freeman and is glaring at me from behind his desk. Now might not be the best time to take out my muffin.

"As I was saying, my second pet peeve, after students who come in late—" he looks at me as he enunciates "—are students who eat in class. You cannot eat and concentrate at the same time. If you must, coffee and water are acceptable beverages, but do not come to class half-asleep. I am not an alarm clock. By the time you are seated in your chairs, I demand that you be well rested and prepared to work."

No muffin?

His eyes dissect the room. "Now that we've gotten my pet peeves out of the way, welcome to Organizational Behavior. I am now passing out the class syllabus and assignment sheet. Note the required reading. And required does not mean optional. It means mandatory. My TA Ronald—wave hello, Ronald—" Ronald waves hello "—will be marking you on your participation. Every time you raise your hand, you'll get a tick beside your name. The number of ticks you have will be factored into your final grade at the end of the semester. Is that clear?"

We nod. I almost shake my head to see what he would do,

but decide this is not in my best interests. He's exhibiting a classic case of small penis syndrome. Which is surprising since I thought that only Jewish guys like me suffered from that affliction. Since no one cares about organizing their behavior, he's obviously trying to scare us.

My stomach grumbles. Loudly. I want that muffin.

"Now, in this classroom, I will teach you theories…"

Maybe if I reach my hand into the paper bag very slowly, then rip the muffin into pieces, he won't notice. I carefully drop my arm to the floor and attempt to insert it inside the bag.

Crinkle! Snap!

Small Penis stares at me. I retreat, and he continues yammering. "You will work in groups to choose the best type of organizational structure. For instance, I will give you a case study about the organization Procter and Gamble. Then I will give you three to five questions you must answer in a few paragraphs. The questions might be, for example, What organizational structure would best suit P and G's current situation and why? Is that clear?"

We nod. My stomach grumbles, again. Kimmy hears and dry giggles.

"Very well. First I will do a roll call, and then, as it states on your syllabus, I will begin by teaching group dynamics."

Fuck it. In one swoop, I reach into the bag, rip off the muffin top and slam it into my mouth.

The bell rings, and I immediately unwrap the rest of my muffin and eat it. "I guess the rumors are true—this class is bogus."

Kimmy looks like she might cry. "What are you talking about? Who said it's going to be bogus?"

"The second-years."

"Are those the second-year girls I saw you flirting with yesterday?"

I give what I hope is a mischievous smile, while trying to

keep my mouth closed so as not to reveal chewed muffin. "Darlin', are you accusing me of cheating on you? I'm shocked and bewildered." I'm kidding, of course. I've been trying to get her alone all weekend, but she keeps coming up with excuses. I'm not giving up. Chasing Kimmy might be my only entertainment all year.

She shushes me with her hand. "That class didn't seem like such a joke."

"Trust me. It is."

She looks confused. "But…but I still don't understand what organizational behavior is."

"It's psychology for business people. Different personality types. The best way to structure your business. That kind of stuff. You worked for a leasing company, right?"

She fiddles with her turtleneck as if it's choking her. "How'd you know that?"

"Because you said it on Tuesday."

"Oh, yeah. Right."

"How many vice presidents were there?"

"Um…" She shakes her head. "None."

"Okay, then who was the boss?"

She blushes. "My dad."

Ah. "Who worked under your dad?"

"There was a finance manager, collections manager, accounting manager, office manager…"

"What did you do?"

"I worked for collections."

Sexy. "Really? You demanded people pay you? Did you threaten physical harm?"

"No, I called them."

I can see her in a tight black leather dress, black stiletto boots and a gun harnessed to the inside of her thigh. I'll have to save that image for later. "Were all your dad's leases in Arizona?"

"No, he does leases all over the country."

"So let's say we take your company and restructure it. You

have five managers, but now they're arranged geographically, each one overseeing an area. West Coast, East Coast, the central states, the South, and the Southwest. Would this structure better serve the company?"

"Oh," she says slowly. "I get it. So we're going to learn theories that we can apply to answer that question?"

"Right."

She nods. "I was a Philosophy major in college. We learned theories and tried to apply them. This I can do."

I stand up and stretch. "Glad to be of service."

"How do you know all that? Did you study business in college?"

My mother wishes. "No, I did a liberal arts degree. But I read a lot."

We have a ten-minute break until the next class, which is in this same room. All the classes we have today are in the same room. I feel like we're back in grade school. The teachers come to us instead of us going to them.

"I'm going to get a coffee," Kimmy says, standing up. "Want anything?"

"I'm okay, thanks."

Professor Douglas arrives while Kimmy is still out. With his dark glasses, large bald spot and five-foot-five skinny frame, he looks more like Woody Allen than a professor. Short legs dangling, he sits on the front of his desk and sips his coffee.

"Mmm," he says. "They have a new flavor this year, hazelnut latte. I highly recommend it to anyone like me who suffers from severe caffeine addiction."

His audience laughs.

"So am I your first class today?" he asks.

"No," says the tall blonde in the front row. "We had Professor Matthews first."

He smirks. "Don't worry about him. His bark is worse than his bite. Although I wouldn't get too close."

Ah, the wanna-be comedian.

"He barked pretty loudly," another student adds.

Professor Douglas laughs a loud, room-filling laugh. "Yes, he does. And he never erases the board. Look at that," he says, and points to the dry board. "You'd think professors would learn to clean up after themselves."

Layla jumps up. "I'll do it."

Oy. What a suck-up.

"No worries," he says. "I got it."

Ah, and he isn't afraid of manual labor. What more could one want in a professor?

Kimmy walks through the door, coffee in hand, Russ beside her. She laughs at something he's saying.

I feel a sinking sensation in my stomach. I shouldn't be jealous. Russ has a girlfriend. He isn't making a move on my dream girl.

"Good morning," Douglas says to them.

"Morning," Kimmy says. Did she just stick her chest out?

Douglas yawns. "I guess it's not morning for you. You suckers had to be here for nine. I just got up thirty minutes ago. But no worries, I'm highly alert once the caffeine kicks in."

I don't know if I can take an entire semester of bad jokes.

"So. Here we are. I'm Professor Douglas, and this is Intro to Accounting. Unfortunately, this is not a how-to course on how to launder money."

More laughs.

Too bad. Now there's a final I wouldn't mind studying for.

Kimmy and Russ are crouched over their meals at a corner table in the cafeteria on the ground floor of the Katz building. Large glass windows are behind them and I have to squint to make them out. "I thought I'd find you hiding here," I say to Kimmy.

"Not hiding," she says, sipping her soup. "Just eating."

"Mind if I join you? What's today's special?"

Russ shoves a forkful of beef into his mouth. "Meat loaf. Not bad, either." He takes a packet of vinegar and dumps it over Kimmy's fries. Now that's gross. I thought I was the Grossman. Now that's funny.

"Will you two still be here after I buy my food?" I ask, trying not to appear anxious.

"Sure," Kimmy says.

"Do you want anything?"

"No, thanks," they say in unison.

"What d'ya want?" a mid-fortyish woman wearing a blue smock and a hair net asks when I reach the top of the food line.

"Well, Stella, what do you recommend?"

"How'd you know my name?"

"I'm psychic."

She peers at me in disbelief. "You are?"

"Not really. You look like a Stella. I can imagine myself as Marlon Brando screaming for you to come back to me. And you're wearing a name tag."

She looks down at her chest. "So what'll you have?"

"What's today's special?"

She leans in toward me. "The burgers are from yesterday and the meat loaf is from Saturday."

"I think I'll have a grilled cheese."

Next, Carl, the guy at the cash register, calculates what I owe, and tells me to slide my student/debit card through the swipe machine.

"You'll have to type in the number," I say. "I haven't received my permanent card yet."

He eyes me with suspicion. "Why not?"

"The bureaucrats lost my picture, again." What am I going to do about this problem? I'm going to need to have a student card by exam time. But if I apply for one in person, I'll be found out. And probably kicked out of school.

Carl nods. Apparently he knows all about the bureaucrats. "It's a mess up there, huh?"

I carry my tray back to my table. Russ and Kimmy's heads are inclined together in conversation. How did they come to be at dinner together, exactly?

Russ says something, and Kimmy peals with laughter. Russ smiles and leans closer. If I didn't know about Sharon, I'd swear that Russ is making a move on my woman.

"So what did you two think of Stats?" I ask, depositing my tray.

"Useless," Russ says. "Professor Gold obviously doesn't want to be teaching an intro class."

"Seems that way," I agree. "She phoned in her lecture."

"What does that mean?" Kimmy asks.

"It's an expression. Like in baseball, someone who phones in a game means he didn't really try. Russ, you a baseball man?"

"Not so much. I play basketball."

Guess we won't be watching the games together.

Kimmy sips another spoonful of soup. She is the slowest eater I've ever seen. "Personally, I prefer male professors."

"Why?" I ask, surprised.

"I've never liked my female professors. They're always bitchy. Like they're trying to prove something."

Russ uses his fork to extricate the meat crumbs in the crevices of his plate. "Like female customs agents. They always try to nail me when I'm crossing the border."

I've never heard of a female student not wanting a woman at the front of the class. "I thought you'd like having a female professor. They always seem to favor the female students."

"No, they don't," she says, shaking her head. "They always want me to fail."

"Maybe the ones you've had were jealous of your beauty and talent," I say, and wink.

She laughs and pushes her soup bowl away from her. "Maybe."

I blow her a kiss. "Unlike the other profs, at least she didn't give an assignment for Wednesday."

"I know," Russ says, shaking his head. "I bet we get just as much work tomorrow," he complains. "Better start my reading now. But first I'm getting a bag of chips."

Yes, Russ, why don't you go study…somewhere far away, maybe?

"So what are you doing tonight?" I ask, once Russ is safely away from the table and in the food line. "Want to see a movie?"

"I…we have a ton of reading to do," she says.

Not what I wanted to hear. I was looking for a more positive response, like maybe, "Sounds fabulous!" or dare I hope for "I'd love to be entertained by both you and Hollywood!"

"Come on, it's only the first day of school. It's just going to get worse, my darlin'. Enjoy it while you can."

"That's true. Maybe. Where's the movie theater?"

"Only a ten-minute drive away. It's just past the Children's Hospital, if you know where that is."

"You have a car at school?" she asks, leaning toward me.

"Yeah," I say smoothly. Score! Who doesn't want to date the guy with the car?

Russ slides into the seat beside Kimmy and slashes open his bag. A ketchup cloud wafts above the table. "Chip?" he offers.

"No, thanks," Kimmy says.

I take a few.

Kimmy turns to Russ. "Jamie just suggested we go to a movie tonight. What do you think?"

We? What we? Who invited Russ? She and I equals romance. Russ, she and I equals group goes to movie.

I try to catch Russ's eye to mime the signal that he should

say no. That subtle male clue would be me frantically shaking my head.

He says, "Sounds good."

He's killing me here. "I thought you wanted to get a head start on your work."

"It's only going to get worse, eh?"

Bastard.

kimmy's double date

"Running late?" I say to Russ as he passes me in the bathroom. Please don't cancel. Please don't cancel. I'm leaving the shower stall, and he's on his way in. I'm holding my towel securely to me. But not too securely. If he wants to tear it off, I won't stop him. Although he'll probably scream in horror at my fat ass.

Russ is holding a green towel around his waist with his left hand and a two-in-one bottle of shampoo and conditioner in his right. His stomach is exposed. One, two, three, four…five…six. Yup, that's a six-pack. "Just a little late," he answers. "But don't worry. I won't leave you alone with you-know-who."

He's coming. Oh. My. God. He's coming. "You'll protect me?"

"Be honored to."

Take that, Wayne! I have a date!

I'm still smiling when I get back to my hovel. I'm smiling and dripping. Problem number thirty-seven with the coed bathroom is that I can't wrap a towel over my head. No one looks sexy with a towel wrapped around her head. You also can't look sexy in a bathrobe. Which is why I didn't bring one. Only towels for me. Ones that perfectly reach from just above my breasts to my mid-thigh. They're also the perfect thickness. Thick enough to keep me warm, but thin enough not to add extra padding to my mid-body problem areas.

Guys love dripping hair and exposed skin.

I discard my towel onto the floor and then realize that the flimsy shade is open again. I keep forgetting to close it. My window faces the dark courtyard, so pretty much anyone sitting outside having a butt just got a nice look at *my* butt.

First I spray perfume in all the places I'm hoping to be kissed. And I am hoping to be kissed tonight. On my date. My movie date. My first B-school date. Kind of. If you don't count that three of us are going. Two guys and me. Could be worse. Could be two girls and a guy. I did that once when I was in college. Me, my college boyfriend and another girl in one of our classes. It was my boyfriend's idea. I wasn't interested in the girl in the slightest, but it was his birthday and I wanted to be the coolest girlfriend ever. He bragged to all his friends, and then I was the sluttiest girlfriend ever.

What to wear, what to wear. I wrap my towel around my hair, and choose a thong, my best jeans, a padded bra and a low-cut blouse. I don't have many variations of outfits, but I buy what works. Same with makeup. I own a red lipstick, a black mascara and a bronzer. And that's all I need. I'd love to use eyeliner, but putting anything near my pupils scares me.

Maybe Jamie won't show. I'm hoping that Russ had a chat with him, explained the situation and told him to fake a cold, that he's getting in the way. I know we hooked up last week, but it's time to move on.

I'm pretty sure Russ is interested. After the hour at the gym yesterday, we grabbed dinner together. And today, even though we didn't sit together in class, we had that connection going on. That aware-of-each-other connection. I'm not hallucinating—I caught him staring four times. And then we sat together at lunch. And then in Stats. And then we went to the gym this afternoon. And then he asked me if I wanted to get dinner. And now we're seeing a movie. If he were any more interested, he'd be wearing a red flag.

At ten past nine, I fly down the stairs as quickly as one can in two-inch heels. I hate these things. I spot Jamie in the entranceway, waving from behind the glass. He's wearing a Marlins baseball hat. Nice try—attempting to cover his bald spot.

Not only is he coming, but he's early. No surprise there. He was early in bed, too.

I open the door and ask, "Where's Russ?" Did he change his mind? Oh, no, oh, no. Maybe Jamie begged him to stay home. Yeah, right, begged him. Listen to me, I think men are begging over me. Who do I think I am, exactly? Aphrodite? I stand up straight, sticking out my chest in case anyone important is watching their TV monitor.

"I don't know," Jamie says, glancing at his watch. "He still joining us?"

Why does he ask that as if he's expecting Russ not to show up? Did the two of them have words? I'm about to cry when I spot Russ through the glass. He's now fully clothed, unfortunately, but still looks hot in jeans and a button-down shirt. His hair has some gel in it. He put gel in his hair for *me*. He likes me. He's trying to impress me. I could have an orgasm right here. Metaphorically speaking, that is. I've never actually had one.

But that's a topic for another time.

Our thighs are touching. It's subtle but happening. He's sitting on my right and is slightly slanted in my direction, and I'm slanted in his direction and we're touching. And not by accident. No one touches by accident. His thigh is purposefully pressed up against mine. Saying hello. Our ligaments made contact about four minutes ago, during a preview for a movie in which Kate Hudson and Matt Damon play opposites who fall in love.

Thigh, make nice to your new friend, Thigh. The heat being generated by the gentle touching of our denim is unbearable. I must rip off his clothes. I simply must!

Something to my left is talking and poking me in the shoulder. "I'm getting popcorn. Want to come with me?" Jamie asks.

"No thanks," we both say.

He shrugs and creeps down the row.

"The previews are my favorite part," Russ whispers, distributing shivers all over my ear.

"Me, too," I lie. Previews are a waste of time. I want to get to the good part. But I'll agree to anything Russ says. Want to have sex right here? Okay. Want to lick the gum off the underside of my chair? Sounds delicious.

Keanu Reeves does some sort of high-tech tae kwon do move on screen. "Doesn't that look cool?" Russ asks. Then the next preview starts. "I definitely want to see this," he says.

I can't help but laugh. "You're a marketer's wet dream. You want to see everything."

"Can't help it. They all look good."

"That's because you only see the best part of the movie. You don't have to sit through the boring dialogue, bad editing and predictable plot."

I feel his eyes on me instead of the screen. He's going to tell me I'm nuts. Instead he says, "That's an interesting way of putting it."

He is so close. I can smell the M&M's on his breath.

Is he going to kiss me? I think he's going to kiss me. Now. Any second.

Suddenly there's a thump in the seat beside me.

"Russ, you greedy bastard," Jamie says, stuffing his mouth

with popcorn. "You have to leave some women for the rest of us."

Huh? What does that mean?

Russ withdraws back into his seat, like a scared turtle into his shell.

"He's not being greedy," I say. Why does Jamie think he owns me?

"Yes, he is. He has Sharon to whisper to during movies. He can't have you, too."

Sharon? What's a Sharon? Any chance Sharon is his sister? This preview is really interesting. So interesting I think I'll keep staring at it. Yup. Keep staring. And not look as though I am upset or surprised in any way whatsoever.

Jamie continues chomping on his popcorn, inadvertently spurting out both kernel remnants and more information. "So Russ, how long did you say you and Sharon have been going out?"

Nail. Slammed. Deeper. Into. Heart. Russ has a girlfriend. I've already named our children, and he has a girlfriend. Maybe they're not serious?

"Hasn't it been since college?" Jamie says, answering his own question.

Russ shifts in his seat. His thigh is no longer touching mine, but is a continent away. I cannot cry. I cannot cry. That would be pathetic. Not more pathetic than me imagining he was interested in me in the first place, but pathetic nonetheless.

This had better be a short movie. Or a sad one.

I will stare straight ahead. Beautiful, tragic movie screen.

The movie starts and I continue staring ahead.

"Do you want some popcorn?" Jamie whispers to me.

"Sure, thank you," I say in a seductive voice, just loud enough for Russ to hear. Ha. You're taken? Fine. Then watch me flirt with Jamie. See how you like that.

My fingers accidentally touch Jamie's and a smile twitches his face. Uh-oh. Maybe this isn't a good idea.

"Where do you think they filmed this?" Jamie asks a few minutes later. A kernel remnant lands on my ear.

Who cares? "New York."

"Yeah? I was thinking Montreal. Isn't that the Olympic Stadium?"

How should I know? "Maybe."

"I think it is. I love Montreal. It's so European. Have you ever been?"

No. And I never will. I now hate Canada and all Canadians. Especially Russ. Jamie better shut up. If he keeps talking throughout the entire movie, I won't be able to properly fixate my thoughts on Sharon. Sharon. She sounds like a bitch. I bet she's blond.

Jamie's still staring at me. "Have you?"

Have I what? Oh, right. Montreal. "No."

Definitely blond. With dainty feet. Men love small feet. I bet the guys in her high school ranked her a ten. The entire package, I mean. Her feet are probably size six.

I hate B-school.

layla makes a
good impression

I love B-school.

And I would love it exponentially more if Professor Martin stopped spitting on me. But he appears to love what he teaches, Strategy, and that's what's important.

He's wearing an army hat. This is because he is trying to make the point that business is war, which is written in block letters on the blackboard and on the class agenda, lest we forget.

As usual, I'm sitting in the front row. This time, I'm regretting the seat choice due to Professor Martin's tendency to spit every time he uses the letter *P*.

Kimmy seems to be enjoying the class even less than I am. She looks horribly uncomfortable in the front row, and keeps reclining her neck as though attempting to get away. She's wearing a look of distaste, as if the maid forgot to empty the kitty litter. And she's not even taking notes. I suppose she's planning on borrowing them later from the library, where the professors keep them on file.

All the men around me are eagerly leaning forward in their seats, enjoying the war metaphor. I'm finding the environment mildly testosterone heavy.

"Do you *people* understand?" Professor Martin spits, waving his hands. "Your com*pe*titor is the enemy. You must be *pre*pared to fight for every consumer dollar and every *p*oint of market share or you will not *p*revail in business."

Too bad I'm a *p*acifist. Why do men think everything is about war?

Yes! The bell rings, and I head to the computer terminals to check my e-mail. The application committee was supposed to get back to me early this week. It's Tuesday. Today is the last possible day for it to still be considered early in the week. Tomorrow is the middle of the week. I type in my e-mail address and password. My password is always the same. It's the license plate I memorized off a cab when I was five, thinking that the driver was the gray-haired man who had killed his wife in that week's episode of *Unsolved Mysteries.* I wanted to call the show, but my then nanny wouldn't let me.

In my inbox: five e-mails from my best girlfriends back home in the city, a bunch of e-mails from the LWBS administration regarding class add/drop dates, a reminder about my ten-year high-school reunion this summer (for which I'm on a committee), an article featuring my mother in *Woman Entrepreneurs,* forwarded by her secretary.

Not in my inbox: a message from the applications committee.

Bummer. I IM with the girls for twenty minutes, wash my hands in the bathroom to cleanse myself of computer germs, and use a paper towel to open the door. I need to buy more of those antibacterial wipes. I'm already out. In the caf, I buy a burger and a Sprite, then search for a familiar face. I look for people in my work group, but can't find anyone. They're extremely competent, but they don't like to socialize. Two of them are married and live in off-campus housing. The third is the orange-haired Japanese student, who mostly hangs out with the Asian student association.

I spot Kevin, the last member of my group, sitting by himself in the corner, rubbing his eyes. He's always rubbing his eyes. And I've seen him do it right after he opens the germ-infested classroom door. In Japan, they hand out warm towels to wipe your hands on before you eat. Kevin could use one.

"Mind if join you for lunch?" I ask. He wouldn't be my first choice for a meal partner, but I'll give him a chance. "Ghjkhjh," he says, mumbling something. He pushes his tray to the side to accommodate me, so I assume that's a yes. Obviously I didn't ask him to be part of my group because of his conversation skills. A former accountant for Ernst & Young, he's a whiz with numbers.

"Are your eyes okay?" I ask, biting into my hamburger.

"They're itchy." Small bits of pus line the rims. He continues rubbing. His fingers are streaked with ketchup. Then he stops, picks up a French fry and licks the ketchup off his finger. A few seconds later, he's rubbing his eyes again.

"Hjkghfj," he says, and then eats another French fry.

I seriously need to make some LWBS girlfriends.

Professor Rothman is extremely handsome. He's almost six feet tall and has sandy-blond hair. And he's in his mid-thirties, tops.

Who knew professors could look like this?

For the first time, all the women in the class are sitting in the front two rows.

Rothman lifts his muscled arm and writes GDP = C+I+(X-M)+G on the blackboard. I copy the new equation.

"Does anyone know what the letters represent?" he asks.

I raise my hand. "The *C* signifies consumer goods. The *I* signifies investment goods. The…" Think! Think! I know this! "The *X-M* signifies exports minus imports and the *G* signifies government spending."

"Well done," he says, and smiles. Wow. That's what I want. A gorgeous, intelligent man. A man who knows his numbers. I look away and continue taking notes. He's talking too fast to stop. I've already written eleven pages, and my hand is starting to hurt. I can't believe he's teaching so much in the first class.

The bell rings, and I finish the sentence. I insert my notes into the second section of my Tuesday/Thursday binder, then hole-punch and add the sheets he handed out at the beginning of class. I hope I didn't miss anything.

"Professor Rothman?" I ask, waving my hand toward him, and a smile lights up his face.

"You can call me Jon," he says, and then looks at the nameplate that's still on my desk. "Miss Roth."

"I'm Layla," I reply. He's so approachable! "Will videotapes of your lectures be available at the library?"

"Yes, the videotapes will be available." He rubs the back of his arm against his chin. "And I would also like to tell you that your contribution today was excellent."

Yes! "Thanks, sir. I mean, Jon. I've always enjoyed working with unknown variables."

"I'm looking forward to having you in my class this year." He continues to hold my gaze. All right. Time to look away. Why isn't he looking away? I smile, look down, close my binder, zip up the rolling bag I bought so I wouldn't strain my back and roll it down the hall.

What was up with that? Why is the professor flirting with me? That is *so* inappropriate.

Integrative Communications is the only class I have that's

not in room 103. IC is in room 207, and I'm looking forward to the change of scenery.

I walk around the podium, sit myself down in the front row and arrange a new area in my binder. The class slowly fills up behind me. A few minutes later, a woman with frizzy red hair and a big smile walks in clapping her hands.

"Hello, everyone, hello," she says as people bustle to their seats. She cups her ear with her hand. "Sorry? I didn't hear you." No one speaks. "That's your cue to say hello back."

"Hello," we mumble.

"Shy ones, are you? This is no place for shyness! One of the most vital aspects to speaking in public is confidence. Let me hear that confidence!"

"Hello!" we say. My hello is especially loud.

"Excellent! I can see I am going to have a wonderful time with you!" She smiles down at me and I smile back.

"My name is Cindy Swiley," she says, and presses a button on her laptop. The title, Professor Cindy Swiley, flashes in red across the screen. "But you can all call me Cindy." Professor and Swiley fade away, leaving a gradually expanding Cindy. "I'll be teaching you Integrative Communications for the next six weeks." New slide appears. "In this class, you will learn how to present. How to handle questions. How to speak without notes. You will be giving two presentations, one halfway through the class and one as your final exam. Your midterm will be videotaped, and then reviewed and critiqued by me. But I'm sure you'll all do fantastic!"

I can't wait! At twenty past four the bell rings. I pile my belongings together, then return to the computer terminal to check my e-mail.

Dear Ms. Roth,
Congratulations! You have been accepted to the Carry the

Torch Committee. Please be in room 302 on the third floor of the Katz building on Friday at 9:00 a.m. for an informational briefing.

Yes! I would pat myself on the back, but I still haven't purchased more of those antibacterial wipes.

kimmy buys her books

I am wasting my day in a bookstore line. And it's not even a fun bookstore. Where are the cappuccinos, the magazines, the scones?

The LWBS bookstore is one long, windowless room, filled with textbooks, course-packs, and nebbish royal-blue sweatshirts that say LWBS in block red letters. As if I'd ever buy one. Maybe a baby tee, but that's as much school spirit as I've got.

There are seven people ahead of me. To add insult to injury, the line next to me is moving exponentially faster. Look at me, throwing around words like exponentially. What do I think I am, an MBA student?

This place is busier than a gym at six o'clock. Not that I have a choice. I have cases to read by tomorrow. My heart pounds at the thought of the never-ending treadmill of homework. My fingers are about to break off from lugging these hundred-pound books. I'm holding one course-pack per class, plus an extra one for Strategy. Even IC has one, which I don't understand. Why do I need photocopied case studies to help me learn to speak in public? I'm also lugging to the cash register the must-have B-school eighty-five-dollar calculator and seven textbooks. SEVEN. All hardcover. All in the region of a hundred dollars. Each. And they don't even sell used copies so I can't skimp on last year's editions. What bookstore doesn't sell used copies? What a waste. I won't even be able to resell them next semester.

True, my dad paid my tuition, but I'm using the money I've saved up over the last few years of working to pay for my books and living expenses. And my dad isn't thrilled about his contribution. He wrote the check with a heavy hand and asked me repeatedly if I was sure this was what I wanted.

I told him yes, even though I have no idea.

I drop the books onto the floor to alleviate the cramp in my fingers and scan the room for Russ. Where is he? I hoped he'd be buying his books now, too. Not that I want to see him. I'm a tiny bit mortified that I've been throwing myself at him all week and he already has a girlfriend. He must think I'm a freak. Obviously a guy as gorgeous as him has a girlfriend.

I avoided making eye contact with him for the remainder of the movie. In the car home, I decided that dodging the subject made me look like I cared, and obviously that wasn't going to help my cause. So I acted like I loved Sharon. Hurray for Sharon. Maybe Sharon and I can be best buds. We'll bake cookies and braid each other's hair. "So when do we get to meet Sharon?" I asked from the front seat of Jamie's ten-year-old Hyundai Excel, putting on my best girly voice, all high-pitched and full of fake cheer.

"I don't know," Russ answered. "She lives in Toronto."

Toronto? Does it count if they're not in the same country?

I avoided him all day. I walked straight into Strategy and sat right in the front. Big mistake, since Professor Martin is psycho. Thinks he's still in Vietnam. I tried the front row again for Economics and IC. Barely saw Russ until he and

Nick passed me on the way out and Nick asked me if I wanted to join them for a four-twenty. Decided to play it cool and say no. And I have no idea what a four-twenty is.

There he is. My mouth goes instantly dry as if a vacuum has sucked out its moisture. He and Nick are standing by the door. Nick stumbles, and the two of them laugh. Then they scan the bookstore and shake their heads in what I assume is dismay at the jungle in here.

Russ spots me and I freeze. He smiles and twirls his index finger near his temple, which I read as his this-line-is-crazy gesture.

I nod. "I know," I mouth. I hold up two fingers and then point at my watch. I'm trying to tell him I've been here for two hours.

He shakes his head again. Then he points to his eyes and then at my books on the floor.

Translation (I think): Can I look at your books tonight?

My mouth goes dry again. I'm glad we're not face-to-face because I don't think I can talk properly. He wants to hang out with me tonight. To do reading. Together.

Maybe he just doesn't want to wait in line.

Or maybe (it's possible) he's looking for an excuse to hang out with me.

I nod.

He says something to Nick that I can't read, winks at me, and then takes off.

There's suddenly a huge gap between my massive feet and the person in front of me in line. I pick up my five-hundred-pound pile, then drop it a foot up.

Sigh. How come the good ones are always taken? Russ is so cute. So perfect. I have the worst luck.

The person in front of me is at the cash register. I push my books forward with my foot.

First Wayne leaves me for someone else, and now the guy I want is taken.

The skinny purple-haired undergrad at the register motions to me. I'm up. I pick up my stuff in two shifts. How am I going to carry these back to the dorm? A boyfriend would carry them for me.

"That'll be eight hundred, forty-seven dollars, and twenty-two cents."

Good thing I didn't buy that baby tee.

russ goes to war

Dribble. Dribble. Big breath. I shoot, I…

Miss. Oh, man.

"You suck, Russ," Nick says.

"Shit." I jog toward the basket.

"You see that net, up there?" he says, pointing. "The ball is supposed to go through it. *Through*."

"Yeah, thanks."

"Had enough for today?"

I nod. Don't think I can speak. "I'm too old for this."

"Gimme a break. You just need some practice, dude."

I empty a bottle of water down my throat and follow Nick outside the gym. The fall air attacks the sweat on my arms and face.

"Wanna go for a beer?" Nick asks.

"Can't. Made plans to study with Kimmy."

Nick raises an eyebrow. "So have you fucked her yet?"

I trip on my shoelaces. "Excuse me?"

He laughs. "You two have been spending a lot of time together. Just wondering what's going on."

"Nothing's going on. I'm a taken man."

He chuckles. "If you say so." When we reach the second floor, he says, "Same time tomorrow?"

"You got it," I say to Nick's retreating figure. I climb the rest of the way on my own, thinking about his other question.

Kimmy and I have been spending a lot of time together. But nothing is going on. Nothing. Who's to say I can only make male friends at school? I'm supposed to be networking. We've been hanging out for legitimate purposes. Studying. Reading. Working out. Nothing sketchy.

And she knows about Sharon, thanks to Jamie. I was going to mention it eventually, honest, but it's not something you can easily work into the conversation without sounding like a hoser. Thanks for the movie invite. Did I mention my girlfriend Sharon really likes movies?

I unlock my room, grab a towel, shampoo and soap, and bolt to the bathroom. As the hot water pummels against my back, I tell myself for the umpteenth time this week that I'm not doing anything wrong. There is nothing wrong with having a close female friend.

I'm full of shit.

She wants me—didn't she say so at the gym?—so, yes, it's wrong to spend so much time with her. It's wrong to lead her on when I don't want her.

I'm *so* full of shit.

Last night I dreamed we were having sex in Professor Martin's class. We were actually under the desk, our combat uniforms strewn all over the floor.

I am an asshole. I am the hugest asshole. (But it *was* a good dream.)

In the dream, under her khaki soldier's clothes she was wearing what she'd been wearing when we studied together last Tuesday night: a black tank top with red bra straps peeking through. Instead of studying, I spent the entire evening imagining what the rest of the bra looked like. I was thinking the lacy, see-through kind. Maybe with a pair of matching red panties.

When I stopped by her room last Tuesday night to borrow her books, she suggested that we work together in one of the study rooms in the library. I thought, why not. Might be more fun. And there we were. Two people, a man and a woman, in an enclosed room. With the door closed. And no windows. And a big, brown table. I wondered if anyone had ever had sex on that table. I pictured us having sex on that table.

We were supposed to read two cases, one for Organizational Behavior, one for Stats. I skimmed the pages, but it was hard to concentrate when she smelled like vanilla and lemon, like something in my mom's kitchen.

I shower slowly, enjoying the memory. Eventually I turn off the water, wrap my towel around me and return to my room. Then I pick up the phone. I told Kimmy I'd call her when I was done with basketball.

"Hi, this is Kimmy, can't come to the phone. Leave a message and I'll call you back."

Her voice sounds sexy, smooth then rubbed with sandpaper. I leave a message and pull on the jeans that were crumpled on the floor, the ones that already have my belt in the loops and my change and credit cards in the pocket. My plans with Kimmy are for around five, and it's five on the nose.

If it hadn't been for Sharon meeting me, liking me, convincing me to go see a doctor about my skin and kicking my ass into the gym, a girl like Kimmy would never look twice at me.

Where's my gel?

The phone rings. Must be her. At least she didn't forget.

"I was waiting for you," I say, finding the bottle under my desk and rubbing some in my hair.

"You were?" says a familiar voice. Sharon's.

"Oh, hi," I say, startled. Sharon. Sharon. My girlfriend. Remember her? The girl who was always there for you? I am such an ass wipe. "I had a feeling you were going to call."

"Yeah? You must be psychic. What's up?"

"Not much. Just got back from playing ball."

"And tonight?"

I wipe the gel residue on my jeans. "Studying, maybe."

"Good idea," she says. I doubt that. Then she adds, "I miss you."

Maybe she can sense my wandering eye. "I miss you, too," I mumble.

Knock, knock. Oh, man. "Shar, someone's at the door, I gotta go. Can I call you later?"

"Who is it?" she asks.

At the moment, I'm hoping Nick.

But no. Voice from behind the door. "Russ? You there?" Kimmy.

"One second," I say to the door. Then I say to the phone, "I have to go."

"Where are you going?"

"To study."

Kimmy knocks again. "Russ? You inside?"

Oh, man. I have a pain in my arm, and I think I could be having a heart attack. Breathe. So I've been flirting. Big deal. No harm in flirting.

"Who are you studying with?" Sharon asks, relentlessly.

"Just some guys," I answer. Now I'm lying. I'm not just flirting. I'm lying and flirting.

"Okay, call me tonight."

"Will do." I try to keep my voice upbeat and blameless sounding.

"Be good. Love you."

"You, too." I leave out the love in case Kimmy can hear. Not sure what else "you, too" could mean. Good luck? You, too. Have a good dinner? You, too. Have fun screwing around? You, too.

Now I really feel like an ass. After all she's done for me, how can I flirt with someone else? I can't treat her like this. No more private study sessions with Kimmy.

I open the door and find Kimmy in combat clothes, slinging a rifle over her shoulder. I blink and the vision disappears.

She's wearing that black tank top with the red bra straps peeking through.

Oh, boy.

"What do you say we go for a beer instead?" I ask.

She smiles. "Sounds even better."

"I think Nick wants to join us."

A cloud passes her face. "Lead the way."

My alarm doesn't go off when it's supposed to. My eyes pop open at ten to nine. Oh, man. How did I do that? I check to see if there was a power failure. Nope. Apparently I set my clock for eight p.m. instead of a.m. Good job.

I jump out of bed. No time to shower. Need clothes. I can keep on the same boxers, since I just put them on after I showered last night. Sharon hates when I don't change my boxers in the morning, but what's the point if I showered the night before? She goes through three pairs of panties a day. One in the morning, a thong at night, and then a clean pair to sleep in. Who has time for that kind of laundry?

Eight fifty-four. I can't believe I'm going to be late for class. I'm never late for anything.

I zip up the same jeans I was wearing last night, and throw on the closest available T-shirt. Did I wear that yesterday, too? I think I wore that yesterday. It smells like I wore it yesterday.

Ready. Must brush teeth. No time to floss. There's never time to floss. I rummage through the papers on my desk, looking for my toothpaste and toothbrush, then sprint to the bathroom, brush, pee, shove my stuff back in my room and sprint to class. Professor Matthews is about to slam the door, when I rush in.

Kimmy waves from the back row, and I weave through the desks and sit beside her. "You were almost late," she says.

"Had some trouble getting out of bed."

"No kidding," she says. She looks at me with speculation. "How come? We didn't get back that late last night."

I don't answer. We left the bar at around twelve-thirty. But then I hung out in Nick's room smoking joints and watching the security monitor till two. Then I called Sharon. We were on the phone till three, and then I tossed in bed till four-thirty.

I slump into my seat. Should have picked up coffee.

Kimmy starts to doodle on the piece of blank paper on my desk. "Are you going to the club fair at lunch?"

Club fair, club fair. "Will there be rides?"

"A Ferris wheel in the center of the cafeteria," she deadpans.

The door creaks open. Jamie waltzes in, coffee in hand. He scans the room for a seat, and climbs up the stairs toward the back. Matthews is watching him, steam shooting from his nostrils.

Kimmy taps me on the arm with her pen. "So, are you coming to the club fair?"

What the hell *is* a club fair? "Definitely."

By that afternoon, I've signed up for the American Marketing Association, LWBS Intramural Basketball, the Entrepreneurial Club, the Microbrew Society, the Ice Hockey Association and the Consulting Association. I think I might be overdoing it. But they all sound interesting, eh?

We're in the main hall of the Katz building, and there's no Ferris wheel. But there are desks set up against each wall, with groups of second-year students manning them, hollering at passing first-years to join them. There are at least eighty clubs, and it's like I'm in an electronics store and all the televisions, radios and CD players are tuned into different stations at full blast. How can there be so much to meet about? And why did I just sign up for all of them?

Somewhere in the sea of people, I've lost Kimmy. I spot Nick at the front of the line of the beer blast booth. He waves me over. "Dude, did you sign up here yet?"

No, this appears to be the one club I haven't signed up for yet. How is it different from the Microbrew Association? Beer is beer, right? "Should I?"

The second-year shoves a clipboard and a pen under my face. I write my name.

"That'll be fifty bucks." The second-year takes back the clipboard. "You're signing up for a year of beer blast. Otherwise it's five bucks a night."

"Fifty American bucks for beer?"

The second-year puffs himself up and dives into his speech. "Every Thursday night there's beer blast in the cafeteria. Companies sponsor them, and the profits go to various clubs. You can spend five bucks at the door, or fifty bucks for the entire year. That's about four for free. Trust me, it's worth it."

If a guy I've never met before tells me to trust him, why wouldn't I?

"Do it, dude," Nick says. "First one's tomorrow."

"All right," I say. "Can I bring the cash then?"

"No," the second-year says. "But there's a bank machine down the hall."

I barely have fifty bucks in my account. "I'll cover you," Nick says, sensing my hesitation.

"Thanks, man." Now that's a friend. A friend will do everything in his power to help you. If I'm going to win this war I'm waging inside myself, I'm going to need all the help I can get.

jamie is a washout

Most men would have taken the hint. I am not most men.

"I can't tonight," Kimmy says, "I'm going to a beer blast." She's standing in her doorway, brushing out her hair. I wonder what it must feel like to brush one's hair. I don't even touch mine, for fear of inadvertently encouraging strands to fall out.

"But you have to eat. You shouldn't go beer blasting on an empty stomach."

She grins but shakes her head. "I can't. I want to get some reading done first. Maybe another time?"

Aha! An opening. "Tomorrow night?"

I know I'm sounding desperate, but the over-the-top-style adoration technique usually works for me. I had to send my last girlfriend, Shoshanna, roses with corresponding poems for two weeks straight before she agreed to go out with me. Let's face it, I'm not going to pick up women with my hot bod and balding head. I need to showcase glitz, romance and the potential for a lot of laughs.

Unfortunately, Kimmy is not taking the bait. Which

poses a problem. Because there aren't so many women at LWBS to begin with, never mind hot Jewish women, I might have to start hanging out in the undergraduate dorms, which would look suspicious. I might be taken for a perv.

I need something to entertain me at this institution. To distract me from the fact that I don't know why I'm here. What a farce. What a lie.

For now my distraction is Kimmy. I wonder if it's the hair. Does she not like the balding? Maybe I should try to grow a comb-over. Oy.

"Maybe. We'll see," she says. "I need to work on that Stats assignment for Monday."

"Stats? I'll give you a stat. A hundred percent you should have dinner with me tonight."

"Funny. But no. Not tonight, anyway."

A maybe is better than a no. I guess I'll go to beer blast tonight. Might as well watch the morons make fools of themselves.

I decide to call my bubbe before getting ready. I feel a twinge of guilt for not calling since I've been at school.

She drops the phone twice before picking up. "Hello?"

"Hi, Bubbe!"

"Hello?"

"Bubbe, it's me, Jamie."

"Jamie? Oh, Jamie! I'm so happy you called." The sentence sounds more like, *I'm so heppy you cult.* She has a thick Yiddish accent. We speak for only a few minutes. We never have that much to talk about, but she sounds like she's in good spirits, as usual. It always amazes me how someone who has been through so much—she's a Holocaust survivor who lost her entire family, including her first husband, in the war, and then her second husband, my mother's father, to cancer, and then a grandchild, the sister I never met, to crib death—can still keep smiling. Which she does. She may not have too many of her own teeth behind that smile, but she's still smiling. Unlike my mother, who's never happy with anything.

"When I gonna see you?" she asks.

I tell her that I can't come home for Rosh Hashannah, the Jewish New Year, which is in a week and a half, but I'll be back for Thanksgiving.

"Good, good. You focus on school."

"Love you, Bubbe."

"I love you. So much."

I change into my terry-cloth navy bathrobe, grab my bucket of products and stroll to the showers, not caring that I don't look macho.

I step into the second shower, because the first one's in use. I wonder by whom. Maybe it's Kimmy. All wet, and hot, and soapy. And then just like we're in a movie, there's a knock on the shower divider. Wow. Maybe it *is* Kimmy and she can read my mind. Just like in a movie, we were meant to be.

"Yes, darlin'?" I say.

"Darlin'? How did you know I was a woman?" It isn't Kimmy, but whoever it is, she sounds sexy.

Me: It was a feminine knock.

Sexy Stranger: Do you have any conditioner? I'm out.

Me: Who wants to know? (I need a name!)

SS: It's…Darlin'.

Me: Playing mysterious, are you?

SS: Always.

Me: My personal conditioner, occasionally referred to as cream rinse, is for extrafine hair. Is that acceptable?

SS: Preferable, actually.

Me: (A clue?) So you have thin hair?

SS: No, I mean I prefer my men with thin hair. (She doesn't actually say the part after "no.")

Me: (While contemplating standing on my bucket and peering over the wall.) Shall I come over to hand you the bottle?

SS: Why don't you throw it?

Me: What if it spills?

SS: Close it properly and it won't.

Me: (Laughing.) All right. Ready? One, two, three. (I don't throw it.)

SS: I'm waiting.

Me: That was a test. Now I'm really going to throw it. Are you ready? I need to know if you're ready.

SS: *Always.*

Me: Are you sure? This is serious stuff.

SS: I'm pruning here.

Me: Don't get cranky. Here we go. One, two, three. (Toss bottle over dividing wall.)

(Clunk. Laughter.)

SS: Oops.

Me: You dropped it, didn't you?

SS: It didn't spill. Much. There's some left. I think.

Me: (While rinsing the shampoo from my head.) I'm going to need it back now.

SS: Why didn't you take some before you passed it?

Me: Why? It wasn't time for the cream rinse yet.

SS: Don't you need a second shampoo?

Me: Real men don't do two shampoos. (Real mean are men like me without much hair and are afraid to wear it out.)

SS: All right. Ready? One, two, three.

(Nothing comes.)

Me: You didn't throw it.

SS: Just testing. Now for real. One, two, three. (Bottle flies in arc over wall, I catch it.)

SS: Impressive.

Me: You should see me juggle.

SSE: (Turns off her water.) One day.

Me: You're leaving me already?

SS: It gets cold standing here with no water.

Me: (While imagining cold naked body and telltale nipples.) Desert me, see if I care. (Bathroom door closes. Sigh. I open bottle of conditioner. Empty.)

(End of Scene)

layla's price isn't right

Tom Price is far too sloppy to be accepted into LWBS. I feel bad, but what can I do? You'd think with a last name like Price, he'd be more market-savvy.

I read his opening statement again: "I think Stern Business School is the perfect place for me to grow as a professional…"

It's Leiser Weiss Business School, not Stern Business School. Stern is New York University's business school. Tom's entire application focuses on what an incredible place Manhattan is. NYU probably got his application to LWBS.

Final score? His GMAT translated into a nine out of ten, work experience is a seven, undergrad marks an eight. For references, I gave him four out of five, essays three, and for overall impressions I'm giving him a zero. That makes a total of thirty-one out of forty-five. Reject file. He was sloppy, case closed.

I feel a tad guilty, but someone has to make the tough decisions.

My favorite is the "overall impression" category, because it can be anything we want it to be. That's where we can give a high score if we think the candidate will add something exceptional to the business school experience. Like if she does Broadway plays in her spare time.

"How'd he do?" asks Dennis, the student sitting to my left. He's young, twenty-four, and looks like a miniature, handsomer Bill Gates, despite the massive round glasses covering most of his face. Not so shockingly, he did in fact work for Microsoft, and wants to go back to Seattle once he finishes his MBA.

Six of us are in the conference room, shuffling applications from the new pile to the first-round pile to the rejection pile. Dorothy gave us brief instructions at the beginning: be fair, try not to be biased, everything we read remains confidential, every application has to be looked at by two of us. The two scores are averaged, and then the applications are put in numerical order.

"Not great," I answer him. "I don't think he'll be joining our ranks next year."

Next. Emily Beckman. Essays…pretty good. Four out of five. Work experience. Good. Seven out of ten. GMATs… not fantastic. Four out of ten. Not terrible, but not as good as Tom Price. References, four out of five. College marks, eight out of ten. But since this is the first female applicant I've come across in nine submissions, I'm giving her five out of five for overall impressions. LWBS is trying to increase its female quota from thirty-two to forty percent. I'm therefore being extremely generous in the general comments section, supporting my sisters.

Emily's total is thirty-three. I write a note on her file: solid female applicant. Please interview.

Two hours later, my eyes are starting to blur, as if I spilled a glass of water over the applications. I've read twenty-two. I'm officially shocked at the overall incompetence of most of the hopefuls. One guy used his father-in-law as a reference. Another had blatant discrepancies between his résumé and essays. Others should have spent more time proofreading.

Their résumés are so linear. Went to college, went to work, want to go to B-school, blah, blah, blah. Bor-ing. I like my candidates to be more well-rounded. Where are the business-minded people who are concert pianists/avid travelers/documentary filmmakers in their spare time?

Perhaps I should hire myself out as an application consultant. Now that would look good on my résumé.

Only two readers are left in the room. Dennis and me. Everyone else has taken off for the weekend. "Are you finished yet?" he asks me.

"Just about," I say, smiling.

"Do you want to grab something for dinner? With me?"

Didn't see that one coming. I give myself whiplash when I look back at the applications, away from him. "I can't, unfortunately. I think I'm going to pick up a pizza and hit the books."

He blushes and says, "Um…okay."

Whilst it may be lovely to have dinner with someone new, and he seems nice, and is kind of cute, I don't think it would be a good idea to date someone I work so closely with. And Dennis isn't my type. First of all, he's too short. I like my men lean and brawny. I'm five foot nine and full figured, and I like to look a man in the eye. Plus he wants to live in Seattle, which is across the country from Manhattan, where I intend to live. And I'm in no rush to date just anyone. My career has to come first. I have to come first. I don't have time to get involved and then realize what a mistake I made.

Like in high school, I fell in love with Darryl McDonald, the best-looking guy at the all-boys school down the street. I had a habit of hanging out at Central Park whenever he played football. And following him home. And calling and hanging up. Finally he asked me out. We started making out in the park. And I discovered he had the IQ of a turtle.

I wave goodbye and pack up my belongings. Maybe I

need therapy for my tendency to obsess. About school. About my career. About ideal men. I've always wanted to have a therapist. All my sorority sisters had therapists, but my parents thought it was a waste of time and money. Work harder, that was their motto. Instead of therapists, I had nannies. Many, many nannies. Most of them blur together into one face. For a while a Brazilian woman took care of me, but when I started talking with a Brazilian accent, my parents became alarmed and fired her. So on to the next. I remember a long blond braid being flicked over a tall woman's shoulder. I remember sitting on a hard park bench while someone explained who I was according to Chinese astrology. Her name was funny sounding, like an amphibian. She told me I was born in the Year of the Dragon. Or maybe it was my sister who was the dragon. Maybe I was the pig.

I remember sitting on the grass in Central Park, refusing to put on my sneakers, being told I was stubborn. Just because I hate being told what to do doesn't make me stubborn. I remember standing in the doorway while one of my nannies disengaged my arms from around my mother's legs. I was begging my mom not to go to China while my father was in Italy. She kissed me on the head and told me to make sure to do my homework, and then she left. She just *left*. From the penthouse window, I watched the black car whisk her away, and thought, At least I have my sister. And my homework. I wanted to score perfect marks on everything so I would make my parents proud, and over time perfection became my ultimate goal. I began to loathe the red marks highlighting my mistakes on my assignments. Loathe the unmade bed. Loathe the dirt on the floor.

Everything had to be just so.

I became a princess watching over my tower.

Maybe I should have demanded therapy, because I'm still that princess, and the prince I'm looking for doesn't exist—

someone smart, gorgeous, ambitious, tall, who intends to build his castle in Manhattan. Unfortunately, no one in B-school seems to fit that description.

None of the students, anyway.

Professor Rothman seems to have a thing for me. He always makes a point of saying hello to me whenever he walks into class.

I think that's a little creepy. He's not married or anything (no ring), but I don't think professors should be flirting with their students. We're here to learn.

I lock the door behind me and set off for the dorm. I wasn't lying to Dennis—I do have a lot of work. I stop at the pharmacy on the way, to pick up antibacterial wipes. Who knows what's on those applications? I also pick up another conditioner. I go through one a week, which I know is absurd.

I shake some fish food into Martha's bowl, then study until ten-thirty when I call my friends back home to say good-night. I should do laundry, but the idea of using those revolting machines in the basement makes me cringe. I tried to find someplace where I can send out wash the way we do in the city (I love the way my underwear comes back folded in cubes), but I learned quickly that Connecticut is not Manhattan.

I head to the bathroom to get ready for bed. Reminiscing about those high-school nights has put me in the mood. Okay, fine, I'm *always* in the mood. Getting off to Darryl could be just the medicine I need to help me fall asleep. And with a smile on my face, to boot.

Jamie and Russ walk in as I'm brushing my teeth. Russ's head is rolling behind him. Someone's had too much to drink.

"Someone got too friendly with Mr. Daniels," Jamie says, his arm around Russ's shoulder. "Need to get to a stall. Care to help?"

Jamie is funny, in a ha-ha way. He was really funny last

week in the shower when he didn't know who I was, but at the moment I am not amused. I spit my toothpaste suds into the sink as Russ spits up on the floor. It splashes onto my leg. I am definitely going to need a shower.

Jamie continues leading Russ toward the toilet. "Stall, Russ, stall. Did I say floor? I did not say floor."

I think I'm going to be sick. The smell of his stomach contents is overbearing. I tiptoe back to my room, seize my shower pail and dash down to the hopefully vomitless second-floor bathroom.

Talk about inappropriate behavior. B-school boys seem to think they're still in high school. But why waste time obsessing over children? Darryl awaits.

kimmy's quasi quarantine

I'm going to fail school.

No, really. I feel like a six-year-old sitting in on a molecular biology class. It's been a month since I got here, and I still have no idea what's going on.

Russ, Lauren, Nick, Jamie and I are sitting in a study room in the library working on our group Accounting assignment, which is due next Wednesday. I already handed in the individual portion, which was due today. I'm sure I failed.

Russ pulls out the case. "Did everyone read it?"

I keep my mouth shut. No need for Russ to think I'm a moron. Which I'm sure he does already. Which I'm sure is why he's been avoiding me.

"No," Jamie says. "It looks huge."

Russ flips through it. "It's not so bad, man. Mostly graphs. These things are deceiving. Some of them are fifty pages long but have thirty pages of graphs, and others are thirty pages with only five pages of graphs."

"It's like fat-free food," I say. "You have to eat twice as

much to feel full and you end up consuming the same amount of calories anyway."

Everyone stares at me.

I spend the next forty minutes executing my reinstated keep-your-mouth-shut plan while the rest of my group does the work. And as usual, even though Jamie hasn't done the reading, either—he hasn't even bought the books yet—he seems to be able to wing it.

"I don't think you all see the big picture," he says, then launches into an explanation. The rest of the group nods. How is it that he can barely skim the case yet still have a deep understanding of it? He usually writes up the assignment as we're discussing it. He's a great writer. Used to be a journalist, I think.

We've already gotten two assignments back, and we got B-pluses on both of them, no thanks to me. I contributed nada.

It's only Wednesday. Another whole day of boring classes. The weekends are more fun, because at night everyone gets wasted, but we still spend the days in this claustrophobic room.

Every few hours, Jamie, Lauren and I get Cokes from the vending machines, and Nick and Russ disappear outside for a smoke. I think they might be smoking more than cigarettes, but I don't ask. I did spot the Visine in Nick's laptop bag. Not my problem. I don't think I have the right to criticize, especially since I'm so useless.

I repeat, I'm going to fail school. Besides the individual portion of the Accounting assignment, I handed in a Stats assignment today and I am one-hundred-percent sure it was all wrong. Jamie had offered to help me, but I was nervous he would try to molest me if we were alone together. I couldn't ask Russ, since I don't want him to think I'm more of an idiot than he thinks I am. Besides, he's been ignoring me. He won't even sit next to me. Today he came into the study room, saw the empty seat beside me, then sat on the other side of the table next to Lauren. What's up with that? When school started he couldn't get enough of me, and now I have SARS? He's the one from Toronto.

Lauren waves her hand in front of my face. "Hello? Do you have an opinion on question number five or not?"

"Sounds great," I say.

She rolls her eyes. Fuck off, I think but don't say. Here's one stat I'm sure of: she's one-hundred-percent bitch.

layla finds her prince
in a haystack

More applications = more losers.

Be nice, I reprimand myself. They're not losers. They're just not right for LWBS.

More unacceptable candidates. More wistful looks from Dennis. I keep catching him staring, and it's making me uncomfortable.

Next one. Bradley Green.

I skim through his file. Undergraduate degree from Harvard. Now that's fancy. And he's worked for the Lerner Investment Bank for the past two years. GMATs? Oh, my. Ninety-ninth percentile. That's pretty brainy. That's the highest you can get, since you can't beat a hundred percent of the rest of the people. Although I suppose if you were the only person who got a perfect score, then you would have done better than everyone else. An issue to ponder another time.

"This guy scored in the ninety-ninth percentile on his GMATs," I say, waving his paper in front of me like a flag.

Dennis shrugs. "I got a ninety-eight."

"But this is the ninety-ninth."

I flip through his application and see an article cut out from the *New York Times.* "Bradley Green III, son of Bradley Green II…" He's *that* Bradley Green? As in Bradley Green, one of the wealthiest businessmen on the East Coast? "…CEO of the media conglomerate PAX Technology, has spent the summer building houses for the homeless in Oregon…"

My eyes skip to the picture. A tall, well-built man with light hair, a cleft in his chin, a dimple in his cheek and a serious look on his face is crouching over rubble.

Oh, my. Bradley Green III is gorgeous.

I pull out one of his essays, entitled "What Matters to Me and Why," and read the first paragraph:

> On my fourteenth birthday I was given a fish tank and two bright goldfish. The tank still sits in the corner of my room, flush against the wall. Along that same wall is my bed with a clear view through the side of the tank. When people walk into the room and take the time to admire the fish they always look at the tank head-on, neglecting the alternate view through the side of the tank. I always hold a high regard for the varied viewpoint offered from my bed that serves as a different, enlightening perspective into the lives of my enclosed aqua-friends. The driving force behind the vast majority of choices I have made is the desire to view issues and experience life through a multitude of perspectives. This is why I have volunteered around the country, traveled extensively and chose to work at the Lerner Hong Kong branch for my first year. I have always attempted to see beyond my own biases into other people's points of views, and I believe that a business degree from LWBS will allow me a challenging new perspective.

He has fish!
Here we go. I'm in love. Again.

Bradley Green III is brilliant, ambitious, gorgeous, well traveled, has perspective, has fish, and builds houses for the homeless. And according to his address, he now lives and works in Manhattan. And he's applying to LWBS.

If he's not the perfect man for me, I don't know who is. If I had the computer program that the guys in the movie *Weird Science* used to make the perfect woman, I couldn't have produced a more ideal man.

The perfect man whose phone number is directly in my line of vision.

No, I can't call him. Extracting information about an applicant for my own purpose would be unethical. I tally up his score. His GMAT translates into a ten out of ten; work experience a nine; college marks—I peek at his transcript—a four point five! He's better than perfect, and here I thought only high school granted extra credit—I give him a perfect ten (unfortunately, I can't give him extra credit); references—glowing, but why am I surprised?—five out of five, essays five out of five; and overall impressions I'm giving him another five. That's a total of forty-four out of forty five. He's most definitely in.

All right. I've done all I can ethically do. If he comes to LWBS, I can introduce myself and let love weave its magic.

But magic aside, why leave anything to chance?

I change his work-experience score to ten. If you're better than perfect in one area, you should be allowed to let the extra credit spill over to an area that's lacking.

It's ten-thirty and I can't sleep. I have to pee. I do not feel like standing up, slipping on pajamas, finding my slippers and walking all the way down the hall. I will not be able to fall asleep if I have to pee. I'll just think about something else. Something fun.

I reboot my computer and click onto the *New York*

Times Web site. I search for Bradley Green, and click on his photo.

So hot. Now for some sexy music.

It's now eleven o'clock and I still have to pee.

I don't have to pee…I don't have to pee…I don't have to pee, I don't have to pee…

I'm never going to be able to sleep until I go to the bathroom. I sigh and search for my slippers.

kimmy's fears comes true

Professor Gold is handing back the assignments. She walks up to me, looks me up and down (probably wondering if I slept with someone to get accepted here), and places mine facedown on my desk.

I wait for the others to receive theirs before I peek. I want to prolong the moment as long as possible.

Maybe it's not as bad as I think. Maybe I did amazing. Who knows? I could be a secret Stats genius. Just because I got back a D in the individual portion of the Accounting assignment today and a D on my last Economics mini-paper doesn't mean I don't have a knack for Stats.

"Yes!" Layla squeals.

"How'd you do?" I hear Jamie ask her.

"An A," Layla answers.

"As usual I bet," Jamie says.

"Always," she says, and winks.

For some reason, the word "always" causes Jamie to drop his mouth. She smiles at him, collects her paper, then heads out the door.

I flip over the assignment.

F.

I flip it back.

I got an F. I have never gotten an F in my entire life.

It's official. I'm going to fail out of business school.

Jamie slaps his hand on his head. "I'm such an idiot."

At least I'm not the only one who screwed up. "You didn't do well?"

"No, I got a B-plus. I just realized who the girl in the shower was."

What the hell is he talking about? I ignore him and stuff the stupid assignment into my bag, and head toward the library. Group meeting number seven hundred and twenty. Not that it matters if I attend or not. I don't say anything, anyway.

F. Failure. Fuck. What a bitch that Gold is. I knew I wouldn't like female teachers. Not that I'm doing much better in any of my other classes. I'm going to fail everything. I am going into debt for nothing. Nothing, nothing, nothing. That's what I am. Nothing. A big fat zero.

That's one statistic I can count on.

I sit mutely through another boring group meeting until it dawns on me that they couldn't care less if I'm there or not, so I feign exhaustion and leave. I'm not even in the mood for dinner. I buy a bag of barbecue chips from the vending machine and climb into bed. I turn on my reading lamp and open a *GQ*.

At eight, someone knocks on the door. "Kimmy? Honey? Are you there?" It's Jamie. I don't answer.

At eight-thirty the phone rings, but I don't answer. It rings again at eight-forty. Jamie, again, I'm sure. How did I get here? Why am I hiding away in a tiny room on a creaky bed? Right. Wayne. I was running from Wayne. I miss Wayne. Where is Wayne? Maybe I should call Wayne.

I know phoning Wayne is a bad idea. But I'm going to do

it, anyway. I pick up the phone and dial his number. I'm allowed to call an ex-boyfriend to say hello. Of course I am. It's not a crazy thing to do. Pathetic, maybe, but not crazy.

One ring. Two. Maybe I should hang up.

"Hello?" a woman says. Cheryl has answered the phone.

I should hang up. But what if he has caller ID? I kick myself for not using star 67. Calling and hanging up when the person has caller ID is worse than calling and saying hello. "Is Wayne there?" I don't like the name Wayne. Never did. I always picture the obnoxious, fat older brother from *The Wonder Years*.

"Who is it?" she asks.

You know who it is, you stupid skank. I should hang up. Slam the phone down in her face. I should.

"It's Kimmy. Who's this?" Take that, bitch.

"Kimmy…hi." She slows down the hi as though I'm mentally challenged. "It's Cheryl."

"Cheryl. How are you?" I put on my fake high-pitched voice, the one I use when talking to my grandmother's friends whose names I can never remember.

"I'm well, thanks." Her tone sounds confused—my question was nice, my enthusiasm high, but she knows I wish she'd be squashed by a falling house. "You?"

"I'm fantastic. I'm in business school now, did you know? I love it. Just love it. Time of my life. And what about you? What are you doing these days?"

She's working as a waitress at El Condo's Mexican Restaurant. That's why I can ask the question. I know what I'm doing is so much better than what she's doing. As long as she doesn't toss up an "I'm waitressing but in my spare time I'm modeling for Victoria's Secret" on me.

"Nothing new." Ha! She can't even say it, she's too embarrassed. "Wayne's not here right now. And I'm running out. Should I ask him to call you back? Is everything all right?"

"Oh, everything's fine." What does that mean he's not

there? Why is she answering the phone? Are they living together? ARE THEY LIVING TOGETHER? "Just calling
to say hello. See how the two of you are." I must find out if
they're living together. How can I find out? Who can I ask?
"Well, take care." Take care not to walk into a passing truck.
Which I'll be driving.

"Oh, you, too."

Slam. I stare at the phone for the next twenty minutes. She
must have left by now. I press the code to block my number
and call back.

Her voice is on his damn machine.

"Hi, everyone! You've reached Cheryl and Wayne and we
can't come to the phone. If you leave a message, we'll call
you back as soon as we can. Bye!"

They're living together. How can they already be living
together? And in the apartment I helped him fix up! I chose
the paint, I shopped for his linen, I picked out the couch—
I spent four hours on various furniture Web sites finding that
couch. Does she like the couch? Have they had sex on it?
What about the comforter? Suddenly I understand why dogs
pee to mark their territory. I've had sex in that apartment,
too, you know. Does she know? Does she know where we've
had sex in that apartment? Everywhere. We had a lot of sex
in that apartment.

I can't deal. I need to sleep. I turn off my reading light,
toss the magazine onto the floor, climb back into bed and,
crusty teeth and face be damned, I close my eyes. If I go to
sleep, maybe I'll feel better in the morning.

Did he buy new sheets? I bet he didn't. Does she think of
me naked when she washes those sheets?

I bet she comes every time. Shrieks and spasms and all. I
bet she told him about how I faked it every time. Telling her
that I thought I was frigid (after we'd polished off a pitcher
of margaritas) was my second mistake. I told her about my
little orgasm problem only because she'd confessed to being

an occasional bulimic, but I realized right away that I'd been shortchanged. After all, she wasn't telling me anything new. At least twice, I'd seen her puke after gorging herself on five slices of pizza.

I also told her how sweet Wayne was, which was my first mistake.

Never brag to another woman about your boyfriend, because she'll want him for herself.

What else could I have blabbed? Thank God I didn't tell her about getting pregnant.

Must sleep. Can't.

I feel like the time I dropped acid in college, saw spiders on the walls, and thought that one of the girls was plotting to suffocate me. I saw everyone in freeze-frame, like a video in a broken VCR. I tried to sleep, but my brain wouldn't turn off.

Like it won't now. Maybe I'll wash my face. There we go, that will give me something to do. It's ten o'clock. I don't even change into my I-look-sexy-even-though-I-happen-to-be-going-to-the-bathroom-in-the-middle-of-the-night outfit. What's the point? No one cares. Russ isn't interested. He has the lovely Sharon back home. Wayne doesn't care. He's living with Cheryl. And I'm a Stats failure.

My door creaks open. The hall is empty. Everyone is partying without me. No one is in the bathroom, either. Just me, alone. As usual.

As I lather the cleanser on my face, my eyes sting with tears. I hate when I cry. I'm not one of those sexy, demure criers. My eyes get red and blotchy and squinty, and when I breathe I sound like I have the hiccups. I rinse my face and sob at the same time, and accidentally swallow a mouthful of soapy water. Great. For the grand finale, the glorious conclusion to a truly spectacular day, I will now choke to death.

And that's when the door to the bathroom opens and I am saved.

layla has a girls' night in

"Are you okay?" I ask.

Kimmy is standing in front of the sink, bawling her eyes out and coughing. She nods and wipes her eyes. "I'm fine."

I pat her on the shoulder. "You are not fine. Why don't you come to my room and we'll talk?"

Instead of looking at me, she looks at her reflection. "Talk about what?"

"About whatever is bothering you."

She hesitates, then says, "Okay. Let me clean myself up first."

"Good idea. And I'll just be a sec." I quickly pee, since that is the reason I came to the bathroom in the first place, and then find Kimmy waiting for me by the door. "I think you need a girls' night."

She opens her mouth to say something, changes her mind, then opens it again. "Where's your room?" she asks as she follows me down the hallway.

"Make a right at the fork."

We walk in silence. Maybe inviting Kimmy wasn't a good

idea. All I really know about her is that she was in diaper commercials. She seems so lonely. And she appears to be in need of a good girlfriend as much as I am. I snap on the light.

She scans my setup. "Wow. Did you get a decorator in here?"

"Not quite. But I appreciate the compliment. Why don't you sit?" I gesture to the purple beanbag in the corner. "Just throw the newspapers on the floor." I have a week of business sections that I've forgotten to recycle. "Do you want some tea?"

She sits. "Tea? No thanks."

"Oh, Come on. I have herbal, and it's good for you."

She shrugs. "Okay." This girl is at the bottom of her emotional barrel.

I plug in the kettle on my night table and then pass Kimmy a chenille blanket and a box of chocolate cookies. She shakes her head. "I'm more of a chips girl."

"More for me, then," I say, and sit cross-legged on the bed. I eat a lot of chocolate. Especially when I'm not having sex. I need to get my endorphin fix from something. "So tell me your life story. What's wrong?"

She opens her mouth and starts to cry.

"Don't cry, it can't be that bad." For the first time since I arrived at school, I feel at home. I miss my girlfriends. I miss my sister. I miss hanging out. I miss drinking tea, eating cookies and talking about everything and nothing.

"It's that bad, believe me. I got a D in Accounting, another D in Economics and an F on the Stats assignment."

I inwardly cringe. "Big deal. It's just one assignment. Or three. And the Accounting assignment was only worth ten percent." Probably not the time to mention my A's or the *Excellent job!* comment I received or that Professor Gold gave me a smiley-face sticker.

"Trust me, Layla, I won't do better on the next ones. I'll probably fail out."

"Fail out! What kind of talk is that? You won't fail out.

You just started. Maybe you're not working hard enough." The kettle hums, and I pour the boiling water into two cups stuffed with chamomile tea bags.

"You don't understand. It doesn't matter how hard I work, I don't understand anything. I don't get it. I'm a moron. I don't belong here."

I hand her a cup. I love these cups. They're from the Calvin Klein mahogany fine-china collection. "You're being ridiculous. Your group will help you."

"No, they won't. I can't ask them. We're having some, uh, issues. One of the guys has a crush on me, and I don't want to encourage him."

Gossip! I've missed gossip. "Yeah? Who?"

"Do you know Jamie Grossman?"

"Oh, yeah. He's in your group? He's hilarious. We met in the shower a few weeks ago." She looks at me with disbelief, and I laugh. "Sounds more sordid than it was. I ran out of conditioner, so I asked the person next to me to lend me some."

She nods. "So that's what he was talking about today when he said he realized who was in the shower."

"Ha! I'm surprised it took him so long. I recognized his voice from class immediately."

"He doesn't shut up in class."

And the point is…? "That doesn't bother me."

"You never shut up, either." She clamps her hand over her mouth. "I didn't mean to say that out loud."

I giggle. "You're right. I like to talk in class. No reason not to get the participation marks."

"I never talk in class."

"You should."

She shrugs. "I never have anything to say."

"Neither do half the people in our Block," I say. "And they still talk."

She smiles. "I didn't mean to insult you earlier. You make good points in class. I'm jealous."

"And I'm jealous of the poetry you get in the bath-room," I say.

"How embarrassing are those poems!" she shrieks, covering her face with the blanket.

They are a little embarrassing, but definitely sweet. "You could probably just wash them off the walls," I suggest.

"I know," Kimmy says, "but I kind of like them." She laughs. "We got together in orientation."

"Really? You and Casanova? No wonder he's writing you poetry. So what happened? He wasn't any good?" I ask, automatically leaning toward her.

She covers her face with the blanket again.

Girl talk! Girl talk! I need some girl talk. "Come on, tell me!"

"Promise you won't repeat?"

"Repeat? I would never." The first rule of girl talk is that one must never repeat. "Spill it!"

"It was terrible. Terrible." She brings her thumb and index finger about an inch apart.

I shriek with laughter.

"It didn't even make it inside of me."

How awful. "No wonder he follows you around. He wants another chance."

"I know. Do you think a guy knows when he's not good in bed?"

Now we're talking. I dip into the box for cookie number three. "I don't know. Does a woman?"

"I think I would know if I wasn't good in bed. Which I am." She smiles. "I have another secret. I have a huge crush on Russ."

Ew. Puke-boy. I attempt to mask my revulsion. "Yeah?"

"Isn't he gorgeous?"

I can't help but picture him with vomit on his chin. "So? What's the story?"

"There *is* no story. He has a girlfriend back home. And I have no boyfriend and I'm failing out of school."

"Maybe I can help you," I offer.

"Find a boyfriend?"

I'm about to throw a pillow at her, but I'm afraid I'll end up spilling the tea on my five-hundred-thread-count Ralph Lauren sheets. "I'm talking about getting better grades. We can work on our assignments together."

"Really? You don't mind?"

Why would I mind? It'll be nice having someone to hang out with. "Not at all. It'll be fun."

She nods and looks around the room. "Thanks. I appreciate it. If you're sure. If you change your mind, I'll understand."

If I change my mind, she'll fail. "I'm sure."

"Is there more hot water?" she asks. She crawls over to my night table and empties the rest of the kettle water into her cup. "Hey, who's this?" She picks up the printout of Brad.

"Uh…no one."

"No way, I told you everything about me!"

That's true. A friendship is based on give and take. "It's just some guy I've been admiring from afar."

"You know, I've noticed Professor Jon has been admiring *you* from afar. He spends all class staring at you."

"He's not for me."

She shakes her head in disbelief. "Are you nuts? He's hot and smart and sexy and he seems to want you. I'd go for it. So who is this guy?"

"I read applications for LWBS. And today I processed an application of the guy I want to marry. Is that weird?"

"A little. And this is him?"

I can't believe I just told her that. "Yeah. But please don't tell anyone, okay?"

"So are you going to call him?"

"No! I can't. It's unethical. His picture will be my sexual fodder for the rest of the year. And who knows? Maybe he'll come to LWBS in the fall." He's already been good to me. I had two orgasms last night, back to back. They weren't *per-*

fect orgasms, but you know what they say: bad sex is better than no sex. That's my quest, to have the perfect orgasm. I figure I'll know it when I have it.

She taps her index finger against Brad's head. "By next year this one will be taken. If he isn't already."

Taken? He could be taken? I can't fantasize about a man who's taken.

She laughs. "Don't look so upset! He might not be. Just call him."

"He ticked off the single box. He's not married. Damn applications. I wish they had a *Do you have a girlfriend?* box. Or *Do you live with someone?* box."

"Call him," she repeats.

"We'll see." There's no way I'm calling him.

I dig into the second row of cookies. Looks like I'll need to stock up on these endorphins.

kimmy does her patriotic duty

I sit next to Layla in Strategy, since it's the one class where she doesn't sit in the front row. The spitting bothers her.

"How are you feeling?" she asks.

"Better, thanks." I can't believe I spilled all that personal information to her last week. I must be a masochist. I whine about how women screw me over, and then I give someone I barely know the ammunition to stick it to me again. Now I have to be nice to her for the rest of our lives. Or at least until I get kicked out of school.

Russ walks in next and sits in the back.

Martin struts into the room, slams the front door and immediately writes BUSINESS IS WAR! on the blackboard, as he does every day. At least he's not wearing the army hat he wore on the first day of class.

Jamie opens the door, waves to Martin and sits in the empty seat next to mine. "Hi, gorgeous," he says, winking.

Layla tries to repress the smile on her face. I definitely should not have spilled the small penis info. Why am I so blessed with verbal diarrhea?

But I have the goods on her, if she turns into a leak, I'm sure the officials at LWBS would be interested to know that she has a photo of an applicant on her night table. For sexual fodder! I can't believe she was so obvious about…masturbating. I've never actually heard a woman *admit* to masturbating. Guys talk about it all the time, but women? I bet if I'd hung around longer, she would have pulled out her dildos. She's so…open. Which I guess is kind of cool.

Okay, I admit I've masturbated. Once. Tried to, anyway. But I couldn't climax, and I just got sore. Yeah, I'm pretty screwed up.

But maybe if I found the right guy…

If Russ wasn't already with Sharon…

"Today, I'll be teaching you the importance of goals and strategy when dealing with a competitor," Martin showers on the front row. "Pretend you are a new company wanting to break into the laundry-detergent industry. Your strategy is your roadmap. If implemented properly, it will help you reach your goals. Your strategic plan should be grounded in knowledge about your customer, research about your competitor, and your firm's current performance."

I so don't understand what he's talking about.

Maybe if applied it to boyfriend stealing…mmm. This could work!

Goal: get Russ to date me.

Now let's see. I need knowledge about my customer, research about my competitor and understanding regarding my firm's current performance.

My customer: Russ. What do I know about Russ, other than he's hot and unavailable? I flip to the Understanding the Customer section of my strategy textbook for appropriate businessy terms.

1. *Brand loyal.* Russ is not very brand loyal. He's joined twelve clubs since starting school and can't decide

on a major. He's always up for a drink, a joint or a smoke break. He can't seem to make up his mind about anything.

2. *Easily influenced.* Russ is easily influenced by peers. He has not cheated on his girlfriend (yet), but he gives off vibes that he has a tough time resisting temptation.

3. *Potential impulse buyer.* Does Russ acquire merchandise on impulse? I certainly hope so, if I'm the potential merchandise.

Not bad. Not bad at all. My heart speeds up. I can do this!

Now, for my competitor analysis: Sharon's goal is probably to marry Russ. What I don't know is how close she is to achieving that goal.

Okay, here we go. Find Sharon's vulnerability and attack. She lives in another country. How can I use that to my advantage and turn "Absence makes the heart grow fonder" into "Out of sight, out of mind"? Obviously, I need to do some research.

Is this horrible? What kind of a person actively tries to steal someone else's boyfriend?

A person like Cheryl.

An *evil* person.

Not necessarily. It's nothing personal, just business, as they say. A matter of economics, supply and demand. (I demand what Russ is supplying?) If business is war, then so must be love! And so, if capitalism is at the heart of the American Dream, I'm doing my patriotic duty.

Besides, if he loves her so much, what the hell was he doing flirting with me?

All right, then. Time to review some vital statistics:

1. He's not married.

2. He's not engaged (yet).

3. He's dating someone who lives in another city. Another country.

4. A guy doesn't get poached unless he wants to get poached. (I'd be doing Sharon a favor if I win; she doesn't deserve to spend her life with someone who doesn't really love her.)

5. And last but definitely not least, I've caught him staring at my boobs on more than one occasion.

I spot Nick in line for lunch. "Hey, you."

"Hey, dude," he says. How can I be called dude with this cleavage? "What's going on?"

"Not much. Just hungry. Where's your sidekick?"

"Marketing meeting. Real estate club. Who knows with that guy?"

For once I'm glad that Russ is missing in action. I want to talk to Nick without interference.

I pick a few vegetables from the salad bar. "Mind if I join you?"

He blankets his plate with a glob of macaroni and cheese. "I was going to head back to my room, but we can eat here if you want."

"Why not? We could use the break." I try to appear blasé, as if a break is the reason I'm here. We chitchat for a few minutes while I try to come up with devious and clever ways to uncover information about Sharon. "How's the studying going?"

"Not bad. Having some trouble concentrating, though."

"A side effect of pot, I'm told."

He smiles sheepishly. "Is it that obvious?"

"The Visine gave you away."

"Russ is the one who's paranoid about anyone finding out." And then finally he throws me an unintentional bone. "He's nerdy that way. Afraid some girl in second year will tell his girlfriend or something."

Covert research is easier than I thought. "Does Sharon have spies?" I ask jokingly.

"I think she has a friend at LWBS."

Oh. I take a bite of salad and try to appear thoughtful. "She doesn't know he smokes?"

"Nope. She doesn't approve." He shoves a forkful of macaroni into his mouth. "This is really terrible."

I try to sway the conversation back to Sharon. "Is she controlling?"

"Who?"

Who? Must I do all the work here? I stop myself from rolling my eyes. "Sharon."

"I don't know. Maybe. She makes him call her every night. I think it annoys him."

Excellent. "Why didn't she move here to be with him? Are they not that serious?"

"They're serious, but she has a job teaching in Toronto. She didn't want to give up her seniority, and besides, it's not easy getting a visa to work here. Immigration laws are really tight. I think he's planning on going back to Canada, anyway."

What? My Prince Charming wants to live north of the border? Don't they live in igloos up there? Kidding. Kind of.

"I can't believe we still have two classes left today," he says, abruptly changing the subject. "Mondays and Wednesdays are way too long."

"At least we have no school Fridays," I say, then quietly finish my salad, absorbed in my thoughts.

I'm told it's easy to immigrate to the U.S. if you're married to a citizen.

I spend Economics updating my strategic plan.

She's closer to achieving her goal than I thought if he's planning on moving back to Canada. I mentally review her weaknesses. She's controlling, she's bossy, she's prudish (schoolteachers aren't slutty, are they?), and she's not here. Time for an attack!

Strategy: Illustrate that unlike Sharon, I am not controlling.
- Tactic: Smoke pot with him.
- Tactic: Never tell him what to do.

Strategy: Illustrate that I am not prudish.
- Tactic: Wear revealing clothing.
- Tactic: Allude to sex during conversation.

Strategy: Since he is not brand loyal, show him that there are other, better brands available.
- Tactic: Show him how compatible we are. Play up the business/LWBS power couple angle.
- Tactic: Show that our schedules coincide and Sharon's and his don't. (Too bad Toronto is the same time zone.)

Strategy: Since he is easily influenced by peers, make sure that his peers approve of me and not Sharon.
- Tactic: Smoke pot with Nick.
- Tactic: Make Nick believe that Sharon is a bitch.

Strategy: Benefit from his impulse-buying tendencies.
- Tactic: Increase my exposure #1
    (i.e. practice borderline stalking).
- Tactic: Increase my exposure #2
    (i.e. wear less clothing).
- Tactic: Increase my exposure #3
    (i.e. combine #1 and #2, especially when his defenses are down).

When the bell rings after IC, Nick pulls back his chair and says to Russ, "Time for a four-twenty."

I lean over their desks in my tighter, lower-cut, redder outfit. "Please, shed some light on this four-twenty."

Nick laughs and Russ looks embarrassed. "It means, it's time to smoke a joint," Nick says.

"I think it's the police code in California for drugs," Russ says.

"No, dude," Nick says. "That's a myth. It was some group in the seventies who met at 4:20 every day after school, and they used four-twenty as their code for marijuana so they could talk about it in front of teachers and parents."

"Ah. Just like you two. And it's now—" I use my right arm to point to the watch on my left hand, thereby pressing together my breasts and enhancing my cleavage "—four-twenty."

Nick nods. "Pretty clever, huh?"

"I think I'll join you," I say. Strategy in motion.

I haven't smoked since college. Wayne wasn't into it, so I wasn't into it. But duty calls.

"Are we meeting now?" Lauren asks, poking her annoying head between the boys.

"No!" I say.

"But what about the Organizational Behavior assignment?"

Why is she butting into my tactics? "We'll meet at five," I say, leading the boys away. Once back at the Zoo, Nick opens the window in his room, then shoves a towel into the crack between the floor and the door.

I plop down onto Nick's bed, my back against the wall. Nick sits backward on his computer chair, as if he were riding a horse.

Russ sits next to me. Excellent.

Nick opens a drawer and pulls out what looks like a wooden jewelry box. He takes out his stash, a shot glass and a long pair of scissors.

Russ closes his eyes and leans his head against the wall.

"Tired?" I say.

He blinks. "Yeah. I think I signed up for too many activities."

Time to commiserate. "This place is a killer. I know just how you feel."

I let my shoulder gently touch his.

He doesn't move away.

jamie snoozes and loses

The alarm on my clock radio sounds again. Eight thirty-nine. Only a moron like me would choose nine minutes for a snooze time. Why not ten?

October 27 floats somewhere above the time. The significance of that date weaves through my semiconscious state. Twenty-nine years ago today, my sister Dara died.

I hit the snooze again. And then again.

Shit. Three minutes to nine. I'm never going to make it on time. I might as well skip the class. I haven't done the reading, anyway. I haven't even bought the books. That's what I'll do. Sleep for another hour and then get my books and make it to Accounting. So tired…

Knock, knock.

"Go away."

"Jamie, you slept through your first two classes, you jackass." It's Nick.

I slither deeper under the sheet. "Tired."

"We're all tired. Open up."

Grumbling, I open the door, then flop back onto the bed.

Nick sits on my computer chair. "We got back our OB papers."

"How'd we do? Another B-plus?" We've already gotten loads of B-pluses. The professors seemed to have made a communal decision that we're good but not *that* good.

"Nope," he says, smiling.

"Not a B-plus? Are you sure? How about a B?"

"Nope." Still smiling.

"A-minus?"

"Nope. An A, dude. We got an A. We're now the A team. Mazel-tov! "An A? How is that possible?"

"We're brilliant, what can I say? Who knew? We're celebrating tonight at Kimmy's. It's her birthday, so now we have twice the reason to party."

Kimmy's room! I'm finally getting back inside Kimmy's room! She's been looking so hot lately. Low-cut shirts, push-up bras, tight leather pants—it's fantastic. She even started bringing lollipops to class—bright, big red ones she licks and sucks, turning her lips bloodred.

"Pat yourself on the back, dude," Nick says. "It was all your wacky ideas and stellar writing that got us the mark."

"I'm the king of the world!"

And my queen awaits me.

After lunch, I stop back at my room to get the list of books I need to buy, and the phone rings.

"Good afternoon!" I say brightly.

"Jamie?"

"Marnie! How are you?"

"Fine thanks, how are you? How's school?"

"So far so good. How's the store?"

"Busy as usual. I wanted to let you know that I delivered the daisies this morning."

"Did she answer the door?" I ask.

"Yup."

"How'd she look?"

Pause. "She was in her bathrobe."

Same as every year. I thank Marnie and hang up.

Twice a year, on October 27 and April 20, Dara's birthday and the anniversary of her death, my mother locks herself in her room and I send her flowers. When I was a kid, I'd sit by her door and listen to my mother cry. The year I was six, I called ten florists until I found Marnie, who agreed to deliver thirteen dollars and twenty-five cents worth of daisies, my mother's favorite flowers.

My mother has never thanked me for them, but she keeps them on her night table until they die. She never talks about Dara, either. Neither does my dad. There's only one album of her, and my mother keeps it in her room, separate from the family albums overflowing with photos of me, Amanda, Erin and Erin's four-year-old daughter, Jenny. There aren't too many photos of Dara, anyway. She died when she was about six months old.

Amanda was only two when Dara died of SIDS, Sudden Infant Death Syndrome, so she doesn't remember anything, but Erin was five and remembers a lot of screaming, a lot of crying, and police and relatives swarming the house.

The flowers are my way of saying I'm sorry, even though I know I'm not responsible.

If Dara hadn't died, my parents wouldn't have had me. My mother had always wanted three kids.

I get dressed and head to the bookstore. Unfortunately, the books I need are nowhere in sight. I find a clerk counting LWBS T-shirts, and I ask for help. He checks his computer and says, "None left."

"Can you look in the back?"

"None left," he repeats. "Sorry." He resumes counting.

Oy. "You've got to be kidding me."

He looks at me like I'm an idiot. "We ran out a month ago. Sorry."

"How am I supposed to do my reading?"

"Tell your professor you waited too long. Maybe he'll order more."

I'm sure that'll earn me an A.

russ spins the bottle

My face is bleeding.

Twenty-six and still don't know how to shave properly. Having to do it in public isn't helping the situation. I don't know how to floss properly, either. The Toronto dentist I went to warned me my teeth would fall out if I don't start flossing. The dental hygienist actually demonstrated the right way to do it: wrap the floss around the middle finger so you can use your thumb and index finger to maneuver it. Every night. Come on! Does anyone floss every night? I bet superheroes don't need to floss.

"Getting pretty for the big night?" Nick says, slapping me on the back.

"Beard was bothering me," I lie.

"See you in Kimmy's room?"

Kimmy's room. Haven't yet been inside Kimmy's room. Did everything possible *not* to be in Kimmy's room. Being in Kimmy's room can't lead to anything good. Actually that's the dilemma. It *can* lead to something good, and I'm not talking ethics. "See you there."

"You can make it? No javelin club or anything?"

Nick thinks it's funny that I've signed up for every club at school. "There's no javelin club."

"No? I hope you're not paying membership fees to all the clubs you've joined."

"No membership fees. Just my blood." Truth is, I may have piled too much on my plate. Yesterday, after class I played some ball, then met with the marketing association, then the real estate association, then with the group to work on our OB assignment, then had a smoke with Kimmy and ended up talking to her for two hours. Sharon would kill me if she knew how much I was smoking. Cigarettes, too. But it seems like such a natural thing to do here. After the smoke, I finished up my presentation for Integrative Communications then called Sharon, and then I couldn't sleep so I went downstairs to the common room. Kimmy was there, said she couldn't sleep, either, so we went for another smoke.

"No one will care if you drop one or two," Nick says.

I think someone will. Especially because I've somehow managed to be on the executive committee on everything except basketball. "Maybe I'll drop basketball."

He clutches his hand to his chest. "A spear through my heart, dude. Anything but basketball."

"See what I mean? I can't choose. I don't think I'll drop any of them. Besides, I like them all. I wouldn't want to miss out."

"I may be out late tonight," I tell Sharon, pressing a tissue against my still leaky chin. "I'm going to a party. Should I call later?"

"How late will you be back? Where's the party? Don't you have class tomorrow?"

Oh, man. Lately Sharon's been grilling me about everything I do, and it's getting on my nerves. And now she's mad at me for not coming in for Canadian Thanksgiving. "Don't know, at a friend's place, and yes, I have class in the morning."

I don't tell her that the friend's name is Kimmy. And that I spent the entire day watching Kimmy licking her red lollipop. I sat in class, mesmerized, watching her insert it in her mouth and out again…in and out…in and out… When I asked her what I should bring to the party, she purred, "Just yourself. Just come." She emphasized the word *come.* At least I think she did. Did she? I think I've been letting my other head do the thinking lately. I've spent all day imagining her in a black push-up bra and matching thong and holding the string of a red balloon.

"Don't be snarky," Sharon says. "I was just asking. Excuse me for taking an interest in your life. Maybe if you came home once in a while…"

"You know I'm sorry I couldn't come home. But I'll come in for American Thanksgiving."

"Whatever. If you have time."

Why is she always making me feel guilty? Doesn't she realize how important my education is? "I have to go."

"Fine. Bye." She hangs up, without telling me she loves me and to be good. She always tells me to be good. I wonder if that means I can be bad.

"Welcome," Kimmy says, opening her door. Instead of a push-up bra and thong, she's wearing a tight, low-cut, short red dress and strappy red heels. Oh, man.

Jamie, Lauren and Nick are already sitting cross-legged on the floor. So far Jamie has been late to every class this semester, but for this he's on time.

A picnic has been set up on in the carpet. Fancy cheeses, crackers, five open bottles of wine and one bottle of Coke. Barenaked Ladies are playing on the CD player, and the speakers are set up by her bed.

"Pour vous," she says, handing me a white plastic cup.

"Thanks. And happy birthday."

"How hot is she?" Jamie says, and then stuffs his mouth with a cracker loaded with Brie.

"Sizzling," I answer, and Jamie throws me a murderous look. "Are we the only guests?" I ask, trying to break the tension.

Kimmy is watching us. Watching *me*. Oh, man. Sharon, Sharon, Sharon.

"Yeah," Kimmy says. "I invited Layla, but she claims she has a group meeting. Whatever. More wine for me."

"I'd like to propose a toast," Kimmy says, lifting her glass. "To a brilliant group, for producing brilliant work."

We all clink our glasses (more of a thud, actually, since we're using plastic cups). "Here, here," Lauren says. I step around the carpet. Kimmy's bed creaks as I sit on it.

Jamie stuffs another cracker into his mouth. "And to you, my sweet Kimmy, for throwing this shindig. And for passing me the Diet Coke so you can fill me up again."

"Diet?" I say. "Didn't realize you were counting calories."

"More productive than counting the number of times you've looked down Kimmy's dress, Russ," Jamie snaps.

Kimmy leans over Nick, topping off Jamie's glass. Her breasts spill over her dress. When she steps back toward her chair, a drop of Diet Coke dribbles onto her knee. "Don't worry, there's lots more where that came from," she says.

"Lauren, dude," Nick says, "why don't you lick that up? You know you want to."

Lauren punches him in the arm. "Don't be a pig."

"Hey, why not?" Kimmy asks. She sits down, crosses her legs and her dress hikes up her creamy thighs. "I'm offended. I'm not your type?"

"Too skinny," Lauren says.

"You know who you look like?" Jamie says to Kimmy. "Sharon Stone in *Basic Instinct*. The interrogation scene. Do you remember it? Are you wearing panties? No, don't tell me. Let me imagine."

She crosses her legs, then uncrosses them again. "You'll never know."

My curiosity has been piqued—along with the southern part of my anatomy. I wonder what her pubic hair looks like. Perfectly manicured? A strip. She seems like a groomer.

I down the glass as if it's a shot. The wine floats through my chest, warming me. Must stop imagining Kimmy's pubic hair. Brown pubic hair. Dark brown or chocolate brown? Stop. Can't stop. If only I had X-ray vision so I could see through her dress. Or is it a skirt? Never remember the difference. Sharon tried to explain it, but I never remember. Sharon, Sharon, Sharon. Wish I had a superpower that could make me stop thinking about…about…Sharon.

One hour and seven glasses of wine later, I can definitely see through Kimmy's dress. My X-ray vision might be alcohol induced, but it's working. I watch her nipples as she bends over the picnic to spin a bottle. It whirls twice and hits the blue cheese. "Did you ever play spin the bottle when you were in grade school?" she asks.

"Does it count if it was with myself?" Jamie asks.

"Too much info," Nick says. "Let's play."

Lauren groans. "What are you, ten?"

Jamie rubs his hands together as if they're cold. "I'm in."

"Of course, you're in," Lauren says. "As if you'd turn down a chance to stick your tongue into Kimmy's mouth."

"Again," Nick adds.

Blushing, Kimmy looks at me. "I'm in if Russ is in."

Everyone stares at me. It's club-registration day all over again. How can I say no?

Spin the bottle isn't cheating. It's a game. Think basketball, I tell myself. "I'm in."

Kimmy picks up one of the bottles, drinks the rest of it, and says, "Someone move the cheese so we can spin this baby."

Nick and Jamie cheer.

"All right, here are the rules," she says. "First time you land on someone, it's a kiss on the cheek. Second it's a kiss on the lips. Third time, there's tongue. Fourth—"

"Blow job," Nick says.

Lauren punches him again. "No blow jobs."

"Don't worry," Jamie says. "We don't mind if you're inexperienced."

Lauren rolls her eyes. "Ha-ha. Third is tongue, fourth you can use your hands, and fifth is seven minutes in the closet."

Nick's face lights up. "If you get Kimmy, can we all go into the closet and watch?"

Lauren threatens him with a nearby bottle. "Only if you get Jamie and we get to watch *you.*"

Nick seizes the bottle and gives it a twirl. "I'm starting. And the lucky winner is—"

The bottleneck points directly at me. Lauren, Kimmy and Jamie cheer.

"No way," I say.

"Pucker up, Russ," Jamie says.

Nick grabs the bottle and turns bright red. "I think I should spin again."

"Don't be so homophobic," Lauren says. "People are just people. Everyone is a sexual being."

"I have nothing against men kissing men," Nick says. "I just don't want to be on the giving end."

I shake my head. "Or on the receiving end."

"Haven't you ever heard of the sliding scale of homosexuality?" Lauren says. "It seems unlikely that both of you are all the way on the hetero side."

Nick ignores her. "I'm amending the rules. Whenever a guy gets another guy, it's a truth or dare instead."

"That's such a rip," Lauren says, stretching her long legs in front of her.

"We'll vote," Nick says. "All in favor?"

Jamie, Nick and I raise our hands.

"No fair," Kimmy says. "We're outnumbered."

"So Nick-man, what will it be?" I ask. "Truth or dare?"

Nick flexes his muscles. "Dare."

"I dare you to make out with Russ," Lauren says.

"Quite the comedienne, aren't you," I say. "I'll come up with a dare. I dare Nick to chug the rest of that bottle." I point to a half-full bottle.

He picks up the bottle and gulps it down while we chant "Chug! Chug! Chug!"

When he's done, he holds up the bottle as if it's a trophy, then hands it to Lauren. "Your turn."

"Why are we going counterclockwise?" Jamie asks.

Lauren spins the bottle. "Because we're wild and crazy." It rolls over a napkin and points to me.

What am I, a bottle magnet? She kisses me on the cheek.

Jamie snatches the bottle and spins. It lands on Kimmy.

He punches his arm in the air. "Wahoo! Come to Papa. Bend over, baby—you never specified which cheek."

"Don't get cheeky with me, or you'll lose your turn." She turns her face to him, and he kisses it, making a lurid slurping noise.

My turn. I spin the bottle. It lands on Nick.

"Truth or dare?" Kimmy says.

"Dare," I say. I guess we're not following any rules about who gets to give the dare.

"I dare you to remove one piece of clothing," Kimmy says.

My face burns like I shaved too quickly, but that could be the booze. I unbutton my shirt. "It's getting hot in here, anyway."

Jamie hums porno music.

Three years ago, I wouldn't have been able to do this. I would have felt too stupid, with my concave chest. I would have come up with an excuse to leave the room. But now…I feel fine. Strong. Drunk.

Everyone stares at my chest when I take it off. "Stop flexing," Jamie says.

"My turn," Kimmy says, still staring at my chest. She spins the bottle and it lands on—

Me? Me? Will it be me? Let it be me.

—between Nick and Lauren. "It's closer to Nick," Kimmy says.

Nick taps his cheek, and she gives him a quick peck. I spin and it lands on Lauren. I peck her on the cheek. Then Lauren spins and it lands on Kimmy. Nick, Jamie and I cheer.

"Fine with me," Lauren says.

"Fine with me, too," Kimmy says. Lauren kisses her on the cheek.

Jamie's turn. It lands on Kimmy. He cheers and tells her to pucker up.

Their lips touch and I feel a prick of jealousy in my spine. Why does he keep getting her?

My turn. Kimmy, Kimmy, Kimmy…it points to Lauren.

My superhero powers are not working. She taps her cheek and I kiss it. She smells clean, like Head & Shoulders.

Kimmy's turn. Around and around and around and…me. Finally. She leans off her chair and her lips hit half on my cheek and half on my lips. I feel her breath on my mouth, and she smells sexy and spicy, and my whole body stiffens.

I finish the wine in my glass. And pour myself another.

Nick spins and lands on Jamie. "Truth," he calls out.

"How many times did you jerk off today?" Lauren asks.

He ponders the question. "Twice."

"Ew," she groans, and rolls back onto the rug.

"You asked."

She nods, suddenly intrigued. "Where do you do it?"

He shrugs. "Anywhere, dude. In my room. In the bathroom. In the bathroom in the Katz building, in—"

Lauren holds her hand up to stop him. "I was only supposed to ask you one question. My mistake. And my turn." She spins and lands on Kimmy again.

Nick, Jamie and I cheer. The girls peck each other on the lips.

Jamie spins and the bottle points at Nick.

"You're choosing dare, dude," Nick says. "Down four shots of vodka."

Jamie shakes his head. "I don't drink."

"Then you don't get to see Kimmy and Lauren make out."

"Don't force him to drink," Kimmy says. "And I don't have any vodka, anyway."

Nick pulls a silver flask from his backpack, and hands it to Jamie. Then he takes out four shot glasses and lines them up on the floor.

Jamie lets out a big, dramatic sigh. "I'll do it. But if I pass out, don't say I didn't warn you."

We count as Jamie drinks and makes sour faces.

My turn. I spin and try to use my mental powers to make it land back on Kimmy. It points to me.

"You have to give yourself a blow job, dude," Nick says.

"Why are you so obsessed with blow jobs?" Lauren asks. "Ha! I bet it's because you've never had one."

"You lose your turn," Jamie slurs. "Kimmy's up."

Not fair. But then Kimmy lands on me and my sense of fairness flies straight out the window.

"Again?" Jamie says. "This sucks. This game sucks."

Apparently booze makes Jamie whiny.

Kimmy leans toward me and slowly, carefully, kisses me. Her lips are sweet and wet and I want to pull her toward me but I don't. She smiles at me as she sits back in her chair.

The game keeps going but all I can think about are Kimmy's wet lips.

Nick and Jamie are cheering because Lauren landed on Kimmy again. "Tongue! Tongue! Tongue!" we all chant.

"Aren't men mature?" Lauren says, leaning toward her. Kimmy holds her hair back.

The girls roll their eyes and both stick out their tongues

like they're making faces at a teacher behind her back, then move in close enough so their tongues touch.

Nick and I groan with pleasure.

"That was too short," Jamie cries. "And I didn't see any saliva."

Nick snorts. "Dude, you're not supposed to see saliva. I guess that's why Kimmy never slept with you again."

Jamie gives him an evil look and spins. He lands on me.

"Say dare," Nick says. He shakes the flask.

Jamie grins. "Truth."

Nick shakes his head in disgust. "Why are you such a pussy?"

"Is that your question?" he asks, looking bored.

"No," he says, taking a sip from the flask himself. "If you had to choose between screwing Professor Gold or Swiley, who would you choose?"

"Professor Swiley. She seems quite energetic. Russ, your turn."

I think I would agree with him. Swiley is energetic. I bet she's peppy in bed. I think I'm pretty drunk. I spin and land on Kimmy. This is number two for us. I lean into her and she leans into me. Oh, man. Her lips part and I part mine and our mouths are all over each other. Her tongue slips into my mouth and tingles against mine.

"Get a room," someone in the background says.

I stop. I feel Jamie staring. Kimmy runs her fingers through her hair. Oh, man. I pour myself another glass of wine.

Kimmy spins. Every part of my body wants it to land on me. Lauren.

Nick cheers. "Giddyap!"

Kimmy walks over to Lauren and sits on her lap. And then, very slowly, they start going at it. Tongue, saliva, the works. We watch, mesmerized, as Lauren raises her hands and caresses Kimmy's breasts.

Then Kimmy caresses Lauren.

Holy shit.

"I think I just came," Jamie says.

Kimmy and Lauren start laughing and pull away from each other.

Kimmy sits down on the bed beside me. My heart is hammering against my rib cage. If we were alone in here, I'd be all over her.

"Can you do that again?" Nick says, bug-eyed.

He spins, and gets Lauren, and they kiss. Then Lauren gets Nick, and Nick says, "Time to turn your back to our team."

Lauren rolls her eyes and they kiss again. Then Nick jumps on top of her, squishing a chunk of Brie, and Lauren knees him in the groin.

"Ball breaker," he wheezes.

"This is getting boring," Lauren says, pushing him off her. "Can we play something else?"

Something else? What else could lead to Kimmy's tongue in my mouth? I need to have her tongue in my mouth. I need to be on top of her.

"How about 'I never'?" Nick offers, still wheezing. "That's where you have to drink to everything you've done."

"I'm bored," Jamie whines. "This sucks."

"So leave," Nick says. "What's wrong with you, dude?"

"I told you, I don't like drinking."

Nick ignores him. "How about truth-or-dare?"

"We already did that," I said. "It was the alternate solution to the alternate lifestyle, remember?"

"I dare the girls," Nick says, "to take off their shirts and bras."

"Yeah, right," Lauren says.

"I'm not wearing a bra," Kimmy says.

Oh, man.

Nick starts to remove his shirt. "I'll take off my mine and the rest of you take off yours. Russ's is already off—you don't hear him complaining, do you?"

Lauren shrugs. "I'm not afraid to take off my shirt. Tell

you what. You streak the floor bare-assed, and I'll be right behind you bare-chested."

Nick jumps into standing position, already in mid-pant unsnapping. "We strip in the bathroom and then run to the second-floor bathroom and back."

"I'm going to sleep," Jamie says, standing up.

"Stop being such a wimp," Nick tells him. "Do you have a camera? Let's take pictures."

Jamie sighs heavily. "Fine."

"You're on," Lauren says. She takes a swig of Nick's flask and runs off, pulling her shirt over her head. Jamie and Nick look at each other and follow after her. The door slams shut behind them.

The CD must have stopped a while ago. It's quiet in here. Kimmy puts her hand on my leg. "Just us," she says.

"Just us," I repeat.

Her face is barely an inch from mine. Her lips are wet and moist. My mouth is dry. She brushes her hair away from her face. "I think we should continue where we left off."

I think she's right. I run my hand through her hair. She looks into my eyes. Slowly I lean into her and kiss her.

Oh, man.

layla tricks but won't treat

The bass of the music reverberates through the vents. Just one more sentence…

No! I forcibly wheel myself away from my desk and close my laptop. I can't work on Halloween. The Economics assignment can wait until after the party. I waddle out the door and down to the common room. I'm already dressed. I've been in costume for the past two hours, wearing a large green shell around my torso, green tights and clunky black shoes. I continue waddling, down the stairs and to the common room.

Must stop thinking about Economics.

The party is in full swing. Kimmy, who is dressed as a geisha girl, is in the corner refilling her drink. Definitely no drinking for me tonight. I must have a clear head when I return to my desk.

"Layla, I have some news," she says. She gestures to me, and I move in closer, as close as anyone could get in a costume like mine. I wonder if she's finally going to admit what's going on with her and Russ. She hasn't said anything, but I can feel the hyper energy between them. Something's going on. I don't approve, but it's not my business to say. I'm a little disappointed that she hasn't confided in me. Maybe she senses that I wouldn't support the infidelity. Or maybe she's mad at me because I missed her birthday celebration. It wasn't my fault, I had to work.

She looks me over. "What are you supposed to be?"

"I'm an M&M." M&M's are not my all-time favorite chocolate. I prefer Snickers. However, the makings for an M&M's costume were far more readily available. I wasn't about to tape nuts and caramel to my body. I stretch out my arm and touch her shoulder. "You look cute." Personally, I would never dress as something that represents subservience, but whatever. She *does* look cute. She's wearing a short red Asian-style dress, and red chopsticks in her hair. "You should have painted your face white."

"A white face would make me look pasty, and I want to look hot." She lowers her voice. "I have news about Brad."

Brad? "Bradley Green?" My Bradley Green?

"The one and only. He doesn't live with a girlfriend."

Yes! "How do you know?"

"I found his number on the Internet and called him. The male voice on the voice mail said he couldn't come to the phone."

I look at her with expectation. "What? When? Why?"

"This afternoon. I've been waiting for you to do it yourself, but it seems to me you're all talk and no action. So calling him was my gift to you for helping me study."

Is she trying to steal my potential man? No, a friend wouldn't do that. Although, Kimmy would. "Thank you. And…?"

Kimmy laughs. "For a bright girl, sometimes you're not too swift. Don't you see? *He* couldn't come to the phone, not *we* as in him and potential skanky girlfriend."

"I can't believe you called him," I say, partly in awe that she phoned him, and partly jealous that she heard his voice. "What did he sound like?"

"Sexy. Serious."

Yes! Two qualities I adore. "You didn't leave a message, did you?" I ask, suddenly panicked. She called an applicant. For me. You can't call an applicant. That's totally unethical.

"Don't be crazy. I just listened to his message. And I blocked my number, so he won't have a record of it on his caller ID. Quick, look like we're busy talking."

"I thought we *were* busy talking."

"It's Russ," she hisses.

Ah. I knew something was going on. I peer around the room. "Where?"

"Stop looking! Keep talking."

"All right. Have you started the new Economics assignment? I've been working on it all week. There is an incredible amount of work to do. At least Integrative Communications is over this week so we have more study time available."

"Not about school. Talk about something else."

Something else? What else is there to talk about? "Then you think of something to talk about."

She sighs. "Why isn't he coming over?"

I eye a bowl of my little M&M's cousins with avarice, but I'm too paranoid about bacteria to indulge myself. Everyone knows that men don't wash their hands after using the urinal.

A blinding flash of light erupts in her face. "Who's he?" Jamie asks, lowering his camera. He's dressed all in black with a T-shirt that reads *The Enquirer*.

"So, Mr. Paparazzi," I say, hoping to help Kimmy dodge the question. "How are you tonight?"

"Pretty good. You look very sexy, Kimmy." He picks up her hand and kisses it. She curtsies.

Then he picks up mine. "Layla, you look delicious."

His fingers are warm and sweaty. I feel mildly uncomfortable whenever I'm around Jamie. I think it's because of my association with Rosen Brothers, and that I was partly responsible for his job loss. I wonder how he worded his getting laid off in his LWBS application so that it didn't work against him. "Thank you," I say, trying to shake off my guilt.

Instead of kissing my hand, he licks it. "I was hoping you'd melt in my mouth."

Kimmy nudges me and whispers, "He's coming over," before taking a long sip of her drink. I spot Russ, walking with Nick toward us.

Honestly, I don't know what she's so gaga about. Sure, he's great-looking, but he seems uncomfortable in his skin, like his briefs are too tight. He's dressed as Superman, with a cape around his neck, a big *S* sewn to his shirt.

Kimmy's posture transforms. She is currently pushing out her chest and sucking in her stomach. "Hi, Russ. Do you want something to drink? Jamie?"

She's certainly running with the geisha theme.

Russ taps the side of his plastic cup. "Sure, thanks."

Jamie shakes his head no. "I only drink when I'm depressed, and I'm in a great mood. Hey ladies, how does it feel to be the best looking women here?"

Kimmy snorts. "We're the only women here. We're like the only women at LWBS."

"Hopefully more women will get in next year," I say. "If I have anything to say about it."

"What do you mean by that?" Jamie asks me.

"I'm on the applications committee," I explain.

"And you're going to let in women just because they're women?" he asks, his voice rising. "Is that fair? What about men who deserve the same right?"

My cheeks feel hot. "When the playing field is level, men can have the same rights. Giving women a slight advantage is more than fair, when you look at the history of discrimination."

"Don't you want the people in your class to be the best

people? And not have to work with people just because they fill a quota?"

"An MBA class is stronger when it's diverse. Just as our work groups are stronger when we're not five engineers, our class is stronger if it's not composed of a hundred white men."

Jamie crosses his arms in front of him and furrows his unibrow. "I think people should be judged on what they bring to the table."

"So do I," I challenge. "I think women bring something different to the table." Then I take a deep breath and try to calm myself down. Jerk.

He raises the eyebrow. "I'm not a jerk because I have a different opinion."

I laugh. "How did you know what I was thinking?"

"Paparazzi knows everything." He eyes the bowl of M&M's. "Let's talk about something else." He scratches his head. "Do you know why our dorm is called the Zoo?"

My shoulders relax. Argument aborted. "No, I don't."

"The real estate magnate Richard M. Zuan built our residence for free as a donation and that's what his friends called him. Zoo. Huh? Interesting stat."

A knowledgeable jerk, then. "Very interesting. When I graduate, I'm going to donate money for a glorious salad bar in the cafeteria. I hate that there's no salad bar. I'm obsessed with the idea. I was contemplating starting a petition."

"Hilarious." Jamie spots the bowl of M&M's and digs his entire hand in. "So what else are you obsessed with? Homework?" He starts chomping away and a piece of green shell sticks to his lip.

"I'm a little obsessed with the Economics assignment." The assignment I should be working on right now instead of staring at a green shell. Does he not feel the shell? Lick your mouth, dammit!

"You've started that already?"

Started? Is he kidding? "I've already written three drafts. I'm thinking of taking off in a few minutes to continue it."

"It's Friday night. And it's Halloween. And the assignment isn't due until Thanksgiving."

"Don't you see? That's what I mean about obsession. I can't stop thinking about it. I want it to be perfect."

He shakes his head, and the green shell bobs from side to side. "You need to relax, darlin'. I think *you* need a drink." He sighs. "The more I think about the assignment, the more depressed I get."

I laugh again. "In that case, since you're already depressed, why not join me?"

jamie is shockingly punctual

"I will be grading you on attendance," Professor Small-Penis Matthews says. "Organizational Behavior is not optional."

It is to some, I think, looking around.

Only ten of us have made it to class today. Ten out of sixty-six. Oy.

I'm not sure what amazes me more, that only ten people decided to come to class or that I'm one of them.

Those absent are most likely nursing hangovers from last night's continuing Halloween bash. The student council bought too much beer for Friday's party, so it decided to keep it flowing all weekend. Last night the common room was humming until three a.m.

"Can someone define Expectancy Theory for me?" Matthews asks.

Layla raises her hand. She has a really nice hand. Her fingers are long and thin, and her nails French-manicured. I'm surprised I haven't noticed them before, considering she's always raising it to answer Matthews's questions. And Douglas's. And Gold's. And Martin's. And Rothman's.

Nick and Russ have taken to rolling their eyes every time she opens her mouth.

The professors love her. Especially Rothman. He's always eyeing her. For all I know they're involved. It wouldn't surprise me that a top student would hook up with the young and hip professor.

"Yes, Layla?" Matthews says.

"The force of motivation is equal to Expectancy times Instrumentality times Valence."

"And all this time I thought it had something to do with pregnancy," I say.

Matthews glares at me.

I don't know how I didn't recognize Layla's voice that time in the shower. It's so distinct. Throaty and sexy. If she weren't in B-school, she could be a phone sex operator.

Strange how Kimmy and Layla have become so close. The two of them are definitely the odd couple. I'd love to be a fly on the wall for one of their conversations. It would be like listening to Mary Ann and Ginger from *Gilligan's Island*.

Kimmy, as well as the rest of my group, are conspicuously absent from class today.

Organizational Behavior rolls into Accounting, and still none of the others show up. Apparently my group has declared November 3 a holiday. The bell finally rings, and Layla stretches then returns her hole puncher, ruler, pink Hi-Liter, yellow Hi-Liter and purple pen to her furry pink pencil case. At the beginning of OB, I watched her remove these items in exactly the reverse order. Pen, yellow Hi-Liter, pink Hi-Liter, ruler, hole puncher. I find her attention to orderliness intriguing. And sexy.

She secures the pencil case in the front pocket of her school bag, then puts away her Accounting binder, the Accounting textbook, the Accounting course pack, and finally, her tape recorder. Layla's schoolbag isn't any ordinary schoolbag. With its wheels and handle, it looks more like a piece of luggage. She rolls it behind her wherever she goes, and I'm beginning to want to know why. I'm beginning to want to know everything about her.

We cross paths at the door. She does an unenthusiastic little wave, as if she's just been crowned Homecoming Queen but has no energy. I try to think of something funny to say, but all I have is, "Good morning." Which just isn't funny. Even with a Spanish accent. Which is what I do, for no reason that I can think of. I am nowhere near Spanish. I don't look Spanish. I've never even been to Spain. Or Mexico. The only Spanish encounter I've had was when a burrito went down the wrong way and I nearly choked.

"Did you have a good weekend?" I ask, quickly losing the accent.

"Yes, I did. You?"

I'm probing my brain for a wheelie-bag-related joke, but my brain's find-key has finished searching the document and the search item has not been found. Lightbulb! Maybe I'll be chivalrous and offer to wheel the bag for her. I open my mouth and close it again. What's wrong with me?

"I'll see you in Stats," she says, and does her little wave again before disappearing down the hallway.

"Bye," I say. And then it hits me. I should have said *When's the flight?* Maybe I can use it later?

Before going to the cafeteria, I pick up the pictures I dropped off on Saturday at the campus drugstore. I sit on a bench in the middle of campus and flip through them. First are the ten pictures of the Halloween party, which didn't come out that well. Too dark. Then there are a few from last week's beer bash. A little brighter. Next, Kimmy's breasts. Covered by a fuchsia shirt, of course. I took it last week in an attempt to liven up our group meeting.

The next ten pictures are of Nick's skinny butt and Lauren's jiggling breasts from their post-spin-the-bottle streak.

Now that was a night to remember. Not that I remember

much of it. The four shots of vodka went straight to my head and made me cranky. The next morning all I could remember was why I shouldn't drink.

I flash back to the accident I had in the ninth grade. I was riding my bike, and the car was making a left turn. The driver didn't see me, and I was thrown right across the street. I was in the hospital for two weeks with a broken jaw, leg and arm. The drugs made me sad and crazy. The days weren't so bad. I got to watch movies. But the nights were unbearable. I stared at the ceiling, imagining myself in a coffin. I thought a lot about death. About what it feels like to die. About the moment just before death. I'd been knocked out immediately when the car hit me. What if I had died? Which is worse, knowing or not knowing the end was coming? And what difference would it make? When you're dead, you're dead.

Did Dara know? *Can* an infant know?

Why does God let a six-month-old baby die?

I should never have worked at the hospital after college. My mother got me the job—she became a nurse after Dara died. She still works at that hospital, loves it there. She claims it makes her feel stronger. In control. But working there had the opposite effect on me. It brought me right back to that horrible frame of mind. After getting laid off, I realized I never want to be in a hospital again.

My grumbling stomach snaps me out of my depressing trip down memory lane and propels me toward the cafeteria line.

Smiling at the lunch-line lady in the hair net, I do my best Brando. "Stella!"

"Hi, sweetie. Take the pizza today."

"Done."

Carl rings up my meal. "Jamie, my man. How are you?"

"Splendid. You?"

"Can't complain." He reads my number from my temporary card and types it into a computer. "You ever going to get a real one?"

"Damn bureaucrats." Fortunately, Carl is the only one who's noticed my sketchy student card. I definitely must amend the situation before it becomes an issue.

Except I don't have a clue how to do it.

Nick, Kimmy and Lauren are sitting by the window. "Good morning, gorgeous," I say to Kimmy, and squeeze in beside her. "And a good morning, oh, I mean, good afternoon, to the rest of you. How are we all feeling?"

Lauren shakes her Snapple in the air above her head. "I slipped in puke. Someone upchucked all over my floor's bathroom again last night. That's three nights in a row. How do you think I feel?"

I cover her quaking hand with mine and ease it down to the table. No one wants a juice shower. "Jealous that you were put on a different floor from us?"

"I'd rather bathe in puke nightly than make conversations with you three when I brush my teeth."

Nick snorts. "Bet you have shit morning breath, Lauren."

I pass the envelope of photos to Kimmy. She howls at the post-spin-the-bottle shots. "These are hysterical," she squeals. "You guys actually streaked?"

Lauren grabs the pictures. "What, you have amnesia, Kimmy? You don't remember?"

She blushes. "I forgot."

"You pervert," Lauren says, focusing on the close-up shot of Kimmy's chest. "Bet Jamie is planning to blow this one up and staple it to his ceiling."

I massage her shoulder. "I've already stapled the naked ones of you, dear. And Kimmy, if you let me take you on a date, I'll give you the negatives as well as all the prints."

Everyone laughs.

"It'll be your dream date," I press on, joking. "I'll rent a limo. Buy you strawberries and champagne. A five-course dinner at Dolce Vita's. You'll never look at another guy again."

With Kimmy it's a routine: I flirt shamelessly, she loves the attention, everyone laughs. It's our own version of the Expectancy Theory. She's come to expect my flirting, and I've come to accept her rejection. Not that I care. Okay, I wouldn't kick her out of bed if I found her there naked, but it's not her I've been thinking about lately. It wasn't her smile that kept me up last night and woke me up this morning. Not her eyes that made me want to be early for class.

Kimmy gives me a *get real!* look and continues flipping through the remaining pictures. "Why didn't anyone tell me I looked so gross on Halloween?"

My turn: "You could never look anything but drop-dead gorgeous."

Through the window, I watch Layla wheel her bag. She catches me staring and does her wave, only this time it's with windshield-wiper high-speed intensity.

I think I'm in love.

russ blasts beer

I hope Kimmy's not here. I hand my beer-bash ticket to the student guarding the door, and peruse the makeshift bar. Forty students are milling around, plastic cups in hand. There's something odd about drinking beer under the glaring halogen lights of a school cafeteria.

I pour myself a cup and make my way over to an already hammered Nick.

"Russ, dude," he says to me. "What took you so long? You only have twenty more minutes to get plastered."

I look around the room for Kimmy, and I feel both relief and disappointment at her absence. I've been doing my best to avoid her since the spin-the-bottle fiasco. Seeing her reminds me of what a jackass I am. Ignoring her reminds me of what a jackass I am.

What should I do? Tell Sharon? Tell her I met someone else? Tell her I hooked up with someone else but it doesn't mean anything? Either way, she'll never speak to me again. Maybe I should talk to Kimmy. Tell her it was a mistake, a one-time blunder.

Why can't I get the taste of her mouth out of my head?

At least I didn't sleep with her. We didn't even take off our clothes. We just kissed. Don't I get credit for that? I feel a small pimple under my chin and play with it.

Nick empties his cup and burps. "Kimmy was just looking for you, but she took off."

Must be obvious that I'm thinking about her, if even the drunk guy can tell.

kimmy goes to bat

"So assets equals liabilities plus stockholder equity."

I wonder what Russ is doing right now. Is he thinking about me? I bet he's thinking about me.

"The stockholders' equity is therefore the difference between a firm's assets and the firm's liabilities, right?"

He is the best kisser ever. Not too rough, not too soft, a little bit of tongue, but I didn't feel like I was playing in a hockey match. His lips were round, plump and warm.

Layla taps me on the head with her course pack. "Kimmy, you're not listening to me. What are you daydreaming about?"

Oops. "Nothing."

"Liar. Tell me."

Can't tell, can't tell, can't tell. "I can't." How has she not figured it out?

It's Sunday night and we're lying on our stomachs on Layla's floor, teacups, textbook and calculators beside us. "Sounds juicy," she says.

Can't tell, can't tell, can't...what the hell. I've held it in since my birthday and that was almost a month ago. That must be a world record. I swing my feet in front of me and sit up. "Okay. I wasn't going to say anything, but I'm exploding."

"What happened?"

"Russ." Even his name sounds sexy and wonderful.

"Russ happened? Is that like an earthquake?"

I give her my best knowing look.

"Did he cheat on his girlfriend with you?"

Yikes. Does she have to put it like that? What about, did you finally physically express your feelings? I shrug, suddenly uncomfortable. "Kind of."

"Kind of? How does one kind of cheat?"

I wish she'd stop using the C-word. It makes me feel whorish. "We didn't sleep together. We just fooled around. Kissed. Some non-friend appropriate touching, but no sex."

She picks up her teacup and, pinky out, takes a long sip. Is she avoiding looking at me? "So what does this mean?"

An excellent question. "I don't know, Layla."

She takes another slow sip, pinky still out. "What about his girlfriend?"

"Don't know."

"Do you think he told her?"

I snort. "Not likely. Men never come clean unless they're leaving." My mother realized my father had cheated only after she heard the message he'd left on her answering machine, telling her he'd moved his belongings to his ho-bag mistress's apartment. But Russ seems more decent. He's probably not the sort to walk out on someone that way. What if he's planning to break up with her but he doesn't want to do it over the phone? Maybe he fell in love with me after we made out, and the reason it hasn't happened again is that he wants to be split up with her before we hook up again. "Do you think he'll break up with her?"

She balances her tea on her Accounting textbook and looks me in the eye. "Kimmy, I don't think what you did was right."

I shouldn't have said anything. Now Layla thinks I'm a big slut. "I'm not in the mood for a lecture, thanks."

She sighs. "What do you expect to get out of this?"

What kind of question is that? What does she think? A record deal? "I want him to break up with her and start dating me."

"But…if he cheated on her, don't you think he'll cheat on you?" she asks, her voice rising.

They all cheat anyway, so what's the difference? "He might. But I would keep a better eye on him."

"That's your long-term strategy? Buy him a leash?"

Can it have rhinestones? "No. Maybe. But giving in to temptation wasn't entirely his fault. I kind of pushed it."

She shakes her head. "There will always be someone like you, pushing it. To be entirely safe, you'd have to keep him under house arrest."

I'm not going to show her my Steal Russ project plan, but she should understand what he was up against. "I got him drunk and orchestrated a game of spin the bottle. Please don't repeat that we played spin the bottle. Or about Russ." Truth is, I want Layla to tell. If everyone knows, he'll have to break up with Sharon. I roll a Hi-Liter between my fingers.

"Who played spin the bottle?"

"My work group."

"Your group has more fun than mine does," she says, sighing.

I don't doubt that. Her group looks like their idea of a fun night is getting together and watching *Star Trek* reruns. (I shouldn't jest. Russ has a Mr. Spock pencil case.) "Anyway, Russ and I kissed during the game. And then when everyone left, we kissed again. And again. We made out for like an hour. And then he left."

She sighs, louder this time. "Has anything happened since then?"

"No. And we haven't even talked about it, either. He's acting totally weird. Sometimes I think he's avoiding me, but then other times he flirts. Like at the Halloween party. We were both drinking, and he would stand a little too close to me, so I thought, for sure we're going home together. But then he left with Nick. So what do you think I should do?"

Layla downs the rest of her tea. "Honesty is usually the best policy. Talk to him. He owes you an explanation. And he certainly owes Sharon an explanation." She puts down her cup. "But now we have to get back to work."

Work, shmurk. "Talking about Russ is much more fun."

"Balance sheets are fun."

I worry about her sometimes.

"I think we should talk about the midterm Economics assignment, which I bet you haven't started yet," she snaps. "It's worth sixty percent of our final grade."

Despite the attitude, she really is a godsend.

By ten-thirty, I (unbelievably) have a basic understanding of what I have to do for the assignment, and I pack up, then leave her to transcribe today's tape-recorded lessons. Yes, she's a freak. My eyes are killing me from the excessive reading, and I need something to drink that does not involve hot water or chamomile. I check for change in my pocket and skip down to the basement to buy a bottle of apple juice from the building's sole vending machine.

And look what we have here. Russ staring at the machine. A balm for my sore eyes.

He spins around, surprised. "I forgot this doesn't take loonies," he says, fingering a gold coin, which I assume is Canadian.

"I don't think so."

He laughs and says, "You don't happen to have an extra dollar do you? I'm not sure why I think we're in Canada."

"Oh, but I do," I say, and hand him one. I pat his arm. "See anything good?"

"I had a craving for Pringles, but all this has is pretzels."

"I have salt-and-vinegar chips in my room." He doesn't respond. I backtrack. "You don't like pretzels?"

He gives me a lopsided smile. "I like chocolate pretzels."

"Those sound gross." I'm trying hard not to point out the massive elephant in the room that we're both ignoring: the fact that he has a girlfriend and we hooked up.

A candy bar pops out of the machine, and he bends down to pick it up. "I shouldn't be eating this," he's saying as I get an eyeful of his perfectly sculpted behind.

"Why?" I ask, very much distracted.

"Bad for the body."

"Your body looks fine." Oops. Didn't mean to say that. I buy a bottle of juice. "Where do you want to sit?" Wasn't that clever? I've implied he wants to sit with me.

"Here?"

We slide down to the floor. I wish there were chairs. No one's stomach ever looks good when we're crouching on the floor. He unwraps his bar and breaks it in half. He consumes his portion in one bite. I nibble on the corners and ask, "How are you doing?"

"Busy. You?"

"You know." You know as in you know I'd rather be naked in my room with you.

He fiddles with the wrinkled wrapper. "I wanted to talk to you about the other night."

Why is he staring at his hands? I'm getting a bad feeling here. He's going to tell me it didn't mean anything. I need to take a different tack. "What night?"

He blushes. How cute is that? "You know," he says, looking at me sideways. "Spin the bottle?"

"Spin what bottle?" I scoot close to him and tap my shoulder against his. "Like this?" I put the lid on my juice and spin it. It hits my knee and stops. "First it's a kiss on the cheek." I kiss him on the cheek, quickly, then spin the drink again. It stops against his thigh. "Second it's a kiss on the lips."

Before he realizes what I'm doing, I lean over and kiss him. He doesn't stop me.

"That's—" more kissing "—what I wanted—" more kissing "—to talk about." His lips are juicy. Sweet like chocolate milk. "I have a girlfriend," he continues. And then kisses me again.

Tongue in my mouth, tracing my teeth. "And?"

"Who I care about."

"And?" I finger the dark hairs on his arm.

He's still kissing me.

I move my hand up to his chest and press my nails into the cotton of his shirt.

"I think we should stop," he says.

"Do you want to stop?"

"No." And then his hand is on the back of my head, pulling me closer, into him, under him. My back is flat against the stiff, cold, basement floor. Something sticky is in my hair. I'm thinking spilled liquid detergent from the laundry room down the hallway. I want to tell him that we should go to his room, but I'm afraid of breaking the spell.

I hear the sound of someone skipping down the stairs, change jingling in a pocket.

That decides it. "Let's go upstairs," I say. He helps me to my feet and I lead him like he's a puppy. (That rhinestone leash would come in handy right now.) We pass someone from another Block and nod hello. Three flights later, we're alone in the hallway. When he pulls his key from his pocket, I rub myself against his back. He moans and opens the door. He doesn't turn on the lights. Instead, he shuts the door behind him and pushes me up against it, then rubs his hands up and down my arms, legs, breasts, stomach, like he's trying to rub off my clothes.

My body's on fire. I pull his hair and kiss him.

He pulls my shirt over my head and discards it onto the floor, undoes my bra and then bites my neck. I squeeze my hands between our bodies and unbutton his shirt and drop it next to mine. Now we're getting somewhere. I squeeze in again for his belt, but he blocks me. Strike one. "Don't," he says, but continues sucking my neck. What is *don't?* What guy says *don't?*

His mouth descends to my nipples. Well, that's better. At least now we're progressing. Last time we hooked up, there was zero nipple action. I take his move as a sign to try for his belt a second time, but again he stops me. Strike two. I've never been on this end of the tug-of-war. In high school it was always me doing the hand block. The guy would stick his hand under my shirt, I'd use a Karate Kid move to stop him. He'd try again two minutes later, and again I'd do the block.

Interesting stat: since coming to B-school, I've tried and *failed* to have sex with two different men, on two different occasions. Is this normal?

My next move is the back-door move—I gently squeeze his ass through his jeans. Is he going to stop me? Nope. Not stopping me. He squeezes mine. Wahoo! We've successfully moved to our body's lower quadrants. I push him to his bed.

He presses Play on his CD player. The song "Hero" from *Spider-Man* comes on.

I go for his belt again.

He doesn't stop me. In high school, I used to give in at round three, too.

Three strikes and Sharon's out.

russ caves in

What am I doing, what am I doing? Don't think, don't think. She's taking me out of my boxers now, stroking me. Must stop. Must say stop. Stop. Stoooooop. Her breasts are floating above me like magical, poisonous clouds.

I don't know how I let this get this far. Honestly. Last thing I remember, I was minding my own business, craving Pringles. And then she was kissing me, I was telling her to stop (mentally), and the next thing I know I'm flat on my back and she's undoing my belt.

Oh, man.

Maybe she has secret Iceman qualities and has (zing!) frozen me to the bed.

Ooh. Ah. She's rubbing her nose on my stomach. Lower. Yes, lower. I don't think I've ever been this hard. This is wrong. So wrong. I must stop. I must say stop. I should not be in this predicament. Can't.

Now she's licking me like a Popsicle. Then she wraps her whole mouth around me and sucks. This is even worse.

Must stop her. So good. Must say stop. Stop. Yeah, right. Instead I say, "I'm going to come."

The good news: she doesn't stop. The better news: she swallows. Sharon never swallows.

At least I didn't have *real* sex.

That's a line I will not cross.

Doesn't that count for something?

Kimmy rests her head on my stomach and I doze off.

Ring. Phone. Shit. *Ring.* Kimmy stirs. "You getting that?"

Ring. Gimme a break. 'Course I'm not getting that. It's Sharon. How can I talk to Sharon when I've just come in Kimmy's mouth?

Ring.

"No." Thank God for voice mail. Imagine having to listen to Sharon's voice echoing through the room. That would be so wrong. Not more wrong than what just happened, but definitely wrong.

Kimmy scoots up to my pillow and kisses my collarbone.

I feel out her ears. The lobes are nothing special, but there's a pointy pyramid on the top of her cartilage that might be fun to play with. I run the pad of my thumb over it.

"My mother used to get mad at me when I did that," she says. "She told me that if I kept playing with it, it would grow."

"Did it?"

"No."

I continue playing with it, until my thumb gets sore. Is she planning on leaving soon? Not that I'm trying to throw her out. I've never been a wham-bam-thank-you-ma'am kind of guy. But—well, I'll have to call Sharon back. Not this second. But in the next hour or so. Anyway, besides the Sharon-telephone issue, this is a single bed. Two people can't sleep comfortably in this baby, that's for sure.

I shift and stretch in the hopes that she'll realize how uncomfortable she is and leave. Doesn't happen.

Ring.

Shit. My spine feels twisted and prickly, my skin clammy. I think the walls of my room might be compressing like the trash compactor scene in *Star Wars*.

Ring.

What does Kimmy expect from this? Does she want me to break up with Sharon? Start dating her? I don't want to break up with Sharon. I love the way she's tough but not too tough to make baby kisses into the phone. I love the way she plays with my hair. She picks one strand and then rolls it in her fingertips while we're watching TV, my head in her lap. I love the way she eats chocolate peanut butter cups. She bites off the rim, peels off the top chocolate layer, and then licks the chocolate off the bottom so that all that's left is the peanut butter circle, which she pops into her mouth. Then she closes her eyes and makes adorable "mmm" sounds.

If I break up with her she'll never do that again. Worse, she'll do it again but not with me.

My stomach hurts. My back's in pain. I can't breathe. I can't break up with Sharon. No way. I have to tell Kimmy that this isn't happening again. Now might not be the best moment. Maybe sometime when I'm wearing my boxers. Maybe if I say I'm going to the bathroom, she'll leave. And then I'll call Sharon back. I pat her forehead. "Bathroom time." I almost said bathroom break, but in the nick of time I realized that she might take that to mean that I'm expecting her to return.

She stretches her arms above her, like Catwoman. "Me, too. I should go back to my room, anyway."

"Yeah?" You don't say. "Okay." I re-dress, then peer into the hallway to make sure the coast in clear. A run-in with Rena would not be good. Coast is clear.

"I'll see you in a sex," she says, heading to her room.

I think she meant sec. Or not. When I see her in front of the sink brushing her teeth, I peck her cheek. "Good night," I say while hurrying out.

"But wait—" she says, but I'm already out the door and pretend I don't hear.

Voice mail from Sharon: "Hi, honey, it's me. Just want to say hello. See what's up. Miss you." She blows a series of baby kisses into the phone and I feel like a bastard.

Second message: "Honey, where are you? I want to go to sleep."

I lie down and dial. "Hi." A strand of Kimmy's hair is on my pillow.

"Hi, honey. Where were you?"

"In the bathroom," I answer. At least I didn't have to lie. Yet.

"I can't wait to see you," she murmurs.

I put on my sweet voice, the one that sounds almost babyish, the one I would never use in front of another guy, ever. "I can't wait to see you, too."

"It's only two more weeks till American Thanksgiving. You have your plane ticket, right?"

My sheets smell musky, like female sweat. "I have my plane ticket."

"I'm so happy you're coming home. Do you want to do anything special? I have a bunch of new recipes I can make you for dinner."

Sure. And would it be okay if Kimmy gave me a blow job for dessert?

How does she not know? All I know is that I can't tell her. Not that I was planning on telling her. You can't tell someone that you cheated only ten minutes after it happened. What's your excuse? Sorry, I was drunk then, but I'm sober now? I didn't realize how special you are, but now I do? I was hard and now I'm not?

What if we get married? Did I just cheat on my future wife?

"Sounds great," I say.

"Any more thoughts on Christmas? I was thinking about a cruise."

Christmas? That's two months away. What if I decide I

want to be with Kimmy? Not that I'm planning to decide to be with Kimmy. I don't know what I'm planning. Except changing my sheets. Smelling Kimmy and talking to Sharon is like watching The Hulk turn orange when he gets angry instead of green. Just wrong. "Um, no thoughts yet."

"Okay, but decide soon or we'll never get reservations. What did you do tonight?"

"Huh?"

"What did you do?"

Better question would be who I did. "Not much." Ain't it the truth. It was Kimmy who did all the work. "You?"

"I had a lousy day. Remember that exam I told you I was giving to my ninth-graders?"

"Uh-huh." If she says so. She's always giving some sort of exam to one of her classes.

"I caught two guys in the back cheating."

I tense at the C-word. "Yeah?"

"They wrote the answers on their shoes. How did they think I wouldn't notice? Do they think I'm an idiot?"

My bed is still warm. So maybe she's not so on the ball. "The nerve."

"I waited till the end of class before I confronted them. They tried to deny it, as if I couldn't see the evidence on their shoes. I escorted them to Sheila's office. She suspended them for two days. They cried like two-year-olds."

Odd that she's chosen today to talk about cheating. If she asked me if I cheated right now, I'd admit it. Right now.

"Russ?"

Shit. "Yes?"

"I love you."

"Me, too."

She yawns. "I'm tired. Time to hit the hay."

"Good night."

"Good night. Be good."

Too late.

I need to sleep so I don't have to think. Unfortunately, I haven't gotten a full night's sleep since I got to school. Lately, I've been able to get more sleep during the day than at night. Maybe I'm a bat. Batman. It's the light in the hallway that keeps me up. It stays on twenty-four hours a day and the outline of the beam through my door is like an eclipse. Maybe I should tape the light out, eh? Make it a bat cave.

Maybe Nick's up. I think I'll start calling him Robin.

layla goes fruity

"It's perfect."

"Really?" I ask.

The career counselor looks at me across her desk and points a bitten fingernail. I want to recommend my manicurist to her, but that might be insulting. "Would you mind if I kept this on file as an example for others?" she asks.

I puff up with pleasure. LWBS offers a résumé critique. Apparently, I have nothing to be critiqued. My cover letter and résumé are perfect, detailing A-plus work and nice, round 4.0's. "Not at all. I'm flattered."

"Great," she says, searching through her files until she finds one labeled Examples. "I'll start sending potential summer jobs your way." She winks. "Who knows? Maybe a good summer job will lead to something permanent. Graduation is still more than a year away, but won't it be nice to have your life all sewn up way in advance?"

It would. "Thanks." I stand up and straighten my skirt.

"No," she says, giving me a meaningful look. "Thank *you*."

I'm smiling as I skip down the stairs of the Katz building

and into the sunlight. It smells like crunching leaves and fresh new clothes. I can't wait to go home for Thanksgiving so I can exchange my fall wardrobe for a winter one. I've placed a few items on hold at Bendel's, including a heavenly mid-length sheepskin coat I saw in *Vogue*. I miss shopping in the city. I also miss the perpetual motion, the high-speed of important people rushing to important places.

As I walk through campus to the library, I'm overwhelmed by all that I don't miss about home—the barrenness, the concrete, the lack of natural color. Here, the red, yellow and orange leaves are a kaleidoscope of color. I'm walking through a Picasso. In the midst of it all, Jamie is leaning against a tree, reading.

As usual, seeing him makes me feel guilty about making the recommendation for the hospital merger. How awful that I'm responsible for him losing his job. I should tell him. No, I can't.

I crouch beside him and glance at his reading material. It's the script to *Casablanca*. "Hard at work?"

He smiles when he sees me. *"Layla,"* he sings. "I bet you get pretty sick of hearing that Eric Clapton song, huh?"

"Not if you're singing," I say, smiling. He doesn't have a bad voice, actually.

"Let me guess, off to the library?"

"I have an exciting hour of Economics research, and then a group meeting."

He stuffs his paperback into his back pocket. "I've made a decision. No more reading for either of us. I'm going to teach you to juggle."

Juggle? That doesn't sound like something that can go on my résumé. "How do you know how to juggle?"

"My parents were in the circus."

Is he serious? "Come on."

"Fine, I made that up. They don't let Jews in the circus."

I don't know what to say about the Jews comment. He's

kidding again, right? "I bet you're lying about juggling, too. I've only seen you throw one thing into the air at a time."

He wraps his fingers around my wrist. "It's time for a lesson. Follow me." I laugh and let him pull me. Oddly, I remember reading something about juggling in the paper, that it enhances your brainpower. In which case, I suppose it could be beneficial.

"Where are you taking me?"

He leads me all the way to the cafeteria.

"Will we be juggling M&M's?" I ask.

"Stella!" he says, voice booming, to the woman at the cash.

"Hi, Jamie!"

She knows his name? He knows hers? Who introduces himself to the cafeteria people?

He sets his elbows onto the counter. "Stella, my sweet, do you have any oranges today?"

"I should think so." She rifles through a basket of fruit. "How many do you need?"

He holds up two fingers. "I think three would be a good start."

He is too weird.

She laughs and cherry-picks the best oranges. "Are you making juice?"

"I'm teaching Layla here how to juggle. Layla, do you know Stella?"

"Hi," I say, suddenly shy.

"Hello," she says. "You're the one who always has her nose in a textbook."

"How much do I owe you?" asks Jamie.

She winks. "Don't worry about it. It's your reward for getting this serious one to have some fun."

I follow him to the courtyard outside, and he stands directly beside me so our legs touch. "We'll start with one orange," he says, dropping the other two onto the ground. "I'm going to throw it to you, and you're going to catch it. And then you're going to throw it back. Got it?"

"Sounds simple enough. I should warn you that I'll probably be good at this. I have excellent aim. Remember that season when Disneyland closed?"

"Can't say that I do," he says, tossing the orange from one hand to the other. "Why?"

"It was because I'd cleaned them out of all their stuffed animals."

He laughs and then throws the orange up, up, up in the air, and it squishes when I catch it. It's heavier than I expected and cold. I toss it back and it soars way beyond his head. A few feet beyond. "Oops."

"The catching is easy, focus on the throwing. Make a nice easy arc."

Nice, easy arc. Can do. He throws it again and I catch it. Then I throw it back to him, in a nice, easy arc. He catches it. Yes! We go back and forth until he tells me it's time for the next lesson. "We're adding an orange. Keep doing exactly what you're doing." He throws the first one and I catch it. Yes! Then I focus on throwing it. Unfortunately, that's when the second orange flies through the air at me. Slam. I miss it by miles.

Am I juggling deficient? Why can't I do this? My heart starts to flutter nervously. "What's wrong with me?"

Jamie laughs. "Nothing. You're new at it."

Big deal. Doesn't mean I shouldn't be able to master it. "Perhaps if I saw you do it, I could learn by example. Let me see you."

He gathers the three oranges and starts juggling. Wow. It's just a matter of aerodynamics. I can do this. If I can stop a company from going bankrupt, I can certainly stop an orange from smacking the ground.

We try again. I wonder if Bradley Green can juggle. He certainly has a lot of brainpower. I drop the orange and it hits the ground.

"Layla," he sings. "You're not concentrating. What are you thinking about?"

I blush. "Sorry."

"Sorry? You were thinking *sorry?*"

We try again. My hand smells like citrus. Should I tell Jamie about Brad? Why not? Maybe I should get a man's perspective. "No. I was thinking about some guy. A guy who doesn't know I'm alive."

"I doubt that."

So true in this case. "No, really. I've never even met him."

He raises an eyebrow. "Huh?"

I know I shouldn't tell, but it's not like Jamie's going to pass along the info to anyone. And I haven't done anything wrong. I wasn't the one to call him. "All right, but you can't repeat any of this. See, I'm on the applications committee for prospective students. And I fell a little bit in love with one of the applicants."

He rolls one of the oranges between his hands. "You fell for a guy's application?"

Why do I have such a big mouth? "Yes. Bradley Green. Is that nuts?"

"As long as his middle name isn't Forest. Or Jade. It isn't, is it?"

He's too much. "Nope."

"Do you think you can love someone you've only seen on paper?"

He makes Brad sound like a centerfold I've taped to my locker. "I know it sounds moronic, but I felt a connection when I read his application. Like I was destined to read it. He's perfect for me. He's my prince." That sounded sophomoric in my head, and it sounded even worse out loud, but that doesn't mean I can't imagine our glorious royal wedding.

"I'm glad you didn't read my application. It was hysterical. You would have started stalking me, too. Let's keep going, you almost had it." He passes me an orange.

Forty minutes later, we're still juggling away and I'm improving. Pass, throw, catch, Pass, throw, catch. I'm having a blast even though my hands reek of orange. I think the citrus might be making me high. My brainpower must be increasing. Yes! Perhaps I should start doing this every day.

"Ready to try it on your own?" he asks.

I nod, very ready and very seriously. He places my feet shoulder-width apart and inserts two oranges into my right hand, one into my left. I fill my lungs with air and throw.

They all hit me in the head.

"Crap!" I scream, falling to the ground. I spot Kimmy and Russ approaching and wave. What is it with those two? Kimmy hasn't filled me in on what's going on with them since the spin-the-bottle experience, presumably because of my disapproval over their kissing fiesta. But I bet they've been at it again.

"What are you two doing?" Kimmy asks, running her fingers along her ear.

"I'm learning to juggle," I say. Uh-oh. I wonder how Jamie feels about seeing Russ and Kimmy together. I know from Kimmy that Jamie likes her, but I don't think Jamie has a clue about what's going on with Russ. Why on earth is she so fixated on Russ, when Jamie is such a sweetheart?

Jamie is rolling an orange in his hand, staring at it.

"Jamie," Russ says, "we're thinking of going over our OB assignment now. Don't want to interrupt you, of course. Busy, eh?"

"Ha-ha," Jamie says. "As if the rest of you could answer the questions without me."

I look at my watch. "Crap, it's already five past five! I'm supposed to meet my group."

"You're late for a group meeting?" Kimmy says, feigning shock. "My, oh, my, you two must have really been having fun."

"You want fun, Kimmy? I'll give you fun." Jamie raises his eyebrows suggestively.

We're going to have to work on his presentation. He obviously didn't pay enough attention in IC. "Hey there's Dorothy!" I say, waving at the Carry the Torch administrator across the field. "Yoo-hoo, Dorothy!" I call. "Let me introduce you."

"You know what, Layla?" Jamie says, grabbing his bag. "I gotta go."

And just like that, he takes off. What was that about? Apparently, we have to work on his communication as well as his presentation skills.

kimmy knows the drill

Another day, another blow job.

I'm getting cynical in my old age. It's almost eleven-thirty, and Russ and I are lying on his bed, wrapped in each other's arms, as though we have just made love and are now basking in the afterglow.

Wrong. We're still not having sex. We kiss, we fondle and we oral, but that's it.

These dates give a whole new meaning to foreplay, but I'm beginning to get a little annoyed. Yeah, yeah, he reciprocates the favor, but since I can't come, I don't get much pleasure. The thing I like about sex is the closeness. While you're doing it, nothing else matters, nothing but the weight of his body, the smell of his neck, the feel of his skin.

My favorite part is now, listening to his heartbeat slowing down, my head nuzzled in his chest. He's wearing a T-shirt but no pants, and I'm completely naked. Sometimes he plays with my ear. It's the same spot that I like to play with and I think this must be a sign.

The Zoo is quiet, and there are a few noises outside, a car

driving off, two friends laughing, but they're in the distance. Any second now the phone is going to ring, furious and loud, demolishing the harmony, like a wineglass slipping out of your hand onto the tiled kitchen floor. Any second now. His clock says 11:29 p.m. and she always calls at eleven-thirty.

If I had any self-respect I'd make a furtive exit. I'd kiss him on the forehead, tell him we'll speak soon, or something equally evasive, and let the phone ring when I'm long gone.

I don't move. The thing is, I need to hear the phone. If a phone rings and I don't hear it, did it really ring at all? Hearing the phone ring is my only way of monitoring the relationship. I wait for the day when the phone will stop ringing.

Ring.

I guess it's not today.

Ring. Ring. Voice mail picks up.

Russ's back tenses. Then he forces himself to relax. At eleven-forty I kiss him on the forehead. "See you tomorrow," I say, and reach for my crumpled panties and socks, which always end up squeezed between the corner of the bed and the heater. I get dressed quickly and quietly.

"Good night," he says. I press my head against the door to see if I can hear anything outside. I'm holding a textbook as my alibi in case anyone is lurking in the hallway. Nothing. I open the door a crack and don't see anyone outside. I wave, and close the door behind me. Then I wait. After a few minutes, I hear him move inside. He listens to the message. And then dials her number into the phone. "Hi," he says. "I'm good…. No…nothing new…. You?"

I hear someone walking up the stairs, and decide to take off before I'm caught eavesdropping. What I should be doing, instead of eavesdropping and giving blow jobs, is writing my cover letter and résumé. I think I want to be a consultant. Sounds glamorous. Lots of travel, high salary, get to be based in New York. Get to play with goals and tactics and strategies all day long. I'm applying to all the strategy consultant firms, including Bain, McKinsey, Accenture, BCG and O'Donnel.

Back in my closet of a room, I flip open my laptop. The job I *really* want is that of girlfriend. But before I can get that job, Russ has to fire the person currently hogging my position. I'm hoping he'll lay her off over Thanksgiving.

I really don't feel like writing a cover letter. Maybe this is what I'll write instead:

HR Jerk
100 Skyscraper, #666
New York, NY 69696
212-no-chance

Kimmy Nailer
The Zoo
1-555-AMB-ORED

Dear Mr. HR:

A consistent objective throughout my life has been to acquire skills that will not in any way, shape or form help me get a job. Such as Pilates and blow jobs. I believe that my skill set can be successfully leveraged as a Summer Associate at your incredibly boring place of work.

Upon graduating from college, I worked for my father in a job I detested, where I spent most of the day phoning my boyfriend. Then the jackass cheated on me and I came to business school to find a new boyfriend.

I possess strong interpersonal skills (two guys in my learning group want me) that I believe would be an asset to you. My experience demonstrates the ability to plan and execute in-depth seducing strategies, with results-oriented goals. I'm hoping the guy I've been hooking up with will dump his girl-friend over Thanksgiving. Why wouldn't he, right? He's obviously not too interested in her if he's been hooking up with me. Not sleeping with me, mind you, as that's where he arbitrarily draws the line. But I'm assuming he hasn't wanted to break up with her over the phone (he's sensitive and considerate) and will take care of it this weekend in person. I'm sure you agree that this is his best plan of action.

Should you also agree that my competencies would make a strong contribution to your organi-zation, I would appreciate the opportunity to further discuss my experience and goals at your conve-nience. My résumé is attached for your review.

I look forward to hearing from you.

Sincerely,
Kimmy Nailer

P.S. If you perform drug-testing for summer em-ployment, don't bother getting back to me. It's a long story, but the guy I've been hooking up with smokes a lot of pot, and in order to prove to him that I'm more agreeable than the prude he actually does cross the line with back home, I've had to do some puffing myself. I wish I could tell you that al-though I smoke, I don't inhale, but that would make me a liar as well as a boyfriend-poacher, and I do have some ethics, after all. Who knew?

jamie wants a sex change/ jamie wants sex, period

I knock on Layla's door to the rhythm of "The Sound of Music." The-hills. Are-a-live. To-the-sound. Of-mu-(long pause)-sic.

"One sec!" She hollers, then opens the door, dressed in khakis and a Polo shirt. I love that this is her study outfit. Everyone else wears sweatpants and flannel to study in. Or maybe that's just me. What's the point in being uncomfortable?

"It's Thursday night. Time to watch the student body drink and make fools of themselves," I tell her.

She laughs and shakes her head. "Are you crazy, Jamie? There's no time for a beer bash tonight. There's a speaking event I want to go to, and do you realize how much work we have due next week? Job applications, Economics midterm, our group OB and Strategy cases, never mind the Economics assignment—"

"You can't still be working on Economics. You've been doing it for ages."

"It's worth sixty percent of our final mark! Have you finished your applications?"

"Nah, I'm not applying anywhere through school."

She throws her arms up in bewilderment. "What? Why not?"

"Because I don't want to be a consultant or a banker or work for a pharmaceutical company. And those are the only companies hiring through LWBS."

"Why don't you?"

"They suck your soul. Did you see *Harry Potter?* Remember the dementors? I don't want that to happen to me."

"It's not that bad," she says quickly. "What do you want to do?"

"What do I want to do, what do I want to do." I lean against the doorway. "I have no idea." Sleep? Watch movies?

"Do you want to hear some fabulous female speakers in the auditorium?"

"Like who?"

"Megan Milton, CEO of E-World."

"I've never bought anything off the Web."

"Get out! Come with me and learn how safe it is."

"Who else is speaking?"

"I think the woman who runs Body Shop and also some nonprofit female executives. Come on!"

Not a movie, but I wouldn't mind spending some quality time with Layla. Last month I couldn't stop thinking about Kimmy. Now I can't stop thinking about Layla. Ever since our Halloween conversation, I can't get her long blond hair out of my mind. I must be a flake. One day I'm proposing marriage to Kimmy on the bathroom wall, and the next day I'm fantasizing about another woman's long bond hair dripping over my naked body.

If I thought Kimmy was out of my league, Layla isn't even in the same hemisphere. At least Kimmy had the Jewish thing going, which I thought would give me an edge. A Jewish girl usually wants to marry a Jewish guy, right? But even if Layla isn't into this whole caste system thing, she has her eye on someone else. Some WASP-y prince. I'd say my chances of wooing her are effectively zero.

Which is a good thing, I suppose, because if I brought her home for Hanukkah dinner, both my mother and bubbe would have a heart attack.

So instead, I'm going to take what I can get, friendship with Layla. "I think I'll come along. Not sure if Megan can put on as entertaining a show as our beer-satiated classmates, but whatever."

"Give me ten minutes to change, and I'll meet you downstairs."

She's changing? The khakis and Polo top aren't good enough? I look down at my sweatpants and fleece sweatshirt, and decide it wouldn't hurt to spruce up a bit.

I change into black pants and a shirt I tuck in, and meet her downstairs. She's wearing a striped pantsuit and looking fantastic. She's holding a leather folder and a fountain pen. I'm assuming she's planning on taking notes. Should be a wild and crazy night. Oh, what one does for "friendship."

She puts her arm on my shoulder. "Jamie, I have to tell you something important."

Is it possible? Does she like me?

"I worked for Rosen Brothers and we were the ones who recommended to personnel at your hospital to scale back. And ever since I found out you used to work there, I've been feeling horrendously guilty."

Damn. Not what I was hoping for. "Don't feel bad. The truth was, I wasn't happy there, anyway. Working at a hospital wasn't the right environment for me. I tend to absorb my surroundings, and I ended up feeling down most of the time. So getting laid off ended up being good for me."

"Wow," she says. "I feel a huge sense of relief."

"Don't worry about it."

"If I can ever do anything to help you get a job, let me know."

I hold open the glass door. "Actually, Layla, I could use one favor."

"Anything." She tightens her coat around her.

I take a deep breath. "This is going to sound very strange. But for some reason, LWBS thinks I'm a woman."

She stops walking and laughs. "Pardon me?"

"I don't know why," I lie. "It's some sort of glitch in the system. Because of my name, I guess. I've tried calling and e-mailing so someone will fix it, but no one has gotten back to me. You have access to the main computer, since you're on the applications committee. I was wondering if there was any way you could set things straight?"

"That's hilarious. Are you on the WOB e-list and everything?"

"I am. I even got an e-mail for tonight." I've gotten three e-mails from the Women of Business society. And trust me, I'd love to join. Talk about an easy place to pick up.

She considers it. "So all I would have to do is change the *W* to an *M*?"

"Yup." I try to sound casual, as though it's no big deal.

"All right." She exaggerates giving me a once-over. "You are, in fact, a man, aren't you?"

"I'm all man, darlin'." I'd certainly like to prove it to her.

Some of the speeches are interesting. Right now a woman named Danielle Grand is explaining her job as executive director at the nonprofit Girls Group in Danbury, which is about ten minutes away. "Girls Group sets up art, athletic, business and career-building programs for young women aged seven to seventeen, with the aim of building confidence, and teaching them that they can make positive contributions to the world," she explains.

Layla starts scribbling furiously.

"Most of you here tonight," Ms. Grand continues, "have probably noticed that only thirty percent of the students at LWBS are women. To significantly increase the number of female business owners and leaders, we have to increase the flow of women into key educational gateways such as business schools. And one way to do this, something that I do at Girls Group, is to motivate young women to prepare for a business career at an early age.

"Nonprofit work is not for everyone. You must have passion for the cause. That's the intangible reward that compensates for less income. And trust me, the income is much, much less than what you'd make at a bank or consulting firm. The cause—arming young women with the tools to make a difference in their lives—is something that fuels my passion."

I fade in and out of the rest of her speech. The truth is, I can't stop thinking about my application lie. About why I got accepted. About why I applied.

It was research. For an article. I had just seen the movie *Soul Man*. The one where C. Thomas Howell pretends to be black so he can get a scholarship to Harvard. There were articles about affirmative action everywhere, and I thought it would be an interesting study. I researched different programs and found that MBA schools claimed that they were committed to diversity but that women didn't have a competitive advantage when applying. I thought it was bullshit and that women would have an easier time getting in. So I decided to apply to ten different schools. Five as a male and five as a female. I handed in the exact same application to all ten schools. The only difference was my gender.

Out of the ten schools I applied to I was rejected at all of the ones I applied to as Jamie the male. For the ones I applied to as a female I was rejected at two, but accepted at one, and asked to interview at another two. I thought, busted! My thesis was proven correct. I would write the article and expose the bullshit.

But there was the acceptance to LWBS. Sitting on my desk. Signed by Layla's boss, Dorothy. Winking at me. Packaged with a brochure promising career advancement, wealth and leadership positions. And I thought—well, why not?

Why not go? Why should women have the advantage? If LWBS claimed they didn't accept based on gender then it shouldn't matter anyway, right?

I look at Layla staring intently at the speaker. She's one person who wouldn't agree with me. Who might even turn me in.

Maybe I shouldn't have asked her to change my official gender for me. But I didn't have a choice. I needed to get a new student card, or I wouldn't be allowed to write my exams. And she's the only person I knew who had access to change the letter *F* to a letter *M*, so my student card could be printed out and not give me away.

And she did get me fired in the first place. Not that I'm angry. I hated being in the hospital anyway.

And I shouldn't worry. If LWBS claims to be gender blind then they shouldn't care about my lie if I ever got caught.

Yeah, right.

I try to stop worrying and pay attention instead.

After the lecture, Layla runs to the podium to thank Ms. Grand for her inspiring speech. I approach the two of them just as Layla is whipping out her checkbook.

"I'd like to make a donation," she says, scribbling.

"I certainly didn't expect to fund-raise at a women's business panel," Danielle says. She glances at Layla's check and looks astounded. "Wow. Thank you. The Girls Group sincerely appreciates your overwhelming generosity. Have you ever considered a career in nonprofit?"

"Me?" Layla says. "No."

"What do you do?"

"I'm in Mergers and Acquisitions."

"So was I," she says, and smiles. "Here's my card. If you

ever want to volunteer, or perhaps apply for a summer job, call me."

We say goodbye and leave the auditorium. How cool is Layla? "That was nice of you to give a donation," I say.

"Yeah? I thought I'd feel good, but now I feel worse for some reason. It would be fun to work somewhere where I felt I was making a difference. And not just…you know."

"Making a fortune? Why don't you apply for a summer job with them, then?"

She laughs. "Yeah, right. I'm a banker. I've worked at banks for the last three years. I'm majoring in Finance. My parents are bankers. I'm going to be a banker. Maybe all I need is an extracurricular activity, like bridge or square dancing. Only something I can be passionate about."

I want to tell her she's welcome to be passionate about me, but I hold my tongue.

layla gets the job done

Print! Print! Come on, come on, you can do it!

I have precisely ten minutes to print out my Economics assignment and haul butt to the Katz building. It's four-fifty. Rothman wants the assignment by five, and he warned us to get it in on time because he's leaving for Thanksgiving. Why did I have to be so nitpicky? I've been working on it for months. What if I'm too late? What if I don't make it? All week classes have been empty because everyone else was working like crazy to finish. I showed up and now I'm going to fail? Where is the justice in that?

Print! Print! Page three pops out. Five more to go!

I don't see why Rothman doesn't let us e-mail our assignments. Why must he make my life difficult?

Print! Print! Two pages left!

I ram my feet into my shoes (no way to treat Prada loafers) and do up my coat. Then I double-check his office number. Six twenty-four. No problem. Time check: 4:54 p.m.

Yes! The final page is done. I slam it into the stapler, and run.

I pass Kimmy in the hallway. "Hey, Layla," she says. "Where are you going?"

"To hand in Economics," I say on the move.

"How'd you find the Stats midterm?" she asks quickly.

"I failed for sure," I answer, and hit the stairs two at a time, and then sprint over to Katz. Stats was impossible. My paper flaps in my hand. I heave open the door to the building. I shimmy between the elevator doors as they're closing and thump the sixth-floor button. Two students are inside, and they seemed to have already pressed the second and fourth floor.

Current time: 4:59. Crap!

The elevator stops at the second floor and a woman in a parka slides out. All right, let's go, off to four. But then the elevator jerks and stops at three. No! A man in a suit steps in and presses…five. Oh, come on, give me a break. This is crazy. Are the Fates conspiring to make me late?

By the time we hit the sixth floor, it's 5:07 and I'm late, I'm late, I'm late. I gallop to his office and—what if he left, what if I fail, what if my entire career is over because of this one useless paper—I stop. His door is open. His lights are on. I hear two men laughing inside.

My heart is still racing from the run. I poke my head around the door.

Jamie is leaning against the wall. "Well, hello there, Layla. We were wondering if you forgot."

"Hi, Jamie. Hi, Jon. Sorry I'm late, sir." I deposit the paper on his desk.

"Hi, Layla. Thanks for bringing it by. You see, Jamie, Layla still managed to make it to class this week even though there was a paper due. I suppose you were sick yesterday, but have since miraculously recovered?"

Jamie smirks. "You hit the nail on the head there, Jon."

The professor laughs and looks directly into my eyes. "Layla, what are you doing this weekend?"

"Going home," I say, and look away. He's doing it again! Flirting with me!

"Have a good Thanksgiving, you two."

I back out of the room. "Thanks, sir. You, too."

Jamie waves goodbye and follows me into the elevator. "That guy has the hots for you."

I blush. "Yeah?"

Jamie raises an eyebrow. But since he only has one, they both veer toward his bald spot. "Tall, dark and handsome not your type?"

"I don't mix business with pleasure."

He nods. "Still after your dream man?"

I sigh. "Yup."

"Have you ever thought about dating someone that exists in real life and not just on paper?" he asks, looking at me out of the corner of his eye.

Enough already. "I told you. I'm not dating Professor Rothman. Too close for comfort." I decide to change the subject. "I gave you a sex change on Friday."

"You did?" He closes his eyes for a second and looks relieved. "Thanks. Much appreciated. Can I interest you in some dinner tonight? I'm not going home until tomorrow morning." He hesitates. "I want to thank you properly."

Aw. "You're so sweet. It really wasn't a big deal. But no, I'm taking the seven-o'clock train back to the city. I decided not to drive so I can start my reading for next week. And I haven't packed yet." The doors open, and I plant a quick kiss on his cheek. "Have a safe flight and a great weekend!" And then I bolt back to the Zoo.

russ returns to the land of the loonies

I'm about to ring the doorbell, when I stop myself. Maybe I shouldn't have come. What am I doing here? She's going to be able to tell. My face will be like a blackboard with my illicit affair written all over it in fluorescent-yellow chalk. If only it could be like in *Superman: The Movie* and I could fly backward around the world to turn back time.

Truth is, I'm not even sure if I want to erase the experience with Kimmy. I like knowing that a sexy woman like Kimmy wants me.

I should tell Sharon what happened.

It's freezing out here. Stupid Canadian winter. I press the bell once, twice, softly as though I'm not sure if I want her to hear.

She must have been waiting for me, because right away I hear the click of the door unlocking.

The soft, silky, short brown hair, the big smile. The perfect earlobes. Sharon. "You're back!" she squeals, wrapping her arms around my neck and kissing me hard on the mouth.

Guilt and sadness surge through me, like I've just stuck my

finger in an electrical socket of pain. I love her, and I always have. What did I do? "I'm back," I say, attempting to keep my voice afloat. Can she tell?

She kisses me deeply and presses her body against mine. Apparently, no, she can't. And I can't tell her. She'd kill me. I can only tell her if I'm willing to lose her, and I'm not. Her tongue feels soft and squishy, like a pillow. I push her up against the door, and I explore under her shirt. My hands feel at home, like Clark Kent returning to Smallville.

She pulls me inside and closes the door behind her.

Decision made. My fling with Kimmy is over.

kimmy waits

Why hasn't he called?

I kissed him goodbye on Wednesday afternoon. I thought he would call the next day. Truth is, I hoped he would call Wednesday night after he landed. Or from the airport while he was waiting for his flight. That would have been amazing. But I wasn't asking for that. No. All I was asking is that he call at some point over the weekend. Is that too much to ask? That the guy I've been hooking up with for the past month call me to wish me a happy Thanksgiving?

I'm lying on my bed, wearing a tank top and panties, sweating and staring at the ceiling. My flight landed two hours ago. I thought Russ would be here by now. The central heating is on full blast, so it's boiling in here. I don't mind the heat; I'm used to it from home. It was gorgeous in Arizona. A nice eighty-six degrees. Here it's forty-two. My body is officially confused. And the Zoo feels like ninety degrees. I saw a guy wearing shorts and a tank top strolling through the hallways. I wonder if he'll keep that outfit on all winter. The same weirdness occurs in Arizona. I'll be wearing sandals and a minidress outside because it's a hundred and thirty degrees, but I need to put on long underwear and a parka to go to the air-conditioned mall.

So far the cold in Connecticut hasn't been so terrible. The gusts of air are refreshing. They make me feel alive. Like sex. Which it doesn't look like I'll be getting tonight. I left my cell phone on the entire time I was home so he could reach me. He could have gotten through while my mother was whining about how miserable her job is. Or while my father grilled me about whether I was wasting my time and money on getting an MBA. Or when I ran into Wayne and Cheryl together at the Rhythm Room and had to maintain a stupid plastic smile on my face.

It was the power-on cell in my purse that kept me sane, reminding me that, yes, there is something good in my life. The very possibility of it ringing was my reason for getting out of bed in the morning.

But now it's Sunday night, and he still hasn't called.

What does it mean? That he wasn't thinking about me? That he was with Sharon the entire weekend? That he doesn't want to see me anymore?

I feel sick and hot and nauseous. I open the window to fill my room with air so I don't faint. Or cry. He doesn't want me anymore. He'd rather be with Sharon.

What do I do? I need a new plan.

I pick up the phone and call him, but he doesn't answer. What if he's decided that he can't live without her? That he's going to transfer to the business school in Toronto?

The open window doesn't seem to be helping the room temperature. What's wrong with me? Why is my heart beating so loudly? I don't understand why I want him so much. Yes, he's hot and smart and serious, but so are other guys here. Why do I want the one guy who's taken? Is it the challenge? Am I worthless if he doesn't want me? Is it the way he plays with my secret ear spot?

I call his room again.

"Hello?" He's back! Why hasn't he come by if he's home?

"Hi, it's me. Can you come by?"

"I…um…" He's stalling. Why is he stalling?

"Just for a few minutes, okay? See you soon." I hang up before he can turn me down.

I open the bottle of red wine, pour two glasses, light two candles, turn off the lights and take off my clothes.

It's all about strategy.

layla hits the books

I push open the heavy oak library doors, slightly astounded that I was the only one waiting for the security guard to unlock them. How are more students not taking advantage of the library's extended hours? From today, the first Monday after Thanksgiving, until LWBS shuts down for winter holidays on December 19, the library will be open from seven until midnight, seven days a week.

The rolling of my bag's wheels against the polished floor echoes through the empty atrium. I ride the elevator up to the fourth floor and head for my favorite cubicle beside the window. First I skim through the business section of the paper while I sip my coffee. Then I pull out my pencil case, Economics textbook, course pack and binder from my bag. I've already done all my reading for today, so I'll start on tomorrow's cases. First thing in the morning is my favorite time to study. It's quiet and serene. Three-thirty is the most frustrating time. Too many people are here engaging in group meetings. My classmates often fail to remember that they're in a library and that others are trying to study.

For the next twenty minutes I lose myself in Economics, until a large hand squeezes my shoulder.

"Mini-muffin?" offers the voice attached to the hand. I turn to see Jamie passing me a small brown bag. "The bakery down the street makes the most amazing mini-muffins. Have you tried 'em? You gotta try 'em."

Don't mind if I do. I peer into the bag and pull out two blueberry and one chocolate chip. "What are you doing here? Do you know what time it is?"

He peers at his watch. "It's seven." Then he gasps. "Oh, shit, is that seven a.m.? I thought I slept through the day. The muffins were my dinner."

"You're hilarious."

"Always." He winks and pulls up a chair. "What are you reading?"

"Econ."

"Yeah? I hate Economics. I'm going to read OB. Do you happen to have your OB course pack so I can borrow it?"

I find it in my bag and hand it to him. "What would you have done if I wasn't here?"

"They keep a few copies on the fifth floor." He flips through the book with his thumb like it's a fan, then gestures to my bag. "So, when's the flight?"

"Ha-ha."

"No seriously, why is your bag on wheels?"

"I like to have all my books with me for reference. No need to strain my back." People should be kinder to their backs. They only get one. "How was your weekend?"

"Warm. It was ninety degrees in Miami."

He doesn't look like he just got back from Miami. He's paler than I am. "Did you have fun?"

"Oh, yeah. My parents live in a retirement community now, so we partied hard. Played some shuffleboard, a little bingo. Had the early-bird special for dinner. Wild and crazy times. You?"

"I had a nice time. My sister and I have a place in the Upper East Side, so I went back there. I saw my parents for Thanksgiving dinner and some friends on Saturday night."

"Bet you have a huge Thanksgiving bash, turkey and all the trimmings."

Not quite. "My mother doesn't cook much, and the maid was with her family, so we just went to Nobu. No big deal." Not really.

"I make a mean-ass turkey," Jamie brags.

"Yeah? Maybe I'll invite you for Christmas dinner. Have you ever been to a Christmas dinner?"

He shakes his head. "Can't say that I have."

"Is there a Hanukkah dinner? What exactly *is* Hanukkah?"

He leans back, balancing his chair on its hind legs. "It's the story of how one small jug of oil lasted for eight long days."

"Do you get presents?"

"No. My parents are misers. You're supposed to get eight presents, one for every day of the miracle. But my mother used to use it as an excuse to replace my socks. So I'd get eight new pairs."

"That's awful." His balancing is making me a little nervous. He could easily teeter over any second.

"I know. My bubbe always gets me good presents, though. She once bought me one of those toy cars that you can drive around your house. You know what I mean? I bet you had one. Never mind. I bet you got a real car for Christmas."

He must think I'm so spoiled. "Only twice." He looks shocked, so I say, "Just kidding. Only once."

He raises his unibrow. Maybe I should just offer to tweeze that thing. Forget it, how rude would that be?

"What kind of car?" he asks.

This isn't going to help the spoiled image. "BMW convertible."

"You have a BMW convertible? Layla, why didn't you bring it to school?"

"I do have it at school."

His chair slips backward, but he grabs hold of the desk before he falls and splits open his head. "What? Why have I never seen it?"

"I don't like to drive."

"Why do you have a car, then?"

"I don't know. My parents wanted me to have one."

"For what? Didn't you live in Manhattan?"

"Yeah, but I needed to get around. You know. To the Hamptons." I think I should just shut up.

"Do you think your parents would mind paying for my next semester's tuition?" He laughs.

Truth is, they probably wouldn't care. Or notice. "I'll ask."

"Wanna get married? I could definitely use a rich wife."

Married? I can't even imagine Jamie as a dating contender. He's too…unambitious. I prefer the serious guy to the clown. "Maybe."

"I'm no Bradley Green, am I?"

Sigh. Perfect Bradley Green. "It's not like Bradley even knows I'm alive. I'll have to wait for him to come to school here, *if* he gets in, and *if* he decides to come."

We laugh and I decide this is an ideal opportunity to discuss his potential relationship with Kimmy. "Anything new with you and Kimmy?" I ask. "Is she back yet?" Over the weekend, I analyzed the Kimmy situation, and I think falling for Jamie would be a far better strategy for her. First of all, Russ is unavailable. Second, Russ doesn't strike me as such a catch. He's nerdy, stoned half the day, and Kimmy needs someone with more personality. Like Jamie.

"I stopped by her room at around six, but she seemed preoccupied and didn't ask me in." He shakes his head with dismay. "I think it's time I give up on her."

"I think you should keep at it. But for now, could you please stop leaning back in that chair? You're making me nervous."

He grins, and slams his chair back on all fours.

"That's better." I don't see why she won't go for Jamie. She hooked up with him once, so she must feel a smidgen of attraction for him. Russ isn't going to dump Sharon, and at some point Kimmy will have to accept that and move on.

"I wonder if something's going on with her and Russ," he says, as if reading my mind.

I look back at my notes and shrug. Am I awful for encouraging him to pursue her, when I know that Russ and Kimmy hooked up after the spin-the-bottle game? At least they haven't "sealed the deal" yet, so maybe there's hope.

"Maybe he dumped his girlfriend over Thanksgiving," he says. "Could be Black Monday for Russ."

Never heard that one. "Black Monday?"

"The day after Thanksgiving, when everyone comes back to school broken up."

I doubt it. "We should get to work," I say, flipping through my notebook. So much work to do before tomorrow! "Why don't we work for thirty minutes and then take a walk around the floor to stretch?"

"Or maybe you'll take me out for a spin in your BMW. Some of us only have a Hyundai Excel in the parking lot, you know."

Matthews spends the morning discussing group interaction patterns, specifically conflict management, negotiations, giving feedback and sharing information.

I'm wondering what kind of information Russ and Kimmy aren't sharing with their group. They're both not here. Kimmy really shouldn't be missing classes when she's desperately trying to improve her grades. Where is she? She should not be skipping lectures so close to exams.

They both waltz in for Accounting. They walk in separately, slyly, and Russ finds a seat in the back beside Nick and Jamie. Kimmy sits beside me. Her cheeks are flushed, her hair tied back in a high ponytail. She looks like she's desperately attempting not to look happy. "Good morning," she sings.

This scenario can't be good for my set-Jamie-up-with-Kimmy plan. Perhaps I was wrong—maybe Russ did break up with Sharon. "Good morning," I say. "How was your long weekend?"

"Horrible," she says. And then smiles. "But all is better now."

I have a bad feeling about her version of better. "Why? Is it Black Monday? Did he dump her?"

Her face clouds over. "I don't think so."

Then what's she so gleeful about? "What, then?"

She raises her well-plucked eyebrow suggestively. "You know."

Oh, no. They sealed the deal! "You slept with him?"

She shushes me with her hand.

"But what about his girlfriend?"

She rolls her eyes. "I told you, I don't know anything more about that."

How could she sleep with him without knowing? Isn't it driving her crazy? It's driving *me* crazy. "Did you at least ask him?"

"Can we not talk about this here?" she hisses.

Well, excuse me!

kimmy studies it up
at the library

At five to twelve, I slam shut my Stats textbook and stand up. Only a few of us are still at the library. Namely, me, Layla and Jamie. I've been reading for the past half hour, and for the half hour before that, Layla and Jamie were tutoring me. (Turns out Layla got the highest mark in the Block on the Stats midterm. Yeah, the one she said she failed.) We only took a few breaks—one for a stroll around the room and another for massage train. A massage train is something Layla used to do at her sorority house. You sit in a line and massage the person in front of you for three minutes. Then the person at the front moves to the back. I started off in the middle. I massaged Layla, and Jamie massaged me. Then I moved to the head of the train, and Layla massaged Jamie. He has pretty good hands. Too bad I didn't ask for a full-body massage the night we hooked up.

"You don't got to go home, but you got to get the hell out of here," Jamie announces. I'm exhausted. After class I went to a case interview session. Jared, the Block president, has organized a three-hour case session once a week until

Christmas, to prepare us for job interviews. As if we have nothing else to do. Surprisingly, though, I'm pretty good at solving the estimation cases, when they ask you something you couldn't possibly know, like how many buses are in America, to see how you would get at the problem. Who knew? Now if only I could finish my cover letters and résumés, then maybe I could actually get to display my recently discovered talent.

But at the moment I have other things to think about. The highlight of the night—private time with Russ. Most people come to the library because they want to ace their exams; I come because I need to keep Russ out of my bed until after he's spoken with Sharon. This was my first new strategy, and it's been working. We used to start fooling around at ten, and go until I evicted myself for his Sharon nightly phone call. Now that I'm at the library until twelve, there's no pending end for our time together.

My second new strategy was to turn my bed into a sex temple, keeping it smelling clean and girly. I bought red satin sheets and pillowcases to match my duvet, making it impossible for him to even consider wanting to leave.

He can stay all night, and does.

He'll have to break up with Sharon eventually. He can't keep up this deception much longer. No, he's going to dump her, soon. Definitely.

When we reach the Zoo, I immediately start preparing. I shower, spritz on my perfume and change into one of my new silk negligees (bought during the satin-sheet-shopping spree).

It's twelve-thirty, and everything is ready for Russ. I'm lying on my silky bed, waiting.

Soft music playing? Check.

Condom box tucked discreetly under bed? Check. Not that I care so much about the condoms, since I'm on the pill, but I know it's the right thing to do. Actually, he's the one who insists on condoms. Maybe he's afraid I'll pass his precious girlfriend something unmentionable.

Hmm. My pill. Yesterday was my twenty-first day, which is a bit unfortunate. That means that in exactly three days I'm going to get my period, which sucks. Russ and I are only together for two more weeks before vacation. I can't be out of commission for one of them. I hop off my bed, open my stuff drawer and search for my next month's pill sheet. When I first went on the pill, my doctor told me to take two months straight. Maybe I should do that again so I won't get my period until winter vacation. It can't be that bad for you if he wanted me to do it when I first started, right? When you forget to take two in a row they tell you to start a new pack straight away, so it must be fine. And I'll only do it this once, anyway. I push one of the white pills through the foil and swallow it before I can change my mind.

A knock on the door startles me, as if I'm doing something illegal.

I open it quickly, and Russ shuffles inside.

Illegal, illicit, what's the difference? His lips are warm and I think I might be in love.

The alarm goes off at six-ten. Madonna is on the radio. I wonder what she would think about my affair. The Madonna of "Like A Virgin" would have approved. The *English Rose* Madonna, not so much.

Russ reaches for his sweatpants and shirt. "See you later," he says.

Love you, I think but don't say. The door shuts softly behind him.

I try to fall back asleep, but I can't. That was Russ's only condition for staying the night. The shrieking alarm at six-ten in the morning so he can sneak out without anyone seeing. Come on, what are the chances that Rena will be standing outside and spot him? I suppose he's concerned that if he gets up at a normal hour, someone will see him doing the walk of shame and mention it to Rena, who will report back to Sharon. He doesn't even want us telling anyone in the group. Fine, I understand. Nick has a big mouth, Jamie would be crushed because of his feelings for me, and who knows what the deal with Lauren is. So it's a secret. For now. Except for Layla, who I had to tell. Eventually he'll break up with Sharon and we'll come out of the closet. Closet, dorm room—pretty much the same thing. He has to, doesn't he? He's not a bad guy; he's just trying to figure out what he wants. And he'll realize that it's me and not Sharon.

I'm sure Russ has no problem falling back asleep. He's been late to almost every morning class in the past two weeks. Matthews launches daggers at him when Russ tries to sneak into OB. I'm worried he's not taking class seriously.

Not like me. Now that I'm up at six-ten, I might as well be studying. I step into my flip-flops and grab my shower supplies.

By seven-thirty I'm at the library. Layla is already there, in her usual seat. "Morning," she says, waving.

"Hey." I'm not much for talking this early. At least not until the bland coffee I picked up from the twenty-four-hour campus store kicks in. I'm almost done studying for Economics, which is pretty crazy, considering the exam isn't until next Monday. OB is on Tuesday, Accounting on Wednesday, Stats on Thursday, and Strategy on Friday. I've also done most of the reading for OB and Stats. Tomorrow is the final day of class, so as of Friday I can start studying full-time.

I like being in the library at this hour. From my perch near the fourth-floor window, I watch the sun crawl its way into the sky, illuminating the campus below. Not too many students are around, but every few minutes someone rushes from one building to another. I spot Jamie, a bag of mini-muffins under his arm, on his way to meet us. He comes here every morning at seven forty-five, follows us to class and then walks back to the Zoo with us at midnight. Funny, I would never have pegged him for a library guy.

Then again, I wouldn't have pegged myself as a library girl, either.

jamie's on fire

I'm having that exam dream—you know the one I mean, the one where you're scribbling furiously in the high-school gym and you realize you're butt naked—when the alarm signaling the end of the exam goes off.

Then I realize it's not an exam bell, it's a fire alarm, and I shoot up in bed. Oy. It's 3:14 a.m. It's probably a false alarm, but what if it's for real? When I worked at the hospital, I saw kids who were victims of house fires, and it wasn't pretty. I grab a pair of sweatpants, sweatshirt, a jacket and running shoes, my credit card and new student card with photo (finally got that in the mail today, can't have it go up in flames already), take my keys and step into the hallway. I don't have too much of value in my room except for my TV and DVD collection. And the mini-fridge I rented for a hundred bucks. (Who doesn't want cold drinks and ice-cream sandwiches available twenty-four/seven?) I try to remember what we were instructed to do in a fire situation. I think the brief on fire safety in my welcome package said to line up at the nearest exit.

The hall is empty. Either I've developed schizophrenia and hearing loud, continuously ringing fire bells is a part of my new condition, or I have quicker-than-average reflexes.

I begin to hear a faint rustling in the rooms.

"Make it stop!" someone yells.

I patrol the hallway to see if anyone other than me has deemed it necessary to vacate his or her room.

Nick is standing in his boxers, topless, looking skeletal and confused. "What's going on?"

"Not sure." I sprint down the stairs to see if I can find anyone who knows why this annoying bell is still ringing. I'm both surprised and impressed with my middle-of-the-night energy and agility.

The people from the second floor are exiting the building. I spot Lauren with an opened coat over red flannel pajamas. Maybe the carbon monoxide has spread throughout the third floor, and for some reason everyone except me is unconscious.

I decide to check on Layla and Kimmy, hero that I am.

I hike back up the stairs, my energy waning, and am poised to knock on Layla's door when she flings it open. She's fully dressed in khakis, a green turtleneck and a long wool coat. She's toting a fishbowl above her head with one hand, her laptop with the other.

She is so cute. "It's a fire alarm, not a flood alarm," I say, and take the fishbowl from her.

"Thanks. I forgot to back up my documents last night. If this computer melts, I'm a dead woman. Are we supposed to go downstairs?"

"I think that would be the best option. I'll just check on Kimmy."

"Jamie to the rescue." She makes a kissing noise and disappears down the stairs.

Funny, she doesn't notice that I rescued her first. She's possessed with the notion that I'm in love with Kimmy.

I wish I could tell Layla that it's her I can't get out of my head, but it's obvious she's not interested in me. If I told her, I'd end up being another class joke, the way I did with Kimmy.

"Hello, Martha," I say to the bowl. Then I knock on Kimmy's door. "Darlin'? That alarm blaring? It normally signals fire. It's best to leave the building so you won't burn."

I hear swearing from inside. Male swearing. There is a male swearing in Kimmy's room. Must be Russ, I figure (not that it would take a rocket scientist to figure it out). Three pj-clad people pass me, and I'm standing by myself in the hall. "You two can come out now. Coast is clear." No sound. "Russ, I know you're in there."

The door opens slowly. Russ is sitting on the desk, wearing jeans and a sweatshirt, looking extremely pale. Maybe the carbon monoxide has gotten to him. Or not.

"Studying late, are we?" I ask.

He ignores me and peers into the hallway. "Do we really have to go out?"

I tug on my ear. "The bell does seem to indicate that."

"Isn't it a false alarm?"

"I assume so," I say. "I don't smell smoke, but I'm leaving the building, just in case. You two do what you want." Like you're doing already. I turn and leave them, disappointment overwhelming me. He should know better. She should know better.

Of course, it's snowing. I find Layla through the flakes, clasping her laptop to her chest. She takes the fishbowl from me and puts it beside her on the ground. Nick and Lauren join us, and a few minutes later Russ approaches us, Kimmy following a few discreet feet behind. There are no fire trucks, no sirens blaring, no flashing lights washing the campus in red, so either this is a false alarm or the firefighters need to work on their game.

Russ is looking around, probably for Rena, the woman I've

seen him talk to, the woman who knows his girlfriend. He spots her and waves. She waves back.

Layla's teeth are chattering. I put my arm around her waist to warm her, but then I realize she might get the wrong idea, or the right idea, so I put my other arm around Kimmy and bring them both into a group hug, Layla's laptop elbowing me in the stomach.

"You know," I say, "an orgy would really warm us up."

"Does your mind ever come out of the gutter?" Layla scolds me.

"What about a massage train?" I ask. Now that was fun. Being touched by Layla and touching Kimmy. I thought I'd died and gone to heaven. I certainly wouldn't mind a repeat performance.

The fire alarm stops.

We wait a few seconds, holding our breath, then collectively exhale.

Russ pats Kimmy on the ass as they go through the door. I wish I could pull that move on Layla, but I think she would assault me with her laptop.

russ ignores his conscience

One eye is open. One eye is closed. Don't think I can study and nap at the same time. Too bad these notes don't come on tape. Then I could let them suggestively enter my consciousness.

Ten-minute nap. I deserve it. I wrote the Economics exam at the ungodly hour of nine this morning. I deserve a ten-minute nap.

I poke Kimmy in the shoulder. She's sitting in the cubicle next to mine at the library. "Wake me in ten minutes," I say.

She glances at her watch. "Okay. Ten minutes."

Mmm. Sharon. Mmm. Kimmy. In my dream they're both giving me an excellent rubdown.

"Wake up," Kimmy says, patting my shoulder.

"Ten more minutes."

"Russ, I let you sleep for an hour."

An hour? I open my eyes and lean back. "I think I need a coffee."

"You've already had three today."

Thanks, Mom.

Over the course of the next several hours and countless cups of coffee I attempt to stick to my study schedule.

"My back is killing me," Kimmy whines at seven.

Jamie pops up and starts massaging her shoulders. He must be doing it to piss me off. He knows I can't really touch her in public. Ever since Jamie saw Kimmy and me together, he's been giving me attitude. I'd like to punch him in the face, but I can't have him spilling split lips to the entire school, can I? Why is he touching her, anyway? He doesn't still think he has a chance with her, does he?

His fingers continue to dig into her shoulders. Maybe he does think he's still in the running. Maybe Kimmy's sleeping with him, too.

Nah.

"Time for a dinner break," I say, attempting to clear my head. I have enough issues to worry about, most prominently my own dual-dating, without having to worry about Kimmy's extracurricular activities.

We go to the caf for some food and then back to the library. At eleven Nick starts making toking motions. I know smoking a joint the night before an exam isn't a brilliant plan, but after all that coffee, I don't think I'll fall asleep if I don't come down a bit. Also dulls the jagged blade of the I'm-an-asshole guilt that now pierces into my stomach lining on a daily basis.

I follow him back to his room, where we smoke a short, quick one. Then I go back to my room to call Sharon.

She decides that tonight is a good time to ask me, "Do you ever think about getting married?"

I'm lying on my bed, still dressed. I wonder if she means to her, or in general, but I don't want to talk too much in case she realizes I'm stoned. She'd kill me for smoking during exams.

"Do you?" I ask.

Often the best way to avoid a question is to deflect the

question with another question. I should have tried that on today's exam. *As identified by the Federal Reserve Bank, what are the three different components of the overall money supply?* I could have gone with, *What do you think the three components are, eh?* Right.

Sharon laughs. "I asked you first."

Guess it doesn't work on her, either. "I'll get married when I'm settled," I say.

"When you're settled, or we're settled?"

Another good question, and another I don't answer. I can't exactly say, *At the moment I'm involved with someone else, and I can't decide who I prefer.* Maybe I should use a food metaphor. I can say, *I'm sitting at a restaurant and there are two menu choices, but both are my favorites. Which do I choose? Chicken parmesan or fettuccine alfredo?* Just what all women dream about. Being compared to food. Objectified and put on a plate. Pass the pepper, please! "When we're settled," I say. I am too chicken-shit to start. Chicken parmesan, please.

Something else I haven't told Sharon is that I've applied for summer jobs in New York. She's under the impression that I'll be going back to the IT consulting firm I worked for before. The firm, too, is under this impression. But since everyone else applied to jobs through school, I figured I should, too. So now it comes down to this: life in Toronto with Sharon or life in New York with Kimmy?

Ten minutes later, I say my *love you, toos* and *good-nights* and *be goods,* then wash up and walk over to Kimmy's room.

She stands behind the door when she opens it so no one can see she's naked. Not that anyone's up. I love that she opens the door naked. I wonder how long she lay there in bed, naked, waiting for me. Or does she strip off her clothes when she hears the knock on her door?

I drop my jeans and sweatshirt and briefs onto her floor, and she puts her mouth on me before I can even get into bed.

Then I push her down and lie on top of her. We rub

against each other for a bit, and I can feel her getting wet beneath me. She tries to slide me into her, but I reach out to get a condom. She pulls me closer.

I know she wants to do it without a condom. She keeps telling me that she's on the pill. But I can't. Even though I know it would be a million times better. Cheating on my girlfriend without a condom reaches a whole other level of repulsiveness.

I really know how to draw the line, eh? The only problem is, the line keeps fading, inch by inch.

I slip on the condom and then push myself inside her. She wraps her legs around my back. I try to make her come with my fingers, the way Sharon likes to, but she stops me.

"Just fuck me," she says, and I do as requested. After I come, I throw the condom into the garbage beside her bed.

"Did you set the alarm?" I ask.

"For eight?" she asks with a half smile. "Don't you want to sleep in before the exam?"

"Don't give me a hard time. Six-ten, as usual." I don't know where I got the six-ten. Maybe it's because I don't expect anyone to be out in the hall at six-ten. Six-thirty maybe, but six-ten? Doubtful.

"Fine. Whatever." She reaches across me, her breasts hanging deliciously over my mouth. "Alarm set. Six-ten." She turns her back to me.

"'Night." I wrap my arms around her so she's not mad. She curves into me, and I kiss her neck good-night.

When the alarm rings at six-ten, I get dressed quickly, then open the door gently. As I expected, the hallway is quiet and empty. The lights are on—they're always on—and the windows over the stairs are mirrors because it's still dark outside, so instead of seeing outside, I see myself.

I quickly look away. I don't think I like what I see.

layla thinks she failed (again)

"Two more minutes," Flynn, the proctor/TA says.

I'm going to fail. Completely fail. How am I going to get a job this summer if I fail? It is humanly impossible for a mere mortal to answer all these questions. I still have so much more to write for this last question. My heart is racing and my hand is scribbling and I have to get this all down. Why can't we write with computers, why why why? Paper and pen are so archaic. How am I supposed to think? To delete? To spellcheck? I should have gone to sleep earlier. I need at least seven hours of sleep to perform properly on an exam. Next semester I'm going to bed early the night before all exams. At eight.

Only four of us are left in the room. Everyone else has somehow finished. How have they possibly finished? I haven't even started proofreading yet.

11a. With a squared multiple correlation coefficient of 78.6 and a standard error of 4.347, these numbers represents a better correlation than the single variable models in 1 and 2.

"Thirty more seconds."

   11b. As long as there is not a significant correlation be-
        tween X1 and X2, a significant multiple linear re-
        gression should give you a higher r-sq and
        therefore a better predictor model.

"Time up, everyone. Pencils down." One more question!

   12. Yes. With such a high r-sq value store size is a good
        predictor of profit.

Done! Flynn picks up my paper. His hands are thin and
hairy. "How'd you find it?"

"Impossible."

"Layla, I'm sure you did fine."

All my TAs and professors know my name. I ask a lot of
questions.

I walk to the door, disgusted with myself. Kimmy is waiting for me outside, smiling. "Not bad, huh?"

"I failed for sure."

"What?" She's shaking her head in disbelief. "No way. It
was everything we talked about. You knew that stuff cold.
You taught it to me."

"There was too much to write and not enough time."

Kimmy gestures to the cafeteria, but I have to get away
from school. "Let's go for sushi," I suggest. "On me." I know
Kimmy doesn't like spending money when she's already paid
for the food plan. I'm getting tired of cafeteria food.

She hesitates. "I want to get to the library. What about sushi
for dinner?"

"Deal."

"I still don't believe you failed," she says as we enter the
cafeteria. "You've claimed to have failed every exam so far.

And you said the same about midterms and you aced them. It's a little annoying, actually."

She's probably right. I do always think I've failed, yet I always do well. But I'm not lying when I say the exam was hard. They're all hard. "We'll see. You found it all right?"

I take a grilled cheese and fries and she just takes fries.

She nods. "Yeah. Not easy, but much better than the midterm." She watches me drench my plate in ketchup. "Would you like some sandwich with that ketchup?"

"Ha-ha." Yum.

We sit in our regular seat. Jamie and Russ aren't here. They left the exam a half hour ago, so they probably already ate and are either studying or napping.

"I've been into vinegar on my fries lately," she says, dribbling the clear shaker over her fries.

"Yeah? Why?"

"Russ does it, and now I'm addicted."

I pop a sopping red fry into my mouth. Yum. "Let's eat quickly so we can get back."

I think I'll miss the library when we're done. Is that weird? I love the quiet, the smell, the sense of purpose. I wonder if the hotel we're staying at in St. Bart's has a library. No, that would be weird. To be honest, I'm going to miss taking exams. The rush. The blood pouring from my brain to my fingers. I know I always think I failed, but I also know I won't.

"Only one more," Kimmy says. Her voice sounds almost wistful. Semester's end means Russ goes back to Toronto. To Sharon.

"Only one more," I repeat. We eat our fries slowly, as though hoping to prolong the day.

russ finishes his exam

Head hurts, hand hurts, who cares, I'm done. I don't know how I did, probably not as well as I could have, but I don't care.

I raise my hand until a proctor picks up my exam. "Have a good break," he says.

Oh, I will. I *need* a break. A break from studying, from clubs, from random exam questions, from my life. Exams are so frustrating. After an entire semester, they choose twenty questions to ask. Twenty random questions. Can those really quantify my knowledge?

What I really need is a break from Sharon and Kimmy so I can figure out what I want, who I want. Wish I were back-packing with Nick in Australia for the month. Now that's a break. He leaves for Sydney tomorrow. It's summer there, so I guess he'll be sitting on the beach and playing with kangaroos. No kangaroos or beaches for me. Toronto has already had three snowstorms. I'll be shoveling, not sunning.

I grab my pencils and student card, and bolt from the room. Kimmy is still scribbling away. She's all dressed up today, in high black boots, a miniskirt and a tight blue turtleneck. She looks hot. So what else is new?

I pick up a sandwich in the caf, zip up my coat and return to the Zoo to pack. Flight leaves at nine. I have to make some decisions in the coming month about where I want to work, Toronto or New York. Maybe I should let my job determine my girlfriend. If I return to my job in Toronto, I'll stay with Sharon. If I'm offered something in New York, I'll stay with Kimmy. Luck of the draw. Maybe random is the way to go after all.

kimmy gets screwed

"Do you like it, Kimberly?" my father asks.

"It" is a day in a Scottsdale spa. Facial, manicure, pedicure, massage. "Love it, Dad. Thanks."

Valued at three hundred dollars, it could all be exchanged and used to purchase books next semester. My father the atheist refuses to call it a Christmas present, but that's what it is. I don't care what he calls it; it's still nice to get presents even if they don't know what I'd want. My mother, who's Jewish, was never good at presents, either, and it got worse when I was eleven and they got divorced. She'd buy things I didn't want, like rhinestone-your-own-T-shirt kits and glittery hair clips. When it comes to presents, my parents don't know me at all.

"Honey, you look tired," my father says.

We're sitting on the patio of a trendy new Mexican restaurant in Phoenix. I've had a few too many margaritas, and my body feels rubbery and indestructible.

"I haven't been sleeping well."

He runs his no-polish manicured fingers through his jet-black dyed hair. "Maybe LWBS isn't the right lifestyle for you."

I shrug.

"You should think about your goals." He's nodding as he speaks, his perfectly chiseled chin bobbing up and down. I wish I looked more like him and less like my mom. I have no chin. Just a neck.

"I do. I have two consulting company interviews through school." Interviews for first-year students are the first week after vacation. Second-years have an extra week off for winter break. I could use that second week of rest, but three and a half weeks is already too long a time to have Russ off philandering with his precious Sharon.

I want my father to be impressed with my potential career, and I say, "Who knows? Maybe I'll nail a fantastic job. Some of them pay two thousand a week."

He cuts his tamale into neat little sections and inserts a piece into his mouth. "So you're looking for a job. That's nice." He chews slowly and swallows. "I was talking about your long-term goals."

To get Russ to dump his girlfriend? "What long-term goals?"

"Marriage. Family."

No pressure or anything. "I'm sure I can worry about that after I find a job."

"I think you're missing my point." He inserts another piece. "I can't pay your tuition this semester."

I nearly choke on my refried beans. "What?"

"Too many leases went sour in the past few months and I need to invest my own capital into the business. I'm sorry."

"But, but Dad…" Oh. My. God. What am I going to do?

"I'm sorry, Kimmy, but money's tight, and I don't believe that sending you to business school is my best investment."

"How can you say that?" I ask, my hands shaking. "What could be a better investment than arming me with an MBA?"

"You won't be in the workforce long enough to make back that kind of money. If you go back to LWBS—"

"I'm going back," I say, suddenly determined. "I'll take out a loan." Russ takes out loans. Lauren takes out loans.

"You want to go forty-five thousand dollars into debt?"

"I'll pay it back after I graduate. I'll get a job that pays well. I told you, I have two interviews lined up—one with O'Donnel and one with BCG." I got rejected by everyone else, but whatever.

"Honey, you're twenty-six now, right?"

I nod, blinking back tears.

"Even if you do get an incredible job after graduation, you'll only keep it for a few years. You'll be approaching thirty and you'll want to settle down."

Settle down? "You can't be serious. In case you haven't heard, two-income families are the norm."

He scowls, and it's not from the jalapeños. "What about the kids?"

I'm not even dating the guy I'm screwing, and my father is talking kids? My back is beginning to spasm from the hard wood chair. "That's what day care is for."

"So you'll ship your kids off to day care? You want your children to be raised by strangers?"

I was shipped off to day care when my mother had to get a job after my father left her. One woman was responsible for about twenty-five of us. I spent the first two weeks crying in the corner, and the rest of the time watching the small Polish woman picking up children by their ears. But anyway, why are we talking about my nonexistent children? "I don't know. Maybe I can get a part-time job."

He points his finger in the air, dotting an *i* in the sky. "Exactly my point. Why spend all that on your education if you can't commit yourself totally to your career? There is no reason for you to have an MBA. You don't want to be a career woman. You want to be a wife and mother. And I don't want to burst your bubble, but in today's economy, managers aren't rushing to hire childbearing women. Remember Melissa?

When I hired her, she didn't utter one peep about wanting kids, and now she's six months along and I have to find someone to replace her while she's on maternity leave. Sure, she says she's coming back, but she doesn't have to let me know until the end of her leave. It's horrible for the company, I tell you."

"I—" I think you're an asshole, I think but don't say. "I'll be right back."

I lay my napkin on the table and scamper to the bathroom, as quick as my unpregnant body can take me. Although, since I haven't gotten my period in weeks, I could be pregnant, who knows? Not a big deal. I could just have it "taken care of." Again.

I lock the stall and sit on the closed toilet, the tears freely flowing down my cheeks, ruining my mascara.

Taken care of. Can you take out the trash, please? I imagine a vacuum being placed up against my vagina, sucking out the debris. When I missed my first period, I'd been surprised. But excited. Wayne hated condoms so he'd been pulling out. I knew I was supposed to be nervous, devastated even, but I ran to the store to buy the pregnancy test, ran up to my bathroom and did it right away. Pink. Pink, pink, pink. Wayne and I had been dating a year; he would be happy, wouldn't he? Scared of course, that was normal, but *secretly* happy. He must have known there was a chance this would happen (they don't call pulling out sexual roulette for no reason). Maybe this was what he'd been planning. I called him at work, told him to come over as soon as possible. We sat in his car in the driveway, engine off. I didn't want my mother listening. I felt like Molly Ringwald in that movie where she and her high-school sweetheart are scared, but they drop out of school and make it work.

After I told him, he stared at the windshield. He turned the wipers on and then watched them go back and forth, back and forth. "Do you need money to take care of it?" he asked.

Take care of it.

I felt the baby die right then. Shrivel up like a popped balloon. "Is that what you want?" I asked, my throat contracting.

"What choice do we have?"

Instead of explaining the choices, I nodded.

In the middle of the night, I crawled into my mother's bed, crying. I hadn't done that since my father left. I told her everything, and that I wanted to keep the baby. Then she started crying, too, and told me that I couldn't keep it, that it would ruin my life, that I had to take care of it, take care of it, take care of it, and two weeks later I did. We sat together in the waiting room, my mother and I. She read the *Redbook* that was on a table and I stared at the safe-sex posters on the wall. Another girl, a tall blonde who looked about sixteen, was also there with her mother. We didn't make eye contact.

I called in sick for the next week. It's easy to get out of work when your dad's your boss. Told him I had bronchitis. Smoked a cigarette before I spoke to him so my voice sounded scratchy. Decided that since I was no longer pregnant, I might as well take up smoking. Went on the pill the next week. Wayne thought it was the best present ever—now he could come inside me.

I doubt I'm pregnant again, since I'm a few weeks into my continuous birth control taking. My trick worked—I didn't get my period during exams. The only problem is, I realized that if I take the entire month, I'll start my next period on January 9, which sucks, because I go back to LWBS on the eleventh. Since I want my period to end on the ninth so there's none of that "aftermath" left by the eleventh, I have to get it on the fifth, which means I have to take my last pill on the second. Maybe I'll keep taking the pills straight until I go through menopause, and then I'll never have children. Then will my father encourage me to work?

What if I never get married? What if I decide to spend the rest of my life as a mistress instead? Under the circumstances, that seems likely. No worries, Dad, I think I'll just spend my life sleeping with men. Especially attached men. Have any friends you can introduce me to?

I sit on the toilet and pee out the margarita. What am I going to do? Drop out? Take out loans? Maybe my father is right. Maybe I don't care about my career. I never used to. I applied to LWBS only because of Wayne. Maybe I am wasting my money. Maybe I should throw in the schoolbag and head up to Alaska. I've heard the male-to-female ratio up there is comparable to LWBS's, but knowing me, I'd probably head straight for the guy with the serious girlfriend. The guy who stops calling as soon as he's out of the country. I pull a sheet of rough toilet paper out of the dispenser and use a square to dry my eyes. Why did I fall in love with a guy who loves someone else?

I'm in love with him. I love that the only music he listens to are soundtracks to superhero movies and that he hums them when he doesn't think I'm listening. The way he plays with my ears. The way he smiles. The way he smells.

I wish it wasn't so cold up in Toronto. He's going to need some body heat.

I take a deep breath and flush. I wash my hands and stare at myself in the mirror, at my bloodshot eyes. Maybe staying at B-school is a waste of time. Maybe I should drop out. My mother would kill me. She's a hundred percent behind me being in business school. Emotionally, not financially. She doesn't want me to end up like her. Happy housewife until she found out her husband was having an affair. And it wasn't a one-night-stand affair that was over; it was an I'm-leaving-you-for-someone-else affair. She got alimony, but she hated taking money from him, and so she got a job as a secretary, which she hated.

She blamed herself, said she'd let herself get treated like

shit. She'd always treated my father like the king he wasn't. Every Sunday she'd pick oranges off the tree in the yard and make him freshly squeezed juice. Each glass would take her twenty minutes, and sometimes he would ask for seconds. She was too tired to make herself a glass. She never made me one, even though I would beg. Once in a while, if my father didn't finish, I was allowed to drink whatever was left, savoring each drop against my tongue.

Maybe I'm more like her than she thought.

Maybe LWBS isn't for me.

My final Stats mark was posted before I left for the airport. Seventy-eight. The class average was a seventy-nine. Not great. Not horrible. Our group assignments probably raised my mark. I guess I did all right on the exam, which is good to hear. But I studied my ass off and came out average. It's a little sad.

What will I do if I drop out? Come back here? I don't know if I could live in Phoenix again. Last night I went to the same lame-ass bar I went to when I was twenty-one, and saw the same people who I hung out with, including Wayne and Cheryl.

Wayne pinched my ass when Cheryl was ordering a Heineken. "You're looking great," he said. I thought I was looking thin. Exams will do that.

"Thanks," I said, wondering if all men cheated. He cheated on me. Now he wants to cheat on her. Russ cheats on Sharon. My father cheated on my mom. Is it their fault? Or our fault for letting it happen?

What have I done? And what should I do now?

Thursday, January 1, 2:10 a.m.

russ rings in the new year

Is it time to go yet? I've had too much champagne and I'm now feeling frisky. I pat Sharon on the knee. "Shar, you ready?"

It's two-ten, definitely time to leave her sister's New Year's party. All that's left of the chips and booze are crumbs and bottles. Most of the thirty guests have left. Rena, unfortunately, is still here. Whenever I'm not paying attention, she corners me to harass me about school.

At eleven she wanted to know if I'd gotten any grades back. I told her I hadn't checked. At eleven-thirty she asked me if I had gotten any interviews.

"Yeah. BCG, Accenture, Stewart & Co. and O'Donnel."

"Good for you!" she exclaimed, while straightening her ridiculous tie. I'm not wearing a tie, so why is she? "Who are you waiting for?"

"Bain and McKinsey."

"I'll see if I can get you an interview with McKinsey. I may have some pull now, you know."

Second-years had their interviews in October, and Rena has been gloating about her McKinsey acceptance all evening.

Sharon kisses me on the cheek and stretches off the couch. "Let's get our coats." She has a pimple on her chin. In all the years we've dated, I've never seen her with a pimple. She fought with it for twenty minutes before we went out tonight, with ice cubes and concealer creams, but it still shines through, red and angry. For some reason, the pimple calms me, reminds me of her flaws. If she finds out about Kimmy and never wants to speak to me again, I'll remember this pimple. Since I've been home, I've found myself rejoicing in all of her flaws. Her short temper with her mother. How she won't let me smoke dope. How she insists on manning the remote control.

I tell myself that this is what I won't miss when she breaks up with me.

Inversely, every time she does something sweet, like bake my favorite chocolate peanut-butter brownies, or kiss my finger when I somehow slice it on a butter knife, or when she wears the purple V-neck mohair sweater that makes me want to lay my head against her stomach and be held for hours, the one she's wearing right now, a knife spears through my heart. And not a butter knife. A machete.

We pick through the pile of haphazardly thrown coats on her sister and brother-in-law's bed until we find ours. My scarf was once stuffed in my jacket's arm, but is now missing.

Beep. Apparently there's a message waiting for me on my cell, which was inside my jacket pocket.

Sharon looks at me with curiosity. "Who called?"

Beep. I should definitely have turned off the message alert. "I'll check later." *Beep.*

"No, hon, check now. It could be an emergency. You never know on New Year's." Her forehead scrunches, and I know her well enough to know that she's imagining her parents stuck in an overturned car, their only means of survival getting in touch through my cell phone. I open the phone and type in my code.

"One new message, left January first at twelve-oh-three.

"Hi, it's me," Kimmy says. Oh, man. I press the phone tight against my ear in the hopes of shielding her voice. "Happy New Year! I'm at a bar right now, drinking!" She sounds hammered. "I miss you. I have something important to talk to you about…" I erase the message quickly and turn off the phone.

Sharon stares at me funny, as if I'm changing into The Hulk while she's watching and she's not sure if she should tell me I'm turning green. "Who was it?"

I shove the offending mechanism into my pocket. "Friend from school."

She's still staring at me. "Female friend?"

Could she hear the message? "She's in my group."

"Stop picking," she says, swatting my hand away from my face. I've been staring at her pimple all night, I didn't realize I had been picking one of mine. "You've never mentioned a female friend in your group." Her fingers are doing up her coat, but her wide brown eyes are still on me.

"I haven't?"

"No. You haven't. What's her name?"

I concentrate on looking for my scarf, which should be somewhere on the bed. "Kimmy. There are two girls in my group." I've decided that the best way to play this is to act as though it's totally normal that she called me practically at the stroke of midnight.

"Who's the other one?"

"Good, here's my scarf." I pick it up and double wrap it around my neck. "Lauren."

"Did she call you, too?"

"No."

"Don't you think it's weird that this Kimmy-girl called you?"

I shrug. She probably wants to listen to the message. That's why I erased it, in case she asks. "No. She probably called everyone in the group." Good one.

"Is she pretty?"

Damn. She can sense something. "She's all right."

She folds her arms across her chest. "Maybe I should come and visit you this semester."

Oh, man.

jamie saves the world
one book at a time

Instead of basking in the Miami sun, I'm back at the over-heated Zoo, quizzing Layla before her interview with Silver-man Investments. I'm sprawled across my bed, my booted feet hanging over the edge. She's pacing from one side of the room to the other. Click-clack (she's on the wood), silence (she's on the carpet), click-clack (other side of the room near the desk), pivot. She accidentally kicks my pile of last semes-ter's textbooks and swears under her breath. (I don't know what to do with those books. The school bookstore won't take them, and there's no used bookstore in the area. Do they really expect us all to buy new books at full price every year when these are available?)

She looks tanned and fantastic. In her knee-length charcoal-gray skirt suit and matching fitted jacket, she looks like a se-rious teacher who might at any moment rip her clothes off.

Sexy Pacing Goddess: Ask me something else.

Me: If you were a flower, what kind of flower would you be?

SPG: That's ridiculous.

Me: That is not a good answer. You will not get the job if you call the interviewer ridiculous.

SPG: Then I'm a Venus flytrap. Because I can trap success wherever I go.

Me: Much better! (She can trap me anytime she wants.)

SPG: (Scowling.) I hate interviews.

Me: You'll be great.

SPG: Thanks. Crap. It's one-ten. I have to go.

Me: Your interview isn't until two. And it's in the Katz building. You don't want to sit there for forty minutes.

SPG: You're causing me unnecessary stress. I have to go. Crap. My shoes. I can't wear these shoes outside. It's snowing. My nylons will get soaked. I can't show up at an interview with soaked nylons. I need to carry my shoes. But what will I do with my boots? I don't want to bring my schoolbag. What do I do? (Her eyes look wild as if she's about to get hysterical.)

Charming gentleman: Milady, I would be honored to accompany you to the Katz building and then return here with your boots.

Layla gasps, then joyfully hugs me. "Thank you!" she gushes. "You're a godsend! Can we go right now?"

I escort her first to her room to get her coat and boots, and then to the Katz building. She sits on a wooden bench in the main hall and reaches to remove her boots. I gently slap her hands. "Allow me, milady. I wouldn't want you to go to your interview with soiled hands." I unzip each boot slowly, relishing the moment.

"Oh, wow, I love you," she says, blows me a kiss and runs to the elevator. "Wish me luck!"

Love you? I wish. "Good luck," I say. I have no doubt she'll get the job. I saw her first-semester transcript by her bed this morning. She had a 4.0. Who has a 4.0 in business school? I only got a 3.3. I wish I were in her group. Both so I can work with her, and so I can watch her work.

I step outside and the snow lands directly on my bald spot, numbing my head. I forgot my hat. Again, why am I not in Miami?

This week is interview week, which unfortunately cuts into winter break, but it's not as if I have any interviews lined up. I just can't bear to work for a bank or a consulting firm. They seem so soulless. I need to have a job I'm passionate about. I guess I can always go back to writing. But I think I prefer to be in a career that involves more companionship than a computer.

So why am I here? Sunshine notwithstanding, I was bored in Miami. And I knew Layla would be back.

I have it bad.

"Excuse me," sings a blond undergrad in a parka and hat. Ringing a bell, she says, "Can you spare some change for the Children's Hospital? We're trying to raise money for the new pediatric oncology department."

I get instantly depressed. Here I am whining about my future. There are people out there, children, who might not even have a future. I reach into my pockets. All I have is a five. "Here you go," I say, placing the bill onto the tray. I wonder how the kids' ward at Miami General is doing without me.

As my bald spot continues to freeze, I have an epiphany, which I decide to share with Kimmy. Back at the Zoo, I knock on her door.

"Hold on," I hear from inside. The door clicks open, and she scampers back under the covers. As far as I can tell, it's just her.

"Kimmy, my sweet, welcome back! Lover-boy not here?"

"No. He's flying back today, I think. His first interview isn't till tomorrow."

"When did you get back?"

She sits up in bed. "Last week."

I lean against her desk. "So early?"

"I had to apply for a loan." She groans. "Don't ask."

I don't. "When are your interviews?"

"I only have two. One on Thursday, one on Friday. I'm glad you woke me, Jamie. I should start researching the companies."

"I'll let you be, then. I just have a question. What did you do with your last-semester books?"

"Nothing. They're piled over there." She points to the corner of her room. "Why?"

"Would you give them to me? I want to hold on to them and sell them to the first-year students next year. I'm planning to donate the proceeds to help fund the pediatric oncology department at the Children's Hospital."

"Definitely," she says. "I'll even help you collect them. That's a great idea. Why don't we make up flyers and then hand them out door-to-door throughout the Zoo?"

Something occurs to me. There Kimmy was telling me she needs to apply for a loan, and she's willing to give up the proceeds from selling her books privately next year. She really does have a heart, after all.

I return to my room, feeling a familiar rush at the idea of making a flyer. I don't think I can handle working for a hospital full-time again—living it, dreaming it, breathing it wasn't right for me—but doing part-time work makes me feel great. Ideally, I should have a career that's creative and that allows me time for charity work on the side. I'll start collecting books tomorrow. Good thing I don't have too many clothes. My closet is about to become a storage room.

Forty minutes later, boots still in hand, I decide I should go pick up Layla. Why not? I don't want her to ruin her adorable shoes.

A half an hour later she spots me in the lobby of the Katz building. "You came back for me? I love you!"

If she tells me enough times, I'm afraid I'll start to believe it.

Thursday, January 15, 10:10 a.m.

kimmy's prepping

I'm sitting in room 316 of the Katz building, waiting for my O'Donnel interview to begin. Five hopeful prospects, including me, are waiting in this mini-classroom, each sitting in a different row. I'm sitting in the back row, and am very uncomfortable in my suit. What is the point of a suit? Really? And why blue? And why a skirt? Of the five waiting to be interrogated, three are guys, and I find their ties even crazier. Why is a rope around one's neck considered formal? And why for a man and not a woman? Maybe I should apply to Ralph Lauren instead of to a consulting firm. Right. As if any clothing chain besides Frederick's of Hollywood would want me working for them.

None of us wants to be wearing a suit; we'd all rather be in sweats, or at least jeans, but nope, suit it is. I'd rather be in my bed, naked, with Russ.

I bought this navy-blue atrocity especially for today. Do I have to get a second one if I make it to the second round? My coat is definitely wrong. All I have is a short ski jacket in candy-apple-red from the Gap. The three guys waiting

all have dull, gray, wool, appropriate coats. Why didn't I
think of buying an appropriately dull coat? At the moment
my highly inappropriate coat is bunched behind me in my
seat. Maybe I should hang it up. When they call me in, the
interviewer won't see the flaming mess and think that *I'm*
inappropriate.

I hang it on the back of the door, then return to my seat.

I'm going to do fine. I will. My eggs aren't all in this basket, anyway. I have an interview with another firm tomorrow. And I've been practicing cases all week. All vacation. I
can do this.

Not sure what to do with my hair. It's in a tight ponytail
for now, which I think makes me look serious. I hope it
doesn't give me a headache. I'm feeling too good at the moment to have a headache. Russ came back last night. I wasn't
sure what to expect, after a month of Sharon.

No one's going to stop me from getting what I want. Not
my dad and not Sharon. And not my period, since I'm still
taking the pills.

As soon as Russ saw me, he slammed my door behind him,
pushed me against the wall and kissed me hard. Phew. Maybe
they're over. Maybe he broke up with her. We haven't talked
about it yet. I didn't want to bring it up when we have so
much else to worry about. (I don't want him to think I'm a
nag.) He has Stewart & Co. this morning, BCG this afternoon, and O'Donnel tomorrow. I just have O'Donnel this
morning and BCG tomorrow afternoon.

A man pushes open the door. "Ms. Nailer? We're ready
for you."

Here goes nothing. Or everything.

it's the doghouse for russ

I shake the interviewer's hand firmly and sit down. We're wearing matching Brooks Brothers navy suits, white shirts and blue ties. He's in his forties, balding at the top of his head. He hands me a pad of yellow paper and a black ballpoint pen, then opens the black leather folder in front of him.

"We're going to run a case," he says. His chin disappears when he talks.

No kidding. I relax my shoulders and try to smile. I need to invoke all of my superhuman mental strength. "I'm ready."

"How many dogs are in the U.S.?" He's looking me straight in the eye to see if I flinch.

Oh, man. Who gives a shit how many dogs there are in the U.S.? I try to remember all that I've learned about answering estimation cases. They don't expect you to get the right answer. They just want to see how you think. How you analyze the problem and come to a conclusion. First you have to show that you can clarify. So here's my clarifying question: "Is that just domestic dogs or working dogs, as well?"

He's still staring. "All dogs."

All dogs. Wait a minute. Maybe he doesn't expect a number, like 2,000,577. Maybe he wants a list of types, like beagles and boxers. What the hell do I know about dogs? Wait. Maybe I'll be creative, and list them by function. "All right. Let's see now. There are domestic dogs, police dogs, show dogs and racing dogs."

"Are you sure that's it?" he says, pointing an accusatory finger.

Am I sure that's it? I have to appear confident. If I can't make choices in my real life, how am I supposed to make them here?

"No. Let's not forget hot dogs."

He smiles.

Afterward I go straight to Kimmy's room. She's lying in her bra and panties. I take off my clothes and carefully arrange them over her chair. (Maybe she'll be inspired to iron them?)

Four hours to relax before my next interview.

Relax. Now that's a good euphemism.

I inhale her warm, vanilla smell. "How'd you do?" I ask.

She nestles her knee between my legs. "All right. I'm glad I'm done for the day."

"Cases suck, eh?"

"Don't laugh," she says, "but I don't mind them as much as I thought."

I mess up her hair. "Did you enjoy yourself? Did you find the cases fun?"

She giggles. "A little."

Knowing how ticklish she is, I go straight for her underarms. "Stop," she squeals, squirming in my hands. Her hands are now under my arms, and we're both laughing and rolling around.

I spent twenty-one years alone, and now I'm seeing two people at the same time.

Shit. I freeze.

"What's wrong?" Kimmy asks, sitting up.

Shit, shit, shit. "I forgot seeing-eye dogs."

second semester

Thursday, January 22, 2:40 p.m.

kimmy's shrinking basket

"We regret to inform you that we will not be hiring you for the position of summer associate."

Fuck. In an e-mail, too. You'd think BCG could pick up the phone to shatter my heart.

All my hopes are now on O'Donnel. All of my eggs in one consulting basket. I think the interview went well, but what the hell do I know?

Not much, apparently, according to BCG. I e-mail Russ.

You hear from BCG? I'm a no-go.

He's sitting diagonal from me at the computer lab, but I like seeing his name in my inbox.

Ding! He says: Yeah. I got a thanks but no thanks.

Ding! An e-mail from Layla:

Hi! What's up? I'm in the library, where are you?
Guess what? I got the second-round interview with the Manhattan Group! Not my first choice but the interview is in the

city and Manhattan Group shares an office building with Lerner Investment Bank—where Bradley Green works! Maybe I'll meet him...must go to futures and options now! XXX Layla

Layla has second-round interviews scheduled all through next week in Manhattan. And each company is putting her up at some fancy hotel.

Sigh.

On the bright side, if I have no interviews, I won't have to miss any classes and become even more clueless.

Speaking of clueless, thank God I don't have to take Futures and Options. It's Layla's elective. This semester our block has Finance on Monday and Wednesday at nine, then Marketing at ten-thirty, and GBE, Global Business Economy, at one-thirty. Today and Tuesday we have Operations at ten-thirty, and after an extralong lunch, Russ and I have our one elective, Corporate Strategy with Martin. We've both decided to become strategy majors. Why not? Martin's class last semester was my highest mark, A-minus; maybe I'll be two for two.

More classes mean more books. Beads of sweat sprout on my forehead. Books I'll have to buy with my nonexistent money. Why is it so hot in here? You'd think the school would learn to regulate its buildings' temperatures. The computers could melt.

I look over at Russ to see if he's looking at me, but he's fixated on the computer screen and typing away. He's probably writing to Sharon. A love letter.

We don't talk about it, but I know he's still with her. What's wrong with him?

Not that he has any incentive to break up with her. Why should he? This way he has his cake and gets to eat it, too. Those are Jamie's words, by the way. Now that he knows about us, he loves to give advice. Yesterday, it was warmer than normal and we sat on the bench in the courtyard, the same one we first kissed on, and smoked cigarettes. I smoked and he talked. He said I deserve better, but I don't know if he meant it or if he's jealous. Either way, he said if I don't ask for more, I'm not going to get it.

I know he's right. I'm being an idiot. I should tell Russ to choose.

But what if he doesn't choose me? I should dump him for doing this to me. Tell him to get lost. He's never going to break it off with Sharon. Why should he?

He will. He's going to break up with her. He'll have to choose between us eventually. He can't marry both of us.

Can he?

No, he can't.

The clock on the bottom of my screen tells me I have eleven minutes till Corporate Strategy. I tap Russ's computer and point to the clock.

As we're leaving Martin's war dungeon, Russ's cell phone beeps.

He clicks it on to check. Is it Sharon? He gives me a thumbs-up. Is that his infantile way of telling me they're over?

"Second interview for O'Donnel," he says. "Do you have your cell on you?"

I left it in my room. "No."

"Do you want to check your messages with mine?"

What if it's a no? Then I'm left with nothing. It's like giving Russ an ultimatum. Then the answer would be in front of me in black and white. At the moment I prefer the unknown of a shade of gray. "Not yet. Wanna grab a smoke?"

"One new message."

My chest cavity is taking a beating from my heart. I sit on the corner of my bed, tapping my heels against the floor. I need this job. Otherwise, how will I pay back my ever-increasing massive debt?

"Hello, Kimmy, this is Claire Moss at O'Donnel. We'd like to bring you down to Manhattan for a second interview…"

Oh. My. God. She keeps talking, but my hand is shaking as I note down the number. Word on the street is that they make offers to three-quarters of those who make it to second round. Oh. My. God.

I dial her number immediately.

"Hi, Kimmy. Thanks for calling back. Would you like to come to the Manhattan office for our second round?"

Oh, no thanks, I'd rather remain unemployed. "That would be great."

"Good. Second round will be next Thursday, and then we're having a dinner for the prospective employees that night."

Amazing. I've never been to New York. Russ will be there, too, and it won't matter who sees us together there. We can sleep in the same bed in the same hotel the entire night without setting the alarm for six-ten. I hate six-ten. I hope I never have to see six-ten again on my clock.

I'm going to need a new suit. And an outfit for dinner. After I make the arrangements, I check my bank balances online.

Bank account: $400.00.

Visa balance: $1,000. (Stupid second-semester textbooks.)

Loans…no need to torture myself and look at that link. Today I'm focusing on the positive. New York. Hotel. O'Donnel. Me and Russ.

layla's stakeout

I am stalking Bradley Green.

All I need is a long-lens camera, a trench coat, cigarette hanging from my lip and dark sunglasses. I bet most stalkers don't wear Chanel suits.

The best part is that I didn't even break in. Since my interview was at one, I just stayed in the building's coffee shop. The woman behind the counter makes a mean vanilla chai. I've set up camp with my *New York Times* directly against a glass wall that faces the elevators. And it's not just the potential of catching a glimpse of my potential Prince Charming that's exciting me; it's the energy. I love working. I seriously love the pulse of getting things done.

Why hasn't Bradley come in for a cup of coffee? Then I can casually bump into him and we'll finally meet. Everyone needs a four-o'clock break. Maybe he's not in his office today. I could be waiting here all day for nothing. I should call him. Why not? I'll call and hang up. I take out my cell phone. No. Sitting here, minding my own business (meeting the man of my future *is* my business) is one thing, but stalking him on the phone is totally unethical.

What the hell. I'll star 67 and block the call. And Kimmy thinks she has nothing to teach me. I dial the company number, which I looked up just before I left for New York, and ask his receptionist to connect me to him.

Connect me to him. That has a nice sound to it.

It rings. I am going to hang up, aren't I? I will. I will not speak to him. I can't speak to him. I'll sound like an idiot.

"Hello, you've reached Bradley Green, it's January twenty-eighth, and I'm either on the phone or away from my desk…"

Fantastic. He's in the office today. I hang up the phone.

At six-thirty, I see him.

It's him. I know I've only seen one picture of him, although I did enlarge it on my screen, but I feel that it's him deep in my soul. It's him. My prince. I'm going to meet him!

He's about six feet tall, and wearing black pants and a silvery-gray shirt. His hair is light brown, and he's talking to a woman in a short yellow suit. He's holding his folded jacket over his arm. Is he leaving? So early? Is he a slacker or is business slow? And who is that woman? And why is she wearing yellow? Vile. That is so not her color.

I hate being catty. It is not nice to be catty. It's time to meet my prince!

I'm paralyzed in my chair.

I can't. I just can't. I don't have an excuse.

The door flaps behind him as he leaves for the night.

I pretend to read the paper.

the green-eyed monster gets to russ

The cab jerks forward and then backward, and then forward again. Oh, man. I try to steady Kimmy by putting my hand on her knee.

"Russ, I think I'm going to be sick," she says.

"We're almost there."

"That doesn't help. I'm nervous."

"What are you so nervous about, eh? You said the interview went great."

"I think it did. But…this is it. If I don't get this, I'll probably end up back in Phoenix." She uncrosses her legs and then crosses them again. "I can't take out more loans if I'll never be able to pay them back."

"You're being ridiculous. You can look for a job on your own. These are just school jobs. There are a million opportunities out there, and not just in New York."

She kisses me on the cheek. "Yeah? What about you? You're not worried about this dinner?"

"Who me? Nah." I'll be more worried if I get the job and

I have to decide whether I want to take it. Which doesn't mean I don't want it offered to me.

I'm not going to pick the pimple that has appeared by my left temple. I'm not even going to touch it. I may not have willpower when it comes to Kimmy, but I have willpower for my picking.

Me, nervous? Oh, man.

The taxi slams to a stop on the corner of Fifth and Forty-seventh. I hand a five over the plastic divider, then we shuffle out onto the street. "Ready?" I ask, holding open the heavy metal door for her. The floor of the lobby is green, the walls a dark wood, the ceiling pale blue. Are they trying to impersonate a golf course?

Kimmy bites the side of her lip. "As ready as I'll ever be."

I scratch at my pimple.

"Hello," I say to the maître d'. "We're here with the O'Donnel party."

He nods. "They're in the private room on the left." I follow Kimmy through the lobby. She looks hot in her tight black pants and red blouse. Clothes that I'm looking forward to taking off later tonight. We each have a hotel room with a king-size bed. We'll have to try them both out. She gives me a nervous smile as we walk into a room full of partners and applicants. I squeeze her shoulder and put on my best fake smile. I've gotten better at being fake this year than I ever thought possible.

"Would you like a glass of wine?" a floating bartender asks us. Apparently my fake smile looks like it could use a drink.

"I would, thank you."

I pass one to Kimmy. We clink and dive into the deep end.

Kimmy seems to be doing better in the deep end than I am. She's been talking to the same partner, some guy named Johnny Dollan, for the past half hour. Doesn't she know she should be mingling? They're standing very close to each other. He keeps laughing at everything she says. Ha, ha, ha. She's not *that* funny.

I've been wandering from group to group, making sure I converse with everyone. I was doing fine until I got stuck in the lame football huddle I'm in now, with three other wanna-bes and one partner.

A short, stocky guy with thick glasses is talking about the collapse of the Internet bubble. Haven't we been talking about that for the last five years? "I think there's still room in the market for technology companies with good ideas," he says.

"American innovation didn't die with the collapse," another drone adds, eager to insert her opinion.

Kimmy just flipped her hair. Is she flirting? Flirting to secure a job is so wrong. Maybe she's flirting to make me jealous. How immature, eh? I'm not going to get jealous. I have a girlfriend. She can do whatever. If she wants to flirt and sleep her way into a company, then fine.

I excuse myself from the huddle. I need more booze.

She's sitting next to him. I can't believe she's sitting next to him at dinner. Doesn't she realize that all the partners will know what she's up to? That he's just trying to pick her up for a one-night stand? It's embarrassing.

She sips her wine, slowly, letting her lips linger on the glass. Is she trying to turn him on?

I gulp down my water. I have to get a grip. I'm not going to get the job if I keep this up. I hear the guy next to me discussing the new *Spider-Man* movie. That I can do. About ten minutes later, Kimmy's *friend* excuses himself to use the washroom. I see her trying to catch my eye.

Yeah, right. Now she wants me? I ignore her. Let's see what she does now.

"Did I hear you say you're from Cali?" she asks the man across the table from her.

Cali? What's a Cali?

"Yes, you did," he says.

"I love California. I spent a summer working in San Diego when I was in college."

She did? Now she's flirting with *him?* I try to block her out and focus on my conversation.

People start leaving, but Kimmy is now deep in conversation with Johnny-boy. I grab my coat and hail myself a cab.

When I get back to the hotel, I call Sharon.

"Hi! I'm so happy you called," she says. "You said you didn't think you'd get a chance."

Her voice sounds soft. I love her voice. I wish she were here with me. "I miss you," I say.

"You do? You're so sweet. How did today go?"

I miss her so much that I can barely breathe. The Kimmy-spell has been broken, dead, finito, now that I see her for what she is. "I want you to come visit."

"Visit New York?"

I flop down on the bed, my shoes still on. "No, visit me at school."

"Honey, you know it's hard for me to get away on the weekends…because of tutoring and—"

"Enough with the tutoring. Call in sick for a weekend. Please?" Kimmy probably went home with Johnny-boy. Finally, my decision is made. I won't get the job, anyway, so I'll go back to Toronto and be with Sharon. No more lying, no more yo-yoing between them. Maybe I'll even marry her. And have two-point-two Canadian children. Or would four Canadian children equal 2.2 U.S.?

"When?" Sharon asks.

"Soon. This weekend."

"I can't come this weekend! I have to book a flight."

"So in February."

She giggles. "Maybe I'll come for Valentine's Day. It's on a weekend."

I forgot about Valentine's Day. "Perfect. Valentine's Day. All settled. And you'll call in sick on Monday, too. It's a holiday here. President's Day." Maybe I'll propose then. Forget chocolates, I'll get her some carats.

"So tell me about tonight. How was it?"

A few minutes later, there's a knock on my door. I ignore it. What, Kimmy's back so soon? Did she give Johnny-boy a quick blow job in the bathroom of the restaurant? She knocks again. I ignore her again. I talk to Sharon for twenty minutes and then say good-night. As soon as I hang up, the phone rings. I know it's Kimmy, but I pick up, anyway. "Yup."

"What happened to you?" She sounds pissed.

"What do you mean?"

"What do you mean, what do I mean?" she shrieks. "I looked around the room and you were gone. I looked for you forever."

"I took a cab."

"Why didn't you wait for me?"

"You seemed a little busy with Johnny-boy."

Pause. "Are you joking?"

Joking? "I don't think so."

"Go to hell," she says, and hangs up.

What? Now she's mad at me? I stare at the ceiling. She can't be mad at me; she's the one who was flirting all night.

I touch the side of my face with the pimple. I should just pop it. One time. I won't start picking again. I'll just do it quickly before I change my mind.

I jump out of bed, stand in front of the mirror over the dresser and pop it.

Ah.

Let's see. Is there anything else that needs to be popped?

Stop. What am I doing? I put my hands on the dresser and take a deep breath. I'm not taking out my anger on my face. No way. I was an ass to Kimmy, I know I was, and I'm going to go apologize.

I grab the room key and march over to Kimmy's.

"It's me," I say, knocking on the door.

"Go away," she shouts.

Uh-oh. What's wrong with me? Why am I so evil? I'm not a superhero, I'm the evil villain. "Please let me in. I'm sorry. I was an idiot. Please?"

Pause. A few seconds later she lets me in without looking at me. Her eyes are red, as though she's been crying.

"I'm sorry. I was a big jerk."

She stands next to the window and looks outside. "I don't get it. Is that what you think of me? That I'm such a slut that I go home with everyone? Do you have no respect for me at all?"

"Well, I..." I trail off. I've been a total ass. How could I make her feel like that? I'm the one who seems to go home with everyone. I'm the slut. "I'm sorry," I say. "I didn't mean to insult you. You're right." I wrap my arms around her waist and feel how tense she is.

"I am right," she says, and then turns around so we're eye to eye. "Don't ever make me feel like that again."

My heart feels so heavy and all I can do is kiss her. No, not all I can do.

I lead her to the bed.

layla writes a marketing plan

"Can you pass me another application?" I ask Dennis.

He shuffles through the papers. "Sure, Layla. So did you hear from any of the firms yet?"

"Yup." I stick the end of a piece of licorice in my mouth. "I got a few offers."

"You did? From Manhattan or Silverman?"

"Both." Plus a few others, but I don't want to brag.

He gives me a thumbs-up. "That's fantastic. Which one are you taking?"

"Silverman."

We sit and read more applications. After a few minutes, I ask as casually as possible, "Dorothy, when do acceptance letters for prospective students go out this year?"

She looks up from whatever she's reading. "I think they've already started going out."

"I'm curious if some of the applicants we reviewed were accepted."

"You can check if you'd like."

"I can?" I wasn't going to ask, but if she's offering...I have to know if he's coming next year. "I'm just curious." I finish reading the application on my desk. I don't want to appear too eager.

Twenty minutes later I stretch and slowly make my way over to the main computer. I add a yawn to show how not excited I am about checking my prince's status.

I'm still furious with myself for freezing up in Manhattan. I should have forced myself to meet him. What in the world was my problem? I won't let it happen again.

I perch on the computer and lean into the screen. No need for everyone to see what I'm looking at. Maybe I should search one of the other applicants first. Whatever happened to Tom Price? The guy who claimed he would be thrilled to go to Stern?

I type in "Tom Price." He's been…rejected. He must have felt awful when he got the letter. The thin envelope in his mailbox. Poor boy. How could I help destroy someone's dreams? I type in Bradley Green. A letter was sent to his apartment, informing him that he's been…accepted! Accepted! Yes! Next year he could be here with me! In the Zoo! That would be amazing. Let's see—if I remember correctly from his application, he applied to four other schools: Columbia, Harvard, Wharton and Stern. Let's say he got accepted to three of them. That means there's a twenty-five-percent chance he's coming here next year! Of course, LWBS is ranked lower than the other four. If both my parents weren't alumni, I might not have come here.

Let's say there's a ten-percent chance he enrolls here. Ten percent. I can't wager my future on ten percent.

"I can't believe I might never see him again," I whine to Kimmy later that afternoon. I'm lying on my bed, and she's sprawled on my rug. We're studying for Monday's Marketing quiz.

Smack.

"Ouch! What was that for?" I ask. There's a red scratch on my leg from where Kimmy just hit me.

She rolls her eyes. "How can someone so hard-core in class be so lame when it comes to getting a guy? Just call him."

"I can't call him. I have no reason to call him. I'm not supposed to fall for an applicant. What reason would I possibly have to call him?"

She appears deep in thought. "What you need is a plan."

"And I'm not lame with guys. I just don't like to play games."

"You don't like to play at all. Are you sure you even like men? You wouldn't flirt with Professor Jon, you wouldn't go out with that guy who's on the application committee with you, who's adorable. What's his name?"

"Dennis."

"Right. And you're not even going after Bradley. What's your problem?"

I feel my cheeks flush. "I don't have a problem. I like men. I just don't like wasting my time with guys who won't end up being good enough."

"But you won't know who's wasting your time unless you play the game."

"Okay, okay, I'll play the game. Let's get Bradley."

She swings her legs around so she's sitting cross-legged. "Time to use the marketing model."

"Glad you're finally finding a use for class."

"About time, huh?" She rubs her hands together as though she's setting them on fire. "These are the five Ps: product, positioning, price, promotion and packaging."

"Perfect."

"Okay, listen up. You're the product. Now according to the textbook," she says, flipping through the pages, "we're supposed to figure out where you are in your life cycle. The choices are introduction, early growth, late growth, maturity, decline. Let's say you're in your late-growth phase."

"Hold on. Am I the product, or is the relationship between Bradley and me the product?"

"You're the product. We're selling you to him. Let's plot you on a perceptual map." She draws a cross on her paper. "Let's make the X-axis represent sexy versus pretty, the Y-axis studious versus fun. I would put you somewhere in the studious/pretty quadrant."

"Hey," I say. "I'm fun."

"More studious than fun."

"And what quadrant are you in? The sexy/fun quadrant?"

She examines her drawing. "Yup. Cool. If we were both products in the same company, we would totally avoid cannibalization for the company."

"Yeah, because no one would want the pretty and smart one!"

She hits me on the leg again. "Are you crazy? Who doesn't want a pretty and smart girlfriend?"

"This is the most absurd argument I've ever had. And why can't I be both pretty and sexy? What's the next P?"

"Pricing."

"Perfect," I say. "I'm free."

"Yeah, right. What about fancy dinners? Jewelry? Roses?"

In relative terms, I'm no longer the insane one. "Next."

"Promotion," she says. "The most important thing about an ad campaign is that it catches the attention of the target audience, communicates key information and is memorable." She looks up at me. "We can work with this one. How should we advertise you?"

Definitely crazy. "I've always wanted to be on a Times Square billboard."

She rolls her eyes. "Can you be serious for a second? Our key message is that you're smart, pretty and available. Our target audience is Bradley Green. Obviously. The positioning…"

"Can I be on top?"

She rolls her eyes. "It's always about sex with you, huh? We should position you as smarter and better than the average girl. The best catch. And now placement. Hmm. That's the toughest one. Where will he see you?"

"He'll only see me if he comes to LWBS next year. That's the problem. See? It won't work."

"Can't you see him in Manhattan anywhere? Don't you know where his job is?"

"Yeah. But I'm not taking the Manhattan Group job. So we're not going to be in the same building. I suppose I could stalk him where he lives…his address is in the application."

She shakes her head. "Not a good plan. You'll be depending on his coming and going, and you need to be the one in control. And there are laws against annoying doormen. Maybe he can have an interview with LWBS? And you can interview him?"

"LWBS only interviews when you're on the waiting list. And he already got accepted. Unless…" Idea! Idea! Idea!

"What?"

"Well, I came for a tour last year. You know, to see the school. Didn't you?" Doesn't everyone?

"No," she says. "I couldn't afford to fly across the country for no reason."

No reason? Only her future! "Anyway, maybe he's planning on coming."

"That would be perfect. You could be his tour guide. He'll fall in love. It'll be perfect."

"So all I have to do is sign up as a tour guide and find out if he's coming."

"Brilliant."

It's four o'clock. Maybe I should go now. To check if he's signed up. No point in me obsessing about it all weekend, if he's not even coming. "Where are my boots? I'm going to see if this is a possibility."

She laughs. "This second?"

There they are. I zip them up and wrap my scarf around

my neck. I won't let myself wimp out again. "Be back in a sec."

I grab my jacket and skip back to the Katz building. Dorothy is still in her office. "Hey," I say. "How do I go about volunteering to do school tours?"

"You walk around showing people where to go?"

Who knew she had a sense of humor? "Ha-ha. I meant, if I want to volunteer, who do I talk to?"

"Just go sign yourself up. The application room is still unlocked, and the computer should still be on. Just use your task-force password and sign up for the groups you want to lead."

I feel like I have the key to the golden city. I sign on, then search through upcoming tour groups, looking for Bradley Green. His name is nowhere. How am I supposed to be his tour guide if he hasn't signed up for a tour?

Foiled!

kimmy has a heart-to-heart

"What do you want to do this coming Saturday?" I ask.

We're lying in my bed. We've already had sex and are now watching *Daredevil*. He's recently realized that his laptop doubles as a DVD player. I keep dozing off. You'd think Ben Affleck would keep me more awake, but with the laptop balanced on Russ's knees, whenever he shifts I see a glare on the screen instead of the movie. I noticed that Layla has the entire *Sex and the City* series on DVD in her room. Maybe Russ'll watch it with me. I've never watched a single episode. I know now that the series is over, people will probably stop talking about it, but I might as well catch up.

Boring. "Russ?"

"Hmm?" He doesn't take his eyes off the screen.

"Saturday night is Valentine's Day." As soon as I mention the V-word I feel stupid. Do you celebrate Valentine's Day with your mistress? Maybe that's a faux pas.

His ears flush. So cute. Does he have something planned? Maybe he's surprising me with a romantic dinner. Or with breaking up with Sharon.

"Actually…" he says.

Pause. "Yes?"

"Well…"

Pause again. "Well, what?"

"Sharon is coming this weekend."

What? Panic grabs hold of my throat and squeezes. "Coming here? To school?"

He squirms, and the laptop slips off his legs, banging me in the knee. "Yeah. She wants to visit."

Visit? What? "Why can't you go and visit her?"

He shrugs. "I was just there. She wants to see how I live."

"You're going to give her the tour?" I wave my arm around the room like a *Price Is Right* girl showing a new car. "Show her where you spend your nights?"

Maybe I should suggest she take one of Layla's tours. Only we'll modify it slightly and make it far, far away.

He pauses the movie. "You know I can't tell her about us."

That's it. I can't take it anymore. I throw the duvet off me, sit up and turn my back to him. This is the last straw. It's one thing to keep dating us both, but to bring her here? How could he? "Why can't you? Why are you sleeping with me if you're in love with her? Who do you think you are? Don't you care at all about me?"

There, I've said it. I know I'm not supposed to say it, not supposed to suggest it, not supposed to think it. But too friggin' bad.

I'm looking at the door instead of him. And he doesn't respond. And then I realize that he's never going to break up with Sharon. He's just sleeping with me. While he's out of the country. I don't mean anything to him. I'm just someone to help pass the time.

I hate him. I feel like shit. Why do I need to feel like this? I don't need this. I don't need him. Two full minutes later he still hasn't responded. What, is he napping? I turn around. Tears are streaming down his face. What? He's…crying?

"I'm sorry," he says, eyes glistening. "I'm so sorry. I know I'm being a jerk. To both of you. It's just that I honestly have feelings for you both. I never thought I'd be—" He interrupts himself to wipe his eyes on the back of his hand.

I can't believe he's crying. I hand him a tissue.

"I know this is no excuse. But growing up, I never thought in a million years that a girl as beautiful and smart as you would ever look twice at me. I was scrawny and geeky. You know, the boy who was always picked last for gym class."

He laughs and then wipes his eyes again. I squeeze his leg.

"I spent my entire childhood buried in comic books. Hung out in the world of superheroes and villains instead of real people. And then in my last year in college I met Sharon."

I hold my breath. He's never talked about Sharon directly to me. "And what happened?"

"We had a class together. Pop lit. It was a mandatory for her Education degree. I took it because I heard that the prof put comics on the reading list. She sat next to me on the first day." He shrugs. "She asked me out."

I try to imagine him, shy, skinny, not knowing what to do with his hands. I can't.

"I don't know what she saw in me. She thought I was funny. I went to the gym with her, started boarding—"

Boarding? I would have pegged him as the downhill type, but what do I know?

"I stopped picking at my face. And then for the first time, I came out of my shell. I didn't run home between classes to hide my nose in a comic book. I talked to people. Started playing ball. Socialized. I'd wanted to go to business school in the States, but only after starting to date Sharon did I think I had a chance of getting in. And then I came here and met you. I couldn't get you out of my head. I still can't, but I can't just throw away everything I've experienced with Sharon, either. I owe her."

I don't know what to tell him. I know I can't tell him what to do or who to choose. Instead of feeling angry, I feel relieved that he's opening up to me. I lie back down and pull him close.

"I want to be with you," he says, his breath soft on my cheek.

"But you also want to be with her."

He stares into my eyes and nods. "I don't want to give either of you up."

I half smile. "Isn't that a little selfish?"

"Yes." His fingers draw loops on my bare arms. "Do you want me to leave?"

Never. "No." I kiss him tenderly on the lips. "But is she really coming for the entire weekend?"

He kisses me back. "Yeah. I'm sorry. I can't tell her not to come now."

Yes, you can, I think but don't say. "Okay. No biggie." I tickle his tummy. "You gonna tuck her in and then sneak in here?"

"Yeah, right." He lays his head against the pillow. "Did you set the alarm?"

Sigh. "Yes, Russ, I set the alarm."

I am *so* bored. I can't believe I'm taking a tour of the school when I could be sleeping. It's nine o'clock Sunday morning as I trail behind the eight potential students, through the Katz building.

My entertainment is trying to guess why these people are here. Two nerd boys in navy suits and freshly shaved faces keep asking questions about how to get accepted. Losers.

Then there's the man who's already been accepted. He's about forty and he's here with his wife. I know he's been accepted, because she keeps saying it, rubbing it in to everyone else on the tour. "If we decide to go here instead of Harvard…" Blah, blah, blah.

Then there's the guy who's on the waiting list and has an

interview today. He keeps checking his watch, as though he's afraid he might be late.

There's a woman here who's on the wait list, too. She's with a nerdy-looking boyfriend who has horrendous skin. Hmm. That could have been Russ and Sharon.

I'm here to give Layla moral support. Instead of coming up with a fake persona, I've elected to keep my mouth shut.

I wonder if Sharon came to check out the campus with Russ, when he came for a tour. I can't believe I'm finally going to meet her. At last, I'll be able to check out the competition. Will she be gorgeous? Skinny? Brilliant? How will she compare to me when no longer in separate countries, but on the same floor? We'll be sharing the same bathroom. I will so not be able to brush my teeth next to her.

"Honey, what do you think of the library? Not as nice as the Harvard library," the annoying wife says.

We end up in the cafeteria, where Layla wishes the group goodbye and good luck, then bolts toward me. "What did you think?"

Today is her first tour, a practice tour for when Brad arrives. When she came back to her room with the news that he hadn't signed up for a tour, I decided to call him to encourage him.

He answered on the first ring. "Hello, may I please speak to Bradley Green?"

"Speaking."

"Hello Bradley, this is Grenadine from LWBS student services."

Layla looked like she was going to pass out. "Grenadine?" she mouthed. "You're a drink syrup?"

I hushed her away.

"Hi, Grenadine," he said. "What can I do for you?" He had a sexy voice. If it wasn't for Russ…and Layla, of course.

"I want to personally congratulate you on your LWBS acceptance," I said. "We're thrilled to have you as a prospective student. We'd like to schedule a tour of the school for you at your earliest convenience."

"Hmm. I wouldn't mind seeing the school. Do the tours run daily?"

"I…I believe the tours run daily," I repeated loudly, looking at Layla expectantly. She nodded. Then I mouthed, "What time?"

She held up three fingers.

"Every day at three," I added.

"Three is convenient," he said. "I have a meeting in Greenwich on Wednesday morning. I could be at the LWBS campus by three for a tour."

Oh. My. God. I gave Layla a thumbs-up. "Fantastic. So I'll pencil you in. Directions are on the Web site. Meet the group in the Katz building at two-fifty. Your leader will be the gorgeous blonde with the clipboard."

Layla covered her face with her hands and I hung up the phone.

Her hands started waving around the room. "How am I possibly going to be prepared to be an LWBS tour guide by Wednesday? I only know a fraction of the school's history, not nearly enough of the architecture—"

"Stop freaking out. We have to start planning the final P. Packaging."

Then she started jumping up and down on her bed, screaming that she was about to meet her husband. She froze in mid-leap, then sprinted off to the library for books on the history and architecture of LWBS, and then back to Dorothy to sign up for Wednesday's tour. Dorothy agreed, but only after Layla agreed to do the early-bird weekend tour as well (nobody likes to volunteer on the weekend). But that was fine, as it would give her a chance to practice, and that's how I came to be in the cafeteria so early on a Sunday morning, congratulating her on a job well done.

I pat her arm. "You were the best guide ever. Award winning. If I were Brad, I would certainly want to sleep with you."

She shushes me. "Fall in love with me you mean."

"Sleep with you, love you, what's the difference?"

"You are kidding, right?"

Kind of.

jamie's wake-up call

Ring.

I jump into the upright position. Who the hell is that? It's six in the morning. Oy.

"Jamie?" The voice sounds hoarse, scratchy.

It takes me a few seconds to place it. "Mom?"

"Honey. Bubbe…"

I'm now wide-awake. "Bubbe, what?"

"She had a stroke. A few hours ago."

My head pounds. Shit. "Is she…?"

"No, she's in the hospital. Miami General. In the ICU."

"I'm getting on the next flight."

"What about school?"

"Don't worry about school. Are you okay?"

She starts to cry. "No."

"Where's Dad?"

"He's talking to one of the nurses."

"Is she cute?" It's my feeble attempt at a joke. What's wrong with me? Why do I feel compelled to make people laugh, even now?

"What, dear?" She didn't hear, thank God.

I pull out my suitcase and start packing. "Okay, Mom, don't worry. Everything will be fine." I know I'm lying as I say it, but I say it anyway.

layla makes her move

"Layla, how do you not poke yourself in the eye?" Kimmy asks me. She's sitting cross-legged on my bed, watching me apply my makeup. My vanity mirror is set up on my dresser, and I've rolled my computer chair so that I'm facing it. "And how do you not blink? My eyes have a natural tendency to protect themselves when a pointy object heads in their direction."

I finish outlining half of my lower eye rim with charcoal-colored liner and move on to my Lash-a-Lot mascara. "Practice makes perfect."

Done. I roll my chair back to the desk and pivot. "How do I look?"

"The red shirt is a million times better," she says. I'd been wearing a collared white shirt under my black pantsuit, but Kimmy persuaded me to change. "Very pretty meets intellectual," she says approvingly. "Miranda meets Charlotte."

"Hey, you watched my *Sex and the City* DVDs."

"Yup," she says. "I'm halfway through season one. Not bad. A little girly, but not bad. I even got Russ to watch with me."

"Did he get any tips?" I've certainly gotten many tips. Like those fake nipples Samantha used. I wore them out once and they were hot.

"Not really," she says.

The sad tone of her voice makes me worry about her. "Are you okay? Playing the mistress getting to you?"

She waves her hand. "I'm fine."

She doesn't seem fine. More to the point, what she doesn't seem is satisfied. "You know, you've never told me how Russ is in bed."

"How does one measure if a guy is good in bed?"

Uh-oh. "I measure it by how often he makes me orgasm. How many times a night does Russ make you orgasm?"

She examines her split ends. "Not often."

So what is it exactly she sees in this cheating bastard? "How often?"

"Never."

I must not have heard that correctly. "Did you say seven?"

"No, never."

"Kimmy, my dear, that's awful. He won't commit or satisfy? Can you please dump him and date Jamie?"

She rolls her eyes. "I'm not attracted to Jamie."

"Fine. Then you have to show Russ what you like. You know, what gets you off."

Her face turns a deep shade of red. "Um…what if nothing does?"

What? "Nothing? What does that mean?"

She plays with her hair again. "It means I've never had an orgasm."

"Bullshit!"

She shrugs and I realize how insensitive I just sounded. It's just that I didn't know that a woman who never had an orgasm actually existed. I always thought it was just a myth. That's like a woman who never tried chocolate. I know there've been women who've never had a sex-induced or-gasm, but this? "You do masturbate, don't you?"

She blushes. "It doesn't do anything for me."

I can't believe this. "You haven't been doing it right, ob-viously. Have you ever tried a vibrator?"

"No. Have you?"

Have I? Have I tried chocolate? "Of course, I have." I point to my sex drawer. "I have a few in there. Do you want to see?"

"Um, sure."

I open the drawer and pull out my Zoombuster and my Magic Banana. "Both are my favorites, but the Magic Banana is better for school. It's heavier but quieter. It's modeled after the Holy Grail of penises, one that curves up at the end so it hits the G-spot during missionary-position intercourse. Some of my girlfriends have claimed they've seen one, but I think it only exists in vibrators. Do you want to see the at-tachments?" I should try juggling these things. I haven't prac-ticed my juggling in a while. I don't want to forget my new skill already.

"Definitely not." She looks so amazed that I almost laugh.

"It's all about the perfect orgasm," I explain.

"I'd settle for any orgasm," she says wistfully.

"I think we should order you one."

"Don't you find it…gross?"

"Gross? No. Celebrating my sexual vitality? Yes." I point to the *Sex and the City* DVD. "Watch episode nine. You'll change your mind." If Charlotte can become obsessed with the rabbit, so can Kimmy. It seems that my next order of business is encouraging Kimmy's personal empowerment. But at the moment I have to go play tour guide. "And I'll send you some sex-toy Web sites so you can see all the var-ious options."

"Why not?" she says, and laughs. "Hey, I wonder if any of this will help us with my work group's Marketing project. We're doing female condoms."

That is so much fun. I wish I were in their group. "Lucky you. My boring work group is doing a new soda. Hey, can you get me samples?" I glance at my watch. "I'm off to meet my destiny. When you leave, make sure the door is locked, all right?" I dart to the bathroom, careful not to blink so that my mascara doesn't smear.

Jamie is getting out of the shower stall, wearing his bathrobe and flip-flops. "I thought you already had a job," he says.

"Jamie, you're looking at the new tour guide for prospective students." I'm about to tell him about Brad, when I notice that his eyes are bright red. "You okay? Did you get shampoo in your eyes or something?"

He takes a deep breath. "My grandmother had a stroke last night."

How awful. I pat his shoulder. "I'm so sorry. How is she?"

"Not great. I'm flying back to Miami on the five o'clock. It's the first flight I can get a seat on."

"You are? What about class?"

He shrugs. "It's just class. I'll figure it out."

"I hope she gets better."

"Me, too." His eyes fill with tears. "I have to get ready. Have a good tour."

"Thanks."

He leaves the bathroom, and I watch the door sway behind him. I hope he's not gone too long. You can't miss weeks of school without falling behind. Is he going to stay there until she dies? Until she's better? What if she stays in limbo for months? Will he drop out? I'm feeling panicky just thinking about it. But no time to worry about it now—it's already a quarter of. Time for my tour. I finish getting ready and head to the meeting spot. Seven people are already standing around waiting. Two single guys, one single girl, a father and his daughter, and a couple. No Bradley.

"Hi," I say to the too-small group. "I'm Layla, your tour guide." What if he doesn't show?

"I love the name Layla," the father says.

He might still show. We still have—I frantically peek at my watch—two minutes.

The father starts to sing the Eric Clapton song, and I'm reminded of Jamie. I hope he's okay.

It doesn't look like Bradley is going to show. And I've wasted five days of my life learning LWBS architecture. Five days that I could have spent elsewhere. Like in the library. I begin reading the names off my clipboard. Slowly.

One minute.

"Sandy Johnson?"

"Here," the father says. Oh. I had assumed Sandy was the daughter. That's nice. A father coming back to school.

And then he pats the daughter on the behind. Oops. Guess she's not a daughter. What is it then? A second wife? A midlife crisis? New wife and career change? I hope they don't plan on living at the Zoo.

I continue reading the names on the list. The minute hand on my watch officially declares that it's now three-oh-one. He's late. He's not coming. Everyone is here but him. "We're missing one," I say. I look down at my paper as if I don't know who it is. "Bradley Green?" I say, looking around. He probably chose Harvard and blew us off. Downhearted, I say, "Well, I guess that's it. Will you all please follow—"

And there he is.

Pushing through the turn door, snow sprinkled on his head. He's just as handsome and perfect as I remember. And he's smiling at me. My body freezes. I force myself to speak. "Mr. Green. You almost missed us."

He removes his coat and tosses it over his arm. "Thanks for waiting." And then suddenly, he's standing beside me. Less than a foot away. Up close, I can see he has a cleft in his chin and a dimple on each cheek. His skin looks soft, as if he shaved only moments ago.

"My pleasure." I lose myself in his ice-green eyes, which

are remarkably framed by thick, dark brown lashes. He smiles again. His eyes flick to my exposed cleavage and then back up. I guess the red shirt was the right choice. "Now, if you'll all follow me, we'll start our tour." And hopefully our love affair.

I lead the group to the auditorium. Bradley sidles up next to me. "Grenadine was right. You are gorgeous."

I smile and bat my eyes. This is going to be easier than I thought.

"Want to grab a quick coffee?" he asks after the tour.

I try to keep my voice nonchalant. "Sure." It worked. I can't believe this insane plan worked.

He orders a café latte and I order a cappuccino.

I sit down at a table in the back, concentrating on my posture. "So, Bradley, where are you from?" As if I don't already know his exact address on Seventy-sixth.

"Manhattan," he says, smiling.

You don't say! "Yeah? Me, too. When I'm not here, I mean."

"Where do you live?"

"The Upper East Side. You?"

"Same. On Seventy-sixth and Park. You?"

"Eighty-third and Park," I say.

"We're neighbors."

"What college did you go to?"

"Columbia," I say. "You?"

"Yale." See how perfect we are for each other? "This is surprisingly good coffee," he says.

I lean over to take a sip from mine. Screw my posture. Might as well give him an eyeful. "So tell me, Bradley, where else did you apply?" I've decided to ask him about everything I already know so I don't mess up and mention it as a matter of fact.

"For B-school? Columbia, Harvard, Wharton and Stern. I've been accepted everywhere except Harvard. I'm on the waiting list."

"What's your first choice?"

"Harvard." He leans toward me over the table. "Am I allowed to say that here?"

I wink. "Yeah. I'm sure most people here would have gone to Harvard if they'd gotten in. I didn't even apply."

He looks surprised. "No? How come?"

I tell him about how both my parents graduated from LWBS, and we chat about our families and our career goals until our third cups of coffee are empty, and the sky beyond the window has turned midnight-blue. We toss our garbage away and stroll toward the door.

"It was wonderful to meet you, Layla."

"It was nice to meet you, too." Is that it? That can't be it. "I hope I'll see you here next year."

"You just might," he says. "At least now there's an incentive. Besides the coffee. Are you in New York this weekend?"

"I…yes." As of this second.

"Do you think you'll have time to get together?"

I try to appear as though this isn't the question I've been waiting for all year. "I don't see why not. When were you thinking?"

"Dinner on Friday night?"

"I can do dinner."

He smiles and pulls his PalmPilot from his coat pocket. "Terrific. Want to beam me your number?"

I whip out my Palm and beam it to him.

He kisses me softly on the cheek. "Till then."

Yes!

kimmy works it

Normally I do either the step class or Pilates class. Today I do both.

"Lift that leg," Gossip, the Pilates instructor, tells me. So I lift.

"Who wants strong legs?" he calls out to the class. I do! I do! In case I have to kick Sharon's ass.

The nerve of her invading my turf. So what that she doesn't know I exist? Not true. She must know that I exist, just not that I'm sleeping with her boyfriend. She must have asked him about his learning group. Surely he mentioned me. How does she picture me in her head? I wonder if he described me.

"Hold it, baby, hold it." The instructor is the most stereotypical gay man I've ever seen. He's wearing pink leggings and a tight purple tank top. He goes by the name, Gossip. Yes, Gossip. It says that on the class schedule.

Maybe Russ told Sharon I was gay. Maybe he told her that Lauren and I are partners. Either that, or he told her I'm ugly. Or stupid.

When Gossip finally tells us to have a fabulous weekend

and make sure to make a lot of love, I hit the gym showers. I stuffed my knapsack with all my shower stuff, hair dryer, change of clothes and makeup. I don't normally bring all that paraphernalia to the gym, but I don't know what time *she's* coming in today. And I can't have *her* walking in all dressed up and crossing my path while I look like a shlump. No, way. Russ will obviously be comparing us, the way men must compare their equipment standing at the urinal.

After showering, I blow-dry my hair straight. Then do my best makeup application. I skip the eyeliner, since it scares me despite Layla's lesson. Sweet Layla. She tried to convince me to come with her to New York.

"No way," I told her. "I have to check out the competition." I was lying on her bed watching her pack, drinking tea.

She folded a green shirt into a perfect square and carefully placed it into her suitcase. "You're being morbid. You're going to be alone here, miserable. Why do you want to put yourself through that?"

"I'm not running away. Besides, you have a date."

"I'll cancel."

I threw a pillow at her. "Cancel? After we pulled off the best advertising campaign ever? Are you on crack?" I still couldn't believe we did it. I come up with the best strategies! I must be a strategy whiz. Martin seems to think so, too—he gave me an A on my last assignment. Yes, an A. I almost asked him if he was sure it was my paper.

My strategy for this weekend is to look superhot. I finish blow-drying and admire the effect in the mirror. Beat that, Sharon. As the final touch, I apply my new lipstick. It's red and called Irresistible. I spent twenty-six dollars on this tube, more than I've ever spent on any piece of makeup, so it had better work. I'm wearing my good jeans, and a tight sweater that shows a little cleavage but not enough to make me look slutty. I'm a ten out of ten, if I must say so myself.

I wrap my red puffy jacket tightly around me and head

back to the dorm. Not that I have anything to do. Or anyone to do. Layla left me the key to her room. Maybe I'll borrow her Magic Banana.

I can just imagine telling my germ-phobic friend that I borrowed her most personal of items.

Ew. No, if I were going to use one, I would buy my own. If I were going to use one. Which I'm not. But maybe I should. Maybe it'll bring on my period, which I haven't gotten in forever. I stopped taking the pills continuously earlier this week so that I would get it—now that Sharon is here for a few days and I have a sex break, it's a good time to get it over with—but it didn't come. What I don't understand is how Russ hasn't noticed that I haven't had it in months. I'm probably just infertile.

Maybe Russ secretly hopes that I'm pregnant?

My running shoes have lost most of their traction and I nearly slip on the ice. I need to buy new shoes. As if I have the money for that.

Almost there. As I'm about to open the door, a cab pulls up in front of the dorm.

There's a woman in the back seat. My heart stops. Sharon.

russ almost blows his cover

Oh, man. She's late. Why is she late? Better question, why is she still coming? My television is on channel 2, the door channel. I'm watching for her arrival. I can't believe I didn't tell her not to come. I should have insisted on buying a plane ticket and going home for the weekend, instead of putting Kimmy through this.

Nick hurries into the foyer. Then he searches his pocket for the key, drops it, picks it up and goes inside. Bastard is still tanned from Australia. Maybe he's fake tanning.

On Monday I thought I was getting out of it. Sharon called me with the flu. I recommended she stay home and get better. I'd even come to see her. She said, no way. She'd get better.

She got better.

I open my food drawer to see if there's anything worth eating. I've already finished a bag of chips and a liter of warm Pepsi that was stashed under my bed.

I was hoping that Kimmy would take off for the week-end. Meeting up in the bathroom might be mildly uncomfortable. Though meeting up in my room could be fun, the three of us rolling around on my skinny bed.

Yeah, right.

Maybe I should break up with Sharon. Maybe I should break up with Kimmy.

Maybe I should make a goddamn decision.

I pace the length of my room. It's not long enough for a good pace. I'd like to pace the hallway, but Sharon needs to buzz from downstairs to get in. I've been stuck in this room for an hour. I have to take a piss.

Kimmy is in the foyer. Her hair is shining, and she's about to unlock the door, when someone enters, rolling a suitcase.

Sharon.

Shit.

Kimmy turns around and stares. Does she know? Sharon's lips are moving. She seems to be asking Kimmy a question. Kimmy nods and says something back. I think I'm going to hurl. What are they saying? It's V-Day, not D-Day!

Kimmy unlocks the door, and Sharon follows her inside.

What do I do?

I pick at my face.

Knock, knock.

I am not opening that door. What if Kimmy spilled the beans? And now they're both standing there waiting to roast me?

"One sec," I say, and I open it.

It's Sharon. Just Sharon. No one else in sight. She's smiling, her hair moist from melting snowflakes, and she looks beautiful. I wrap my arms around her and pull her to me. She smells like home. Actually she smells like airplane. In mid-hug I twirl her around to scan the room to insure that everything is presentable. Bed made. Drawers closed. No boxers on the floor. No condoms, God forbid. I kick the door closed. We're kissing, more kissing, it's her, here, she tastes perfect, her shirt is off, my shirt is off, our pants are off.

Now the floor is a mess.

And we're on the bed, me on top, and then I'm inside her and we're making love, fast, it's been over a month. For her, anyway.

"Do you want to come now?" I ask.

"Later. Don't worry. Go ahead, come now, it's okay, I figured we should get the first time out of the way, since it's been so long for you."

Probably not the best time to tell her I had sex less than twenty-four hours ago with the woman she just met downstairs. Now that was wild sex. Kimmy was on top but facing my feet. I came in about five seconds. Stop imagining sex with Kimmy. Stop. Can't. I come, and hold Sharon tightly. "Well," I say. I run my fingers over her earlobe. "Nice to see you."

She wiggles to get comfortable beside me. "Not much room in here, is there?"

"Oh, it's fine." I'm about to add, you get used to it, but I catch myself in time.

"I can't believe I almost didn't make it because of the flu. It was so gross. I was puking all over the place."

Now there's an image I'd rather forget. "But you're here," I say. "You made it."

"Made it."

"Made it straight to my room. Um…how did you find my room, anyway?"

She runs her fingers through my hair. "A girl in the foyer offered to show me the way. She knew you, actually. When I told her who I was looking for, she said that I must be Sharon. You must talk about me a lot, huh?"

"Uh. Yeah."

D-Day diverted.

layla gets bubbly

"You look marvelous, darling," Ronnie, my little sister, says, patting down my hair.

I'm sitting at my vanity table in my room in Manhattan, enjoying the space, lining my eyes. "Thanks."

In the mirror she looks like a miniature version of me. A few years younger, her facial structure is daintier, her eyes smaller, her hair shorter. She graduated from Brown last May and is now at Teacher's College. I tried to talk her out of it. With so many options available to her, why does she want to be just a teacher? But she ignored me. She sets her glass of champagne on my night table.

"That better be on a coaster," I say. The apartment is not quite in the condition I left it in. I've noticed numerous scratches on the coffee table.

"We're going to head over to Mack's tonight," she says. "So you can be alooooooone with Bradley."

Mack is Ronnie's long-haired boyfriend who isn't good enough for her.

"Have you spoken to Mom?" I ask. "Is she in the city?"

Ronnie rolls her eyes. "Who knows? I haven't heard from her in months."

"Don't be rude," I say, and pick up the phone. "Let's call her now."

Her voice mail picks up. I leave a message.

"I'm shocked," Ronnie mutters, and walks away.

"She'll call us back later," I call after her.

"Whatever."

At five to eight, the doorman calls up. "Bradley is here."

"Thank you, send him up."

When the buzzer sounds, I'm balancing myself on the arm of the couch, holding a glass of champagne. I can't believe this is happening. Bradley Green is picking me up on the eve of Valentine's Day. The hockey game is blaring in the background from the flat-screen TV. Ronnie opens the door.

Bradley is wearing a black suit, and is holding a bouquet of roses. A dozen long-stemmed red roses. How perfect! He tugs one out of the bouquet and hands it to Ronnie. "It's a pleasure to meet you," he says.

"How sweet!" my sister shrieks.

I approach the door, and he plants a kiss on my cheek. My entire face tingles.

"For you," he says, handing me the bouquet.

Aw. "Thank you."

As I find a vase to put the roses in, I hear him discussing the hockey game with Mack. Seems like he knows just what to say to everyone.

By the time we leave, both Mack and Ronnie are swooning. When Brad's not looking, Ronnie mouths, "Wow." I believe they are impressed.

In the elevator, I wonder if we're going to walk to the restaurant or flag a cab. But a black sedan outside the door answers the question. Is that his car? Did he hire it for the night? I'm feeling mildly light-headed. I'm unclear if it's from the champagne or the roses/suit/car combination.

He takes me to La Grenouille, and does everything right. He knows his wines, listens while I talk, asks all kinds of questions. After dinner, he drops a platinum American Express card on the table, and asks, "Would you like to go to Plush?"

Plush is the new VIP hot spot on Forty-second Street. This is turning into the best Valentine's weekend ever.

jamie's
valentine's day curse

This is officially the worst Valentine's Day ever.

I lift the phone in the ICU waiting room and wait for the nurse to answer.

"ICU?" the nurse says.

"Hi, Donna, it's Jamie. Can I come in?"

"Of course. Your mom is here."

"I know. Thanks." I rub the antibacterial cream into my hands and open the door. I wave to the nurses.

My mother is sitting on the wooden chair in my bubbe's room, staring vacantly out the window. Her eyes are heavily shadowed, as though she hasn't slept in months.

I sit on the metal stool beside her. "How is she?"

"The same," she answers, her voice shaking. "Terrible."

My grandmother is lying on the bed, eyes closed, too thin, too pale. Her heart is too weak. Her almost transparent skin sags around the thin bones of her face. There is nothing the doctors can do.

"What did the nurse say?" I ask softly.

"Any time now."

I'm not shocked. You always expect your grandparents to die. My other grandparents are already gone. But they'd always been old. But not my bubbe. I thought she'd be around forever.

Okay, I can deal with her leaving, but I can't deal with it if she can't. I want her to call me over and tell me it's okay. That she's okay about dying. That she's looking forward to the next step. Looking forward to being with Zadie. That she's not scared. I can deal with no longer seeing her anymore, but I can't deal with her fear. After going through the Holocaust, and burying her husband, I can't bear to have her go through any more pain. How horribly unfair.

I'm exhausted. I've been making jokes for days, trying to keep my bubbe going, trying to make her laugh. Yesterday, I even juggled bananas for her. She tried to smile.

I hate being here.

I hand my mother a heart-shaped chocolate. She doesn't smile.

Valentine's Day has always been disastrous. At ten, Maddy Weiner, the tiny brunette who sat in front of me in the fourth grade, ripped my homemade Valentine's Day card in quarters and tossed it like confetti around the schoolyard. I went to the nurse and told her I had to go home, because my heart was broken.

In high school, I sent a dozen red roses and a singing telegram to my girlfriend of two weeks, right in the middle of biology. She broke up with me at lunch.

And then there was the bike accident. Which happened to be on February 14.

All in all, never a successful holiday for me. But I've never felt more alone.

I wonder if Layla misses me.

I take my mother's hand and squeeze. And we wait.

kimmy is pissed

I'm lying on Layla's bed, slightly drunk from a bottle of Chardonnay I'd bought in a futile attempt to cheer myself up, flipping through channels, trying to find something on TV that isn't about stupid Valentine's Day.

Irresistible, my ass. That lipstick is going right in the garbage.

Everyone else in the world has something to do tonight. Even Nick and Lauren have dates. With two undergrad roommates, oddly. And I have nothing. I have to pee, but I'm afraid to run into Russ and his precious Sharon. I crept out of the building at ten a.m. and spent the day at the library, and so far I've managed to avoid them. I'd planned on showing up in places I'd thought they'd be, so that Russ could compare us in the flesh (and thus find her lacking), but I couldn't bear to see them together, laughing and kissing, arms intertwined.

It's now almost midnight and I can't even see what's going on in the common room downstairs, because what if Russ and Sharon walk by and see me sprawled pathetically on the infested couch, stuffing my face with chips?

I flip the channel again and see Russ and Sharon in the entranceway.

Oh. My. God.

I still can't believe this average albeit attractive woman is *the* Sharon. When I met her in the entrance the other day I was shocked. *This* is my rival? *This* is the other woman?

I should have told her right then and there who *I* was.

Okay, fine, technically I'm the other woman, but nevertheless, she's not what I expected. I thought she'd be tall and blond and waiflike, but she she's kind of average. Like Joey from *Dawson's Creek* but with less angst. She has shoulder-length brown hair, big brown eyes and a small slightly turned-up nose.

He opens the door for her, slowly kissing the spot on her neck between her chin and scarf.

I don't want to see this. I don't want to see them all loving and happy.

I keep watching.

She takes off her gloves and runs her right hand through his hair.

My eyes fill with tears, angry tears, sad tears, the screen blurs, and the next thing I know they're gone.

How could he kiss her like that? How can he act like he loves her but then sleep with me? What is wrong with him?

Why do I let him get away with it?

Right now they're climbing the stairs. I should meet them at the top. I should tell him to go fuck himself. I should tell her what he's been doing—screwing me. I should shake my fist and scream and make her realize the truth, make them both feel as shitty as I do.

Maybe I will.

I smooth my hair and slide out of Layla's room.

The hallway is empty and I stomp toward the staircase. I open the stairway door, listening to their voices coming from the second floor.

"I think I had too much wine," she says, giggling.

"You only had two glasses," he answers, and from where I am, I can see him patting her on the head.

"I'm a cheap date," she says. Then she adds, "I had a terrific time tonight."

I clench my hands into fists and anchor them to my hips.

Sharon stumbles over a step and giggles again. "I'd better not get sick tonight," she says, still laughing.

"I'll take care of you," he answers.

They're about to turn the corner in the stairwell, where they'll see me. Any second now.

I think I'm going to be sick.

I can't do this.

I step out of the stairwell, back into the hallway, unlock my door and, just as I hear them approaching, I close my door, tears streaming down my face.

jamie thinks about life

One shovel of earth. Two.

The rabbi is saying the mourners' prayer, and my mother is tightly holding onto my father.

My bubbe died at eleven-forty Saturday night. I was downstairs getting my mother a hot chocolate. Bubbe was sleeping. I came back to the room and found chaos—my mother was wailing, my sisters and niece had shown up and they were also crying, and the doctor was trying to calm everyone down. I was drowning in both panic and relief. Relief that she is no longer afraid.

No more fear. Now she's in a box, buried next to my grandfather, whose headstone reads, Abraham Rosinsky, 1912–1990. Summary of their lives: they married in Warsaw in 1937, survived the camps, met up again in 1946, emigrated to America in 1948, had two kids, my mother and my uncle, had seven grandkids and are survived by six of them.

It comes down to that, a summary.

Is she with my grandfather now? I don't believe in an afterlife, but what do I know? Did my bubbe believe in one?

Maybe she did. Maybe she wasn't afraid to die. I wish I had asked her.

How do you ask someone who is about to die if she's afraid?

If I had really wanted to know, I would have asked.

I glance around at the clusters of gravestones. Two rows over, a tombstone says Nathan Mandel, 1975–1992. Poor Nathan Mandel. How did he die at seventeen? What happened to ill-fated Nathan Mandel? Leukemia? Car accident? Drug overdose?

The sun is shining directly on my head, burning my scalp. The bright weather makes the cemetery seem almost obscene. My mother grips my hand tighter.

My bubbe's death is sad, but I wouldn't call it a tragedy. She had a full life. Nathan Mandel, that was a tragedy.

But why is longevity important when we're all going to die, anyway? Is the purpose of life merely life? What about courage and integrity? What about loving and being loved?

I feel a rush of panic. Life is short, and I don't want to waste it. I want to make sure that every day is filled with things that make me and others happy.

Layla. Why haven't I told her how I felt about her?

When I called the dorm earlier today, wanting to hear her voice, I got her machine: "Hi! This is Layla. I'm in New York for the weekend. You can call me on my cell at 212-555-6782 or leave a message. And happy Valentine's Day!"

She was probably in New York for another interview. Good for her! I smiled at her chirpiness, then hung up before saying anything. I didn't know what to say. I debated calling her in New York, but decided against it. What would I say to her? Standing here in the hot sunlight, looking at the coffin and the gravestones, I know what I want to tell her, but it's the sort of thing that should be said in person, not over the phone.

I want to tell her I love her.

russ gets nailed

"Russ, sweetie, time to wake up. It's already afternoon. Happy President's Day."

I blink my eyes open and pat Kimmy's hair.

My eyes shoot open. Oh, man. *Sharon's* hair. *Sharon's* hair, not Kimmy's.

My heart speeds up. Better hope I don't confuse their names out loud. I open my mouth to say something but then close it, not trusting my own voice.

Having Sharon here is confusing the hell out of me. On the one hand, I love seeing her. How could I not? I love those ears. On the other hand, having her in such close vicinity to Kimmy fills me with dread. Don't like when worlds collide.

She sits up and stretches. "What do you want to do today?"

"Relax?" Let my heart rate go back to normal, for starters. I need to get out of the Zoo. Out of the bed I've slept in with Kimmy. It's freaking me out. "Let's go shower, then take a walk and get some lunch."

We get out of bed and Sharon starts straightening the

linen. She reaches between the comforter and wall to pull out the pillow that fell over. "Russ?"

"Yeah?" I say while searching for a clean towel.

"What's this?"

She's eyeing me suspiciously and holding the DVD jacket of *Sex and the City,* season two.

Shit. Kimmy must have left it here.

Now why would I be watching season two of *Sex and the City?* As far as Sharon knows I've never even seen season one. There's no superhero in *Sex and the City.*

Her eyes are squinting in mistrust.

Shit. Shit. Shit. The only reason I would I have *Sex and the City* here is because I was watching it with a chick.

Or…

"I borrowed it from a female friend to use as porn," I blurt. Heart pounding. What the hell did I just say? That's just gross. Did she buy it?

She continues staring at me, then shakes her head. "That's so pathetic."

"Yeah, well, it's been a long time. And I need to release myself sometimes."

She laughs, tiptoes over to me and kisses me on the lips. "You should call me next time. We can have—" she lets her hand roam over the seat of my pants "—phone sex."

How did I manage to turn a potential disaster into phone sex, eh? I am a superhero. "Shower and then lunch?"

"Can we shower together?"

She loves showering together. I don't. I get cold while I'm waiting for her to rinse out the conditioner.

"I only have one pair of flip-flops," I say.

She swats me lightly with my one clean towel, grabs the flip-flops and heads to the bathroom.

Five minutes later there's a knock on the door.

Kimmy. Oh, man. This is not a good plan.

"Hi," she says. "Your *girlfriend* was preoccupied so I thought I'd say hi."

"Hi. All good?" I scan down the hallway to make sure Sharon isn't on her way back. I don't want to engage her in a conversation. I don't want Sharon to even see her here. She'll be able to tell if she sees us together. I know she will.

"I'm okay." She tries to make eye contact but I'm not letting her. I can't flirt with her when Sharon's here. Just can't. I feel bad for Sharon. Hell, I feel bad for Kimmy, too.

She touches my arm. Is she crazy? I shake her off.

"This isn't a good time," I say, lowering my voice. "Can we talk later?"

She steps back like I slapped her. Her eyes fill with tears, and she turns and starts walking away. Oh, man.

"Wait, Kimmy, don't be mad," I say to the back of her head. I hate what I'm doing. To them both.

She shrugs without turning around.

"Can't we talk about this tomorrow?"

She doesn't answer and continues walking.

I'm about to go after her, when Sharon appears at the other end of the hall, in her towel.

Shit. Did she hear?

Kimmy raises her arm and gives me the finger.

Oh, man. Did Sharon see that?

I guess not. Sharon waves at me, and continues her journey down the hall. "My feet just don't feel clean when I wear flip-flops," she says, laughing.

I turn off the shower water and try to turn off my brain, as well. That was so close. I can't believe how near I came to blowing everything.

I wrap my towel around my waist and peer out of the stall. Not in the mood for another Kimmy run-in. I'll deal with it tomorrow.

I hurry back to my room and unlock the door. My stomach grumbles. "Are you starving, too?" I ask Sharon. Sharon is sitting on the bed, wearing just a bra and underwear, staring at something in her hand.

She's staring at a condom wrapper.

Oh, man. Shit. Shit, shit, shit.

Sharon and I don't use condoms.

An icy chill travels down my body.

She looks up at me, her face pale, her lips quivering. "My hair gel rolled under the bed. And look what I found."

"Sharon, I…"

She tries to throw it at me, but it falls pathetically to the floor. Her hand starts to shake. "Are you cheating on me?" she squeaks.

Shit. Shit, shit, shit.

I open my mouth, close it, then say, "Yes."

I lean against the door for balance, then slide down to the floor. "I'm sorry…I…" My voice trails off. Shit, shit, shit. "I'll stop."

"Who is she?" she asks, her voice rising.

"Kimmy."

She flings herself off the bed, picks up the wrapper and waves it in the air. "Kimmy, the one who called you New Year's Eve?"

I nod, my throat too tight to speak. "I'll stop," I breathe out again.

"You'll stop?" She holds her stomach, and I wonder if she's going to be sick. "You'll stop?" she repeats, screeching. "Well, thank you, I *so* appreciate that, you slime bucket. How often, Russ? How many times did you do it? How many times has this *fucking* happened?"

Oh, man. "A few," I whisper meekly.

"A few with Kimmy? Or a few women?" Her eyes look wild, and her hands are waving all over the room.

"Just Kimmy," I croak. I don't know if just Kimmy is better or worse.

"I can't believe you could sleep with me all weekend, even though you've been sleeping with someone else." She covers her mouth and groans. "We don't even use condoms, you jackass, and you know why? Because I *fucking* trusted you!"

I'm crumpled on the floor, feeling sick to my stomach. "I'm sorry. I'm so sorry. But you don't have to worry. Kimmy and I always used condoms, I swear."

Her hands are shaking. "Yeah? Did you use condoms when she gave you head? I've taught Sex Ed. If you get something from that slut, so help me, I'm going to kill you, do you understand?"

Bile rises in my throat. "I love you," I say, because I mean it and because I don't know what else to say.

She kicks me in the thigh. Holy shit. She's never kicked anyone in her entire life.

She kicks me again. Ouch. Good thing she's not wearing shoes. "Fuck you!" she screams.

"I love you," I repeat desperately.

She starts getting into her jeans. "Save it. If you loved me, you wouldn't have slept with someone else. End of *fucking* story."

"I'm sorry," I say. "I'm so sorry. I love you."

"Too *fucking* bad." She opens her suitcase and throws her hair dryer inside.

I have to stop her. "Don't leave," I say, sadness welling in my throat. What do I do? I don't know what to do. I jump up and try to hug her.

She pushes me away and sobs, tears running freely down her cheeks as she finishes getting dressed. "I thought I was going to marry you." She looks up at me, and her wet eyes look beautiful.

I gently touch her arm. I want to tell her it didn't mean anything, but I can't. It did, and I can't lie to her anymore.

She zips up her bag and shakes her head. "It's over, Russ.

I can't even look at you. Being in the same room as you makes me want to throw up."

"Please don't go," I whisper. "Don't leave like this."

She takes a deep breath and shakes her head. I don't move. She pushes me out of the way and opens the door.

"Your flight isn't until tonight," I say, desperate to make her stay.

She walks out the door and doesn't look back. And then she's gone. The hallway is silent. Oh, man. I feel dizzy and lean against the wall. That was so goddamn dramatic. Surreal. I can't believe what just happened. I go back to my room. Why didn't I check under the bed? How could I have left that wrapper?

I sit on my bed. Then stand up. Then sit again. A two-hundred-pound weight is pressed against my chest. My head feels like someone is squeezing it.

I lie on my bed and spend the next few hours picking at my face and staring at the ceiling.

kimmy gets lucky

I'm lying in bed staring at the ceiling. I hate him. How could he jerk me around like that? How could he ignore me?

I hate him, I hate him, I hate him.

There's a knock on the door.

"Not here," I say. I don't feel like talking to anyone. It's not like it's Russ. He's too busy with his *girlfriend*. No time for me. I'm sick of it. So sick of it. He can have his precious Sharon. I don't care. He can go to hell.

"It's me," Russ says.

Huh? What, did he send Sharon on an errand so he could get a quick blow job? "Go away."

"I need to talk to you."

"I don't want to talk to you." I can be strong.

Pause. "I told Sharon the truth. She left. Can I come in, please?"

What? I scurry off my bed and open the door. He looks sad and disheveled.

He told her. He broke up with her.

He told her. He broke up with her.

I wrap my arms around his neck and pull him inside. He chose me. I can't believe it. A helium balloon of happiness rises in my chest. I kiss his neck.

He loves me.

I nap and wake up feeling happy. It doesn't matter that he was a jerk. He realized his mistake and chose me! I turn over and see that he's staring at the ceiling.

"Do you want me to set the alarm?" I ask. What I'm really asking is, Do you still plan to sneak out?

"What time is class tomorrow?" he asks.

"Ten-thirty."

"Why don't we sleep in and get up at ten?"

I fall back asleep, smiling, my head nuzzled in his arms.

When the phone rings the next morning I'm still smiling. I reach across Russ for the phone. The call display says O'Donnel. Oh. My. God. "Hello?"

"Hello, may I please speak with Kimmy Nailer, please?"

Please be yes. Please be yes. Please don't ruin this perfect morning. Damn you O'Donnel, give me good news. "Speaking," I say, my voice shaking.

"Hi, Kimmy, this is Claire Moss from HR at O'Donnel. We're pleased to be offering you a position of summer associate."

Oh. My. God. Hurray!

"The summer program is ten weeks, beginning June first. Your salary has been set at fifteen hundred dollars a week."

I can pay back some of my loans! "I accept!"

Russ's eyes pop open. I give him a thumbs-up and mouth, *O'Donnel.*

"Wonderful," Claire says. "The only provision is that you'll need to maintain a B average in your classes."

"That won't be a problem." Better not be.

"Let me confirm your address," she says, "and we'll send you all the necessary paperwork."

When I hang up, Russ hugs me. "Congrats," he says. "I'm proud of you."

He must have gotten in, too, right? "Check your messages," I urge.

He hesitates, then picks up the phone and dials his voice mail. Two minutes later he smiles.

"I got it, too," he says, looking dazed.

"Wahoo!" I scream. I don't believe it. How amazing is this day?

He scoops me up and whirls me like the twister ride at a fair. I bend my knees so they don't hit the wall.

I can't believe how good my life just got. He broke up with Sharon. For me. We both got jobs. In New York. Where we'll be working together all summer. Maybe we can even live together…. Maybe I should wait a day or two before bringing that up. Don't want to push my luck.

We walk to the showers smiling, his arm tightly around me. Two people from another Block spot us. "Morning," I sing.

"Morning," they say, eyebrows raised.

I think we're finally out of the closet.

jamie returns to the zoo

I walk up the stairs of the Zoo, feeling dazed. It's only been a week and a half, but it feels like I've been gone for months. I hear laughing through the rooms, doors slamming, people walking from one room to another. I wonder if anyone even realized I was gone.

I drop my bags off in my room, and then try to snap out of it. My family will be fine. They don't need me watching over them. I'll be back in two weeks to make sure they're okay.

At least I'm not behind on my assignments. I sent them all in by e-mail. Right now I have to get my life in order. I need to talk to Layla. I knock on her door. I'm not sure what I want to say to her, but I want to see her.

"One second!" she yells. I hear her laughing inside. She opens the door and hugs me. Tight. Maybe she feels the same? "Hi! You're back! How are you?" The phone is cradled between her ear and neck. "Hon, let me call you back, okay?"

Hon? Who's hon?

"Five minutes, I promise." She giggles. "Me, too. Bye." She

hangs up the phone and hugs me. "Jamie, how are you?" She pulls back and puts on her somber face. "You doing all right?"

"I'm all right. Who's hon?"

She claps her hands. "It's him! The essay guy, Bradley Green." She mouths the word *essay* so no one in the hallway will hear. Not that there's anyone in the hallway. "Come in. I'll bring you up to speed."

As usual, her room looks as though she's spent all day organizing and fluffing it. I flop on her bed and make myself comfortable. Who knows? Maybe she'll join me.

Nope. She sits on her desk chair. "First tell me about you. How's your family doing?"

"They've been better." They were better when more of them were alive. "It was all pretty sudden."

"Poor you. How are you?"

I don't feel like talking about me. "I want to know about Bradley. *Nu?*"

"He's wonderful," she gushes. "I met him when I did the prospective students tour. Then I met him in the City last weekend."

Last weekend. When I called. "That's where you were."

"What do you mean?"

"I called you."

"You did?"

"Yeah." Should have left a message. Should have told her how I felt two weeks ago, then maybe she would never have gone to meet this Bradley guy. Maybe she would have chosen me. "Never mind. So you went to visit him last weekend."

"Yes, and he took me to a fabulous restaurant, and we had an incredible time."

"Get some action?" I lift my eyebrows suggestively. My stomach falls simultaneously.

She smiles. "Wouldn't you like to know."

Bradley Green. Kermit had it wrong. It is easy being green.

I feel an unmanly lump in the back of my throat. Oy. "What else is going on? Russ and Kimmy still on the sly?"

"No, that's the other big news. He broke up with Sharon. And now he and Kimmy are all over each other in class. You'll see tomorrow. And they both got offers at O'Donnel."

Throat lump increases exponentially. "Am I the only one without a job?" I need to figure out what I want to do.

"No, I don't think Lauren got one yet."

"But she'll take any job. She swings all ways."

Layla giggles. "We're all going to the Monsoon Bar on Johnson Street tonight to celebrate. And it's Nick's birthday. You'll come, won't you? We missed you. We miss our comedian."

I fake smile. "Celebrate we shall." What's not to celebrate?

kimmy has a *boyfriend*

I'm sitting next to Jamie along the bar. "What do you call a four-hundred-pound stripper?"

"What?"

"Broke." I laugh, waiting for him to join in. Instead, he sits with a dump-truck-just-ran-over-my-puppy look on his face. "You okay?"

My adorable *boyfriend* and Nick are playing darts and doing tequila shots, and Layla is on her cell phone, talking to Brad. I love my boyfriend. I started taking my pills again so my *boyfriend* and I can start having sex without a condom.

"Fine," Jamie says. "What about you? You've hardly touched your beer, and we've been here two hours. You feeling okay?"

"Ha-ha, funny man. I can tell you're masking your pain with jokes. Are you going to tell me what's wrong?"

"Glenda," he says to the waitress, "can I have a beer?"

"What?" I say. "You're drinking? You don't drink."

"I do now," he says, staring at Layla.

Huh? "Do you…do you like Layla?"

He shrugs.

What? Since when? What about *me?* "But she's seeing someone."

"Thanks, Sherlock."

"So that's why you're upset," I say, and take a sip.

"You are quick."

I could do without the attitude. "Stop being such an ass, Jamie. I'm trying to help."

He shrugs. "What can I do? It's not like someone like her would ever go for someone like me. I'm not quite her handsome knight in shining Armani, am I?"

Not quite. "You never know."

He's gazing at her with big cartoon puppy eyes, and it's making me jealous.

Why is this making me jealous? I thought Jamie had a thing for me. When did he start having a thing for Layla? What does Layla have that I don't? Besides blond hair and a smaller ass?

"What does Bradley III have that I don't?" Jamie asks. "He must be hung like a donkey."

I should hope so. Those vibrators were pretty well endowed. "She hasn't told me."

"You think she's slept with him already?"

Um…yeah. "I don't know, Jamie."

My *boyfriend* gets a bull's-eye and then does a little dance. Can't he stay still for one second? He's always moving. I thought that now that the cheating was over, I wouldn't have to share him, but he's still always running from club to club, basketball to real estate, friend to friend, me to the dartboard. Why can't he stay still?

Jamie pings me on the leg. "Is he tall?"

"Who?"

"Is Prince Bradley tall?"

"I don't know. I've never met him. Why?"

"Because tall men are usually well hung."

I burst out laughing. "Are we still talking about Brad's penis?"

"Yes," Jamie says. "I can't help but worry."

"Why?"

"Because how am I going to compete with a man with a huge *shlong*? You know what I'm talking about. I look as if my last girlfriend was Lorena Bobbitt."

Beer snorts from my nose, I'm laughing so hard. I thought all men think they're Goliath. "You're not that small," I lie.

He dismisses me with his hand. "Yes, I am. I don't care. There's a lot of magic in that wand. Occasionally Cinderella's coach turns back to a pumpkin before midnight, but normally she can party all night, you know?"

At this point, I'm screaming with laughter, and my *boyfriend* appears protectively by my side. "What's so funny here?" he asks.

Jamie points his finger at Russ's crotch. "We're discussing *shlongs*. Care to join in?"

I weave my arm around Russ. "You can't discuss *shlongs* with my *boyfriend*." I monitor his facial reaction to my use of the word *boyfriend*. Neither his lips nor his eyebrows flinch. That's a good sign, isn't it? I'll assume we're officially dating unless advised otherwise.

Russ squeezes me back. He reeks of beer. "Why can't he?" he asks.

I'm not sure he knows what a *shlong* is. "You want to discuss your genitals, go ahead."

"That's the problem with coed bathrooms," Jamie says. "In the days of urinals I could check out the competition. Now I'm forced to battle blindly."

"Do you pee blindly, too?" I ask. "Someone keeps hitting the floor in the third stall."

Jamie shakes his head. "Not me, I have perfect aim."

Russ nods. "So do I. I just kicked Nick's ass in darts."

Jamie wags a finger at me. "Maybe it's you, Kimmy."

"Me? Woman can't have bad aim."

"You leave the toothpaste all over the sink," Jamie says.

"No, I don't!"

"Yes, you do," Jamie says. "I've used the sink after you do, and it's no pretty sight."

Great. Now Russ thinks I'm a slob who pees on the floor. "Jamie, do I make fun of you?"

"Yes," he says. "All the time. We just spent the last twenty minutes making fun of my *shmekel*."

Layla finally turns off her cell and joins us. "What are you guys talking about?"

"My *shmekel*," Jamie says, looking desolate.

"Isn't that the Yiddish word for a small *shmuck*?" Layla says.

Jamie obviously needs my help winning over the opposite sex. Maybe I should write a book; I've certainly had a lot of success recently. First tactic: do not bring up one's small penis in front of one's object of affection (unless, of course, you're actually bringing it up, ha-ha).

Layla smiles. "Small isn't always bad. It's all about the shape. Sometimes big is too big."

Then why are all her vibrators twice the size of a normal man? The guys look surprised. They obviously haven't seen what's inside her pleasure drawer, or listened to one of her masturbation lectures.

Jamie leans forward, eagerly. "You prefer small?"

Could he be more obvious?

Layla scratches the side of her face in thought. "I find when it's smaller, you can have sex more often, and you don't get sore."

Nick's eyes are popping out of his head. "How often do you like to have sex?"

She appears thoughtful. "When I'm in a relationship, you mean?"

"Or not," Jamie adds.

"Once or twice a day, I suppose."

I spit the beer I was drinking back into the bottle. "Oh, please." Give me a break. She's batting her big blue eyes at her adoring fans. "You do not have sex twice a day."

"I don't?"

"Come on!" What, she needs everyone's attention? It's not enough that she has the perfect boyfriend, but she has to steal Jamie and now Russ?

"It destresses me. I can't sleep if I don't orgasm."

Great. The masturbation discussion. Again. Why do we always have to talk about masturbation?

"Do you have an orgasm every night?" Russ asks. He can't take his eyes off her. My back tenses. Is he going to fall for her now? Start sleeping with her? What if I become Sharon and no one tells me he's screwing someone else? If he did it to her, why not do it to me?

"Of course," Layla says. "Don't you?"

"I do," Nick says.

"I think you're the first woman to ever admit to masturbating," Russ says.

Layla looks shocked. "What are you talking about? My friends at home and I talk about it all the time."

"You do?" Nick asks. "Now there's a conversation I'd like to overhear. Can we call them?"

"I'm not embarrassed about my body. Women have to be in charge of their own pleasure." She gives me a meaningful look.

"Charge away," Nick says, and everyone laughs. Everyone except me.

Back at the Zoo, Russ asks me to masturbate for him. I don't really want to touch myself down there. "Can't you do it?" I ask.

He gently bites the top of my ear. "I want to watch you do it."

This is highly stressful. I don't want to touch myself with

him watching. I don't even know what to do. But I don't want him to think I'm a prude. And what if Sharon used to do it? I can't not do what Sharon used to do. I can do this. If every other woman can make herself come, so can I. If it takes way too long I'll just fake it. I'm good at faking it.

"It might take me a while," I say.

"I'm not going anywhere."

Unless he meets someone else.

I dip my hands into my pants and attempt to arouse myself. I feel like an idiot. But I pretend I'm finding this arousing. I continue rubbing myself and it starts to feel better. And better. I feel him getting hard beside me. This apparently turns him on. Which turns me on.

I continue stroking myself, faster, harder, lighter, slower. He starts to stroke himself beside me. My legs and arms start to shake. My hands and feet start to feel cold, but we don't stop. We're each breathing so hard, we could have asthma.

Eventually I feel overwhelmed with heat, like an itch that desperately needs to be scratched, and then...

So that's what everyone keeps talking about.

I love you, I think but don't say.

russ becomes a copycat

Score is four nothing, us. I'm tired, but I gotta keep going. I can't remember the last time I slept. When is my super-strength going to kick in? And why is a fucking asshole sec-ond-year blocking me? Have to get past him. Move. Sweat. Can't get it, shoot, block, miss, fuck.

Crack.

Ow. Ow. Ow. Ow.

Ow.

I try to shake out my hand, but it hurts too much.

Ow.

My eyes sting, my hand kills. This sucks. There is no time for this.

"What's wrong, Russ?" Nick asks, out of breath.

The middle finger on my right hand looks abnormally bloated, and ferociously angry. Ow. "I think it's broken."

"You're kidding."

"I don't think so." Ow. Maybe if I just shake it out—ow.

"I think you need to go to the health center, dude."

★ ★ ★

Three hours later, I'm back at the Zoo, and my finger is wrapped in a metal plate. I am not happy. The nurse told me that MBA men have the highest broken-bone ratio of any group of students at the university. Apparently we all think we're eighteen. This week she saw one broken leg, two pulled-out backs and one sprained neck.

"Where were you?" Kimmy asks when I knock on her door. "I thought you wanted to work on our Corporate Strategy assignment."

I show her my hand. "I had a run-in with a basketball."

"Looks like the basketball won."

"Funny. It's sprained."

"I really wanted to go over the assignment, Russ. I'm done, but I wanted to check it against yours, in case."

Hello? My hand? *Well, excuse me,* I say, annoyed.

She locks her door behind her. "We have to meet the group now about the female condom project. Sorry about your hand," she says, almost as an afterthought, then leans over to gently kiss it.

"I'm okay," I say, suddenly trying to be the tough guy. I guess I shouldn't tell her I haven't even read the Corporate Strategy assignment yet.

Nick and Lauren are waiting for us in Jamie's room. "How are you feeling, dude?" Nick asks.

I shrug. Kimmy and I sit on the floor, our backs against the wall.

Jamie claps his hands together. "All right children, let's get to work. I e-mailed each of you my part last night. Did anyone read it?"

"I did," Kimmy says. The rest of us nod, but we're looking at the floor.

"Did any of you finish your parts?" Jamie asks.

Nick and Kimmy simultaneously say, "I did."

I'm staring at a very interesting crack in the paint on the wall.

"Guys, we have to finish this. I wrote the intro, but I can't write the conclusion until you all give me your sections. It always helps when the intro and conclusion have something to do with the rest of the paper. And we have to practice. We're presenting it as well as handing it in. Has anyone thought about props?"

When did he become so psycho? "Jamie, man, you have to chill," I say. "The paper isn't due until Wednesday." I have other pressing priorities. Clubs, Kimmy, my finger. Another assignment due tomorrow. I thought breaking up with Sharon would free up some time, but I've been busier than ever these past two weeks.

Gotta keep moving, as they say. You have time to think when you stay still.

"I have a surprise," Kimmy says. "I spoke to the retailer, and she sent me a box of freebies to give out to the class."

Freebies? We would need them, but we're not using condoms anymore since she's on the pill.

We make plans to work during all our free time tomorrow and on Tuesday. We break up at around eleven.

"Are you coming to bed?" Kimmy asks, yawning.

"I can't. I have to finish Strategy."

"Now?"

"Yes, now."

She sighs. "Why don't you use my work to fill in anything you're missing? And let me know if I've forgotten anything major."

Sounds good to me.

I go to my room, and start copying: "The all-stock purchase of Time Warner (TW) by America Online (AOL) was perhaps the ultimate display of Internet-era exuberance. The merger represented a supposed model for the future, where an endless stable of content was delivered anywhere at any time through seamless networks that integrated with effortless hardware."

When did Kimmy become so articulate? Who knew? I'm impressed. And aroused.

I flip my chin between her paper and my keyboard, typing what I see. I change a few words to make it sound like mine. Forty minutes later, the words start to swim in front of my eyes.

Telephone rings. "Time for bed?" Kimmy purrs.

"Definitely," I say, and hit the print key.

layla's library libido

"Our initial product rollout for the women's condom will target areas that fall within the triangular shape formed by Boston, Miami and Chicago," Jamie says, as the PowerPoint slide behind him illuminates a gigantic triangle. "A strategy we refer to as the golden triangle."

Everyone in the class snickers. He is too much. I can't stop laughing. How can someone make a Marketing presentation so funny? I'm not the only person howling, either. It feels like Comedy Central in here. And the place is packed. I bet everyone came just to hear him present. I wonder if he's ever thought about show business.

"People," he says, "get your mind out of the gutter. The product packaging is gold."

I feel a pang of jealousy when all five in his work group start laughing. I wish I were in that group. My group did a presentation on the soda industry, and they've been doing condoms every night. Where's the justice?

When the group finishes, they hand out freebies. Cool. It's like getting a loot bag after a party, except with this stuff in hand, the party comes later. Hopefully I'll be able to use this over spring break when we finally have sex.

At the end of the day, I stop at the Internet terminals to check my e-mail. One from Brad, asking me if I want to see the Broadway play *Avenue Q* during March break. He's gotten really into e-mails and phone calls lately. Almost obsessively. It's almost suffocating. Oh, well. At least he's booked my break with dinner reservations and concerts. And he's taking off two days so we can spend some time during the day together.

Library time. I knock on Jamie's door to collect him. No answer. Oh, well. I trudge through the snow on my own.

I find him at our regular spot on the fourth floor. "I'm so happy you're here," I say, sitting on the chair next to his.

"I'm happy *you're* here," he says. "It's time for a walk."

"But I just arrived!"

"All the more reason to take a break. Hey, Jason," he says to the guy sitting at the table. "Will you watch our laptops?" He extends his arm to me, and we stroll through the library, waving to the people we know. His short arm hairs tickle my skin. We're both cold and goose-bumpy. In the hallway in front of the elevator he performs a yogalike stretch. "I think I've lost all feeling in my toes," he says.

"How long have you been here?"

"Since three-thirty."

I look at my watch. "It's only three-forty five."

"Exactly."

"How's the job search going?"

"I thought this was our break?"

"Sorry, Jamie. I was just wondering what your story was."

"Avoidance."

I remember my earlier observation. "Have you thought about going into show business?"

"Yeah, why? You think I could be a star?"

"I was thinking you'd like to work for a film company. I have a friend in the city who works for Miramax. I'm sure he'd be happy to talk to you."

"That would be amazing." He faces me and puts both hands on my shoulders. "You're always looking out for me, huh?"

"Always," I answer. "Let's get back to work."

"What do you say we work for forty minutes and then do a massage train?"

Who knew my Alpha Phi massage train would be a hit at B-school? "It's not a massage train with only two of us. It's just a massage." He looks forlorn, so I decide to compromise. "Fine. But first I work for an hour."

"Half an hour," he negotiates.

"Forty minutes," I say. I set my watch and return to my work.

Forty minutes later, my alarm goes off. I stop it before the librarian boots us out for disturbing the peace. "Me first," I whisper. He stands up behind me, rolls his sleeves, and begins massaging my neck. Tighter…oooh…ahh…It's sooo good. I feel sooo relaxed. I feel sooo good.

I feel sooo…aroused?

I probably shouldn't be feeling aroused at the library. I probably shouldn't be feeling aroused by a man who's not my boyfriend.

kimmy saves
her *boyfriend's* ass

Russ doesn't answer when I knock on his door, so I knock again.

I hear the *Spider-Man* soundtrack. Why isn't he answering if he's inside? Is it possible…is he…is he in there with someone else? Bastard. He's probably sleeping with some slut. Who? Who can he possibly be screwing? Lauren? Layla? Some coed?

"You'd better open up," I say, seething, and continue pounding. "I know you're in there. Open the damn door!"

The door creaks. I kick it wide open. "Where is—"

Russ's hair is ruffled, and his eyes are half-closed. He's wearing jeans and his favorite green Roots sweatshirt. He's alone. "Were you napping?" I ask, feeling stupid.

He nods and lies back down. Why was he napping when he was supposed to be studying Finance? The midterm is tomorrow. And it's impossible. For me, anyway. I don't understand any of this stuff. I'm going to fail. It's only worth twenty percent, but still.

Russ also has to finish his part for the GBE project. He

promised Jamie that he would have his section done by five. Jamie has to finish putting it together and hand it all in tomorrow. Just like he did for the Marketing assignment, Russ is the last one to finish his part for the GBE. "Did you finish studying for Finance?"

"Almost."

I think he's lying. "Yeah? Good. Let's work on Operations, then."

He groans. "Let me get a cup of coffee."

Nick sticks his head in the doorway. "Russ, aren't you coming with me to ref?"

Ref? What is he talking about?

Russ slaps his good hand across his forehead. "Oh, man. I forgot."

"What's ref?" I ask. Don't tell me he's blowing off studying for basketball. Again.

"I promised I'd referee the game tonight, since I can't play." He waves his sprained hand at me.

"You promised to referee a game when we have a midterm tomorrow? Are you crazy?"

He scratches his head. "It does seem stupid, now that you mention it."

"You can't get out of it now, dude," Nick says.

Why is there a basketball game right before a midterm? That's the dumbest thing I've ever heard.

"I'm just refereeing the first game and then I'll be back," Russ says. "Give me an hour."

Is he an idiot? "You think you can finish studying and also finish your part of the assignment all tonight? Does this mean you're going to be pulling another all-nighter?"

"Probably." He kisses me on the forehead and scampers off. That boy seriously needs a vacation.

I review my notes for Finance and then take a ten-minute break to play on Travelocity to find a last-minute vacation.

Apparently I cannot afford Barbados. Maybe Miami? Seems like every undergrad in the world is going to Miami. I need something cheap. Romantic. Did I mention cheap? Montreal pops up. Montreal? Is Montreal cheap?

"Go on a romantic ski resort vacation in Montreal!" the computer cries out to me. Fireplace. Hot chocolate. Cuddling. Lots of cuddling. Skiing. French. It's like going to Europe but much, much closer. Canada it is. I have always wanted to go to Canada. Really. Mountains. Clean air. Fun. How cold can it be? I've always wanted to learn to ski. Slaloming down the mountain. Sexy. In one of those sexy ski outfits. Tight and impractical. Look, I'm a ski bunny! Skiing in Montreal it is. And there's a last-minute special.

At ten, Jamie comes by looking for Russ and his part of the assignment. "He said he'd have it done by five," he moans. "It's due tomorrow."

"He's almost done," I lie.

"Tell him I'm going to bed early, and that I'll put it together during lunch tomorrow."

At eleven, yes *eleven,* Russ knocks on my door. "Do you think I can finish the assignment tomorrow?"

Is he joking? "Russ, you need to get it to Jamie *tonight.*"

He fidgets with a pimple scar on his cheek. He's been breaking out a lot lately. What's wrong with him? "That's slightly problematic," he says.

"Look, why don't I help you with it? It won't take more than an hour."

We work on it until one. He keeps glancing at his watch.

"What?" I ask. "You turning into a pumpkin?"

"I just want to start studying for tomorrow."

Oh. My. God. "Did you just say *start?* It's 1:00 a.m.! Are you crazy? Why didn't you tell me you haven't started? Why haven't you started?"

"I've been busy."

"I've been busy, too, but I still managed to study for my

midterms. Especially the one tomorrow, which let me remind you is worth twenty percent."

He looks at his watch again.

"Go," I say. "I'll finish this and send it to Jamie."

"You sure?"

"Yeah."

He kisses me on the lips. "I love you."

I love you? Did he just say the L word? He looks surprised that he said it. I don't know if he meant to, but it's too late. It's out there, suspended in the air like potent cologne. He loves me. "I love you, too." Mission officially complete!

jamie's muse
makes him miserable

I finish my Operations midterm and hand it in. "Have a great week, Professor Sholtz."

"Thanks, Jamie. You, too."

And that's it. Another half a semester gone. Three-eighths of my postcollegiate education is over.

Layla is still scribbling away with furious intensity as I pass her on my way out. She's shaking her head angrily as she always does during a midterm, which is her way of claiming that she failed.

Yeah, right.

Now, how to enjoy my next week? Oh, right. Torturing myself with visions of Layla screwing Kermit. And looking for a job. I'm excited by the idea of working for a movie studio. I don't know what it is about Layla. I think she might be my muse. Before I met her, everything seemed like a waste, a joke, and now I want to do something with my life. Make something of myself. Partly to impress her, but mostly because she makes me want to be a better man. Where's that line from? Oh, *As Good As It Gets*. See, I'm made for the movies!

I pretend to use the Internet terminals in the hallway while I wait for Layla to finish writing her exam. Ten minutes later, I spot her and wave.

"I failed," she says.

"Sure you did."

"I didn't have time to finish! How could he give us only an hour and a half to answer eleven questions? It's absurd." She's wearing her hair in a high bun, and tendrils are framing her face.

"Absurd."

She laughs and leans against the terminal. "I have to pack."

"What time are you leaving?"

"As soon as I can."

"Last chance to spend the week here with me. It's going to get crazy here at the Zoo."

She laughs again. Thinks I'm kidding. Thinks I don't really want her to stay. She pats me on the head and says, "You sure you don't want to go home? It's going to be lonely here. Do you know that Kimmy and Russ are going to Montreal?"

"Quiet will be good for me. It'll make me focus. So tell me, how's Kermit?"

"So far so good. He's the type of guy I could fall in love with." She shivers. "Saying that out loud just scared the crap out of me." She kisses me on the cheek. "I must go pack. Your job over the vacation is to find yourself a career. Got it?"

"Got it." I watch her and her bag roll away and I feel like crying.

russ is annoyed

Kimmy squeezes into the hotel bathroom, hogging my space. "Russ, which shirt do you like better?" she asks for the third time.

Oh, man. "That one."

She sighs, apparently exasperated. "Before you said you liked the other one."

I'm rubbing gel in my hair, trying to decrease my head's static. In the mirror I look like a porcupine. It's our second night at a boutique hotel in Old Montreal. Tomorrow morning we're going up to Mont Tremblant to ski. At the moment she's contorting her body so she can see herself in the mirror behind me. I move, so she can have a full view. Again. "Yes, because you look good in everything."

"No, I don't. I looked like a fat cow in that one."

Kimmy is constantly criticizing her body and her looks. "You do not look fat."

"So you're saying I look like a cow? I should never have eaten that poutine today."

"I told you it was filling."

"Who eats fries, cheese curds and gravy? It's disgusting."

"You, apparently." She felt differently while she was inhaling it.

"I hate this shirt," she says. "I'm changing." Ten minutes later, she's still changing. I'm sitting on the bed, flipping through the channels. TSN. CTV. CBC. Good old Canadian television. I miss my channels. I miss Peter Mansbridge.

"What do you think of these pants?" Kimmy asks. "Does my ass look big?"

I keep my eyes trained on the TV. "No." I don't understand. If she didn't like the way any of her clothes looked, why did she bring them?

"You're not even looking."

Oh, man. I look at the clock. "Are you almost ready? We're going to miss our reservation."

"I'm trying. I'm trying to look nice—for you." The last segment comes out as a sob. She storms into the bathroom and slams the door. What is her problem? Why is she acting like such a baby? She comes out, five minutes later, eyes red.

I turn off the TV. "Are you going to tell me what's wrong?"

"Nothing's wrong."

Then why is she crying? I don't get it. When Sharon was pissed, she told me. "Fine." I'm not going to fight with her. When she wants to tell me what's wrong, she'll tell me.

She changes back into the first outfit she tried on.

"You look great," I say, meaning it.

"No, I don't. Let's go. Do you have the room card?"

"Yes." I stop her with my hand as she opens the door. "You look great, eh?"

She smiles. "Really?"

"Yes, really."

"Thanks." She kisses me and we head out the door, only ten minutes late.

I ask the concierge how to get to the restaurant.

"You can walk, *monsieur*," he says. "Eez only tree block down."

The cold air attacks us as soon as we step outside. "Why can't we take a cab?" Kimmy whines. "It's freezing out here and my feet hurt." She hasn't stopped complaining about the cold or her feet since we got here.

Oh, man. "Why didn't you wear the hat we bought you yesterday?"

"I can't wear a hat out at night. I just blow-dried my hair for thirty minutes. I'm not ruining it with a ha—" Swish! She slips on the ice, and her legs split apart like she's an action-adventure star doing a stunt. I seize her arm so she doesn't fall.

"Maybe we should slow down," she says. "It's not easy to walk on ice in stilettos."

Maybe someone shouldn't be wearing stilettos in the middle of winter, eh?

layla's new fantasy

Don't tell me…did he just fall asleep? With his hand on my clitoris? While he was trying to make me orgasm? We just had sex, and he came, and now it was my turn to come. Or it would have been if he hadn't fallen asleep.

I'm not impressed. Just because he's well endowed doesn't mean he can take naps in the middle of coitus. He's too big. It hurt when he inserted himself at certain angles. His penis is very straight, and could use a curve, like my banana.

Now what am I supposed to do? I wish I had my banana. No movement. I nudge him again. "Hello? My turn."

Dead to the world.

Maybe if I catalogue the contents in his room I'll fall asleep. His closet is open and I can see one, two, three, four, five, six…ten…no fifteen pairs of shoes. How many shoes does one man need? Shoes aside, I'm still aroused.

Maybe if I think about something non-sexy, like snow, I'll be able to fall asleep.

Lots of snow. White snow. Wet snow. Wet.

Now I'm getting all aroused again. I guess I'll have to do

it myself. I turn over and slip my hand downward. He doesn't move. I start to rub just a little bit. All good. He still isn't moving.

As I start getting a little more into it, I notice that the bed is shaking. Not shaking a lot like in the *Exorcist,* but just rocking like we're having a minor earthquake.

I stop and the bed stops shaking. Then I start again, slowly. He groans and turns over.

I freeze. But his eyes are still closed. I start again. Then stop.

This is kind of a turn-on. Once again I start. This time I picture a scene from an erotic novel I read years ago. A man and a woman are dancing at a party. The guy lifts up her skirt and undoes his fly, and they have sex right there in the middle of the dance floor. People are dancing right next to them, but no one can see a thing.

My legs start shaking.

And I imagine I'm dancing, moving around the dance floor, and he's whispering into my ear, how good I feel, how good he feels, and it's…my God, it's Jamie!…and my legs are shaking, and the floor is shaking, and the bed is rocking…uh-oh, the bed is *really* rocking, and I'm about to orgasm—

"What are you doing?" Brad asks, sitting up.

I stop. "Trying to orgasm."

"You're shaking the bed," he says, then turns over.

Well, excuse me! As I wait for lover-boy to fall back to sleep, I realize something: he doesn't have any fish. I didn't see an aquarium anywhere in the apartment. Why did he write his whole essay on fish if he doesn't have even one? What kind of lying freak am I dating?

I knew there would be something wrong with him. I sit up, put back on my clothes, leave him a goodbye-and-don't-call note, and sneak out.

When I'm back home in bed, I return to the party.

Jamie, huh? Passionate, loving, caring Jamie.

Oh, Jamie!

Thursday, March 18, 9:30 a.m.

kimmy boards
the train to pain

I. Am. In. Serious. Pain.

"Time to get up," Russ says, jumping out of bed.

Can't. Move. "Ghjrfhft," I groan.

"Ready to get going?"

Going? Going back under the covers. "Going where?"

He laughs. "What do you mean, where? Boarding."

He wants to go snowboarding…again? "I can barely move from boarding yesterday."

We flew into Montreal on Monday, spent two days touring, then rented a car to drive up to Tremblant. Apparently my dreams of slaloming were outdated. "No one skis anymore, Kimmy," Russ said. "We board."

It was fun at first. The sky was a brilliant blue, the air fresh, the sun warm on my face. I wore my new ski pants and puffy jacket (what debt?), sunglasses and gloves, and rented boots and a board. We took the chairlift up, and up and up, stood at the top of the mountain and…

I fell. Again and again. And again. Russ was a champion at it, flying from side to side. Show-off.

"I was thinking that today could be a cuddle-by-the-fire-place-and-drink-Baileys day," I say hopefully.

"But we paid for two days of boarding."

Does he always have to be doing something? "But I want to relax."

"But it's beautiful out."

But, but, but. My butt is killing me from all that falling. "But I'm not a good boarder."

"You won't get better by not practicing."

Even talking to him is exhausting. "Can't we just relax? We've been running around all week." We've shopped, we've Metroed, we've boarded and we've hiked. Ever since his hand has healed he's wanted to do every possible activity imaginable. "This is spring break, not spring workout."

"I was happy to stay at the Zoo for the break. You were the one who wanted to get away."

"Get away for a vacation. Not to make myself even more worn-out."

"But we're here. Let's not waste any time."

"Since when is relaxing a waste of time?" Is cuddling a waste of time? Next he'll be saying that being with me is a waste of time.

"But the tickets!" he says, jutting out his chin.

"So go." I storm out of the bed and go to the bathroom. Sometimes he's so annoying. I sit on the toilet, and then see a splotch of red in my panties. Shit. I'm bleeding. It's my period. Damn. I don't know if I should be happy or upset. On one hand, I'm relieved I'm not pregnant; on the other hand, I can't believe I got it now.

Damn. I've ruined the vacation. He's going to start fanta-sizing about someone else. He'll meet some sexy boarder on the hill who knows all the right moves, and he'll forget all about me. And then who will I live with this summer? Not that he's asked me yet, but why wouldn't he? There is no point in us having our own places when we sleep in the same bed every night, anyway. I haven't suggested it outright yet, but I've been hinting. I'd prefer if he came up with it on his own. Unfortunately, I don't think skipping boarding will help my cause.

I find my emergency tampon in my makeup case, then turn the shower on and call, "We better hurry if we want to hit the slopes."

The bathroom is full of steam. He steps into the shower and I wrap my arms around his chest. If I give him a blow job now, he might want to skip sex tonight. Here's hoping that the slopes wear him out.

jamie talks the talk

Ring, ring.

Phones ringing in the middle of the night make me nervous. I pause *Casablanca* and pick up.

Me: Hello?

Voice on phone: Hi, ya! It's Layla.

Me: Everything okay?

Layla: Of course.

Me: *(Exhaling in relief and then singing her name song.)*

Layla: You're up!

Me: So are you, apparently.

Layla: I can't sleep.

Me: Where's Bradley the frog?

Layla: *(Loud sigh.)* That didn't work out.

Me: *(Heart soaring into the sky like a kite on speed.)* What happened?

Layla: He wasn't as perfect as I thought.

Me: After all that?

Layla: It happens. How are you? How's the job search going?

Me: Job search? Is that what I'm supposed to be doing?

Layla: Does that mean you haven't found anything?

Me: Actually, I did find something. Your contact gave me a bunch of names. I've decided I definitely want to get a job in movies. And I've spoken to a few production companies. They all seem interested, but none of them want to pay me. I'd be a kind of intern, aka slave laborer.

Layla: With half an MBA you shouldn't be working for free.

Me: It's not always about the money.

Layla: You're right. You are so right. I love that you're following your passion.

Me: (She's *my passion. Maybe I should start following her.*) You do?

Layla: I have a confession to make. I'm jealous that you're not going for the money, that you're going to do something you love.

Me: (*What I'd love to do is you.*) You love what you do.

Layla: I love working. But I wish I worked somewhere where I could make a difference, instead of pushing papers and million-dollar deals that don't mean anything.

Me: What would be your dream job?

Layla: Remember Danielle Grand? The executive director of the Girls Group in Danbury? I would like to do what she does.

Me: So why can't you do that?

Layla: Because I already have a job. And you don't get to wear Chanel suits at a nonprofit. And—this is going to sound horrible—working at a nonprofit just feels like such women's work.

Me: Excuse me?

Layla: It's such a stereotype. Like teaching. My sister is in Teacher's College. And I'm disappointed in her. I thought she could do better.

Me: (*I hate that she said, "I thought she could do better." For sure she'd never go out with me.*) Teaching shapes the minds of our youth. Isn't that one of the most important jobs there is?

Layla: I know, I know. Rationally, I know. But I would still worry about people putting down what I did, like it was some kind of woman's hobby. (*She sighs loudly.*) Isn't that dumb?

Me: Yes. Do you want to be a banker?

Layla: My mother is a banker. My father is a banker.

Me: That's the worst answer I ever heard.

Layla: (*Laughs.*) I love working. I'm just not crazy about the projects I work on. (*She sighs again.*) Let's talk about something else. So is it quiet there? Empty? Is it weird?"

Me: It is weird. Like that scene in *Vanilla Sky* when Tom Cruise is walking through an empty Times Square.

Layla: I loved that movie. So what did you do all week?

Me: I instant-messengered my mom. Never show a lonely mother how to use the Internet. She'll use it against you.

Layla: My mother wouldn't have time to IM me. She works twenty-five-hour days. But if we didn't communicate by e-mail, I would never hear from her.

Me: What about your dad?

Layla: Same.

Me: You must have seen them this week while you were in New York.

Layla: Nope.

Me: That's so sad.

Layla: Isn't it?

Me: Were you a lonely kid?

Layla: I had my sister. And my friends. And my work. Yeah. I guess I was. (*She laughs again.*)

Me: Maybe you want to be a banker because you think it'll bring you closer to your parents.

Layla: (*Pause.*) That's very astute of you, Jamie. Maybe you should look for a shrink job instead.

We stay on the phone until I look out the window over my bed and the light has started to eat its way over the empty campus, turning the sky vanilla.

Sunday, March 21, 7:00 p.m.

layla's epiphany

I can't wait to see Jamie. He's funny and sweet and smart and passionate, and he organizes book drives.

I pull my car into my underground parking spot and take a deep breath.

Jamie's the one.

He's perfect for me. He gets me. I don't know how I didn't realize this before. As soon as I see him, I'm going to tell him. No, I'm going to throw my arms around him and show him. Unless he's still in love with Kimmy.

How silly of me, encouraging him to go for Kimmy when he's so perfect for me.

I shift the gear into Park, grab my bag and lock the door. If only the Zoo had a valet. Or a doorman. This is taking too long! I have to know if he feels the same way I do.

I sprint out of the garage, into the Zoo and up the stairs, run right to his room and pound on the door. "Jamie! It's me! Open up! I have something to ask you!"

From behind the door I hear, "You want the truth? You can't handle the truth." He's watching *A Few Good Men*. I love that movie. See? We're made for each other.

He opens the door and I throw my arms around him.

"Hello to you, too," he says, looking vaguely flabbergasted by my greeting.

"Are you still in love with Kimmy?"

He snorts. "Noooo. Why?"

Before he can say anything else I tilt my head down and kiss him hard on the mouth.

He just stands there.

Oh, no.

He doesn't want me. What did I do? I didn't even stop to think, I just did it and…wait a sec. He's kissing me back. Yes! He's kissing me back! His tongue explores my lips, my mouth, my tongue. Tingles explode down my face and neck and chest and arms. He tastes sweet, like ice cream.

It's a perfect kiss. I knew it. I am so clever. I pull away and smile.

He looks shell-shocked. "If that's how you say hello after a week apart, what will you do after summer vacation?"

"I have no intention of keeping you in suspense," I say.

russ gets busted (and drags kimmy down with him)

I'm high and lying on Kimmy's bed.

"I found a great sublet in the West Village," Kimmy tells me.

"Yeah?"

"It's a one-bedroom, and it has large windows, and a rooftop patio with a charcoal barbecue. How amazing is having a barbecue?"

It does sound amazing. I want a charcoal barbecue. I haven't even looked for an apartment yet. "Wanna shack up for summer?"

I can see the possibility rolling around in her mind. Come on, Kimmy, say yes! I want a barbecue!

"Why not?"

I love how spontaneous she is. And I love that she doesn't care that she did all the work. Truth is, I'm not sure if I love her. I know I told her I did, but I didn't mean it. I like her a lot, and I'm in lust with her, but—love?

She kisses me and I forget what I was worried about.

★ ★ ★

I walk in fifteen minutes late to class, and sit in the spot Kimmy reserved for me.

She points to her watch. Thanks, Mom. She can't get over the fact that I'm late to every class. I pat her on the knee. She pats back.

The trip was great, except for her excessive how-do-I-look and do-you-think-that-chick-is-hotter-than-me whining. How is someone so awesome so insecure?

Sharon wasn't insecure. Shouldn't think about Sharon. Can't stop thinking about Sharon. Did I make a mistake? No. Kimmy is right for me. We're moving to the same city. We're working at the same place.

When there are only a few minutes left of class, Professor Martin pulls out a stack of assignments from his briefcase. "The class average was a seventy-three, which isn't too impressive," he says. "Apparently the majority of you failed to understand the difference between synergy and leveraging."

I don't even remember the assignment. Not a good sign.

I brace myself for a low sixty. I couldn't have failed. I assume that if you bother showing up you deserve a passing grade. And I've shown up. Some of the time.

Martin hands back the assignments. Hands back every assignment but mine. Kimmy nudges me. She doesn't get hers back, either. When the bell rings, Martin is out of papers. He returns to the front row and says, "Russ and Kimmy, I'd appreciate it if you two could stay after class."

Did I forget to hand in my assignment? That's possible. There's so much to keep track of. After the class empties out, Kimmy and I make our way to the front of the room.

"It has come to my attention that you have both breached the MBA Code of Conduct and Honor Code of Leiser Weiss Business School."

What?

Kimmy's face drains of color. "Excuse me, sir?"

"Both of you signed the honor code, which states that as a student of LWBS, you would not plagiarize another student's work."

Oh, man.

He places two papers, side by side, faceup on his desk. Kimmy's has an A on it that's scratched out. "Now herein lies the problem. I received these two almost identical assignments. According to school rules, plagiarism must result in disciplinary action, and any person found guilty will, at the very least, receive a failure for the course."

Shit.

Kimmy starts crying. "But…I…"

I give her a look to be quiet. Crying is not going to win us points. "Sir, we discussed the assignment together. It was just a coincidence, a crazy coincidence that the papers look alike. I don't think it's unheard of that a couple discusses an assignment."

Martin stares at us. "I believe this goes way beyond bed-time chatter. The two papers were practically identical. I believe one of you plagiarized off the other, and I suggest that you speak up now."

Kimmy looks at me with beseeching eyes but doesn't say a thing.

"I see," Martin says. "Let me add that by protecting the guilty, the innocent is just as culpable. Both of you can expect a notification from LWBS's disciplinary committee. They'll be sending you a notification regarding the day and time you'll be pleading your cases. You're dismissed."

We leave the class, shell-shocked.

"What's the worst that will happen?" I ask.

She wipes the back of her hand against her eyes. "We'll both be expelled."

jamie's rise to stardom

There's a knock on my door, which I ignore, as at present I'm in the middle of negotiating a movie deal over the phone.

"We can't pay much," says the VP Business Development of Light Productions. "Only a stipend really, but we'd love to have you onboard."

They want to pay me a thousand-dollar stipend for the four months, but that's one thousand dollars more then I was expecting. It's a viable offer, an offer I'm taking. I'm going to use my business skills at a production company. And I'm going to major in Media and Entertainment next year.

Cool.

Another knock. Louder. I kick the door in an attempt to make whoever it is go away. I hope it's not Layla. I'd hate to piss her off so early in the relationship.

I smile to myself. I can't wait to be in NY. I get to spend the entire summer with Layla. I can't get her out of my mind. I'm flying far and beyond cloud nine. Cloud nine*teen*. I can't believe the woman of my dreams likes me. Everything happened so quickly and it's so wonderful.

So wonderful—and scary. She's somehow got it into her head that I'm her perfect match. I have to admit her tendency to idealize men and then knock them off their pedestals in one swift kick makes me nervous. Kimmy says that one of the reasons she broke up with Kermit was because his penis was too big. While that's good news for my little friend, I didn't know that was possible. That's one of the reasons I haven't slept with her yet. Not because she'll think my penis is too small and dump me (although that *is* a concern), but because I want to make sure she's really in love with me first. Let me tell you, it wasn't easy putting her off Sunday night. But I want to take things slowly. I'm already so crazy about her—if we start having sex and then she dumps me, I'll spiral into another depression.

"When can we expect you?" asks the movie man.

"My final exam is Thursday, April twenty-ninth. I can start work the following Monday." A piece of paper ripped out of a notebook is shoved under my door. What is their problem? I pick up the paper and read: *Huge problem. Come find me. Layla*

I hurry off the phone and open the door. Kimmy is pacing up and down the hallway, her face streaked with tears. Frowning beside her, hands on hips, is Layla.

"What happened?" I ask, immediately hugging Kimmy.

Layla sighs. "She's been accused of *p*lagiarism."

Come again?

Kimmy wipes her eyes. "Come into my room." We follow her inside and she closes the door behind her. "Russ borrowed one of my papers," she says, sobbing. "Martin accused us of copying. We have to go to the disciplinary committee."

Russ copied from her? The guy who's been reading *Forbes* since the womb is copying from the woman who didn't know what OB was? "I'm sure Russ has admitted he copied from you, right?"

She hesitates. "He hasn't."

"What do you mean he hasn't?" Layla shrieks.

"He went back to his room to think. What should I do?"

Layla snorts. "Go tell Martin the truth before you ruin your life. You could get expelled. You have to turn him in."

"I can't turn him in," she wails. "I can't turn in my boyfriend."

I rub small circles on her back. "I think Layla has a point, Kimmy. You're jeopardizing your future here."

She shakes me away. "Don't you see? If I tell the truth I could still lose everything. The code of ethics says you're not supposed to show anyone your work, so I'm still responsible for what happened. So what's the difference?"

"Kimmy," I say, "showing someone your work is not the same as abetting in a crime. What are you more afraid of losing? School or Russ?"

She doesn't answer.

"Are you crazy?" Layla yells, eyes flashing. "You didn't work your ass off all year just to throw it all away to save some guy. Are you not pissed? He used you. He's been using you from day one. We're marching right to Martin's office to tell him what happened."

Kimmy's hands start to shake. "You don't understand. He didn't use me. He loves me. We're in love. This MBA thing…I didn't even want to be here. I came because of Wayne. I'm not losing Russ."

"Have you thought about what would happen to you if you take the rap for this?" Layla shouts. "Do you think you're still going to have a job at O'Donnel?"

"I'm trying to be realistic," Kimmy says.

"What the hell does that mean?" Layla asks.

"It means that this MBA doesn't mean as much to me as it does to him. In a few years, I'll want to start a family—"

"So what? Why does a family mean you can't have a career?"

"I knew you wouldn't understand," Kimmy says. "You live

in a dream world. You can't have everything. You can't have kids and a husband and a company."

Sometimes I'm amazed at how differently women view the world, from us and from each other.

"Of course you can," Layla retorts. "Lots of women do."

"Like who? Your mother? How many times has she called you since you moved here? Did you even see her when you were in town?"

Layla's face flushes as if she's been slapped. "She works. Hard."

"I don't want my kids to grow up with a Brazilian accent is all I'm saying."

"Do what you want," Layla says, and storms out.

Silence.

"Jamie, what do you think?" Kimmy asks.

"I think I'll support whatever decision you make," I say, "but I don't think Russ deserves you."

"Thank you." She starts to cry again. "I wish it was you I was in love with."

I rub circles on her back until she stops crying.

kimmy rationalizes her future

I know it's Layla in the stall beside me, but I don't say anything. I know she's disappointed in me, but I can't turn him in. I just can't.

She's been avoiding me since our fight. I think she's being harsh. She won't talk to Russ, either, just keeps glaring at him. Not that he's noticed. They didn't talk much before, anyway. Things with Russ have been good despite all this. Honestly, I think we're closer than ever. When we go to the disciplinary committee on the twelfth, we'll tell them that we talked about the project, that we apologize, that we didn't realize what we were doing was wrong. And I've done some research. Actually, Jamie did some research for me, and he said that it's not like we're the first ones to ever get caught plagiarizing, and that out of the last five cases, three got off and the other two failed the course. No one got expelled. So big deal, I'll fail a course. I can take it again. We can both take it again this summer. So we won't go to New York. We'll stay here. Big deal. We'll stay here together and take summer credits. And then we'll be together next year and maybe we'll move into couple housing instead of living at the Zoo. And then next year we'll move to New York and get great jobs. Get engaged. Get married.

Married. That's what I wanted anyway, isn't it? Mrs. in front of my name.

And what if they don't buy it? Maybe I'll tell them it was me who cheated. Because, let's be honest, I was never here to learn how to climb the corporate ladder. And even if O'Donnel were to hire me later full-time, what happens then? I work for two years until I get pregnant, and then what? Let some stranger raise my kids?

I shudder at the thought of day care, remember the ear-picking-up woman, remember how tired and cranky my mother was when she arrived to take me home. Is that the type of woman I want to be? No. So it doesn't matter if I don't get my MBA. I want Russ to be happy.

I flush the toilet. Layla flushes beside me. We both hit the sinks at the same time. The silence feels heavy.

"You're making a mistake," she says.

"Don't bother," I answer.

"It's my job to bother. I'm concerned. The guy you're giving up your future for is the guy who cheated on his girl-friend for six months. He's not long-term potential."

How dare she? "It's none of your business."

"You shouldn't trust him." She turns off the tap and leaves me staring at myself in the mirror.

layla streaks

I soap my body. Then I rinse the conditioner out of my hair. Then I turn off the water and reach out of the shower curtain for my towel. For my towel. Where is my towel?

I open the curtain. My towel is gone. My bathrobe is gone. What happened to my stuff? I stand there dripping, totally confused. And then I hear it. A pitter-patter of giggling from outside the stall.

"Hello?" I call over the door. "Has anyone out there seen what happened to my stuff?"

"Your stuff?" Jamie asks. "What stuff?"

"I had a bathrobe and a towel and…oh, you jackass." I suppose this is what you get when you're involved with a jokester.

"April Fools'!" he screams from the other side of the wall.

"This isn't funny," I say but can't stop myself from laughing.

"What's not funny?"

It doesn't seem like I'm getting my towel back anytime soon. So what are my options? I look around. The curtain is hooked up to the shower rod. I could always unhook it and wrap myself in it. I could, if it wasn't germ infested.

I'd rather be naked. Kind of sexy. I'll just sprint. Only other problem: my keys are in my bathrobe pocket. "I'll make you a deal," I say. "I'll come out, if you pass me my keys."

No answer.

Here goes nothing. I take my shower basket and place it in front of my crotch. It doesn't do the job. Good thing I've been keeping my bikini wax up-to-date. Then I sneak out from behind the curtain into an empty bathroom and sprint, grabbing two paper towels, one per breast, as I run.

A flashbulb goes off.

The door to my room is open and Jamie's howling. "That," he says, "was the funniest thing I've ever seen."

"Hilarious." I pull Jamie into my room and kiss him. I know I should be angry with him, furious even, but it is April Fools' Day, and it's not as if anyone else saw me streaking through the halls, not that I would have really cared one way or another. But still...I wish sometimes he'd be less of a clown. "You know, I like you when you're serious, too. You don't always have to make a joke out of everything."

"Okay, just one more. What does an MBA call dating?"

"What?"

"Test marketing."

I shake my head. "Come here, funny-boy," I say, then kiss him again.

russ's depression

Seventy-five issues of *Forbes,* two hundred issues of the *Economist,* and three hundred viewings of *Family Ties,* and now I might never graduate from business school.

Unbelievable.

"Anyone else?" Jamie asks. "Any arguments against why, as domestic producers who export half our goods to foreign markets, we would be hesitant to support an import quota? Russ?"

I shrug.

I'm leaning against the door to Jamie's room, barely paying attention to what anyone is saying. We're working on an assignment for GBE that's due sometime this week. Unfortunately, I can't concentrate. I don't know how Kimmy can be so focused when we could get expelled next week.

I still don't think we did anything that horrible. Who cares? Everyone borrows.

"Nothing to add, Russ?" Jamie asks. Again I shrug. I know Jamie's pissed at me. But what does he want me to do? Admit I copied Kimmy's paper? If I admit it, I'll probably get expelled. If they can't prove it, then the worst that could happen is that I fail the course. None of this is Jamie's business, anyway. And Kimmy begged me not to tell. She thinks this is the better way to go. Even if we both fail the course—big deal. We can take it again. She doesn't even think that O'Donnel will rescind its offer.

Someone knocks on the door, and the pounding reverberates against my back. I scoot over so Nick can squeeze inside. Droplets of water from his wet hair slide down his face. He smells like minty shampoo. "I know I'm late, man. Basketball went late. But I wrote up some arguments for the GBE assignment in favor of the quota I thought we could use."

I haven't been to basketball all week. I don't feel like doing anything anymore. Maybe my apathy is from burnout. I took on too many projects and am now devoid of energy.

With great power comes great responsibility. That's the theme line from *Spider-Man*. Back in September I had great power. I thought I could do anything.

I screwed everything up.

layla sees the truth

"Hi, Dorothy!" I sing. "Hi, Dennis! Hi, everyone!" Today ends the last week of the task force. Truth is, Dennis and I are the only ones who have weathered it out. The other volunteers have all dwindled away with exams and interviews. But not me. I stick by my commitments.

"Hi, Layla," Dennis says. His glasses are crooked, and I resist the urge to straighten them.

Dorothy is biting into an apple and packing up her stuff. "Layla, I have to run out early. If you could update some files for me, I'd really appreciate it."

"No problem." I pull up a chair in front of the main computer and start inserting data. Deepak Hussein will not be joining us in the fall. Has decided to remain at his job for the time being, and would like to know if he can defer his acceptance until the following September. Sorry, Deepak. No deferrals. Try again next year.

Forty-five minutes in I spot Brad's file. He has decided to go to Harvard Business School. Apparently, he's never been dumped before and I've soured him off LWBS completely.

Oh, well. Not sure how well he would have done at the Zoo, anyway. The closet might not have had enough room for his shoes. The entire dorm might not have had enough room for his shoes. He didn't write about his shoes in his application. Would have been an interesting add-on under hobbies. Not.

I click on his name and add the information to his file. I shouldn't make fun of him. Just because he's a prince, doesn't mean he's *my* prince. You can't fall in love with a man on paper, is all.

I close the file on Bradley Green, and you know what comes almost right after Green? Grossman. Can't hurt to peek at his file, just for fun. I've been here for three hours; I could certainly use a break. I peer around the room to see what Dennis is up to. He appears to be totally engrossed in his keyboard, so I click on Jamie's student file. The screen with his student number pops up. I scroll down and click on the icon for his application. I'm giggling in anticipation. How crazy could he have gone?

The document opens and I see where he typed in his name and Florida address. How cute! I picture him sitting on a wooden patio, a sand beach in view, typing away his address on his laptop, pursing his adorable lips. He's a great kisser. I'm really happy. Everything is perfect. Fine, not perfect. He's a little shorter than my dream man. And balder. And he has a unibrow. But other than that he's perfect for me. I hope. I think. Is he?

And here's his birthdate, this July. We'll have to do something fabulous.

And then the F for female…

F? Why was there an F anyway? Ah. No wonder the school records had him down as a woman. He applied as one! Silly Jamie.

Mild panic. *Why* did he apply as a woman? Maybe secretly he *is* a woman. That would explain why he didn't want to have sex. I exhale with relief when I remember Kimmy's less than fervent description of his genitalia. I know that she's seen the equipment, what there is of it.

Silly Jamie. He must have accidentally checked the wrong square when he applied. There is no way that he'd do that…purposely.

Unless he thought that applying as a woman would give him a competitive advantage. An invisible vacuum sucks all the air from my lungs. No. He wouldn't have done that. Would he? People make typos all the time. I saw them myself. Applicants wrote in the wrong schools. If someone could write in the wrong schools, then surely I can expect someone to write in the wrong letter. Except, the M square on the original application was nowhere near the F square.

A fog of nausea overwhelms me. I have to ask him. Now.

I say goodbye to Dennis and return to the Zoo. Jamie is sprawled on his bed, watching an old black-and-white movie I don't recognize.

"Hey darlin', have you ever seen—" He breaks off at the shocked look on my face. "What's wrong?"

I close the door behind me. It must have been a mistake. This sweet man wouldn't do something that despicable. "Did you apply to LWBS as a woman?" I blurt out. As soon as the question is out of my mouth, I realize how ridiculous it sounds. I may as well have asked him if he is, in fact, transsexual.

His cheeks flush. The balding part of his head flushes. And then I realize he did it.

He smiles like a kid who just got caught dipping his finger in the cake's icing. "Kind of funny, huh?"

Tell me he doesn't think this is a joke. I attempt to stop my hands from trembling. "Excuse me?"

"I said it's kind of funny. Or it *was* kind of funny." He sighs. "Obviously you don't seem to think so, so why don't you sit down and we'll talk about it?"

Instead of sitting, I pace the room.

"Layla, sit. I just washed my sheets. No germs I swear."

And that's when I blow up. "Not everything is a joke! This isn't funny! What were you thinking?"

He crosses his arms in front of his chest. "I didn't plan it."

"It was an accident?" Please tell me it was an accident.

"It was research. For an article. Affirmative action was a hot topic and I thought it would make an interesting study. I applied to ten different schools, five as a male and five as a female." He's talking quickly, the words pouring out of him like water on full blast from the tap.

"But why male versus female? Why not pretend to be Hispanic or African-American?"

"Because people always think the name Jamie is female. If the only discrepancy was my gender, then I could keep my name and get my college to send my real grades."

"But what about the rest of the application?" Someone in the hallway smashes into the side of the room and laughs. We both ignore it, and I continue pacing.

Jamie sighs. "I wrote the essays, the GMATs—that's all legit." He pales. "But I had to write my own letters of reference."

Holy crap. "That is so illegal."

"I know, I know, but I couldn't ask former professors to write them, could I? People normally use gender pronouns in their letters."

"And you got in."

"Yeah."

"You took advantage of the system."

"Maybe the system is wrong," he says.

"An MBA class is stronger when it's diverse. Just as our learning groups are stronger when we're not five engineers, our class is stronger if it's not a hundred white men. So what if diversity needs a little help? But that doesn't mean you have the right to take advantage of it."

"I didn't see it as that big a deal. I thought, why not?"

"Why not? Because it's wrong!" I yell.

"Why is it wrong? Why shouldn't I get the chance to be here?"

I feel dizzy. "How has no one noticed? How is that possible?"

"You'd be amazed how irrelevant gender is in school life. My only problem was my student card. The picture ID says female or male on it. And we need to bring those to exams."

I feel nauseous all over again. "And that's when you asked me to change the F to an M so you could get a new student card."

"Yeah. Thank you. I don't know how I would have written my exams otherwise. I guess I could have risked it, but I was nervous one of the proctors would look at it and start wondering." He pauses. "You don't look so good. Are you okay?"

No, I'm not okay. "How could you do that to me? You asked me to commit a felony! What if I had gotten caught?" I'm pacing again, this time faster. "What if Dorothy thinks I'm an accomplice? And I get expelled? What if you ruined my life?"

He leaps off the bed and puts his arms around me. "Calm down."

I push him away. "Don't you dare tell me to calm down. I can't believe you would do that to me. Put my future at risk."

"It wasn't that big of a deal. It's really kind of funny, when you think of it." He smiles hopefully.

Why is nothing ever a big deal to him? "It *is* a big deal. Not everything is a joke, Jamie. I could be in front of the tribunal with Russ and Kimmy. I could lose my job at Silverman."

"You don't even want your job at Silverman," he points out.

"What I want is not to be manipulated." What I want is to get out of his room. "You're no better than Russ."

I jerk the door open and storm out. I hear him protesting from inside, but I don't care. I'm angry. Furious. Steam-shooting-out-of-ears pissed off. And I'm feeling something else, too. Something really familiar.

Relief.

some news for russ

I'm lying on my bed picking my face. It's gross, but I don't care. I need to. I can see the blood on my fingers. I look in the mirror and see how ugly I am. There are patches of raw, red skin on my chin, on my forehead, around my nose. Disgusting. Just how I feel.

The phone rings and I quickly pick it up. "Hello?"

"How is it possible that for the six months we were still dating you never once answered the phone and today you answer practically before it even rings?"

"Hello?" I repeat. "Who is it?"

"How do you not recognize my voice? It's Sharon."

"Oh, hi." Her voice sounds so soft and I feel empty, and I realize how much I've missed her. "I didn't expect to hear from you."

"Hi. I didn't expect to call you. How are you?"

"I'm all right." I reach my hand back to my face and continue picking.

"That's good. Are you coming back to Toronto this summer?"

"No, actually, I accepted a summer position in New York."

Pause. "I thought that might happen now that we're no longer together."

"There's a lot of opportunity in the U.S.," I say. "And because of the MBA I have a visa to work here for a year after I graduate. But I'm having a few issues…" I want to confide in her even though I know I have no right.

"I need to tell you something. I don't expect you to come home, but I hope you'll contribute financially. It's up to you how involved you want to get."

What is she talking about? "Involved with what?"

I hear her take a deep breath on the other end of the line. And then, "Shit." The next thing I hear is the sound of her puking.

What, did she drunk-dial me?

"Involved with your baby, Russ. I'm pregnant and I'm keeping the baby."

jamie's advice

Life's a bitch and then you die.

Oy. Beer has made me feel even worse. Instead of drowning my pain, I'm now just drowning. Should have stuck to my nondrinking guns. Now all I can think about is how useless getting up in the morning is. What's the point? What's the point in anything? Why bother living when life is filled with so much unhappiness? I lean my head back against the leather cushion of the booth in the back of the Monsoon. Suddenly I have nothing. There's now a massive hole in my life. An emptiness. What's the point in going on with this kind of pain? I swallow another gulp of beer.

Why am I feeling so pathetically melodramatic? I'm all joked out. Even trying to lose myself in a movie doesn't help. I can't stay focused. I tried calling my sister, Amanda, but she wasn't helpful. "You dated her for two seconds. Snap out of it."

A blast of cold air blows in as the door opens. It's Russ. He steps inside and looks around, confused, as though he has no idea how he got here. Kind of how I feel. His eyes are wide open like saucers.

He sees me, looks baffled, as if he doesn't recognize me. Maybe he's been hitting the bong too often. He orders a beer at the bar and then approaches the table, sliding into the seat across from mine.

"Oh, man," he says.

Exactly. I don't have much to say to him. I think what he's doing to Kimmy is shitty. How he can take advantage of her makes me sick. I take another sip of the beer. Not that what I did was any better. Oy. Am I really no better than Russ? I lied to the woman I love. I used her to get what I want. Might as well drown in my own pain. I chug half of my beer and wave at Glenda for another. Then I go to work on the remaining half. I wonder if there's a limit to how much beer a person can drink before exploding.

Russ runs his thumb around the rim of his beer. "I'm going to be a father."

I spit the final mouthful back into the bottle. "What?"

"I'm going to be a dad."

Holy shit. "Kimmy's pregnant?"

"No. Sharon."

Oy. "What did Kimmy say?" I ask.

"Haven't told her yet."

Glenda passes me a new bottle and I take a long sip. I don't even like the taste of beer. "That might be something you'd want to consider letting her know," I say.

Russ starts laughing and can't stop. He drops his head onto the table and bangs it against the Formica. "I'm so fucking scared. I might get expelled and I'm going to be a father. I'm not ready to be a father. I can't even floss properly. How am I going to be a father?"

Instead of feeling sorry for him, I feel envious. I wish the right thing to do in my life was so obvious. I wish I were the one becoming a father. He has everything and I have nothing.

"Once a night before bed and dig into those gums," I offer.

kimmy's ejection

My nipples are frozen. It's so cold in here. Where is Russ? I'm sitting on a wooden bench outside the disciplinary committee boardroom in the Katz building, wearing my blue interview suit. At least it's good for something.

He's late. Surprise, surprise. I knocked on his door, but he didn't answer. I assumed he'd already left. Although why he'd leave without me, I don't know. I don't know what the hell has happened to him in the last twenty-four hours. Yesterday he didn't even come over. Called to tell me he wasn't feeling well. Asked if he could borrow my laptop. Said his was broken and he wanted to finish an assignment. Hope he didn't stay up too late. Hope he doesn't sleep through this meeting. That would essentially be academic suicide. He has to be here in person to plead his case. He still has a few minutes if I go in first. Apparently we have to go in separately.

The clock above the hallway says eight fifty-eight. He has two minutes. Maybe I should have knocked harder. Louder. Tried calling. If he doesn't show up, it will be entirely my fault. I'd better call him. I whip out my cell and am about to dial his number, when Russ appears in front of me.

"Kimmy," he says. "I have to tell you something." Even though he has thick bags under his eyes, he looks calm, like he's just had a smoke, or a bath. (Do men take baths? I long for a bath. The sublet I got for the summer has a bathtub. Probably not a great one, considering it's in Manhattan, but still a bath is a bath.)

I can't tell if he has good or bad news. "What is it?"

He takes a deep breath and squeezes my hand.

"Russ?" The door opens and a second-year student who always reminds me of Bart Simpson because of his spiky blond hair, pokes his cartoon head into the hallway. "We're ready for you."

My heart plummets right down to my work pumps. "Good luck," I say.

He kisses me on the forehead and disappears inside.

We've rehearsed our stories. We're going to say that we talked about the assignment, but then each wrote our own report. They might buy it. I compared Russ's to mine and they aren't exactly the same. Pretty much, but not identical. I think we can get away with it. And if not? We'll take the course again. Not a big deal. There's no way they'll expel us both. Even if we lose the O'Donnel jobs, it's not the end of the world. We'll still be together. Sure, I think I'd like working in strategy, but I'll get another job eventually. What matters is that Russ and I stay strong and together.

I wish I could hear what's going on inside. Would it look weird if I put my ear against the wall?

Ten minutes later, the door opens, and Russ kisses me on the forehead again. "How'd it go?" I ask.

"Perfectly."

"Good." I stand up and straighten out my suit. "My turn, then?"

"Yes." He uses his fingers to brush my hair away from my face. "I hope you can understand," he says.

"What? Understand what?" What's he talking about?

"Try not to be pissed at me. I'll meet you at the Zoo after, okay?"

Bart pops his head out. "Kimmy, we're ready for you."

I want to ask Russ what he's talking about, but he's already halfway down the hall. I have a bad feeling about this. What is he sorry about? What did he do? Did he—did he tell them I copied from him? No. No way. He wouldn't do that to me, would he? Maybe he would. Business school was always his dream. Maybe he decided that he deserved it more than I do. That I couldn't care less about being here and that it wasn't fair.

He's right. He does deserve it more than I do. I only came to school to meet a guy. And I did. Maybe I owe it to him. I love him and I owe him that. So if that's what Russ said, I'll back him up.

The dean, Professor Martin, Bart and another student are sitting behind a long desk. I feel like I'm standing before the Supreme Court. The dean does look like The Hulk, as Russ once described. The other student, a second-year redhead, looks familiar, too. Bart introduces me and tells me to have a seat. I try to calm my shaking hands.

The dean clears his throat. "Thank you for coming, Kimberly. After speaking with Russ, it's come to our attention that you—"

Plagiarized his work?

"—are not to blame for this situation and are excused. I will advise, however, that in the future, should a situation like this come up again, you report to the authorities immediately. Thank you for coming in today, but we will no longer be needing your testimony."

"Excuse me?"

"You're dismissed."

Dismissed from school? He's smiling at me, so I don't think so. Professor Martin is giving me a thumbs-up.

I nod and back out of the room, unable to wipe the smile off my face. What did Russ say to get us off the hook? How did he do it? I run back to the Zoo and knock on his door. When he answers, I throw my arms around his neck. "I can't believe you did it. You are a superhero."

He squeezes me tightly and then pulls away. His eyes are rimmed with red.

"What's wrong?" I ask. "Aren't you relieved? We're off the hook! What did you tell them?"

"I told them that I borrowed a printed version of your assignment without your knowledge and then copied it."

I don't believe it. That is so sweet. I love him. He must love me if he sacrificed himself for me. "But what happens to you now?"

He pats my hair. "I'm not coming back to LWBS next year."

The wind is knocked out of me. "What? You got expelled?"

"No. I'm going to fail Corporate Strategy, but I didn't get expelled. I've decided not to come back next year. I'm going home."

What is he talking about? I back away from him and balance myself against the door. "What about O'Donnel? What about our sublet?" What about me?

"I can't take the job in New York."

"Yes, you can. Of course you can! They didn't expel you. Don't be crazy."

"Sharon's pregnant."

The room starts to spin.

"And I have to go back to Toronto to be with her. To be there for her."

"And where does that leave us?" I ask, my voice soaked with tears.

He hugs me again and I let him. "I'm sorry," he says. His

voice is soft and sad. "I have to go back. It's the right thing to do."

I can hear his heart beating against my tear-streaked cheek. I reach up and kiss his neck. And then his cheek and his lips and then he stops me.

"I can't," he says, looking into my eyes.

I try to swallow the lump in my throat. "How do you know she'll even take you back?"

"I don't," he says. "But I have to try."

I hate this place. I'm lying in bed, covers drawn over my head, crying my eyes out like a two-year-old. What the hell just happened? She totally planned this. She wanted to get pregnant so she could steal him away from me. This is so not fair. Not fair. What did she do, stop talking her pills?

What if she's lying? What if she's only saying this to get him back?

Stupid, stupid, stupid. I should have told him I was pregnant as soon as I missed my first period. We might have been married by now.

We just had sex two nights ago. Maybe the sperm is still inside of me. Maybe I can get pregnant, too. Then what would he do?

I hiccup loudly. And then laugh at myself. I think I've lost my mind, as well as my boyfriend. Suddenly the fact that I'm not going to fail Corporate Strategy doesn't even matter to me. Who cares? Nothing matters to me if I can't have Russ. I feel fat and ugly and bloated, and I want to pull out my hair and skin. I'm worthless. Empty. Nothing. I don't want to go to New York. I don't want to work at O'Donnel. I don't want to come back to LWBS if Russ isn't going to be here. I want to go home.

There's a knock at the door. Maybe it's Russ. Maybe he's changed his mind. I jump out of the bed and open the door.

It's just Layla. "How'd it go?" she asks.

I feel confused and disoriented. And why is she talking to me now? "How did what go?" The end of my romantic life?

"The committee? Hello?"

I sigh and crawl back under the covers. "It doesn't matter anymore."

She sits on the foot of the bed. "Of course it does. What did they say?"

"They said that everything's fine. Russ admitted that he copied from me, and now he's going to fail the course. But he doesn't care, since he's dropping out to go home to his pregnant ex. And it doesn't matter to me, because I'm going home, too. I hate this place. I hate the cold, I hate the bathrooms, and I want a bath."

"You're being absurd," she says. "You're not dropping out. You're doing well here."

"You don't understand. Do you know how much money I owe? I'm in debt for fifteen grand. And I'm going to go into debt for another thirty if I come back next year."

She's shaking her head at me, not listening. "You'll earn money at O'Donnel. Did you say pregnant ex?"

"Yes, Sharon's pregnant. She gets a baby and I get to pay for the entire sublet now that Russ isn't coming. What I should do is go home and start looking for a full-time job." Maybe my dad will take me back. Maybe Wayne…

She waves her hands over my bed. "You're talking crazy. You're not worthless just because Russ dumped you."

I pull the covers over my face. "I don't want to talk about this anymore. I want to go home."

"Stop being such a wimp!" she yells. "We need to talk about this. It's crazy. "

I drop the blanket. "If you don't mind, I just found out that my boyfriend has impregnated another woman and as a result is now dumping me. Do you think you could insult someone else? I don't feel like talking to you at the moment. Why don't you go bother Jamie?"

She arches her back. "I am never speaking to him again. I can't be involved with someone who would behave the way he did."

I don't know what it is Jamie did, but I'm sure it's something minuscule. She's got to get that poker out of her ass. Jamie is a great guy, and if she can't see that, she's an idiot. Not going for him back in September was probably the biggest mistake of my life. He would never cheat on his girlfriend. He would have worshiped me. If Layla doesn't want him, maybe I still have a chance. He liked me first. "I think you have unrealistic expectations about men."

She snorts. "I have unrealistic expectations? Hello? You're the one who expects men to save you. You lap up whatever a man says and would screw over any woman for your man. Karma-wise, you had this Sharon-pregnancy thing coming."

How dare she talk to me like that! "Since I'm such a horrible skank, can you get out of my room?"

She slams the door behind her. I wonder if I'm mad at her or if I'm so pathetic that I just want to be mad at her so I can seduce Jamie.

layla's birthday

Happy birthday to me. Happy birthday to me. Twenty-seven today. Twenty-seven sounds a lot older than twenty-six, doesn't it? Twenty-six sounds young and blond and fun, whereas twenty-seven sounds serious and possibly brunette.

I'm at the library in my usual spot, studying Finance. Alone. I don't know where Jamie and Kimmy are studying these days, but I haven't seen them here. I hope they're not letting their work slip. All I can say is that I'm thrilled I'm not in their group.

Tense, tense, tense.

My friends from home all sent me e-cards. No one here knows it's my birthday. My bank balance increased by a thousand bucks. Which means my mother or father transferred money into my account. That's what they do every year. I think it's on automatic-transfer so they don't have to remember to do it.

I didn't expect the people here to know, so I can't say I'm disappointed. I've never mentioned the exact date. Besides I'm not talking to them. Jamie was a mistake and it's best to sever the ties now. And Kimmy hasn't apologized since kicking me out of her room.

My desk creaks as I shuffle in my chair.

So no party this year. Not a big deal. I'll celebrate in a few weeks with my real friends, when I'm home. Training for the job starts May 3 and runs for a week, and then I work for three months. The back of my head hurts when I think about three whole months of redundancy reducing, overhead eliminating, cost cutting, economies of scale…I wish I had a job that made an actual difference in people's lives. Like Ronnie. Or Danielle Grand. I wonder if they love their jobs. If they're happy. Was I happy at the bank? Will I be happy? Are my parents happy?

Does it matter?

sister kimmy

"We done?" Nick asks. We're sitting morosely in his room, all of us thrilled we've finally finished our last group assignment. All of us wishing we were someplace else. "I gotta jet," he continues. "Hot date."

"Hot date?" I wonder aloud. "With who?"

"A large-breasted art major. She lives in the Sphere residence. Cheers."

"You mean the syphilis residence?" Lauren asks. "I heard that place is an STD hotbed. I have a date, too."

"With who?" I ask.

"Cindy." She gives us a big smile.

"Who's Cindy?" Nick asks.

Lauren stands up and collects her things. "Swiley," she answers, and then dances out of the room before we can comment.

Oh. My. God. "Our IC teacher?" I say.

"Let me know if she's all that I dreamed," Nick calls, sticking his head into the hallway. Lauren and Nick both got jobs in Boston this summer so they're sharing an apartment.

I hope they'll get it over with and sleep together already. I guess there's always next year…

Jamie stands up and stretches his arms above his head. The bottom of his shirt pulls up, exposing his pale stomach. "And on that note, ladies and gentleman, our first-year work group comes to an end. Not with a bang but a whimper."

I laugh. I think he makes me laugh about once every two minutes. "I hope the whimper is not because of genital pain?" I banter.

"Syphilis makes you crazy if left untreated," Jamie says.

"I guess that means you already have it," Nick says.

Russ isn't here. He hasn't come to any of our last group meetings. He finished his parts for all the assignments and then e-mailed them to Jamie. He's probably too busy reading the *Dummies Guide to Being a Daddy*. But it's better this way, his staying away. This way, I don't have to talk to him.

I find myself staring at Jamie. He's such a fun guy, really he is. And he's a lot better-looking than I used to think. I wonder what my year would have been like if I'd fallen for him instead. A million times better. No tactics, no sneaking around, just bliss.

"What are you doing now?" I ask him in the hallway.

"I'm thinking of trying scuba diving. I've always wanted to swim with the sharks."

I laugh and rub his arm. "Want to grab some dinner away from the caf? Maybe that little Japanese restaurant on Main Street?"

"Sure. Why not?"

I should be studying for finals—that's why not. I'm okay for most of them. All except Finance. I have no idea what's going on in that class. It's like they're speaking Korean. I'm not sure how I'm going to pass the exam. Even though I'm not planning on coming back next year, I still want to pass. No need to leave on a bad note. I still can't decide what I should do about this summer. I don't want to be in New York by myself. If Jamie and I hooked up, maybe we could share an apartment in the city. And maybe I could be persuaded to stay at LWBS.

Twenty minutes later we're seated at a table for two near the window. He takes my coat and pulls out my chair for me. Two things Russ never did. A tea candle burns in the middle of the table, and I pour the wax on my hand and make him a heart.

"Thanks, darlin'," he says. "I shall wear it on my sleeve."

The waitress asks us if we want something to drink. Jamie surprises me by ordering sake.

"I thought you don't drink," I say.

"I didn't drink. Presently I find it helps me dwell in my melancholy."

My heart sinks. "Because of Layla?"

"Yes," he says, and gets choked up. "She won't even talk to me."

I don't know what to say, so I sip my water. When the sake comes, he pours us each a cup, then raises his in mock salute. "To unrequited love."

"To unrequited love," I repeat.

He downs his cup and refills. "Why do we always have to love the people who don't love us? Maybe it's just me. I think I should go back to not trying. Coasting. That works. Not caring. Not caring about my future. Not caring about women. Before Layla, everything was just a joke to me." He downs his second cup.

My lip begins to tremble. "What about me? Didn't you care about me? Way back in September?" I need to know he cared about me. I need to know I matter. I need to know that I wasn't a joke.

"Of course I cared about you, Kimmy. But we barely knew each other. But when I met Layla…"

I give my best smile. "Right." But he knows me now. I lean in close so he can get a better view of my padded cleavage.

I get soy sauce all over my shirt. "So what do you want to order?" I ask, forcing my voice to sound chirpy. "Want to share a California roll?"

"I've moved beyond California rolls, Kimmy. I'm ready for the real thing, now. Bring on the spicy tuna."

Three platefuls of sushi and four more carafes of sake later I'm still laughing.

"Maybe we should take one of the carafes back to the Zoo and instigate a floor-wide game of spin-the-sake," Jamie says, his voice about two octaves higher than usual, his eyes bright, his cheeks flushed.

"Sounds like a plan."

Jamie signs his name in the air for the bill. "Do you think that's the international sign for bring-me-the-bill? We should ask Nick if in Australia they sign upside down."

He drops four twenties on the table and waves my hand away when I reach for my wallet. "My treat. You've finally allowed me to take you for dinner."

"Thank you," I say, sincerely.

"Don't touch my mustache," he replies.

I peer at his face. "You don't have a mustache."

"Doitashimashite," he says. "That's Japanese for 'you're welcome.'"

Because of our inebriated state, we leave his car on the street and walk the five blocks back to campus. He tries to do a fox-trot, and I can't stop laughing.

When we get to the Zoo, he can barely make it up the stairs. He puts his arm around me to help him balance. Instead of focusing on the act of stair climbing, he's singing, off-key, some song about falling in love. No surprise there, considering that most songs are about love.

Giggling, we half carry each other to his room. He unlocks his door and falls face forward onto his bed. I climb in beside him. He's still singing. He knows I'm lying next to him and he hasn't told me to leave, so I snuggle into his arms.

He smells like warm wine. He fingers a lock of my hair and closes his eyes.

Now's my chance. I can take my clothes off and let his hands wander, or I can start kissing his neck. And then we'll be exactly where we were in September. With Jamie being in love with me. Instead of with Layla.

I close my eyes and pull him close. He doesn't pull away. I inch my mouth to his.

He's no longer singing, he's humming, but it's the same song. *I fell in love with you…*

Where's that from? I know that song.

Right. Eric Clapton.

Layla.

I sit up with a start. What am I doing? My head pounds, my mouth feels drier than the Arizona desert, and my stomach feels queasy. What the hell is wrong with me? Layla's helped me through everything this year and I try to screw her just because my self-esteem's been shredded to pieces? Why am I such a horrible person? Jamie doesn't love me. He loves Layla. And she loves him, no matter what she says.

I can't always be the weak link in the band of sisterhood. I disentangle myself from his arms and back out of the room.

He hangs his head over the bed. "I think I'm going to be sick."

I rush to grab his garbage pail and place it directly in his potential target zone. Then I sit back down on the edge of his bed. "You know what? So am I."

jamie's mom knows best

White noise blares through my alarm clock.

Happy birthday, Dara.

I slam my hand against the alarm. Head. Hurts. Room. Smells. I open one eye and throw off my covers. I'm fully clothed yet nicely tucked into my bed. It smells like ass in here. Oy. That must be because of the garbage pail of puke beside my bed.

What happened last night anyway? The last thing I remember clearly is drinking too much sake. But somehow I must have found my way back here. And set my alarm. Or maybe Kimmy did it for me. Who knew she had the mother gene? I'm not getting up today. I shall mourn Dara's birthday in bed. Nothing matters, anyway. My head is broken and my heart is broken. Why bother getting up?

I turn the alarm off. No thanks.

The phone rings.

"Hello?"

"Jamie?"

"Mom, hi."

"You weren't still sleeping, were you?"

"Sleeping? What's that?"

"Are you getting enough sleep over there? Have you tried those earplugs I sent?"

"Yes, Mom. Thanks, Mom."

Pause. "I'm calling to thank you for the flowers."

Flowers? Oh, right, flowers. I forgot I ordered the flowers. Wait a second. She never calls to thank me. "You are?"

"Don't sound so surprised, Jamie."

"Well, Mom, I've been sending them for twenty years and you've never called to thank me before. Not that I need a thank you. I'm just wondering why this morning I get a phone call."

"You're right," she says, and I hear her eating on the other end. "I'm seeing things differently, since my mother died. I wanted to tell the people I appreciate how much I appreciate them before it's too late."

"Well, then I appreciate you telling me that you appreciate me."

"I appreciate you, I appreciate you. I always have, since the day you were born. Even though I didn't want to have you."

"Um…thanks?"

She laughs. Laughter on Dara's birthday? "That didn't come out right."

I can't believe we're having this conversation. "So why did you decide to have me?"

"Your father thought it would be good for me. And he was right." She pauses, and I think I hear her sniffle. "Honey, just know that pain becomes manageable. I know you're hurting, but it'll pass. You have to take solace in the good things in your life. Like your exciting new job."

Wait a second. "How do you know I've been depressed?"

"Shush. A mother knows everything."

"Amanda spilled the beans," I say.

"I'm all-knowing. So you're going to try to keep your chin up, Jamie? For me?"

"Nothing like Jewish-mother guilt to kick-start me from bed."

"Do I hear you smiling?"

I smile. "Yes, Mom."

"And one more thing. How about getting your niece into one of those movies you're producing? Don't you think she could be the new Shirley Temple?"

I agree. In this world, anything's possible.

I hang up the phone and jump out of bed. I need to study. I have exams to ace.

russ has a fleeting regret

I put down my pencil and raise my hand. Third exam over. I stretch my legs under the desk. Wait for the proctor to come take my paper. Insert my student card into my front pocket.

Kimmy is sitting three rows ahead, scribbling furiously. It's weird to think that after Friday I might never see her again. Nick told me she's planning on going back to Arizona. She's not taking the job at O'Donnel, either. I called last week to tell them I changed my mind because of family obligations, and they weren't too thrilled. Oh, well.

Kimmy runs her fingers through her hair, and I feel a pang in my chest. Part of me still wants her, and probably always will. Maybe our paths will cross someday. Maybe we'll both be visiting New York and will be crossing Fifth Avenue at the same time and our eyes will lock. If I expect Sharon to forgive me, or at least let me be a part of our baby's life, I can't have any contact with Kimmy. It's the right thing to do. I care about her, but I have to be responsible.

I'm going to have to grovel. I asked Sharon if she wanted

to get married and she told me to go to hell. But you never know, eh?

"All done?" the proctor asks, taking my exam.

"Yes."

"Good luck."

"Thanks," I say. I'll need it.

layla's calling

I'm feeling a little ambivalent as I pack my belongings into my bag and roll myself out into the library elevator for the last time this year. On the one hand, I'm happy to be finished exams; on the other hand, I love the adrenaline rush they give me.

The elevator stops at the third floor. Kimmy walks in, blurry eyed, like she forgot to close her eyes underwater. She tenses when she sees me. We haven't spoken since our argument.

"How are you?" she asks.

"Good. You? Ready for tomorrow?"

"Um, yeah."

I flash back to images of her staring at the professor cluelessly. "Are you sure?"

She hesitates again. "I'll be fine."

I know she's lying, and suddenly I don't want to be mad at her anymore. "Do you need some help?"

She shakes her head. "I'll be fine."

"Define Arbitrage."

"It's…um…" She shakes her head. "I'm fucked, huh? I'm totally lost."

I giggle. "You're not. Come over and we'll review."

"It's already midnight. You like to get a good night's sleep before an exam."

"I'm plenty rested. We're reviewing," I tell her, feeling charged. The idea of helping her invigorates me the way nothing else has all week. "You get the snacks, I'll make the tea, and we'll meet in my room in five, okay?"

"I don't deserve it," she says.

What kind of talk is that? "Yes, you do."

For the first time ever, Kimmy hugs me. "Thank you."

"My pleasure."

Kimmy gives me a thumbs-up as she leaves the exam room. She's smiling. Even though I'm not finished yet, and I'm never going to finish, and I'm the only one still in the room, and I'm too exhausted to think straight, I can't help but feel elated at her smile. She did it. We stayed up all night laughing and studying, and she did it. I've never felt more proud. Of someone else or, I realize, of myself.

After the exam, which I most definitely failed, I make a decision. I call Danielle Grand and ask her if she's still looking for a summer associate.

"Wow, Layla, I would love to have you onboard, but I don't have anything left in the summer budget."

"I don't need a salary for the summer, just the experience. I want to help and see if I like the work. I need to find work I can feel good about. My only request is that you don't put me to work as a gofer. I want to do *real* work."

She laughs. "You're going to love it. And there's plenty of real work for you to do that will utilize your skill set. Like managing the fund-raising, budget, taxes…the list is endless."

I smile. "I'm looking forward to it."

closure for kimmy

Almost done. My books have been stacked in a storage area downstairs for Jamie to sell next year, and I'm almost finished packing my clothes.

I lie back on my bare mattress and take a minibreak. I'm exhausted. Physically, mentally and emotionally. I haven't pulled an all-nighter in a while, but it was worth it. I think I might have actually passed the exam. Layla is a genius teacher. She'd make a great professor one day. I hope I have some time to hang out with her before I leave today. My flight home isn't until eight. I wonder if Russ already left. Guess he didn't want to say goodbye. Too awkward.

All right. Break over. I stand up and stretch. I should probably call back Claire Moss. I tried calling her earlier this week to tell her I no longer wanted to work for them, but she wasn't in and we've been playing phone tag ever since. Not that I've been trying very hard to get in touch. I'm not looking forward to the conversation. Between me and Russ revoking our offers, they'll probably stop hiring LWBS students.

I find the number and pick up to dial. Why isn't it ringing? Has the phone company already cut off my dorm line?

"Hello, Ms. Nailer?" says a gruff voice.

"Yes?"

"Professor Martin here."

Not again. Please tell me Russ didn't copy my exam. Haha. "Yes?"

"I'm calling to congratulate you on your final mark. You scored a ninety-five on your exam, which means that combined with your assignment marks, you scored the highest mark in the class."

Oh. My. God. "I did?"

"Yes. And I don't know if you're aware of it, but the top students in all three second-semester Strategy classes will receive the Hunder Strategy Award."

An award? They're giving me an award? Are they crazy? I don't deserve an award. I don't deserve anything.

Maybe it's time for me to become someone who's award-worthy.

"Thank you, Professor," I manage to squeak.

"With the award is a scholarship for fifteen hundred dollars, and I hope it will encourage you to specialize in Strategy next year."

They're giving me money, too? Holy shit. "Um, that's what I was thinking of doing." Well, I am now.

"Also, I'd like you to consider applying for a teacher's assistant position next fall for the Strategy Intro class."

Wow. "I could do that, too."

"Great. I'll be mailing the scholarship and TA application to the address the school has on file in Arizona. And I look forward to seeing you next year. Have a great summer."

"Thanks," I say, unable and unwilling to stop smiling. "You, too." I can't believe a professor has so much faith in me that he wants me to help first-years. Who knew?

The phone rings again. Maybe I won the Finance scholarship, too. Maybe I should stop dreaming.

"Hello?"

"Hello, is this Kimmy Nailer?"

"Speaking."

"Hello, it's Claire Moss returning your call from O'Donnel. Sorry for the phone tag we've been playing."

My heart jumps to my throat. "Oh. No problem. Thanks for calling me back."

"Do you have any concerns?" she asks.

Do I have any concerns? Yes, about a million. I'm concerned that I'm going to spend the rest of my life being someone I hate. I'm concerned that I won't be tough enough to make it in the corporate world. I'm concerned no one will ever love me.

The thing is, I want this job. I want this life. I want to come back to LWBS next year. I want to be a TA. I want my own damn freshly squeezed orange juice. "I want to confirm that the starting date is June first," I say quickly, before I can change my mind.

"Yes. And orientation is May thirty-first."

"Looking forward to it," I say. And I am.

My entire year is packed into two duffel bags. How sad. The walls look bare and small dust bunnies peek out from the corners of the closet. Gross. My hands are filthy and I smell like I forgot to use deodorant this morning. I've packed the clock, but my watch says it's four-fifteen. Still a while to go.

Knock, knock.

"Hold on." Maybe Layla is coming to say goodbye. I can't wait to tell her about New York. She's going to be so proud of me. I open the door and a lump instantaneously forms in my throat.

It's Russ.

"Hey," he says.

"I thought you were gone." I look at the floor.

"Leaving now. Can I come in?"

I nod and hold the door open, still not meeting his gaze.

"How'd you find the exam?" he asks.

"Fine. You?" I lean against the empty desk that came with the room. I don't think I can take much more of this small talk. The lump is threatening to expand and block my speaking capabilities, possibly choking me.

"I came to say goodbye," he says softly. I continue staring at the floor, the disgusting dusty floor, and he touches my arm. "I needed to say goodbye." His voice trembles, and I finally look up.

And then my eyes lock with the bluest eyes I have ever seen, and I fall headfirst into them all over again. His eyes are glistening, and he's trying to blink away his tears. I wonder if I'll ever lose myself in eyes like those again.

My cheeks are wet, but I don't care. "Goodbye," I say.

"I'm sorry," he whispers.

I know, I think but don't say. Me, too.

He hugs me tightly, and I let his smell overwhelm my nose and throat. "You're doing the right thing," I whisper into his ear, and realize I mean it.

"Yeah?" He sounds relieved.

"Yeah."

Would we have worked in the long run? I thought so, but I'm not sure. Eventually the *Spider-Man* soundtrack would have driven me crazy.

That and the fact that I didn't trust him.

"Good luck," he says.

I pull back. "Good luck to you."

He kisses me on the cheek. "Be good."

I laugh even though I can barely breathe. "You, too."

He squeezes my hand and lets himself out. And I sit back on the bare mattress and cry.

layla claims her prince

Kimmy rubs her eyes with the back of her hands, and I gently pull her hands away from her face. "Don't do that, sweetie. Here's a tissue."

"Thank you," she says through her hiccups. "Thanks for making me feel better."

"That's what I'm here for. Do you want some more tea?"

"No, thanks. I'm feeling better." Kimmy looks up at me and smiles. "Thanks for letting me stay in your apartment this summer. Are you sure you don't mind having me?"

"It makes perfect sense for you to stay in my place. Why should you spend money when my room is empty? My sister's at her boyfriend's all the time, anyway. And I just spoke to the Zoo and they keep the dorm open for summer students, and since I'm working only ten minutes away it makes more sense to stay right here." I can't believe I'm staying in this dorm longer than necessary. But there's no point in moving when I'm working so close by. Hey, I just had a thought. Maybe I'll be the only one on this floor. Wouldn't that be great? I'd get the bathroom all to myself.

I could even go streaking down the hallway, stark naked, if I want.

"I really appreciate everything you've done for me, Layla," she says. "You've been a true friend. And now it's time for me to return the favor."

"Don't be silly, I don't expect anything in return."

"I know you don't. And I also know you hate being told what to do and when you're wrong. And you know I normally hold things back, and don't say everything I think, but I want to tell you something."

"Sounds ominous," I say. "Okay, shoot."

"You're being an idiot about Jamie."

"Now wait just a min—"

"No. You've taught me all year, and now it's your turn to listen. Jamie loves you. And he's an amazing man. He's funny and sweet and smart, and he would be a wonderful boyfriend for you."

"But he was unethical and he lied and—"

"Yeah, I know what he did. So he's not perfect. No one is, Layla. No one will ever be. You've got to get over your obsession with perfection. No one can live up to it. News flash—you're not perfect, either."

"Maybe not, but I'm not deceitful."

"Oh, really. Tell me something, did you ever tell Bradley where you first heard about him?"

My cheeks do a slow burn.

"Now listen up. You're bossy and obsessive, and you know what? Your friends love you, anyway. *He* loves you, anyway. So he made a mistake. Learn from it, and move on." She takes a long sip of her tea. "You know what I think? I think you use this obsession you have with perfection as an excuse not to get close to someone. If you have to have something wrong with you, the least you could do was get something a little more original."

I pick up a pillow and throw it at her, and it hits her hand. And knocks over her tea. All over my bedspread.

"Aw, crap." I'm about to sulk, when instead I think, Is it possible she's right? I got freaked out by Brad, but terrified by Jamie. I do a mental recap of all my past relationships. Oh, my, she *is* right.

"You're right," I say, my heart racing. "About everything. Especially about Jamie. He *is* an amazing man. He's generous and sweet and loving and hilarious and sensual. Sometimes I wish he'd stop joking and be serious, and other times he looks so sad, as if he's carrying the weight of every sick child on his shoulders, and it breaks my heart. And he has a unibrow. And according to you, a small penis. But I like him."

Wow. Did I just say that? I leap off the bed. "I have to fix this, now."

Kimmy chokes on her tea. "Of course, only you would have an immediate epiphany and want to take action. You are the most spontaneous and passionate person I have ever met. But I think he might have already—"

"No time for thinking!" I spritz my Chanel No. 5 across my chest and sprint down the hall. I pound on his door. No one answers, so I open the door. The room is empty. Stark-naked empty. I can't believe it. I've missed my chance.

"Maybe he's still packing up his car," Kimmy offers, standing next to me.

"You're right!" I skip down the stairs to the garage.

"You're not wearing any shoes!" Kimmy yells after me. "Or a coat!"

"It's spring!" I yell back, and run to the garage. Is he there? Is he still here? Please let him still be here.

And there's his Hyundai. And he's shoving a box into the trunk.

"Hi," he says, surprised to see me.

I kiss him before he can say anything, then pull back and

look at his face. "I am so sorry. I should never have freaked out the way I did. You are a terrifically imperfect man who's perfect for me."

That so didn't come out right. He doesn't say anything, just stares blankly. Maybe it's too late. He got over Kimmy. Maybe he's over me. Is he now going to turn this all into a joke and blow me off? "Well?" I ask, hands on hips. "Tell me how you feel. Straight up. I can't take a joke."

He brushes my hair away from my face, then runs his finger from my ear, across my cheek, to my lips. He looks into my eyes and I lose my breath. And then he kisses me.

summer break

Wednesday, June 2, 1:30 p.m.

kimmy's elevator

The sky over Forty-second Street is a gorgeous milky-blue, and I can't stop smiling. I love this city. The honking, the energy, the tossed salad I have tucked under my arm (as per Layla's passionate suggestion). I especially love Layla's apartment. I've already been there a week, and I still can't get over the place. The floors are hardwood, the bathroom has a Jacuzzi and toilet with a seat warmer, the bed is a pillow-top-king draped in Ralph Lauren sheets softer than a kitten's fur, the view is of the entire city, and a housekeeper comes every Monday. And Layla refuses to charge me rent, since she owns the place. She didn't even stay with me on the weekend when she visited—she shacked up with Jamie at his sublet. They appear to be madly in love, always cooing in each other's faces and referring to each other by nicknames. He calls her his orange, and she calls him her banana. I'm guessing the orange thing has something to do with their juggling adventures, and I so don't want to know about the banana. "You missed out" is all I'd let her tell me.

I wave to the doorman and click-clack against the marble

floor in the lobby toward the elevator that will take me to the forty-eighth floor. Yesterday, my first day at work, I spent ten minutes confused as to why the elevator I was standing in didn't have any buttons that went past forty. I thought I was in the wrong building, walked back outside, came back in…then realized that there were multiple elevators, each assigned to a block of twenty floors. Who knew?

This elevator, my elevator, only stops on floors forty to sixty. As my elevator zips skyward through the building, my ears pop, and I watch the news on the flat-screen TV, smiling. I know eventually that I'll stop feeling like the entire city is paved with gold, but for now I'm enjoying the ride.

I'm happy. Despite having my period. I threw out my pills the day Russ went back to Toronto. My body needs a break. Time to find its natural rhythm again. Whatever that is.

We come to a nice smooth stop. I'm about to step out when a cute dark-haired guy in a blue-striped suit steps into my path. Oops. I realize we're only on the forty-fifth floor, not my stop.

"Hey, Kimmy, good to see you," he says, still standing in front of me. He looks vaguely familiar, but I don't remember his name. I think he's the partner I talked to during the interview dinner, the man who made Russ so jealous. Smiling, he says, "I'm Johnny Dollan, in case you've forgotten. We met back in January. Didn't mean to block your path. Is this your floor?"

He shuffles in beside me, smiling at me over his shoulder.

"No," I say, and hit the door-close button. "I'm going up."

More great reads by international bestselling author Sarah Mlynowski

Fishbowl

Roommate Compatibility Test

1. Would you sleep with the boy your roommate has been lusting after since college?
2. Do you keep the door open when you pee?
3. Have you ever left the stove unattended?
4. Do you value your privacy?

If you answered yes to No. 4…tough. There's no such thing as privacy when you're living in a fishbowl.

Get ready for a humorous glimpse into the lives of three roommates as they brave fire, kitchen repair, guys and each other on their way to a friendship everlasting.

RED DRESS INK ™

More great reads from international
bestselling author Sarah Mlynowski

Sex, lies and reality TV...

ſarah
mLynowſki

"Mlynowski is acutely aware of the plight
of the 20-something single woman... she offers
funny dialogue and several slices of reality."
—Publishers Weekly

As Seen on TV

Sunny Langstein has done what every modern-day
twenty-four-year-old shouldn't do. She's left her life
in Florida to move in with her boyfriend in
Manhattan. But don't judge Sunny yet, because
like any smart woman she has an ulterior motive—
to star on *Party Girls,* the latest reality-television
show. Here's the catch—*Party Girls* have to be
single. Free designer clothes and stardom versus
life with her boyfriend. What's a girl to do?

RED DRESS INK

TM